I0564042

Sunlight

and

Dappled Shade

a novel

by

Dantie Smith-Brown

Written by Dantie Smith-Brown 2014

Copyright ©Dantie Smith-Brown 2014

All rights reserved. No reproduction, copy, or transmission of this publication may be made without prior written permission of the author and/or her designee.

All characters in the story are fictional. Any resemblance to actual persons, living or dead is purely coincidental.

Sunlight and Dappled Shade is purely a work of fiction and is in no way autobiographical.

ISBN 10: 0692238158

ISBN 13: 9780692238158

Acknowledgements

My grandmother (who passed away far too young), the indomitable Mavis Campbell who placed a premium on education, and my mother Curline McHayle whose love and care helped bring me to this moment. They are both from the quaint and vibrant Bethel Town, Westmoreland, a small town in Western Jamaica.

My husband Larry Brown who gives me inspiration every day.

Marcia Erskine my friend, for her invaluable advice and assistance.

Vangella Hazle Buchanan, my Editor who inspires me to write and who has given me so much help with this novel.

Table of Contents

-Prologue-

Crowing roosters welcomed a new day as Miss Etty sat cross-legged on the floor of her three bed roomed wooden cottage, hands clasped as she called on the spirits. Octavius, her husband of twenty-five years, had long gone to the field where he planted his tobacco, yams, pumpkins and other ground provisions. Ashanti, Miss Etty's dark-eyed assistant, sat with her head bowed. Miss Etty no longer heard the birds chirping or the donkeys braying outside but was filled with the peace and quiet that she needed to communicate with the spirits.

At that moment, her bright brown eyes that were far too young for her face were focused on the glass jar before her filled with water, as if she would find the future written in it.

"Yes," she said, "I see script written here. It will come to pass that the ruler will lament the loss of her son. She will know the secret of life and will follow the path laid out for her. They will follow the path where the gifts of the father will take them."

Ashanti waited until Miss Etty was finished. It was better to simply wait because the spirits didn't like to be interrupted. Miss Etty's voice rose as she stood with both hands in the air before spinning three times in an anti-clockwise direction. Her hands dropped; her head bowed as she settled back onto the cushion on the floor. The spirits had spoken again.

Ashanti spoke as the intensity in the room seemed to increase:

"It is ordained that she will be the first female Prime Minister of Jamaica and it is our purpose to guide her in the right direction."

"I had to be absolutely sure that this is what the cards were showing me. I had to be sure," Miss Etty said, her face warm with a strange glow.

- Chapter 1 -

B ell Town was a quaint little village with a set of softly undulating hills and green valleys tucked away in Westmoreland on the beautiful island of Jamaica. It had always supported its people even in difficult political times when the two rival parties, the People's Leading Party and the Jamaica National Party, were at war with each other. Family, friends, and Church were the glue that held this community together. It was filled with deep rooted culture: cricket, dominoes, reggae, soccer - and you cannot forget the rum bars.

Sixteen year old Alex Keanon stretched lazily and attempted to blink herself awake but sank back under the bed covers. Her long black hair was wrapped in a blue scarf to keep it intact. Her narrow, high cheek-boned face was smooth with a small dimple that showed when she smiled. She loved the quiet of the morning as Bell Town slowly awakened.

"Cock-a-doodle-doo."

She could hear the roosters crowing in the backyard. The hens were responding with their morning cackle.

"Alex are you up yet?" her grandmother called. "It's time to open up the shop. My customers are going to be here soon."

Alex peeped through the window at the early daylight. The grass and trees glistened with early-morning dew. In the garden, the sunflowers, pink and white hibiscuses, multicolor Joseph coats and crotons swayed in the breeze, displaying a profusion of colors. She felt the sudden rush of the anticipated day as she removed the scarf from her head and threw it on the bed.

"I am going to be downstairs in five minutes, Auntie," she shouted to her grandmother.

Her mom, Eve stuck her head in the doorway.

"It's more like another half an hour. You are still lying in bed in your nightgown," her mother commented with a wry grin.

"Oh, mom," she groaned, "you know I am a fast dresser."

It was obvious that it was still early morning because the sun was barely peeping through the almost cloudless sky. The scent of jackfruit wafted in through the open window as did the sound of voices calling greetings back and forth to each other. Alex tossed her head back and inhaled slowly. God, she loved Saturdays! It was her favorite day of the week. Saturdays were busy. Her grandmother whom everyone called Auntie or Miss Florentino owned a grocery store, a bar, and two meat shops. Outside on the open square, her grandmother allowed the villagers to set up a mini market where they sold vegetables, fruits and ground provisions on Saturday mornings.

"Breakfast will be ready by the time you come down," her mother smiled at her. Alex's mother, Eve, was a tall, solid looking woman who carried herself with an air of elegance that belied the indignities she had suffered in her relationship with Alex's father. She was proud of her daughter, watching over her like her own mother had kept watch on her when she was younger. Time sure does fly fast. Here was her baby, growing up, long legs and all.

Twenty minutes later, Alex was showered and

dressed. As she walked into the spacious and airy living room, she looked around at its warm cream walls and understated mahogany wood furniture. The word to describe the living room was homely. She ducked her head into Tata's room to say good morning.

"Morning, Tata. They bring up your breakfast already?"

"Long time, Alex. Saturday is a busy day for your grandmother and I like to be up and dressed so she won't have to worry about me while she is busy in the shop."

"Okay, come Tata," she said as she helped her grandmother's husband who had suffered a stroke some time ago. His gait had slowed somewhat but his mind was as brilliant as ever.

"I'll bring you a June plum at lunch time, okay Tata?"

He reached over and kissed her on the cheek.

"Okay, run along now. I'll be sitting on the verandah soon so I'll see you when you go wandering out onto the open square."

She smiled at him. Tata was always watching out for her. She headed downstairs to a myriad of delicious old fashioned and homely smells that generally waft from a Jamaican kitchen. This morning, the main aroma was that of steaming hot cocoa tea, made from cocoa that had been roasted and boiled. For some reason, Alex always dipped her lightly buttered slice of hard-dough bread into her tea. The taste was to die for. Not only that but there was partly sun-ripened *roasted breadfruit* and fried pork for her and because she didn't eat pork, there was ackee and saltfish for her mom. Alex thought about her girlfriend, Ciarra

Johnston who would still be in bed fast asleep at this time. She had no idea that she was missing out on one of the best parts of the day. Alex savored her meal.

Auntie was already hard at work when Alex finally entered the shop.

"Alex can you finish this order for me? I need to go check on the meat shop to see if they need any help over there."

Auntie patted her on the back as she turned to leave. Alex grinned at her as she took the list from her. A few hours later, Alex was finally able to take a break. She hurried out to the square where she was met with an abundance of color: oranges and tangerines ripened by the sun, ortaniques, which were favorites, both kinds of star apple begging to be eaten with green or purple skin looking so luscious, pineapples displayed in wide straw baskets, all kinds of bananas including *gros michel*, yellow and green freshly cut from the trees, red, juicy tomatoes, onions, scallions and thyme bunched together, displayed so proudly with other wares.

She looked down the street and there she saw Mass Ken, Tommy and some other people chatting in front of Mr. Mackie's store. Children and women were strolling along in the sunshine, chatting with each other. Bright eyed old men sitting on bar stools raised their cups in greeting as others passed by. As a country bus was passing, a group of boys hopped onto the back, some hanging on with one hand, their shirttails waving in the wind.

Alex picked up two star apples and two June plums from Miss Leah's neatly arranged basket and held out her dollar. Miss Leah slapped her hand and would have packed her up with more but Alex's hands were already full.

"Put your money away, Alex. Shame on you giving me money. You insult me."

"I cannot take your stuff and not pay for it, Miss Leah. Auntie would kill me if I asked you for the food you are selling without paying for it."

"Don't worry about her. I give it to you because I want to, not because I have to. Your grandmother is good to all of us here so we repay kindness with kindness."

Alex was not convinced because Auntie was always telling them that they spoiled her.

Miss Leah was shouting, "Dottie, did you hear what happened last night? Vie catch George with Rantie. Me hear sey when Vie start to put the lick pon them, Rantie she run lef her drawers."

"Lord have mercy, what you saying to me? But Rantie say she is a Christian. Every Sunday she gone a Church and taking holy communion. Imagine that. She and her pickney them behave as if they holier than everybody else. If I was there I would help Vie bus' her ass."

"But Dottie, you know sey them a hypocrite. Pretending to be what they are not. George have him money and a use it to mind she and her pickney them. Me, my life is an open book. Them can always open it and turn the pages. I don't have a thing to hide. I don't have anybody man. Is somebody have mine and any day I catch that dry foot gal Mimsi with him, is hell to pay."

"Talk of the devil and him show up. See Mimsi a come here," Miss Leah and Miss Ruth said at the same time.

Alex was so busy listening to the gossip that she didn't hear her friend Ciarra shouting her name. Her star apple fell to the ground as Ciarra grabbed her from behind.

"Alex, you didn't hear me calling you?"

Ciarra and Alex were the same age and had been best friends since they were little. With Megan and Andrea as part of their team, the girls had got into too many scrapes together but they always looked out for each other. Growing up together in Bell Town had given them a somewhat ideal childhood which had helped them forge a bond that had lasted this long. The two friends stood watching the citizenry of the community, like scenes from a movie.

Now, every Saturday at about noon, Mass Joe would arrive with homemade ice cream and snow cones. The ice cream would be in a big bucket and he would pack big chunks of ice around it to keep it from melting. All the children would flock around to buy Grape Nut, Rum and Raisin or Chocolate ice cream. Some would buy snow cones in the cup or shaved ice in their hands.

"Look, Tata is waving to you," Ciarra said as she pointed up to the verandah.

Tata was calling to Alex to come and get her money for her ice cream. Ciarra was busy licking at her own ice cream.

"Did your father leave, Alex?" Ciarra asked when her friend returned with her ice cream. "Mama said she saw him last night."

"You should know better than to ask that question. He comes to visit. He doesn't come to stay. He had to go back to Kingston. That is where he stays with my grandfather. He flies back to New York in a few days," Alex answered as she wiped her hands on a napkin.

"Do you ever miss living with your father?" Ciarra asked.

"What is there to miss, Ciarra? I live with my grandmother whom I love, my mom and Tata. I have all the love I need right here...and remember, I have an aunt who sends me foreign stuff so I'm not missing anything. I didn't get it when I was like five or six. He wasn't here but he would blow in sometimes, so I had this picture of him in my head. Kinda like I idolized him. He left when I was a baby and came back years later with his wife and kid to meet me. I like my life the way it is."

"So, what is she like? His wife I mean?"

"I guess she is OK. I heard that my grand aunt wanted my father to marry her because she is light skinned, plus she live a foreign. My mom wasn't light enough so she didn't meet the criteria."

With her mouth full, Ciarra debated who was better: a father who lived at home or a father who lived in New York.

"You know what, Alex? I guess you get foreign clothes and US dollars, which is cool but I have mine right here, although he terrorizes us to keep us straight," she said with a laugh.

"Come on, let's go inside. I am helping in the shop today. Auntie is in the meat shop."

Ciarra looked around.

"Where is Miss Eve? I don't see her."

"She is in the bar. Lucy is late."

"You like being in the shop, don't you, Alex? You get a lot of respect from old and young when you're back there behind the counter."

"Umm, it's not that. I listen to everyone while they are waiting for their purchases. They tell you things about their life. A few of them ask me to come and read or write a letter for them because you know some of them cannot read or write. Some of them can't even trust their own to do that for them. You know how that is Ciarra."

"Yeah, I know. Look at Miss Bibi. She sings every song in Church because she memorizes them. She knows the scriptures. Anyone would think she can read but the truth is, she can't." Ciarra shook her head as she said this.

"It is embarrassing for them to let anyone know that they cannot read or write. They come here with their money or to change the checks that their relatives from foreign send them. If it is too much, I go get Auntie or my mother and if they are too busy, I go to Tata who will do the transactions for me."

Ciarra nodded. She understood perfectly.

"So what time you going to Church tomorrow? I am gonna get there early so I'll make it for Sunday School at nine in the morning."

Alex answered, "No I am not getting there so early. It's going to be more like ten-thirty. By the time I get there, it will be time for Church service. Megan said she is not getting there early either."

"That's okay with me as long as you guys show up." Ciarra slapped her hand on her forehead. "I almost forgot about the cricket meeting this evening by Mass

Octavius. That means I am going to have to go back home to let Mama know. Papa won't be there so I won't have to tell him. Mama will when he gets home."

Alex laughed out loud. They walked back outside since there were no customers in the shop at the moment.

"You do know how to play your parents sometimes, don't you? "

"Yeah but they catch on real fast, I have to tell you. Sometimes I fear that Papa and Mama can somehow read my mind because if I am not careful, they see through me too easily when I am lying." Ciarra said this as she rolled her eyes.

They were standing in the street now. A car hurtled by. Alex screwed up her face.

"I wish that Rory didn't have to be there. Have you noticed how full of himself he is these days? He pisses me off constantly these days. When I was thirteen, fourteen, we used to be cool with each other. He read Sidney Sheldon books and so did I. We talked about music and politics. I practiced with him on my Scrabble game and I got damn good but he has become a total pain-in-the-ass. I tell you, Ciarra, I can do without being around Rory." Alex said this with a bit of anger in her voice.

For a few seconds Ciarra looked closely at Alex. She had been trying to figure out what the hell was going on between her and Rory.

"I noticed that the two of you can't be around each other for long before there is some kind of tension. You guys used to be such good buddies. Maybe it's because you are not a little kid anymore. I am just saying because I don't know. I saw him kiss Joan a few weeks ago. He didn't see me standing in the dark waiting for Tayo."

Alex shrugged her shoulders.

"Whatever."

The girls hurried back to the shop as a customer approached. It was the idler they called Bongo Man. Alex felt a shiver run through her as their eyes locked. She just couldn't stand him. Him and his friends who just stood on the street corner and called to the girls as they passed. He knew better than to mess with her. Everybody in Bell Town knew you did not mess with Miss Florentino's granddaughter. He wanted a packet of cigarettes. She handed it to him and collected the money, taking care not to let her hands touch his. The girls wrinkled up their noses at his retreating back.

- Chapter 2 -

There wasn't much space in the living room of the two-bed roomed house in which the Richardson family lived. The dining room table and the couch with the love seat took up much of the room. Smack in the middle of the room, there was a coffee table with china figurines. During the night, the room served as an extra bedroom for the boys. On this Saturday morning nineteen year old Rory had much planned for the day. He squirmed in his chair and gulped a large spoonful of banana porridge. The porridge was hot and burned his tongue and the back of his throat. His eyes watered. His brother Andy began to laugh. Mass Kenny looked at them.

"You are in a rush, son? Where is the fire? And you, Andy, put a lid on it. How many times your mother talk to you about slopping down your food? You okay, Rory?"

Rory nodded.

"Yes, papa."

Miss Linnet put her hands on her hips. She was a tall, attractive lady who always wore her hair pulled back in a pony tail.

"Boy, how many times I warn you about eating your food so fast? Here-drink some milk."

"Him rushing, Mama, because Tayo coming to meet him. Them going to look firewood and then this evening they going to meet by Mass Octavius. It's cricket time," his sister Margaret volunteered.

Rory glanced over at his sister.

"Shut up and mind your business!"

As much as he loved his sister, sometimes she could be a pain in the butt.

"What is that noise I hear?" Miss Linnet asked.

"Oh, it's Tayo. Always noisy," Andy explained.

Before his father could answer there was a knocking at the door and Tayo, Rory's best friend was shouting:

"Rory!"

Mass Kenny walked to the door.

"Why are you knocking down my door so early, Tayo?"

"Oh, good morning, Mass Kenny. Something smell good."

Mass Kenny smiled. By the time he could say come on in, Tayo was already sitting at the table. Tayo was skinny, with the wide grin of a perpetual joker. Miss Lin served a plate of mackerel and bananas with sweet potato and fried dumplings.

"Thanks, Miss Lin. I should move here on the weekends. The food always taste good."

"So you boys playing a cricket match next week? You have your bats and pads and everything you need?" Mass Kenny asked as he rejoined the family at the table.

"No, papa," Rory answered. "Mass Octavius giving us two bats and helping with the wickets."

"There is something I need from behind the cabinet, Rory. Can you see if you can find it for me?" his father asked. "I don't know how my wallet got back there."

Rory stood up and walked to the cabinet, peeping behind it to see if he could see the wallet. He was careful with his mother's valuable treasures which rattled a little as he moved the cabinet slightly forward. A brand new cricket bat leaned against the wall behind the cabinet. He grabbed it and swung it in the air.

"Be careful with that thing," his mother chuckled.

"Oh, papa, whose is this? I have wanted a bat just like this."

"Well, if you are going to be the great cricketer you said you are going to be, it's time that you have your own personal bat. It's for you to use. It's light, it should fit right into your hands and your ball is over there."

"Oh, Mass Kenny you are the best!" Tayo exclaimed.

"Thank you, papa!" Rory said with excitement in his voice.

He felt so proud to hear his father speak that way that he had to turn his head away to hide his feelings, but not before he caught his mother looking at him with a smile.

"I am going to be a famous cricketer. Just watch me. Mass Octavius said he is going to ask you to be umpire again."

Mass Kenny looked fondly at his son and silently thanked God for the family that he had. The boys wolfed down their food, picked up their plates, walked down the steps and outside to the kitchen where they hurriedly added soap and water to the dishes, rinsed, turned them down in the dish drainer and headed out into the yard to try out the new bat.

"Hey Rory," Neil, another of Rory's best friends was shouting as he approached the house, slowing his bicycle by using his foot as the brake. "Ready yet? I hope you have some lemonade in there. I am thirsty."

Neil's shaggy hair always seemed to be out of control and in need of a good trim. He was also always the last to arrive.

"Neil, you are always thirsty or hungry. Don't you eat at your yard?" Tayo questioned. "We don't have any lemonade. We are ready to go."

Neil leaned his bicycle against the wall.

"You don't live here Tayo, so don't give me no argument."

"Here, take the lemonade. Come on and leave the people's house in peace," Tayo offered.

Rory couldn't help laughing because Tayo always acted in this way. He truly behaved as if this was his family. He guessed that came from his parents' treating him as if he were their son. In order to get to Mass Octavius' house, the boys in Bell Town had to pass by Rory's house. This was their meeting place where they would make the decision as to who would be on which team. They were all excited about Rory's new bat which he refused to let anyone else touch.

The boys chatted about their proposed visit to Mass Octavius who had promised to mark out the field for them in his back yard later that evening as they walked toward Bell Town All-Age School. They took turns practicing their skills on the open grounds which included a track which was always in use as the children of Bell Town practiced their athletic skills in the hope that some day they might become champions. Shouts of "how's that?" were heard and a group of small children watched their play. The sun was getting a little too hot and they decided to cool it. They sat under a tamarind tree and yapped for a while.

When they had cooled enough they decided it was time to head out. Neil pushed his bicycle along as he walked with the rest of the boys on their way to Mass Octavius'.

"I passed Ciarra and Alex down the road this morning. Alex was talking to Rafe," Neil commented as the boys made their way toward Mass Octavius' house.

Tayo looked at Rory.

"You hear that? She is talking to Rafe. I hear that boy wants her."

Rory shrugged his shoulders.

"Why are you telling me this? Well at least Ciarra is not the one talking to him because you, Mr. Tayo, might be tempted to punch his teeth out."

"We weren't talking about me," Tayo answered.

Neil looked at Tayo with a grin on his face.

"We all know how much you like Ciarra so don't even bother pretending."

It was almost five o'clock when the boys turned up the narrow dirt path to Mass Octavius' house. Rory squinted at the sky as he walked. It was hot and he didn't want to show any signs of sweating when he finally showed up. Mass Octavius was sitting on his verandah smoking his pipe with Miss Etty by his side, rocking in her chair. It was said that Miss Etty had the "gift". She could see things, just like the time she told Mass Tommy that there was going to be fire and destruction and two days later, his house burned to the ground. Even though some people said they did not believe her, if she said she saw harm befalling someone, the person would nevertheless take precautions in order to prevent destruction, keeping in mind that it is better to be safe than sorry.

In his old years, Mass Octavius was now a rebel; gone was his well kept hair that he was known for in his youth and in its place were dreadlocks. He was a storyteller who specialized in telling ghost stories. In addition, he was a farmer who had a love for the land. In his back yard he planted watermelons, papayas and sugar cane so when the children came to play in his back yard, there was always something to eat. A few miles away, he planted peas, corn, yams, potatoes and other vegetables on land he owned, the produce from which he used to feed his family. He also gave some away and sold the excess. Some people said that he used to work for the court system; others said that he used to be a big football player in his time. Rory was not sure about those stories but what was for sure was that when it came to cricket, he was the master.

The house was set on a hill about half a mile away from the main road. It was very quiet up there: there was no television. Only the blaring of the radio, the chirping of birds, the sound of the woodpecker using its beak to chip away at the cedar tree, and in the distance, the everlasting braying of the donkey owned by Miss Jackson, the lady who lived next door, could be heard.

"So Rory, you and Tayo sweet-talking the girls already? I knew you when you were both at my knees. Look at you now, all grown up into fine boys," Miss Etty greeted as they entered the yard.

"Lawd! Etty, you mek the boys them squirming in their pants. Don't mind her at all, sons."

"Thank you Miss Etty," Tayo answered as he stuck out his chest. "I like when people tell me that I am handsome."

He sat down suddenly on the verandah railing, swinging his legs as the girls Alex, Ciarra, Megan, and Andrea walked in. He was engulfed by the sudden feeling of something flipping in his stomach. Ciarra glanced at Tayo a little shyly.

There it was again. That aura that was present whenever Alex was around. Miss Etty could tell that Alex was special. She had the gift of seeing but she wasn't aware of it just yet. Miss Etty knew that she would have to find a way for Alex to become more aware of her gift. She smiled at the girls as they said hello to her and kissed her on the cheek. Rory could not help looking at Alex. He felt all funny inside, in a good way, whenever she was around but for some reason they were always at loggerheads. He was convinced it was because she thought she was so smart.

"Hey Andy, What's going on? Long time no see." Alex smiled at Andy, almost ignoring Rory.

Andy walked over and hugged Alex, kissing her on the cheek. Rory frowned. He could have decked his brother for hugging her. Andy looked at him and smirked.

"You know I am on your team, right Alex?"

"Of course, big fellow," she answered.

"And we want Megan on our team," Rory answered back.

"Okay, children settle down," Mass Octavius interrupted. "Let's call this meeting to order. Before we choose sides we need to have a look at the field." He puffed on his pipe. "Back when people said the word field, they meant massa land where our ancestors worked in the hot sun for eighteen hours a day and during their lunch break they were expected to work in his provision ground. Sit down a while and let me remind you kids about your history. We have the freedom for me to sit on my verandah and tell you all stories, for you to play and do whatever you like to do because of Cudjoe and those who fought hard for freedom." The fire had died in Octavius' pipe and he knocked it against his leg before packing it once more with tobacco. "They said the very fierce slaves remained in Jamaica."

"Yeah, there is no doubt about that. I am a descendent of the *Coromantees*. They were said to be the fiercest. They were the slaves from the *Ashantis* who spoke *Twi* and they were feared by the slave traders," Tayo interrupted, showing off that he also knew some of his history.

"It is from those people that the Maroons emerged," Alex interjected. "The Maroons fought hard for freedom."

Miss Etty clapped her hands together. She could almost hear Queen Nanny speak.

"That is enough history for the day. We have work to do." Octavius stood up. "Time to get to work. We have to mark out the field, decide where the wickets will be. You all understand there is a bit of work to be done."

Sunlight and Dappled Shade

There was a crescendo of voices as everyone responded with a resounding yes.

As the sun dipped in the sky, they picked their spot: a flat stretch of sun-kissed grass and, working together, they marked the field. It was still warm and the sun had crouched even lower when they finished the business of talking cricket. Rory and Tayo began cutting sugar cane from Mass Octavius' field while the girls pointed to the ones they wanted. Mass Octavius and Neil peeled the cane and passed it around. They were all on the verandah - Rory sitting next to Alex, Ciarra leaning against the rail with Tayo by her side. The fresh air was fragranced by the scent of a multiplicity of herbs and flowers while the impending darkness was tinged with orange hues darting across the sky.

"So, Mass Octavius, did you truly see a rolling calf?" Neil asked, chewing on a stalk of cane, the juice dribbling down the sides of his mouth.

This was all Mass Octavius needed to hear to tell a story.

"It was a Friday night and I had a friend, a pretty young lady. So after the usual socializing - she chatting with her friends and me playing dominoes with my boys, it was late so I walked her home all the way to Galloway bottom. Remember there was no street lights back then in the sixties. It was quite late by the time I was walking home. All of a sudden, I hear like chains being dragged along the road. My head swell big and I get hot. When I look around I see nothing but two eyes breathing fire.

I say to myself, *"this rolling calf is not going to breathe fire on Octavius."* 'Lawd Jesus, you up there?' I bawl out. I had two drinks earlier and I start to cuss the bad word them. So I cuss is so I wield my ratchet knife. I had a little flask of rum with me so I throw it on my ratchet and use my lighter to light up a fire. When I finish cuss the bad word them and look around I don't see a rolling calf. That night I must have suddenly sprouted wings because I can't even remember running all the way home. All I know, I was home."

Everyone was silent, caught up in the story. The donkey suddenly started braying as if he knew the tale had come to an end. Alex screamed. Neil jumped and a few of them started to get to their feet. The sudden noise had frightened some of them.

"Okay, I am turning the light on," Miss Etty said as she got up and switched on the light. "You are scaring everyone to death. It's getting late so it's time for you young people to go home, anyway."

She looked at Alex as she said this. There it was again, that light around her that only she could see. She would have to say something to Alex very soon because someone would have to teach her about her special powers.

"Next time you can tell us about the three-foot horse," Tayo said with excitement.

"Yes, next time," Mass Octavius answered.

"Good night Miss Etty, Good night Mass Octavius," everyone echoed as they made their way down the path.

Rory could see that Alex was jittery and a little scared.

"Do you mind if Tayo, Neil, Andy and I walk you, Ciarra, Andrea and Megan home?" he offered.

Alex shook her head and stared down at her hand as Rory took it, noticing how much bigger his was. Her heart was beating an erratic tempo in her chest as her gaze traveled to his face. Rory watched her and, as their eyes met, he held her gaze. He used his eyes to calm the frisson of fear he sensed rising in her. He stared into her wary eyes and squeezed her hand gently. She smiled at him, a smile that lit up her entire face. Rory kept thinking to himself how pretty she was and in that moment, although he didn't quite know what love was, he fancied himself in love with Alex. Puppy love is what his mother called it.

-CHAPTER 3- –

Four days later, Rory studied the plan and checked equipment: flashlight, rope and a bottle of alcohol. Neil was bringing the walkie-talkies because that would be their mode of communication. Tayo would be bringing cotton pads. The alcohol and cotton pads were for any scratches, bruises and cuts they might sustain from crawling into the cave. They were taking the long route to the cave. They would walk up the barely discernible tract a quarter of a mile before entering.

If there was one thing Rory knew about himself, it was the fact that he was stubborn and determined. He knew that no warning was going to stop them from finding out what this cave was all about. The plan was to meet when it was dark. He and Tayo would leave together and wait at a half-way point for Neil and Andy. He was dressed in a black tee-shirt and a pair of black pants. Everyone agreed they should all wear dark clothing so that they would not be easily seen.

He heard Tayo's whistle, snatched up his knapsack and headed out. The teens tapped the front of their fists together and continued walking cautiously up the road, cutting across to the narrow tract until they came to the meeting point. They heard the others whistle and whistled back. Andy and Neil emerged from the darkness.

"Let's check our supplies. I have the walkie-talkies and a flashlight," Neil whispered.

"I have a flashlight and the rope in my knapsack. Has anyone changed their mind because if you have, there is still time to back out," Rory made it clear to all.

"Screw you, Rory. I have cotton and alcohol pads. Keep walking bro," Tayo answered.

"I have beer to settle our nerves after," Andy chimed in cheerfully.

The night was clear and the sky full of stars as they moved through the bush towards the cave. A stray dog ran across their path and the boys paused in their tracks. They chuckled and continued on their way. Glancing around, they approached the mouth of the cave cautiously. They removed the bush and thatch that someone had used to conceal the entrance.

"Okay, Tayo, it's you and Andy on the lookout and Neil and I are going in. If you see anything funny, alert us on the walkie-talkies. Tie this rope around my waist for safety."

Rory moved ahead and disappeared into the black hole with Neil bringing up the rear. Tayo could hear them moving around and heard Neil curse because he had stubbed his toes.

"Find anything?" Tayo whispered.

"Not yet! It's narrow down here, as you know. Hold on. We are coming to a fork in the tunnel. Wait a second. What's this? This looks like weed," he exclaimed as he shone his flashlight on the neatly stacked packages in front of him.

"What kinda weed?" Andy grabbed the walkie-talkie, asking excitedly.

"I mean ganja, cali weed, whatever you call it!" Neil shouted back. "What the hell else we call weed?"

"We didn't see this extra space when were all down here before," Rory remarked. "It's like the extra space was covered. There are boxes and a chest. There is money in here. I don't believe it."

"Shit! Someone is coming. We see lights, repeat, someone is coming," Tayo warned.

Tayo and Andy lay flat on the ground, crawling on their stomachs away from the caves. Below Rory broke into a sweat. The boys glanced at each other and Tayo signaled to Andy. Using their slingshots, Tayo and Andy fired into the trees, startling the sleeping birds. Moving as a flock, the birds flapped their wings eerily as they flew into the night sky. The two men who were approaching the cave whirled around, startled. The boys remained crouched and as they crawled away, they again used their catapults, this time to hit the stray dog who yelped and dashed away through the darkness. They watched as Bongo Man, the taller of the two men, stopped and looked around. Bongo Man and his companion Fiat looked at each other, then turned and walked hurriedly back up the narrow tract in the direction that they had come from. Tayo and Andy were weak with relief.

"Get your asses out of there," Tayo hissed into the walkie-talkie. "For now they are gone but they may be coming back. Exit through the bush and cut out at the back of the Church. We'll meet you there."

Crouching, Rory and Neil ran in the shadows, colliding with the bushes that lined the path behind the Church. They only stopped running when they were leaning against the back of the Church, their breaths coming in spurts. They dusted dirt from their clothes and leaves from their hair. Peering around, they circled the Church only to discover that Megan,

Ciarra and Alex were doing late night practice runs on the dirt track behind the church.

"Shit, we have another problem," Neil said in frustration. "The girls are using this place as a track field."

"There is absolutely no problem here," Rory responded. "We'll just wait until we see Tayo riding up. Then we'll slide around to the front. Tayo will distract them. We'll tell them we walked behind the school."

Neil and Rory slipped out of their hiding places as they saw Tayo riding up with Andy. They must have been telling the girls a funny story because they had them laughing. They ran to the side of the school and then joined the group.

The night was cool and Alex had her hair pinned and twisted at the top of her head. Rory tried to ignore the fact that her shorts were very short. He could see she had been sweating. Ciarra did not seem to be noticing anyone but Tayo, and Megan was busy stretching for her runs. The boys signaled each other. They had to meet without the girls. Five minutes later, after promising to run a race with Megan, Neil, Andy and Tayo hunkered down, sitting on the wall by the little school.

"There is a lot of ganja in that cave. I didn't expect anything like this." Rory shook his head. "They have to be supplying someone big. They are probably taking it out by helicopter as they do in other places."

"I almost pissed in my pants when I saw Bongo and Fiat heading towards the cave. I think we scared the shit out of them when we shot into the trees and then hit Mass Tom's dog with our catapults. Man, you should have seen their faces. It was like they thought the spirits were after them." Andy recalled. "If those guys had caught you two or caught us I don't know what would have happened," he continued.

"Catch who? Me? You mad, Andy? I would have come out with my flying kick. Those guys sell weed. They are not the ones with guns. Remember we knew they were coming but they didn't know we were there. We had the advantage. Isn't that so, Rory?" Tayo asked.

"I wonder if this is why Mass Octavius told us to stay away from the cave. It doesn't make any sense. He couldn't be mixed up in this," Rory said fiercely. "We are going to ask him."

"You think if we borrow some of their weed, they'll know it's us? We can make some money too," Neil said with a grin.

"Hey, you guys seem to be in some kind of intense talk. It's time for my race, Rory. Come on," Megan interrupted.

Tayo held on to Ciarra's hand.

"Can I talk to you?"

"Now? This very minute?"

Her lips twitched. Tayo looked at her pouty and delectable looking lips. They walked further into the darkness, entered the open school classroom and sat on one of the benches. She squeezed his arm.

"You have muscles, Tayo. What do you want to talk to me about in the dark?"

"I always need to spend time with you whenever I can. It's hard to get you to myself half of the time."

He slid his arm around her. His mouth came closer and closer and then his lips came down on hers. She sucked his tongue. He pushed his hand inside her jeans. His fingers slid lower and lower. Ciarra jumped as she heard Alex calling her name. Tayo pulled his hand away as Ciarra pulled up her pants.

"Ciarra, I love you," he said.

She nodded.

Two days later...

The Bell Town All-Age schoolyard was the main place where Megan practiced. This was where Ciarra and Alex made her run up the hill from the School Gate at the bottom of the private road to the Churchyard at the top of the hill. They started out slowly and after a couple of weeks, she no longer felt winded after making it to the top. They had gone so far as to mark out a one-hundred-meter field and a two-hundred-meter field. Although she was known for doing well at track and field she had had previous doubts about beating the girls from Vere Technical High School but now she was filled with confidence. She knew without a doubt that she would break that hundred-meter record set by Vere.

She liked to jog in the late evenings. She lifted her face to the sky, reveling in the cool night air. This was her world - running. Her body was finely toned, her legs that of an athlete. "*I will get that scholarship,*" she mused. "*This will be my ticket out of here. How else am I going to get to college? Papa already used the money on my sister, Patricia...as always. She is my sister and all but*

I have yet to see the benefit of all the money that he has wasted on her. This is my way out." The thought went around and around in her head as she stretched and flexed her muscles.

"Megan, you did 10.9 seconds flat. Between your coach and us you are on your way to winning the hundred meters next week, girl!" Ciarra was jumping up and down shouting excitedly.

"Yeah, with a little more practice you can drop to under ten seconds," Alex said looking at the stopwatch in her hand. "Scholarship, here comes Megan Thomas. Actually, we're shooting for nine seconds. I don't know of anyone doing that time for a hundred meter sprint."

Megan was sitting on the Church steps with her arms wrapped around her knees, her head in Alex's lap. Her shoulders shook as she began to laugh.

"Can anyone tell me how carrying a bucket of water on my head has helped me to improve my speed? Who trains like this?"

Alex and Ciarra had devised the plan where they made Megan carry a bucket of water on her head. It helped with focus and strength. The first few times, the bucket fell or the water spilled but eventually, with discipline and focus, she had been able to balance the bucket with water.

"We have come a long way, sister, but we have a little more distance to go because you will get that scholarship. Where is your sister any way? Is she going back to Kingston or is she living here now?" Ciarra asked.

"Don't get me started on that subject. Papa and Mama have given so much to her. School in

Kingston. He sold land and used the money to send her to Canada. She has been here, there and everywhere and is asking for more. Why? Because she has accomplished nothing. She is twenty-two years old for God's sake. It's six of us and when it comes down to it, I end up with crumbs."

"I didn't even know that you had another sister until she showed up. Did she move to Kingston to live with her uncle when she was young?" Alex asked.

"Yeah, high hopes for her! She attended high school and we all thought that she would have done much better but I guess that's what happens when you are too privileged. She has made no effort to excel and my parents are still catering to her. Why? Because of her good looks?" Megan queried no one in particular.

"Listen to me, Megan. You are so much better off than she is. We were there for you and hung out with you all these years and you see? You are talented, a phenomenal athlete and a loyal friend. Sometimes it's not where we grow up but with whom. Look at where we are, training you for the ultimate Olympics," offered Ciarra.

"You are right about that," Megan said with a laugh. "Being with my best buddies is priceless. What's going on with all that hand holding with Rory anyway? Whenever he is around he stares at you when he thinks no one is looking. That boy likes you, Alex."

"I am sure the same way Neil like you and Tayo likes Ciarra."

"Neil kissed me," Megan blurted out.

"What! When did this happen? Spill, you secret hoarder." Ciarra jumped to her feet, her arms akimbo. "You've been holding out on us."

"It was Sunday night after Youth Fellowship. He insisted on walking me home. You both know it can be quite lonely walking home after everyone else turns off to go up to the housing scheme. Alex, you won't even walk home from the square after dark by yourself. So after we got to my gate, I thanked him and said goodnight but he wanted to talk some more. He told me he had his eye on me and how much he liked me. I guess I was smitten and with it being full moon and the stars were in the sky, I felt good about letting him kiss me. It was good."

"And you're just telling us this?" Ciarra sat down on the steps as if her legs were giving out.

"I am sixteen going on seventeen and he is nineteen. It's time that I get kissed. I mean a real kiss, not the fumbling, sloppy ones. I am ready for something more," Megan laughed.

"Did you see Rory holding my hand last Saturday? He had me cracking up at his jokes. I didn't know he had such a good sense of humor," Alex said with a slow grin.

"What about you and Tayo? What's going on? He is your boyfriend, we know that but your relationship has advanced. It's more intense, more serious," Megan said to Ciarra.

For a few seconds there was silence.

"Well?" Alex prompted.

"Tayo got as far as to touch my breasts. I let him get to second base. He almost got to first base but I don't want to go any further," Ciarra finally answered.

"I can't believe it!" Alex and Megan both exclaimed at the same time. Ciarra bolted straight up.

"You let him do all that?" Alex made a face at Ciarra. "You better be careful."

"Isn't that Neil and Rory riding up this way? Lover Boy is coming to check up on you."

The boys rode their bicycles up to the step.

"Hey, ladies," they greeted.

Neil hopped off his bicycle, gave Megan a hug, then he turned and hugged Ciarra and Alex. Rory sat on the steps.

"I would hug all three of you but since Neil did that for me, I will just kiss Alex for myself".

"Don't worry about us," Ciarra answered. "Where is the other one? Why did you guys leave poor Tayo behind this evening?"

"Poor Tayo? There is nothing poor thing about him. He will be here in five minutes and he is not alone. Ethan and Andy are with him. We are your protection team, both from the living and from duppy. I am sure you have all heard about the piano being played when the Church is supposed to be empty," Rory answered.

"Stop talking nonsense! You really believe that?" Alex asked.

"Yeah, my uncle said that he was going home one night and heard the piano being played when the Church was dark." Neil had to put his two cents in.

"Let's change the subject," Megan suggested.

"So, Megan, I hear you're almost under the ten-second mark. I am backing you and volunteering my help. If there is anything I can do, let me know. We are all going to be there at the stadium to watch you win - I mean break a record. It's in another two weeks - the first week in April?" Rory said.

Megan was animated by the thought.

"It's my first High school track and field competition at the National Stadium and I have every intention of succeeding. I have worked hard." She stood up and looked around at her friends. "I am glad I have you guys as my support team. It means a lot."

Alex tried to lighten the mood.

"After the track meet and Rory's cricket match why don't we have a little party for summer vacation? We can have some fun then."

Rory hoped that what he was thinking wouldn't show on his face. It was a great idea because that way, he could dance up close with Alex.

"Great idea! We have to plan and save. I can ask Papa to ask Uncle to sell us his ram goat for cheap."

"That was a quick yes from you, Rory, but I am in agreement with this so we will have to come up with a plan. We are going to the Church Rally in a few weeks so I hope all you guys will come," Alex said.

A week later...

Alex was up early for the one-day cricket match to be held in Mass Octavius' back yard. She wanted to be there ahead of time. She had promised to make sandwiches. She grabbed the corned beef and tuna from the cupboard, then cut the onions and pepper into small pieces. She quickly spread the corned beef and the tuna on the already-sliced bread. She should have enough sandwiches to feed the whole team and beyond.

"Alex," her grandmother said as she walked into the room, "you can take half a dozen sodas – make sure to take some Kola Champagne as well. I don't want you to be hungry out there."

"Oh thanks, Auntie," she replied with a smile. "Ciarra and I will be riding with Andrea. Her father will be picking me up so I won't have to walk."

"Oh, good. I'll come out and say hi to Charlie when he gets here," Auntie replied.

Alex arrived early to find Rory, Andy, Neil and Tayo with Mass Octavius sitting under the mango tree and deep in conversation. Whatever it was must have been important because Tayo wasn't being a wise ass but instead he was totally involved in the conversation.

"Hello, my dears," Miss Etty greeted them. "You guys look fit and all ready to give them boys a run for their money today." She laughed as she said this. "Bring the sodas. Let's put them in the ice bucket." She preceded them to the outdoor kitchen. Alex walked to the window, eavesdropping on the conversation outside.

Mass Octavius was saying, "I wanted you boys to stay away from that cave. I heard that it's being used to hide away some things. If they find out that you know about it, there may be trouble and things could turn out dangerous for all of you."

"We're going back soon," Rory told him. "It's just that right now, there is so much going on."

Caves? *What caves are they talking about?* Alex asked herself. She jumped as Miss Etty called out her name and hollered for the others to come on out to the mango tree. She moved from the window to the mango tree outside. Miss Etty was standing by the folding table that was covered with a multi-colored cloth. On it was a bowl of water and in her hand a bottle of rum. Her bracelets jangled on her arm as she poured three drops of water around the circle calling on *The Lord of All* and her ancestors. She lit her cigar and started puffing away. She drank from the bottle of rum before spitting some on the floor and then she dipped her fingers into the bowl of water. One by one, she touched each of their foreheads with her fingers while asking for protection and guidance for all. Alex was intrigued and carefully watched the ritual. She felt drawn to it as if she had some inkling of what it was all about. A soft feeling of warmth engulfed her.

Tayo whispered to Rory, "This should give me the creeps but it doesn't because I find it funny. I have never seen her spin like that. She's spinning really fast like a gig. What do you think this is all about?"

"You heard what Miss Etty said - it's a form of protection. Either you believe or you don't," Rory answered.

Alex raised her brows.

"The old timers say that belief kills and belief cures. I heard you all talking about a cave and I want to know what that was all about," she whispered to Rory.

"Okay I'll tell you later,"' he answered. "And by the way, do you all feel any lighter than you did twenty minutes ago?"

Ciarra looked at him and rolled her eyes.

"I don't. What about you?" she asked.

"This is entertainment to me. Who knew Miss Etty had moves like these?"

Megan laughed. Now that she had done what she could, Miss Etty felt relieved, light, as if a great weight had been lifted from off her shoulders. She wasn't about to stand idly by and watch those she loved get harmed in any way. There was something dark and mysterious about that cave but these young people weren't about to pay heed to advice to stay away.

Rory's team won the match by two wickets. His next match would be with the boys from the Youth Club. There would be a combination of players from the different clubs in Westmoreland. This was one of the big matches because from this, the best players would be chosen to play on Jamaica's national team.

- Chapter 4 -

First week in April

It was early morning; the sky was still a pale blue. The sun had yet to put in an appearance. Betsy, as they called the Montego Bay High School bus, pulled out of its parking spot packed with eager, bright-eyed students and teachers on their way to the High School Track and Field Championship being held at the National Stadium in Kingston. They were leaving a day early to get to Kingston because athletes needed to be relaxed and rested in order to compete.

Megan settled in her seat for the four-hour drive, repeatedly opening and then closing her book. She was distracted. They passed the Town of Rose Hall, which featured swaying palm trees lining the entrances to hotels such as Sandals and Half Moon Bay, and villas filled with tourists. The Rose Hall Great House stood in majestic splendor, white against the green hills. They left the Parish of St. James behind and entered the Town of Falmouth where they stopped to pick up another student, Maxine Jameson. What once could be described as a bustling place where people as far away as Montego Bay used to come to shop for clothes and shoes, Falmouth was now reduced to a sleepy town with buildings that looked like mausoleums.

"Hey Megan," Taneisha broke into her friend's reverie, "Miss says it's okay to get off the bus to buy box juice. Are you coming with us?"

"Yes, I am coming. *Gimme* a second to put on my shoes."

Megan bent to retrieve her sneakers from where she had kicked them earlier to make herself more comfortable. Half an hour later, they were back on the road. Megan gazed out over the straight road leading into Kingston, her eyes looking everywhere. She had formed such a bond with Alex, Ciarra and Andrea, it was like a gathering of souls, pulling them together knowing that even if they became separated they would have the will to find each other again.

They understand who I am and that I have chosen to follow my independent path outside the rigid structure of my upbringing. I don't want to be a lawyer or a doctor or a preacher. I am an athlete who wants to be a teacher. Megan liked to think of herself as a rebel. A smile lit up her face because tomorrow her friends would be at the Stadium to support her. She peeped over and saw that Taneisha was asleep. When they got to Discovery Bay, she tapped Taneisha on the shoulder as the bus pulled into Puerto Seco Beach where they were making a brief stop. As usual, the beach had a casual atmosphere and was patronized by many locals, with its reggae bands and food stalls that brought on the familiar tranquil feeling.

"Wake up," Megan whispered.

"Okay, ladies," their coach warned. "We are allowing everyone to get off the bus. Those who would like to take a quick dip are allowed into the water but there is a boundary that everyone here has to observe. Am I understood?"

The coach and teachers smiled proudly as the girls dashed from the bus, squealing in delight, and ran towards the pearly white sand kissed by sparkling, turquoise water.

"Miss, aren't you going for a swim?" someone asked.

The coach shook her head as did the teachers.

"We have to keep watch over you girls and we cannot be distracted."

The students all laughed and shook their heads at the excuse offered by their teachers.

"Nice excuse, Miss," Taneisha said with a chuckle.

The girls laughed in delight and splashed and frolicked in the clear, blue water. They had jelly coconuts with fried fish and bammy; but after what seemed like too short a time, they had to leave this mini paradise.

Their route took them through Ocho Rios, passing by Dunns River Falls then through Fern Gully and after that the town of Moneague with its many hills and valleys criss-crossed by stone walls. The warm salty water of Puerto Seco Beach and the drive lulled Megan and the rest of the girls to sleep. They woke up to find themselves on the Boulevard leading to Kingston, the ever-growing capital and cultural and commercial center of Jamaica. From every street corner reggae music could be heard blaring from big sound systems set up outside of bars and places of entertainment. Megan peered through the window and saw that they were now in Halfway Tree. Minivans competed with municipal buses while drivers shouted at pedestrians and complained that they were behaving as if they owned the road because they sometimes crossed the street when it was not their right-of-way and prevented traffic from moving.

Their coach pointed out the Halfway Tree Clock. Though it was a Jamaican landmark, but what struck Megan was the many vendors displaying their wares.

There was a man selling coconut water. Rubbing elbows with him was a vendor selling sunglasses and others selling sugarcane and the list went on. It was only half a mile from Halfway Tree to the Jamaica Pegasus Hotel where the team was staying and in fifteen minutes, they were turning into the driveway of the hotel. Megan gazed in awe at the building. She was a long way from Bell Town and its small wooden structures the people called home.

The following morning, Megan slid out of bed and inhaled and exhaled. This was it. She felt rested, having gone to bed at her regular time and sleeping like a baby. *Not bad for a country girl staying in a posh hotel*, she thought to herself. She had seen some of the girls from out-of-town schools because many of them were staying at the Pegasus and a few at the Courtleigh Manor. No yam or dumplings for her this morning. She would have some banana porridge and a fish sandwich.

"Nervous?" Taneisha asked. "We're going to win today," she continued. "And let's say for argument sake something goes wrong, we'll make a quick comeback."

"Yeah, that is true", Megan replied. "Let's get a move on. We have to meet Coach and the rest of the team in another hour. Let's check for spikes, running shoes, track bottoms...the whole shebang. Okay, Taneisha girl, let's go have some fun."

They hugged each other, smiling. The bus pulled out once more, taking the athletes onto the streets of Kingston down Mountain View Avenue to the National Stadium, above which was the opulent neighborhood of Beverly Hills with its mansions.

Near to the Stadium were the not-so-opulent communities of Nannyville and Back Bush.

By the time Megan and her team walked out on the field, there were other runners stretching and warming up. There were swarms of students from every school in Jamaica and Megan's friends were sitting in the crowd of spectators. Megan looked up in time to see the star player of her school's biggest competitor, walk over. She looked Megan up and down.

"Hey, Megan, when you see me coming, move out of my way. I wouldn't want to run right over you and this goes for the rest of you too." She gestured to the team.

"You know what, yam foot? You won't even see me coming. What you will see is my shadow flying by," Megan answered.

"Yeah, you know the song, 'If you run down your shadow now, you'll never catch it'? That's us so why don't you bounce right back over to where you came from?" Taneisha taunted back. "She have some nerve bringing her tough ass over here."

"Megan," another classmate answered, "Now we know they are afraid. They would not have come over here if they were so confident that they would win the race so our advantage is our confidence."

Megan paced back and forth. She had run, perspired and pushed her body beyond endurance. She wasn't looking for fame but for respect and for a scholarship. As an athlete, she had learnt that hard work yielded great rewards. Everyone at her school, Montego Bay High, including her coach and her friends, Ciarra, Alex, Andrea, Neil, Tayo, and Rory, believed in her. They were all here at the National Stadium to support her. When she had started out, she had no idea that track and field would have meant so much to her and that this sport would have come to define her. Other races had been run but now it was her race. She walked out to the starting block and stood at the starting line.

"On your marks, get set..."

She heard the roaring of the gun in her ear, and exploded out of the box. She was a natural. The turf seemed to rise up to meet her feet. "Go Megan, go!" She smiled as the chants grew louder and she glided away from her competitors. This was her love. This was what she lived for. Not looking back as she charged down the field, she sprinted to the finish line where she threw up her hands in the air.

"Megan Thomas has set a record 9.24 seconds for the hundred meters. She is going to the Penn Relays. A very talented, very dedicated athlete."

This announcement came from Jay Barnes, the commentator. Alex was cheering and screaming. Megan looked towards the stands and waved.

"She is really good!" Neil was jumping up and down.

"Let's go to the fence to talk to her."

Alex and Ciarra squeezed through the crowd and ran down the steps towards the fence.

"You did it, Megan, you did it!" Alex said excitedly.

"Tayo and the guys are up there. They are all excited. Congratulations, Megan," Ciarra added.

"When I came out of the block, I didn't see anything else but the finish line. I did it, didn't I?" Megan said exultantly.

"Alright, see you later, Megan. I think they are looking for you to do your interview. *Nuff respect.*" The girls threw her a kiss before walking back to the stands.

Monday was the next time Alex caught up with Megan who had become an overnight sensation. Before she even left the Stadium, her name was known throughout Jamaica. This was a huge accomplishment for Megan, the new rising star. The Bell Baptist Church offered up prayers for her in the Sunday service and she was now a celebrity in town. The girls all sat together in the school library. This time they were not discussing sports but a more popular topic: boys.

"So, Ciarra, all of a sudden I am Miss Popularity. Charlie, who never spoke to me before- you know, the goalie for the football team from Cornwall, is giving me the time of day."

She screwed up her face as she said this.

"Don't say that around Neil because he might decide to punch him out," Alex laughed.

"The Church rally is coming up. We need to figure out what we are going to wear to this event. If we are going to have new dresses made, we have to start working on that now," Ciarra said.

With that in mind, Ciarra took out her sketch pad.

Rory stood outside the Churchyard with Andy, Tayo and Neil by his side, his back erect, his shoulders straight, looking quite handsome. He was waiting for

Alex to show up. The Church was filling up fast. It was the annual Church rally and it was going to be jam-packed and would overflow to the courtyard outside. All those who rarely, if ever, attended Church would be here tonight and people from all the churches in the surrounding areas would be in attendance.

The rally gave people a chance to dress up, get out, socialize and hear great singers entertain. It was one of the village's most popular events for a good reason. Alex's grandmother, a member of the Church committee, was one of those who had spent much time planning to make the rally a success. She had sent as far as Canada and the United States of America to solicit donations for the Church rally. There had been a big competition to see who could collect the most money. The funds donated would be used to fix the roof or do repairs to the Church building.

"Here they come," Tayo whispered as Megan, Ciarra and Alex walked up the steps to the boys.

Megan had trimmed her hair in a curly, low cut. She was wearing big hoop earrings that showed off her face to perfection.

"Oh Megan, you look cute with your hair like that," Alex complimented her.

"Well, if I had long hair like you and Ciarra, I wouldn't have to trim it so low. Pulling back your hair like that, Alex, and with that touch of eyeliner, it shows up those pretty eyes of yours."

"Thanks. Let's go in and secure some seats."

They left the boys standing on the steps while they headed inside. As Alex entered the Church, she saw the Bell Baptist Church Choir to her left, dressed in their purple robes with gold sashes. At the front were members of the Bell Holiness Church with their guitars and drums. There was always an interesting mix of churches in attendance on the night of the rally and the expectation was that there was going to be some good old hand clapping and rocking to the music.

The organ blared and the choir sang, "*Alle, alle, alle, lu-u-ia, alleluia, alle-lu-ia!*" Standing in the pulpit, Reverend Malroon asked that everyone bow their heads in prayer while he invoked the name of Jesus. Next, he spoke about the annual rally.

"And the Bible says it is better to give than to receive so tonight we will give what we have and God will bless us."

Megan was welcomed as a rising star in the sports world and received a thunderous round of applause. The choir opened the rally singing, "All Hail the Power of Jesus' Name." As the song ended, the group from Castle Mountain came up and began to sing:

> *Rock my soul in the bosom of Abraham.*

The bass chipped in:

> "*I looked over Jordan and what did I see?*
>
> *A band of angels coming after me; Oh, rock my soul.*"

The crowd shouted enthusiastically, "*Encore! Encore!*" People jumped up and started dancing and stomping, making a loud noise in the Church.

Someone shouted, "A hundred dollars to take them down!"

Auntie shouted, "Two hundred dollars to hear them again!"' It was fun and it got even better when the Castle Mountain group started singing:

> *Swing low, sweet chariot, coming forth to carry me home.*

On the stage, the drummer beat out his rhythm while the guitarist played a mento rhythm, which had some people dancing in their seats. Alex saw her mother's head bobbing up and down to the beat. She was enjoying herself.

Tayo leaned forward and whispered to Ciarra. "I am going outside. Do you want to meet me out there?"

She whispered back with a frown on her face, "Maybe" but ten minutes later, she was on her way out the door.

"You had better be careful, Ciarra," Alex said with concern in her voice, "because if your daddy or mama catches you sneaking around tonight with Tayo, you will get slapped."

"I won't get caught. I'll be careful," Ciarra answered and tip-toed out the back of the Church.

-Chapter 5-

The morning sun held the pleasant warmth of what promised to be a beautiful day with a few wisps of white cloud drifting beneath the clear blue sky. Alex walked the quarter mile to Bell Town Square where she would meet up with her friends and catch the bus to school in Montego Bay.

Alex didn't have the courage to tell anyone, not Ciarra or Megan that come next semester she would be moving to Mona Heights in Kingston. Instead of finishing sixth form at Montego Bay High she would be transferring to St Hugh's. It was her last year of waking up when the roosters were crowing, last day of walking in the dark to catch the bus to school. She wondered if Rory would miss her. Oops, where did that thought come from? It made no difference to her whether he would or not.

Her uncle with whom she would be living was a Member of Parliament in the People's Leading Party. No more catching the bus to school. She would be chauffer-driven to school instead. Where had the time gone? Five, six years had flown by. It seemed as if changes were coming. Living in Kingston was a different way of life; it had its advantages and disadvantages. She mingled with the upper crust of society. Visiting her relatives during the holidays there she had noted the difference; she visited the mall in Halfway Tree, not only browsing but buying because her uncle gave her an allowance and she went to the movies at Carib Theatre which she always enjoyed.

She couldn't deny it, she also loved politics. David DeCampo inspired her. Honestly, she was a little in love with the man. She spent hours listening to his speeches. Whenever she referred to him she always said he had such panache and spoke with such eloquence. Her brow wrinkled as she thought about the snooty girls in Kingston who talked non-stop about designer clothes and the cars their fathers drove. These friends she had here in Bell Town were genuine.

I really don't want to leave Auntie at all, Alex thought. If she had a choice, she would stay here in Bell Town to be under her grandmother's frock tail as they say. Auntie was smart and savvy and Alex loved her so much. All these thoughts rolled over her. The pleasant smell of potato pudding and dukanoo wrapped in banana leaves baking. Oh, the treats her granny could make. She tried to follow what she learned from her grandmother and to find reinforcement in her mother, the rituals taught to her, allowing her to move between two worlds. Her cousin was already helping out more in her grandmother's store, already taking her place. Her mother had just been hired by a company in the big city but she was still debating whether she wanted to make the move. Her mother also hated to leave Auntie and go too far.

Alex started as someone tapped her on the shoulder.

"Girl where is your mind? Do you know how many times I called your name?"

She straightened up and turned around. Ciarra and Andrea were standing in front of her.

"You almost gave me a heart attack, Ciarra. I didn't hear you both sneaking up on me."

"I think we should walk down to Galloway to meet the bus this morning. Look how crowded the square is and I definitely don't want to be late. It's the last day of school and we have much chatting and stuff to do," Andrea said.

"You have your bag with your swim suit and stuff?" Ciarra asked Alex.

"Sure do. Today is going to be so much fun. Last day of school and a whole bunch of us at the beach. I am so looking forward to it," Andrea chimed.

Buses didn't run on schedule from Bell Town. They ran whenever, all throughout the day. There were many buses plying the route to Montego Bay but if there was a roadblock, meaning random police check points to ensure that documents such as insurance and license to operate a bus were up to date, bus men knew to hide until the road block was over because many of them were driving with violations.

The bus this morning was packed and, under normal circumstances people would cuss that a driver is squeezing in too many passengers; but not today. The conductor, knowing that people were desperate to get to work and about their business, was still asking passengers to small up themselves.

"Alright people, we not leaving not a soul this mawning because Crick bus bruk down and Chinaman bus just pull out full to the brim, so small up yourself, everyone want to go to work."

One passenger bawled out: "Lawd Jesus man you step on my corn toe. Driver a how you a fling the bus round the corner so? Take it easy man."

The driver answered: "Ma'am, you want to reach work on time this morning, right? So the bus can go round the corner on two wheels. Please bear it for a second and if someone should slide down in a them seat and squeeze you against the side of the bus, don't cuss them, bite you tongue and don't box that person. It is I, the bus driver a tek corner."

The man in the back of the bus joined in the banter: "Bway, Mr. Driver, you have nuff chat this morning. You must a eat fowl feather last night or some other part."

The entire bus started to laugh except for Christian Mathilda sitting in her seat with her face mek up like when rain a go fall.

"Rat, pass your fare up front because me not chasing you this morning fi my money and stop pretend to fall over in the woman lap because you can hold on to the seat." The conductor spelled it out clearly.

"Why you a put me on blast, conductor. You a mek me look bad like you have problems everyday with me and your money."

With all the new cars on the road and roads being fixed, traffic was backed up from Barnett Street to Reading. Catherine Hall Highway was no better; traffic was crawling. Alex almost fell out of her seat as the driver increased speed because he was dipping in and out of traffic.

"You a go kill me this mawning, driver. Me heart no good," Miss Tiny bawled out.

"Don't worry, mammy, the driver have it unda control," the conductor tried to console Miss Tiny.

The driver almost made it to the top of the line but traffic cop Bags spied him. Bags pointed and shouted:

"Man, just turn around and go back to the end of the line."

The passengers were fed up and started to cuss. The bus finally reached downtown and the driver decided he would drop Alex and Megan on Union Street by their school, Montego Bay High. They waved goodbye to Ciarra who attended Mt. Alvernia High.

To celebrate the last day in the school year most of the girls usually spent the day at the beach. Today was no exception. They walked the distance to Doctors Cave in high spirits. Alex loved the beach. Flip flops went flying a she jumped in the water. She floated on her back and then flapped awhile. Andrea threw a ball; Alex caught it and threw it back. Others joined in the game. They splashed around, played beach ball, ran along the shore having fun before walking back to sit on the sand or collapse on the beach chairs. Alex allowed her mind to drift. She was going to make sure that Rory and his cronies understand that she wanted in on the planning to go back to the cave.

With the late afternoon sun and the breeze on her face Alex paddled towards the shore, crossed the sand and flopped down under the umbrella. She lay flat on her back, staring up at the cloudless sky overhead and let her thoughts drift. She thought about Rory and smiled to herself. She didn't want to admit it but she had a secret crush on him.

Her granny had sat her down just the other night and given her a lecture about being around Rory too much. Her granny didn't like what she was hearing because after all he was nineteen and an experienced man already and she was a sixteen year old innocent.

Alex sucked her teeth. Rory was going to be a famous cricketer and she was going to be the Prime Minister of Jamaica, well maybe not but probably a politician or a high profile lawyer. Each Wednesday all those who couldn't afford health care could attend the local clinic where they would be seen by Cuban doctors free of charge. To some this was unacceptable but to others this was a blessing. This was one of the programs introduced by David DeCampo. Under his government also through the Ministry of Agriculture he had introduced the "Backyard Garden Program." Where each person was encouraged to plant "ready crops such as tomatoes, callaloo, vegetables, peppers and much more. The goal was to establish self-sufficiency and independence.

If I work towards this goal, she kept thinking, I *could do lots of good for this country.* But more urgent right now was the plan to get Rory and the rest of the boys to take her along on a trip to the cave. Something smacked her in the stomach, startling her out of her reverie. Her eyes flew open as she sat up rather abruptly to see Ciarra laughing at her.

"Did you have to hit me with that damn ball?" Alex demanded. "It hurts you know."

"Sorry, but I needed to get you attention. Where does your mind take you to these days? Boys alert. I ran into Tayo with some girl. I know he wasn't expecting to see us," Ciarra reported. "He was shocked to practically bump into me."

"What? Where?" Alex asked as she looked around.

Ciarra pointed in the opposite direction.

"They are over there with a bunch of girls."

Alex didn't say a word. She got to her feet and began to walk across the beach. She turned and looked at Ciarra.

"Come on, let's go. I am going over to say hello to Tayo."

They walked along the sand but he must have seen them coming because by the time they got to his side of the beach he was doing laps in the water. Ciarra huffed out a breath.

"He think he is a smart ass or what. He thinks that by jumping into the water it is going to get him out of his predicament."

"That's what he thinks," Alex answered. "He can only run so far and no more."

The sun was beginning to slide down a sky that was turning orange color when Alex began gathering her stuff to leave.

The following morning Alex woke up, showered and helped her grandmother in the store. At mid day she told Auntie she was going to the library but made her way to Rory's house instead. She had no idea if he was already home from school on vacation but that didn't deter her. She banged on the door and, after banging for a minutes she was about to give up when the door opened. A sleepy looking Rory opened the door. He opened the door wider, looking around.

"Are you here by yourself Alex?" he asked.

She shrugged.

"I don't see anyone else here but me."

"Look Alex, it's not a good idea you being here. There is no one else here but me and you coming in might set tongues wagging as innocent as this is. I don't want to bring your mother's wrath or your grandmother's or anyone else for that reason on my head. Papa has already given me a talking to about you."

Rory stood there blocking the door. There was a split second of silence while Alex tried to figure out whether to leave or stay; then she decided to stay.

"I want to know when are you guys going back to the cave? I told you before that I am curious to see what the inside is like. I can help you with a plan where the stuff in the cave is concerned." "It's too dangerous, can't you see that, Alex?" Rory answered.

Physically he had gone into overdrive. He avoided being alone with her. It was amazing how close they used to be, she tagging along with him; but something had changed. Rory smiled to himself. Alex just didn't know how sexy she was and he had to be very careful around her.

"And another thing, are you going to keep me standing here?" Alex asked with attitude.

Rory looked up and down the street before opening the door and ushering her in. The minute Alex entered the room Rory knew that he liked having her there. They sat at the table discussing school, talking about Tayo and Ciarra's relationship before the topic of the cave came around.

"Rory, why don't we relieve those guys of some of their weed and maybe money too?"

He looked at her as if she had two heads.

"Alex, are you crazy? Listen to what you are saying. You are saying that we should steal from Bongo and Fiat and the rest of their gang. You must be mad to even think of stealing ganja from men like those."

Alex sucked her teeth and held up her hands.

"Hear me out before you dismiss the entire idea. I didn't say steal I said to relieve them of some, not all of their weed. What do they do with all that money? They don't use any of it to do any good so I suggest that we get our hands on it and the money we make we use it to do some good for the community, throw a bash or something on one of these holidays."

Now it was his turn to hold up his hands.

"Wait a minute here. I see you have given this some thought, Alex, but that's a big deal. Stealing weed? It's not something I have thought about. Can you imagine what they would do to us if they caught on to us not to mention what your grandmother, Morphine Sulfate Florentino would do to you and me if she knows you were mixed up in something like this?"

"It will be fun plotting and planning a heist like this, not to mention the good the money will do. We could supply Sunday dinner to members of the church who are shut in and give to those who are on the poorer side." Alex was grinning. She licked her lips. "So, you think I am crazy, hah?" She reached across and smacked him lightly on the hand.

Rory tilted his head to the side and watched her with interest.

"On the contrary," he stated. He stood up from his chair to pace back and forth. "I'll think about it and I will discuss it with Andy, Tayo and the others. I'll have to bring Mass Octavius into it too because he might be able to help us and I trust him not to spill to any of our parents."

He moved closer to her, only inches separating them. She stared back at him. She jumped as the sound of thunder rumbled and lightning scudded across the sky, breaking the spell. He reached out and touched her chin. A smile formed on his lips.

"You don't have to be scared of the lightning and thunder, Alex, you are safe with me."

It was no longer sunny but had started to rain. Alex walked to the window, watching the trees sway in the wind. Rory moved behind her to close the window. As she turned to walk back to the sofa, Rory was in her path. She held her breath. He stood looking at her. She met his eyes and then he took a step forward, touching her, using his hands to frame her face and then he bent his head. She felt his breath against her lips and then the feel of his lips against hers. Her lips parted and their tongues met. Alex felt a surge of pleasure as the kiss deepened. She wrapped her arms around him, wanting to rub her body against his.

Rory's lips caught hers in a hot, demanding, hungry kiss. He wanted more; he could feel his erection rubbing against her belly. She was a weakness that he could not afford. If Papa ever found out that in spite of the warning that he had been given he was messing with her, not to mention only God could help him if her grandmother, Miss Florentino or her mother found out. They were very protective of her.

He wrenched his mouth from hers, breathing hard, and backed off. Her eyes flew open and she blinked up at him.

"Alex, I don't know what came over me. It won't happen again, I'll make sure of it."

Rory didn't know what else to say. She was different than the other girls he messed around with. She appealed to him on a higher level than anyone else. It was as if a piece of him was for her and her only but he knew better than to follow up on his feelings. She wasn't one to play with because she made it clear she wasn't going to be any one's play thing.

"Look Rory, it's getting late. I have to go. There is no need to say anything more."

"Wait, it's dark outside. I'll walk you home. Just give me a minute to go change. He walked towards the bedroom door, closing it firmly behind him. He moved to the bed and sat down with his head in hands. Damn, he had messed up.

They walked together in the darkness.

"What are you thinking, Alex?" Rory asked. "I hope you are not mad with me or anything like that.

"Look, whatever just happened was a mistake so it's already forgotten. I wouldn't want you to get in trouble with your girlfriends. I wonder what Joan would have done if she had caught you kissing me. She would have been one angry lady."

Alex was fuming. Rory didn't have an answer so he just kept going. He walked Alex to a few steps from her doorstep. He didn't want to be seen by Miss Florentino and, although he had promised only a few minutes ago that he wouldn't be kissing her a second time, he held her hand, bringing it to his lips before wishing her goodnight.

Rory led the way down the narrow path which led into a more densely forested area. Alex had only ventured into this area once or twice before. Tall trees towered above them, the leaves rustling in the slight breeze. She stayed close to him, watching as he stepped over rocks and tree roots, copying what he did. The pathway narrowed even more the further in they walked, the silence surrounding them broken by the snap of a dry branch or twig beneath their feet or the far away sound of a dog barking or the sound of a truck engine revving up Castle Hill. Rory parted a clump of bushes, allowing her to pass through ahead of him.

"There it is up ahead." He pointed the flashlight. "See that rocky shelf? The cave is below that." He moved the flashlight back and forth.

She followed his lead and when it came to climbing over the sharp edged rocks didn't resist when he offered his help. She slipped her hand in his and his warm fingers closed around hers with reassurance as they came to the entrance of the cave. Alex stared at Rory in alarm. She stood uncertainly at the entrance to the cave, staring through the inky darkness of the black hole.

"You are scared, aren't you?" he asked.

"No," she snapped.

But she made no move to take another step. It was quite clear why Bongo and his group had chosen this place as a hiding place. The thick bush that surrounded them, acted as a screen for privacy. Only those who knew that this cave was here would venture this way unless they knew with absolute surety where they were going. Rory scrambled down the incline and turned, holding his hand out to her, shining the flashlight in her face. She held her hand up against the glare of the light.

"Come on," Rory coaxed. "There is nothing to bite you down here. Remember I've been here a few times but, if you would like to go back because you have changed your mind, that's fine too."

"What do you mean there is nothing to bite me? Why are you so sure there are no rats down there and, of course, I haven't changed my mind. I am the one who wanted to come. It seems to be rocky ground and I don't want to twist my ankle or worse break my leg."

She was pleased with her explanation. It didn't give away her fear. It sounded reasonable enough to be convincing. He helped her down into the semi darkness of the cave. She shivered as Rory led her further into the cave. She scrambled across rocks jutting out from the ground with Rory lighting the way with his flashlight.

"You are shaking Alex. Are you scared?" Rory asked.

"Kind of. It's just that I am in here with all these walls around me. It's as if I am locked in here."

She stared up at the roof of the cave. This is where the slaves used to find sanctuary and have their secret meetings. She tried to imagine how the slaves might have felt knowing that their hiding place might be discovered at any time.

He grasped her hand, his fingers closing around hers before pausing to light the lanterns hanging from a mainframe of temporary structures built.

"Is that better now that we have more light and you can see more clearly?"

"Look at this place. Oh, my goodness, I never imagined that something like this existed right under our noses."

The light played over the walls and Alex was shocked to note that there were drawings on the wall, pictures of birds, turtles, people hunting with spears.

"It is said that these drawings were done by the Taino Indians. They were peaceful people who lived here in Jamaica even before the Caribs. They were skilled artisans who left their paintings on the walls of many island caves," Rory informed her.

They followed the pathway which forked into other openings until they came to the main cathedral room.

"What I do know is that they were peaceful people," Alex answered.

"There is more," Rory continued. "They worshipped spirit gods and images called *Zemis* and it is said that they buried their dead in pots in these caves. The priests who were the medicine men used herbs for treatments and they would sometimes store their precious bush and herbs in many of these caves."

"This is fascinating stuff," Alex replied with excitement. "They had their own Gods and religion played an important part in their daily life. They had a God of rain, wind and hurricanes but one God was the supreme *Yocahu*, God of the Sun. Look at this, past and present merges. I can't believe that these guys have a bed in here."

Rory led her deeper into the cave.

"Look, Alex, this is where they store the weed in plastic bags and the chest is further in to the cave."

"I wonder if anyone ever got lost in here. There must be another opening that leads into this cave but I am not about to go search for one."

Something touched her arm and Alex screamed. It was a bat. Alex was trembling. She stopped and looked around, listening to the strange noises that were part of the cave.

"Alex, look at me. Come here, you are shaking."

Rory turned her to face him. The confined space and diffused light created an air of intimacy. They were totally alone. She stared up at him in the darkness, his gaze holding her captive.

"Do you think Nanny or any of the other slaves met their lover here because here they could be totally alone?" he suggested.

"Maybe. Nanny was a woman of great passion so I can imagine that she would have rocked any man's world with hot and steamy sex."

Alex's mouth was dry and her heart was racing.

"Are you scared of being here in this cave, locked away from everything, Alex, or are you scared of being here alone with me? Alex, I know I am supposed to be sensible and let you go without even kissing you, but I cannot because what I feel for you is so strong that it transcend commonsense. I have known you for almost all your life and I discovered that so long ago what I felt for you is more than friendship, so I tried to stay away but it's been really hard."

"I am not scared of you, Rory. I am scared of what I might do with you. I know we are young and I know how I feel about you but to have sex is a big step. In another few months or a year I will be history. You will move on and all this that we share now will be forgotten. I want to make love for the first time with someone who values me, with some one who loves me."

She stared at Rory and didn't resist when he held her tight. Her hands crept up, hugging him. The intensity of her feelings for Rory flashed through her body. His mouth hovered closer to hers.

"Can't you see that I really, really like you? That's why I stay away from you. You are younger than I am and I don't want to do anything to hurt you."

Then his lips came down on hers, hot and demanding, belying his words, his body pressing against hers. She felt desire as his mouth seduced her, commanding her response and she gave what he demanded. The world outside failed to exist. She was wrapped in the heat of her own awakened desire.

He released her and stepped back, leading her to bed. Alex felt breathless and dizzy. She knew that she was poised on the edge of change, a change that would impact her forever.

"Kiss me, Rory," she whispered.

And he did. His warm breath caressed the side of her neck as he bent his head to hers.

"Whenever you want me to stop just say the word, Alex, and I will."

His lips met hers, his tongue licked at her lips and then her lips parted giving him access. Her tongue met his. Excitement whipped through her body. She clung to him. She had read about this, watched movies but this was her night. His palm cupped against one breast, then his mouth covered it, sucked it, causing her to cry out. She had never felt any thing like this in all her life. Such exquisite pleasure.

His hands moved over her hips and down. Alex felt the moist heat between her legs. Her body felt consumed by liquid fire. She groaned low in her throat as his tongue plunged hard and hot into her mouth. He raised the hem of her dress and caressed a path upwards. He pushed aside the silk of her panties and his fingers grazed her swollen folds. Then, with one finger, parted flesh and pushed against her entrance. She arched in a desperate plea for more.

"Alex, oh my God, Alex baby. I need you naked," Rory groaned.

He stripped her of her clothes. His hand slid up to touch her breast. She jerked his shirt open, spreading her fingers over his chest. There was a throbbing ache between her legs. His fingers stroked the throbbing nub of her arousal. She reached down, fumbling with his zipper and he covered her hand with his, helping her with the task.

"Open your legs for me, Alex. Part your legs."

Her hips arched. His fingers surged deeper as she lifted to them, shrieking with pleasure. It took all his strength to pause and reach for protection; but he had to protect her in every way. He rose to his knees, opening the packet, working the condom over his heavy, thick erection. His hand stroked over, spreading her juices over the latex before preparing to enter.

"Are you sure, Alex? After this we can't turn back."

"Kiss me," she whispered in response. Her whole body was alive like it had never been before.

He couldn't wait to possess her. He needed no urging. She was giving so much more than he had anticipated. He wanted nothing more than to satisfy her needs and his. His senses were so heightened he could hear and see everything with such clarity as if he had developed a sixth sense. He felt her fear and when he looked at her he could see it written so clearly in her expressions. It made him pause for a minute. He saw the tension, the dread reflected in her face.

"Alex, did you hear voices?" he asked quietly.

She shook her head but he could swear he had heard voices. He came to his senses. What was he thinking having sex here with Alex? Rolling away he sat up. Picking up her clothes, he handed them to her.

"I think you should get dressed."

He grabbed his pants from the floor, pulling them on in haste.

Alex was confused.

"What's the matter, Rory? What's wrong?"

"It's not the right time, Alex. It's not right."

"Did I do something wrong?"

Alex was on the verge of crying. She was humiliated. She stood up, pulling on her panties which had been discarded so easily and carelessly only moments before. She dragged the rest of her clothes on to cover her nakedness.

"Alex, sweetheart, I want you with all my heart. You have no idea how much strength I had to summon to put a stop to making love to you, to take your virginity. You are sixteen and I am nineteen, a not so innocent nineteen. It's not just about sex with you. I can get that anywhere."

He could imagine he would be laughed at by his peers if they found out how far he had come and turned back; but he had too much love and respect for Alex to take it all the way. There would be too much at stake.

Alex was burning with shame.

"Did a fairy just sit on your shoulder and whisper in your ear, reminding you of the age difference? You are cruel."

He turned his back.

"Believe me, one day you will understand why I had to do this."

He couldn't stand to see the shame and embarrassment on her face.

There was an awful silence. He didn't know how to turn around to face her but he had to so he turned holding out his hand to touch her. She ignored it. She started walking towards the entrance of the cave. She couldn't believe what had just happened. She was dying inside. Rory had rejected her after she was prepared to give herself to him. Well, the stars had fallen from her eyes. She couldn't wait to get away from him.

"You don't have to walk me home, Rory. I am fine. I can find my way home," she said in a small voice.

"Just walk," he said in a hoarse voice as he stepped in front of her, then began to lead the way out of the cave.

Not a word passed between them until she was home. He tried to touch her but she stepped away. He started to say he was sorry but she cut him off. She didn't say goodbye or goodnight. Rory wasn't sure Alex would ever speak to him again.

Alex was finally home. A place of love and happiness. The house had never looked so warm and inviting. Her refuge. Her sanctuary. Golden lamplight spilled from the windows upstairs. She avoided the entrance to the shop, slipping through the backdoor and tiptoeing upstairs. She didn't want to run into her mom or grandmother. She ran to the bathroom and stared at herself in the mirror. The face that stared back at her seemed to have lost its innocence. The pain and humiliation she had suffered from Rory's rejection were visible on her face. She washed up, went to her room, removed her clothes, and crawled into bed. She pulled the pillow over her head trying to block out the events of the last few hours.

She was finally falling asleep when there was a knock at the door and her grandmother entered.

"I wanted to check on you to see if everything is okay."

"I am fine but a little sad that I will be leaving my friends behind when I go to Kingston. We have all been so close. I don't know if I'll find friends like Ciarra and Megan."

Her grandmother sat on the bed in her pink terry robe, her hair in curlers.

"It's a part of growing up, Alex. You will have new experiences. Some friendships you will maintain and some you will lose. As you get older, people and situations will change, but your mother and myself will always be here. Enjoy your childhood. Don't rush too fast to be too grown up."

She rubbed Alex's head as she used to when she was younger.

"Come, I made you some mint tea."

As Alex followed her into the kitchen she wondered if Auntie had any inkling of what had happened earlier. Auntie left her to drink her tea in peace. Alex had a feeling she knew more than she was letting on. The hot tea warmed her belly and soothed her somewhat. Returning to her room, Alex lay on her bed, reliving the moments with Rory in the cave. She could still feel the thrill of his touch, his kiss. Her body would not quiet itself. Finally, Alex fell into an exhausted sleep.

Sunlight and Dappled Shade

Alex propped up her head by stacking her pillows into one pile. She looked down her body. It looked the same, flat stomach, long legs. She sighed and rose to stand at her window, watching the sun rise. The start of a new day. A different Alex. She laughed at herself. One moment in time, last night had changed her. She had avoided making a mistake. And she had Rory to thank for that.

She played with the drapes at her window. She would feel better soon. She had so much to look forward to. But did she wish for more of last night's adventure, more of him? She turned from the window, not wanting to answer that question. She sat back on the bed, leaning once more on the pile of pillows reminiscing. She must have drifted off to sleep and she somehow became aware that there was someone at her door.

"Alex." It was Ciarra banging on her door.

"Alex." Ciara knocked again. "Wake up."

Ciarra didn't wait for permission before entering.

Alex dragged herself up. Half an hour later she was showered, dressed and sitting on the verandah, not only with Ciarra but also with Megan, eating breakfast. As they sat chatting and eating, Alex had flashbacks of what she had done with Rory last night. It didn't take long for Ciarra to get around to:

"What's going on? Rory wanted me to come over to see if you are okay. He seemed very concerned."

"Yeah, I am okay. I was having a nasty headache yesterday and I happened to see Rory. My face was all screwed up because I was in so much pain so I guess that's why he wanted to know." Alex had to fight to keep a straight face.

Sitting back in her seat, Megan took a good look at Alex's face.

"I sense that there is more to it than what you are saying and the vibes in the air is telling me that you are not saying everything. If it's something that Rory did I'll go kick his ass for you. Okay girlfriend. Look at me, I am serious."

Ciarra and Alex started cracking up at Megan and her antics. She was being funny, trying to lighten the mood.

"Everything is all good between me and Rory. It's nothing like what you guys are thinking."

"So we are still on for tonight? I can't wait to see what the cave is all about. All that mystery that surrounds it is pulling me in. I want to take my time exploring," Ciarra said.

"Maybe we'll find historical artifacts hidden away that no one has yet found," Megan said cheerfully. "That would take some digging I am sure. After all, they wouldn't be sitting there for anyone to walk up and pick them up. If there was anything visible of significance it would have long been gone," Alex pointed out.

Ciarra threw herself down on the lounge chair beside Alex.

"Look at these stars in this magazine with their heavenly bodies and expensive clothes. We can be those stars and better if we discover anything of importance in this cave. We could sell a few of the stuff, get rich and donate the rest to the national museum."

"Cute," Megan stated as she flipped a page in the

magazine, "but I am cuter than most of these girls. We all know that."

"Hmm, my nails need to be filed and polished, Ciarra. There is no time like the present."

Alex held her hands up for inspection. Ciarra threw a cushion at her.

"When you pay me, and that's like never, but because I like you. Here is your chance to tell us what really happened between you and Rory. I'll even do your   toes."
 Alex closed her eyes and laid her head back on the chair.

"I kissed Rory and then I got mad with him because he is still with his girl, Joan. That's what happened."

"Oh damn. I am going to hurt that boy. He should know to leave that girl before he step to you," Ciarra muttered.

Alex laughed.

"It's cool, we understand each other now. We sorted it out. As of now I don't have much to say to him any more."

They both looked at her and said "yeah, right."

"Let's listen to the radio. See what they are playing." Alex turned the knob on the radio and Coco Tea song blasted from the airwaves:

> *I have been checking you out*
>
> *But you are too young*
>
> *A girl like you will cause*
>
> *Worries in my world….*
>
> *Go home to your mama*

Go home to your papa.

As they rocked to the beat Alex couldn't help thinking about the lyrics and her life. How fitting.

-Chapter 6-

It was almost the end of May and Megan was back in town, beaming with pride at her success after attending the Penn Relays in Pennsylvania and the International Track meet in New York. She had the gold medals to show for her effort. As for Alex, she had not seen Rory in over a week. She had avoided him and had ignored the messages she had received from him via Ciarra. Today was Labour Day, a national holiday and, as usual, there would be a cricket match in Bell Town, after which there would be a party. It was a big day for Rory because he was a major player on the cricket team.

Alex was dressed in white shorts, a greenish spaghetti strap top and matching sandals showing off her pretty feet and toes painted pink. Around her neck she wore the gold chain with a cross for a pendant that her mother had given her as a gift. All four girls Andrea, Ciarra and Megan, were sitting in Alex's bedroom. Megan wore a short sundress, Ciarra a backless jumpsuit and Andrea jeans with a white sleeveless cotton top and white sandals.

"Megan you look very relaxed and mellow. You set out to accomplish your goal and you are doing fine. Did you meet anyone famous that I would want to meet?" Ciarra asked.

Megan laughed.

"Of course I did. Stick with me and I'll make your dreams come true," she said impishly. "I have a choice of where I want to go to school. I was offered scholarships to two schools in the U.S. and I can attend the University of the West Indies on a scholarship for four years. The only thing I would be responsible for is my books."

"That's my girl doing her thing," Alex joined in. "Mission accomplished."

"We have another star to cheer on today. It's Rory's big day. If he does well, he will be on his way to the Jamaican cricket team. I saw Joan with him last night and she and her *posse* will definitely be there today. I just thought everyone should be aware of this."

Ciarra gave Alex a quick look.

"Hey, Joan is no big deal because if any one of us wants Rory, we can take him from her, right Alex?"

She tried to reassure Alex while rocking her back and forth.

"I don't know about that. I am not trying to take Rory from Joan. Anyway, let's talk about something else. Megan, since you have no idea what is going on, let me fill you in on the cave. There is a secret meeting to discuss some important matters coming up with Rory, Andy and the others. As soon as I find out the place and time, I'll let you know," said Alex.

"Alright, that's cool," everyone agreed.

"Come on let's hit the road because I personally want to say good luck to Rory before the game begins," Andrea said as she scrambled off the bed.

Rory saw Alex as soon as she walked onto the field where the match was being held. His eyes had constantly searched for her as the crowd began to grow. He saw when Tayo walked over and tapped Megan on the arm and they all walked back to take shade under the big cedar tree where they all sprawled out. Ciarra touched Alex on the arm.

"There is Rory; let's go wish him luck."

He pretended not to see them hurrying towards him but his heart skipped a beat when Alex touched him on the arm and wished him luck.

"I think I need something better than that. Why don't you give me a kiss right here," Rory pointed to his cheek.

Alex screwed up her face.

"Yeah, right."

"Why? Are you afraid someone is going to see you, Alex? I dare you to kiss me."

Alex stood on tiptoe and lightly brushed his cheek, whispering:

"I'll be thinking about you."

"By the way, that's from all of us," Ciarra said with a smile.

Alex felt someone brush her shoulder and turned to see Joan. The first thing she noticed was that her eyes were darkened with eyeliner and she was wearing light-colored pink lipstick on her pouty lips. She wore a pair of sexy-looking shorts, showing well toned skin.

"I came to give you your good luck kiss." She planted her lips firmly on Rory's. "Oh, damn!" she said. "My lipstick is all over your mouth. Let me wipe it off for you, baby." She used her fingers to remove the lipstick before looking at Alex with a smirk.

"Rory, we'll be over there cheering for you," Alex smiled at him before making her way back to her seat under the shade.

She waved to Mass Octavius and Miss Etty as she passed by. The crowd settled down, drinks in hand, to watch. Some had a Red Stripe beer or a Heineken, others a glass with Appleton Red or White rum; people like Miss Etty had coconut water and Alex and her friends each had a soda, although they tried to get away with Ginger Wine.

The visiting team won the toss and stepped in to bat. The Westmoreland Youth Club failed to pick up any wickets in the first hour and the crowd started to get restless. As the bowler ran up and threw a low ball someone shouted:

"Knock out the boy's wicket! What's wrong with you today?"

The crowd laughed. The bowler, Noel ran up again and bowled. The batsman blocked it. Noel appealed Leg Behind Wicket but it was denied. It was becoming a battle between the two teams. Thirty runs and no wicket in an hour; but Noel recovered and dismissed the first member from the opposing team by sending his first wicket of the day flying. The crowd sprang to its feet shouting:

"That is how you play ball!"

It was hard work but the visiting team was finally dismissed for one hundred and twenty-one runs. Now it was the Westmoreland Youth Club's turn to bat. Rory stepped onto the field and tapped his bat, watching and waiting. His father had certainly known what he was doing when he had given him that bat. It was like it had an energy all its own. The bowler ran up swiftly with his ball. He started out with an awfully wayward ball that made the wicket keeper dive for cover.

"What the hell are you doing out there?" a fan yelled.

The bowler ran up again and Rory waited. This time the cricket bat met the ball. Rory drove the ball down the pitch past the ravine and the crowd went wild.

"Six!" the crowd roared. "Good heavens! Did you see how that ball went flying?" someone in the crowd shouted.

There was no turning back from that point onward. It was a close match but finally, the Westmoreland Youth Club outplayed their opponents and won the match by one wicket. The match was over and Rory was the man of the hour. He caressed his bat like a familiar lover. The party moved to the community center. Rory made his way over to Alex and the rest of the gang who hadn't moved away from their seats under the cedar tree. Andy slapped him on the back.

"You did well, my friend." Megan rolled her eyes as Joan walked over and sat next to Rory.

"Are we heading over to the center or do you have something else in mind?" she asked while leaning on his arm.

"Yeah, but not right now. I am hanging out with my friends here for a while."

Even after Joan left, Alex sat there thinking about the kiss she had shared with Rory. She tried to join in the banter but she was angry at herself for having played second fiddle to Joan. She jumped to her feet and avoided Rory's eyes as he looked at her in a probing manner as if he were trying to read her mind.

"Come on Ciarra, let's get something to eat."

She dragged Ciarra along as she walked towards the jerk chicken vendor.

"Hey, wait a minute, we're all coming with you," Megan shouted.

Rory, Tayo, Andy, and the rest of the group trailed behind as the girls kept walking.

"Is there something going on between you and Alex that we don't know about, Rory?" Tayo asked. "Sensing a bit of tension between you two and it seems to be more than the usual."

Rory sucked his teeth.

"Stop reading into things, Tayo. There is nothing going on between us."

"Well, it became quite icy after Joan ran over and popped a kiss right on your lips. Let me give you a piece of advice. I wouldn't play with Miss Florentino's granddaughter because she might just slap you down if you hurt her pride and joy."

Rory shook his head before mopping his brow and looked up in time to see Tayo and Andy exchanging glances.

"I'm not stupid, you know. I would never hurt Alex. At least not intentionally. Why are you all on my case about her anyway? Tayo, you don't want to get me started on you."

They arrived at the community center where they could hear the sound of music blaring from the sound system. It was already crowded inside when Alex walked into the hall. There were couples twisting and bumping and grinding to the music. Alex started swaying to the music with her hips gyrating sensually. Rory watched as Max approached her and whispered in her ear. Whatever he said to her made her smile. He moved towards her but Joan was standing in front of him, blocking his path.

Sunlight and Dappled Shade

"Coming to find me?" she asked.

She hugged him around the waist and pulled him onto the floor. He moved in time to the music with Joan, hugging her and bumping and grinding with her. He twisted and turned to keep eyes on Alex who did her best to appear to ignore him. He heard Alex's laughter. He turned his head to see her smiling up into Max's face. He was getting agitated. The song ended and he moved to the bar to get a drink for Joan. He turned to see Alex standing in the far corner of the dance floor in deep conversation with Max. Tayo and Ciarra danced over to him and Joan. Ethan wasted no time in grabbing Joan and spinning her around to the music. Andy slapped Rory on the back.

"Come here, Rory. Your long lost cousin over there wants to buy you a drink."

Rory made his escape walking in the direction of Alex. He paused to tell her that he was coming back for his dance.

"How did you know that I wanted to get away from Joan?" he asked Andy.

"A blind man can see what's going on with you and Alex. If you like her that much, you need to be honest with yourself. Let whatever is happening between you and Joan fade out because if you are thinking about playing a game, forget it. You are not the only one who is interested in her. Look at Max over there with her. He really likes her."

Alex was standing at the edge of the dance floor when Rory bumped into her on his way back from the bar.

"Sorry to cut in, Max but Alex promised to dance with me."

He smiled his usual sexy smile as he held out his hand to her. He led her through the throng of dancers and twirled her around to the music until she laughed. When the music slowed, he pulled her to him and then held her even closer. She relaxed against him, her arms wrapped around his neck. His hand moved to her lower back pressing her body against his. She had no reason to pretend. She felt good in his arms. The music ended but Rory didn't release her. He had made a decision.

"I am taking you home tonight, Alex. You are not leaving here unless it's with me."

She frowned.

"How are you going to do that when your woman is here? Give me a break."

"I'll be back in a little while."

Alex stared at Rory as he walked across the room.

-Chapter 7-

Ciarra turned the door knob and listened. All was quiet. She pushed the door and crept in quietly. Nothing. She breathed a sigh of relief. She should have been home ages ago. It was long past midnight but she had stayed at the community center with Tayo and her friends. While she was having fun, the thought that her parents would come down hard on her had entered her head but it had not fazed her. Her father was a deacon at the Baptist Church and her mother sang on the choir. She had heard from her father so many times that he had a reputation to uphold and that he could not have his daughters running the streets. However, now that she was home, all that bravado had disappeared.

Tayo was a good kisser. He could make her swoon anytime, especially when he rubbed or kissed her nipples. If her parents ever knew what she had done with him, they would disown her. She tiptoed into her bedroom. Her heart almost jumped into her mouth and she stifled a scream. There was someone sitting in the chair by her bed. Her mother held the switch that she had probably gone out to get earlier in her hand. Ciarra's feet barely carried her to the bed as she plopped onto it.

"You are frightened, Ciarra? How many times have I told you not to come in here past midnight? Thank your lucky stars that this is me and not your father. Where are you coming from at this time of night? Do you have any idea what time it is? Answer me! I am talking to you."

Her mother was furiously firing question after question without waiting for an answer.

"Mama, you know there was the cricket match and after that we went to the Community Center with Megan and Alex."

Her mother stood up as Ciarra backed away.

"That was hours ago. It is now past two in the morning and you're just walking into my house. Ever since you've been fooling around with Eden's boy, you've been slipping, but I am not having any of it."

"What are you talking about, mama? I don't know where you got that from but I'm not fooling around with any boy. We are friends and that's it."

Ciarra shook her head because she knew that sooner or later, her involvement with Tayo was bound to get back to her parents. Where she came from nobody minded their own business. Here she was now in the hot seat to boot!

"Ciarra, Tayo's mother is a cantankerous woman. The only person she cares about is herself. There is talk that she's mixed up with obeah and you've gone and gotten yourself involved with her son."

Her mother was pacing back and forth.

"He's not like his mother so don't say that about him. He's funny and smart."

Her mother grabbed at her but Ciarra slipped away.

"What did you say to me, Ciarra? I'm going to have to tell your father about this because you're not going to bring any baby in here!"

The commotion must have awakened her father because when Ciarra looked up, her father was standing in the doorway. She groaned inwardly. The situation had gone from bad to worse. Whenever her mother wanted her brothers and sisters to comply with her wishes, all she had to do was tell them that she was going to report their behavior to their father. Ciarra was not the only one who was afraid of her father. She could handle her mother but that was not the case with her father.

Oh shit, she thought.

"What the hell is going on in here?" Her father's voice boomed in her head.

"Your daughter finally decided to come home at this time of the morning." Her mother gestured with her hands. "She is getting out of control."

"I'm not doing anything mama; just hanging out with my friends. You are blowing everything out of proportion."

Her father was quiet for a few seconds. Ciarra knew he was summing up the situation.

"I'll send you to live with your aunt if this continues. You are **not** going to come in here all hours of the night and disrespect my house. If that's what I have to do to get you away from this boy, I will do just that, mark my words, Ciarra. Come Myte, let's go back to bed. It's late."

Her father turned and left the room with her mother. Ciarra threw herself into the bed. She couldn't believe her father. Why did he always boss her around like that? Now he was talking about sending her to live with her aunt. She wasn't going anywhere and she knew that her mother would never agree to that. Why did her parents always have to make a big deal of everything? Didn't they ever do anything wrong when they were growing up? Her last thought was of Tayo and his hands on her body before she drifted off to sleep.

Rory sat on the railing of the verandah of his house with his back to the wall and his feet stretched out in front of him. Labour Day had come and gone and if they were indeed going to raid the caves, they would have to start planning and setting things in motion. At least once per week Rory, Tayo, and Andy had kept an eye on the cave, making note of who visited. They also observed when and how Bongo Man, Fiat and their gang stored their bounty. Rory would be leaving in another month or so, first to cricket camp in Kingston and then on to Antigua. It was time to set things in motion. He watched the butterflies and insects buzz around in the sun and waved as Roxston, another of his buddies tooted his horn as he drove past.

Dammit! He couldn't stop thinking about Alex. There was a connection between the two of them. He could feel it. He didn't have time for a serious relationship right now. He needed to concentrate on his cricket, to be one of the best. He had known Alex for many years; they had thrown stones at Papa's naseberry tree together, picking up the sweet fruits from below when they knocked them from their stems. They also used to play Scrabble together but they were younger then. He couldn't figure it out but the hold she had on him played havoc with his senses. He admired her fierce sense of loyalty but she also knew how to exact revenge when she was crossed. He ran his hands over his face at the thought of Joan and Angie. He was cool with them; there was no fear of being with them. However, with Alex, it was different; he wanted to be with her and he didn't want to. It bothered him when he saw other guys trying to come on to her. He needed to make up his mind and soon. He watched as Ciarra and Megan walked up the steps and onto the verandah and in dramatic style, Ciarra threw herself down into one of the low slung verandah chairs.

"I've been ordered not to spend too much time in your company, Rory, and also Tayo's. You guys might corrupt me by mere association."

She looked at him with such innocence that he laughed.

"Really, Ciarra? So if you don't want to be corrupted, what are you doing here? Aren't you supposed to be in Church or saying prayers somewhere else?"

She laughed.

"Mama and Papa pray enough to save my soul. It's hot and I'm thirsty so bring out the lemonade with lots of ice," Ciarra instructed Rory.

Rory touched knuckles with Tayo as Tayo arrived.

"Hey man, Ciarra is asking for lemonade. Why don't you get it for her?" Rory said.

"Talk about putting a man to work as soon as he shows up! The sun was beating down on my head as I walked from my house to yours and you were sitting here in the shade, stretched out and relaxed," Tayo answered.

"Jeez! I might as well go get the damned lemonade," Rory said as he slid from his perch on the verandah railing.

"I hope you spiked it," Tayo called out, "and if you didn't, do it before you bring that jug of lemonade out here."

Half an hour later, the entire group was assembled on the verandah, with the exception of Alex who had awakened late and was now taking her time walking slowly towards Rory's house. She kicked at a stone in her path. The last time she had gone to Rory's house, he had kissed her or rather she had let him kiss her. When she arrived, she heard the sounds of her friends' laughter amidst their conversations. Rory looked up at her as she approached them.

"Alex you took your sweet time getting here, didn't you? I have been here waiting for you to show up for an hour now," Megan started up petulantly.

Alex mimicked Megan's voice:

"Some people have things to do before they can leave home. I don't know about you or anyone else for that matter, Megan, but when my mother gives me chores I have to do them."

"What is that bag you are carrying? Something smells good."

Tayo tapped the bag with his hand. Alex laughed impishly.

"See? This is why I am late. Auntie baked Toto Jamaican cakes, and grated coconut cakes so I waited until she was finished so I could bring you all some. She also gave me sliced bun and cheese to share. Aren't I a sweetheart?"

Sunlight and Dappled Shade

Megan laughed.

"Let me help you with the bag, Alex. You should have told me that you were bringing food. I could have helped you instead of having you cart around that heavy load."

Rory stood up and relieved Alex of the bag. He kissed her on the cheek and then went to look for paper plates for the bun and cheese and Toto cakes.

"Come on, Rory. I want my Toto while it's hot."

Tayo stretched out his hand.

They all sat down to enjoy their bun and cheese and Toto cakes. Andy drank lemonade to wash down his Toto and wiped his mouth on his shirt sleeves.

"Did you all hear that the other night when Jack was driving home late at night, he saw Miss Dassa hitching a ride? I'm very serious," Rory said jokingly.

Andy snorted.

"Like that could be true. The woman is dead and buried six feet under."

"Thank God I don't live anywhere close to her house. I have no reason to be down in Galloway Bottom, especially at that time of night," Alex said with a shiver.

"Let's talk about why we are here while we eat," Ciarra piped up. "I don't want to hear any more ghost stories. We, girls have done some scouting and so far, we've figured out who needs walking sticks, lamps and lamp shades. Also for one month, all those old people who are shut in will have food delivered to them every Saturday."

"How much do you think we need to take to be able to do all that and have a fun day with free rides and food?" Alex asked. "If we decide to give groceries, we can buy them from Auntie's store and wherever else. If we give away cooked food, someone will have to be hired to prepare it."

Alex was eager to pull this off. This was an adventure that she did not want to miss. The mere thought of doing something like this gave her a rush of excitement. Neil stepped over to rub Megan's back with his hand.

"The school has a cafeteria. The same people who cook there could do the cooking if that's what we decide to do." Neil turned to Rory. "I say a total of ten thousand dollars should be enough but the bigger question is where are we going to store the weed and how do we exchange it for money? We can figure out how to hide the hard cash."

Ciarra's head popped up.

"Connections, we have connections. Mass Octavius' son lives in Montego Bay. He knows people. Octavius will help us. All we have to do is ask. He will tell us where to hide the weed. I trust him."

Rory nodded.

"You're so right. Tayo and I discussed it with him and he will help us. Octavius is much smarter than some people think. He had the solutions that we needed. We have to get to this cave soon. I don't have a date as yet but I'm going away to cricket camp in another two weeks or so."

"And I am leaving also for Kingston. That's where I will be finishing up sixth form," Alex said quietly.

All heads turned in her direction.

"You can't be serious!" Ciarra exclaimed.

"Why are you moving away, Alex? Did something happen? My gosh! That's a big move. I thought we were all going to be riding the bus to school until we leave high school and go to college," Megan joined in.

Rory didn't say anything. He just gave her one of his questioning looks. *If only they knew*, Alex thought. She really did not want to go away. She stood up and walked to the verandah railing looking across at Mr. Virgie's common where the cows were out to pasture. The fowls were in the yard eating whatever food they could find. Here she was with her friends sprawled all over Mass Kenny's verandah eating Toto cakes and drinking spiked lemonade. This was home to her. Moving to unfamiliar territory did not appeal to her very much.

"I'll travel back and forth and I'll be here every other weekend and for holidays too. It's been arranged already. So I won't be gone too long."

"Did you hear that Rory? She's going to be in Kingston where you attend college. Both of you can get together sometimes but the sad part is that she may be leaving before the holidays are over. You have to make hay before the sun shines."

Tayo was making light of the situation and getting on Rory's nerves. Ciarra suppressed a smile. Megan placed her hand over her mouth.

"You just don't know when to shut up, do you Tayo?"

Rory was upset but with whom? Himself, Tayo, or Alex? Emotions were ripping through him like a flash fire. He wasn't sure what was eating at him;

was it fear that he wouldn't be seeing much of her anymore? Maybe he and Alex were never meant to be together; but he did not believe that for a minute. Rory walked over to Alex who was standing by the railing.

"So how long have you known this? You just dropped the bomb here as if your going to school in Kingston is no big deal."

"What's your problem? I would have told you, Rory but you are always so busy these days. I didn't get around to it," Alex retorted.

"Jeez, why don't you just kiss her, Rory? You know you want to. There is so much tension between you two, I can cut it with a knife," Tayo teased.

He stood up and began singing John Holt's song:

> *On the silent step*
>
> *It will creep up on you*
>
> *In a mystic fog*
>
> *It will kiss you too*
>
> *It will make you run*
>
> *Until you want to cry*
>
> *Hurt yourself*
>
> *Make you want to sigh*
>
> *Be careful, be careful love got a hold on you*
>
> *Like a thief in the night*
>
> *Stealing, stealing, stealing.*

"John Holt is a great singer. You can listen to his songs over and over. Take for example this song. It's timeless.'" Andy said.

The group echoed the sentiment.

"That's true."

"...and the song seems to apply to two people around here."

"Oh, shut up, everyone!" Rory and Alex shouted in unison.

"Let's get back to the subject of picking a date and going to the cave. There is no time like the present," Tayo suggested.

They decided that they would visit the cave in a week.

Miss Etty was up early with the rising sun. She left the house with her head tied with a colorful scarf and walked outside to the kitchen, looking at the horseshoe nailed above the door. She sprinkled water by the door. She had this strange foreboding that all was not well. If she could not prevent Alex and the others from going on their adventure, she had no alternative but to protect them. No matter what she did, she had premonitions of disaster for Alex, Rory, Ciarra, and Megan. She was tired of seeing shadows and rolling mists. Her sleep was repeatedly being interrupted by dreams of the Church and ancestors long gone so this morning she was going to channel her energy and call on the spirits. The temperature was going to go up today, well into the 90s and so far, it was somewhere in the 70s.

After Miss Etty had completed her first load of washing, she emptied the wash pan with soapy water onto the ground and filled it with rinse water. *She was not imagining things; the water had changed color. It was now blood red!* She touched the pentagram on the chain she was wearing around her neck and continued with her washing. She finished hanging the clothes on the line and, with a determined look on her face, she walked into her sewing room. No one would interfere with the people she and Octavius loved. She pulled out her box of tricks as she called it. Her altar was covered with linen and on it sat a bowl of water in which she dipped her fingers. She stood six white candles and her beautiful white rock. She lit her incense and sat for some time in meditation. She stood slowly, lifting her hands in the air.

"In the name of all that is true and pure, I call on you, Lord of all, on my ancestors, the Wise Ones and the elements to protect those whom I love."

Miss Etty then began to dance.

-Chapter 8-

*I*diot! Idiot! Tayo repeated this over and over in his head. He should have told Leah to leave from the minute she arrived but he had not and now Ciarra was standing outside knocking on the door. She pushed the door and stepped into the room and the anger was evident on her face. Leah was sitting on the bed holding an ice pack, which she clamped to Tayo's ankle while he lay enjoying the comfort.

"Hi, Ciarra. I brought Tayo something to eat since he is sick in bed. You know what I mean. He needs some tender loving care right now."

Ciarra could not believe what she was hearing or seeing.

"What's going on here, Tayo?"

After what she had been through this morning - the hell that her mother and father had raised, the bitching from her so-called perfect brothers and her uppity sisters, she wasn't about to take any crap from anyone, be it Tayo or Leah. In another minute or two she was about to do some serious damage to somebody.

"Looking for a man, Leah or you are just looking to get screwed? Which is it?"

Leah looked at her almost in amusement, licking her lips slowly.

"Tayo may not be my man but I have taught him things that you can only dream of. We have had such fun together. Be careful, Ciarra, because I might have to claim him as mine soon."

Sunlight and Dappled Shade

"Do you want to play games with me, Leah?" she warned. "I am not in the mood for your bitchiness. Why don't you fly out on the broom you flew in here on because we might both regret it if you don't."

Tayo was laying flat on his back with his left foot elevated. He had sprained his ankle while playing soccer. That was the reason they had had to put off their big invasion of the cave. He wanted to disappear.

"Ciarra, what happened to my kiss, woman? You're standing there breathing fire. Come over here and give me my hug."

He ignored Leah who was walking around.

"You're being possessive, Ciarra. Where were you when he was in so much pain last night?"

"Enough from you, Leah. You and I both know that you were here last night with a bunch of other people so give Ciarra a break."

Ciarra turned to Tayo.

"Why is she still here?"

"She came over to help me with my ankle, I swear to you, Ciarra. That's all."

Leah's lips curled into a mocking smile.

"Poor Tayo. He needs a real woman. Someone who can match him ride for ride and that's not you. Someone who makes him cry out."

Ciarra moved towards Leah. She was in the mood to spill blood.

"Do you have a death wish?"

Tayo closed his eyes tightly. He knew that trouble was ahead. He tried to get up.

Sunlight and Dappled Shade

"Leah, it's time for you to go. You did a good thing helping me out and all but what is happening here is out of hand so leave."

Leah shrugged her shoulders.

"I'll be on my way. Of course if you need any help, Ciarra, call me. I'll be here."

"Thanks, bitch, but I can manage on my own," Ciarra assured her.

She was calmer now, and more in charge of her emotions. Tayo tried to get between the two women but his leg was not strong enough and he fell back on the bed.

"Leah, why are you starting trouble? You know how it is so leave now!"

Leah strolled pass Ciarra and said:

"Make sure he takes the painkillers and don't forget to use the icepacks on his ankle."

The door closed softly as she left Tayo and Ciarra alone.

"I saw her with her arms around you, Tayo. It feels good to have more than one woman, doesn't it? It felt good having her all over you, didn't it?"

"You know there wasn't anything going on. My ankle hurts and I want the swelling to go down as soon as possible. Because of me, everyone has put off going to the cave. Do you understand my frustration?"

"You've slept with her, haven't you?" She stared at him furiously. "You've known her for a much longer time than you have known me."

He wasn't going to lie to her. He couldn't lie to her, not about this. It was unimportant but not harmless.

"I did sleep with her."

He could see the tears welling up in her eyes.

"So that's why she said she was giving you what you wanted. She is older and more experienced. Is that it?"

"Ciarra..."

"Answer me, Tayo." Her voice was filled with pain. "What was it? You spent minutes, hours, doing her? You spent the night in bed with her?"

"All night?"

"Answer me, dammit!"

"Ciarra, come on let's not talk about it now. That's in the past."

"In the past! Are you serious? That doesn't answer my question. Did you spend all night with her?"

"Yes."

She felt such pain.

"I can't call you a liar now, can I? I am too much of a virgin for you? You spent hours making love to her. Oh God. You make me sick!" Ciarra held her face in her hands.

"Ciarra, listen to me. That's in the past. If I hurt you, I am sorry."

"You blasted jerk. What do you take me for? Some kind of fool? I'm not your toy! You call Leah to come back because I'm leaving!"

She slapped him on his ankle for good measure and was satisfied with the look of pain on his face.

Sunlight and Dappled Shade

"To hell with you."

She walked out, slamming the door behind her. She could hear him shouting.

"Ciarra, come back here!"

Ciarra sucked her teeth and kept walking. *Damn him,* she said to herself. As far as she was concerned, he could stay there and suffer. She was having no mercy on him.

Miss Etty knew what she had to do but she would not be able to navigate the bush and rocky trail to get to the caves. She wanted to give to the sprits the rum that they were accustomed to. All this trekking back and forth in the caves was only disturbing the ancestors. She would do what she had to do but Octavius had to do the final part - that of leaving four drops of rum, one each to the East, West, North and South. He dared not leave the bottle of rum there for the ancestors so the four drops would have to appease the spirits. The spirits were restless. Their territory was being continually invaded by these strangers and they wanted assurance that they were not being displaced. She smiled at the thought of one of these ghosts showing itself to Rory or Tayo or one of the girls. It would be hilarious to see but still she did not want it to happen. If this should happen, she wanted it to be a friendly spirit and not an angry one.

-Chapter 9-

*B*uzz...*buzz...buzz!* The noise interrupted the pre-dawn stillness. Groaning Alex rolled over and silenced her alarm clock. She hadn't slept well at all. She had a bad feeling about going to the cave. She had dreamt again about the woman. She was tall and dark as midnight. Her dress was white and shapeless and she had a scarf tied around her head. It was as if she was trying to show her something she couldn't see. She sleepily rubbed her eyes, looking down in the darkness at her alarm clock. It was three-thirty. Today was the day they were all meeting at the cave.

As the sleep left her eyes, she became energized. Megan and Ciarra would be downstairs waiting in another twenty minutes. She flew out of bed, brushed her teeth, dressed hurriedly and pulled on her cap. Her parents would have no need to fear because as far as they knew, it was just another early morning jog with her friends. The only thing was it was two hours earlier. She crept downstairs in the darkness and was grateful for the street light that enabled her to see as she made her way into the soft, cool pre-dawn air, which had not yet been heated by the sun that would brighten the charcoal sky as it slowly started its ascent over the hills in the next two hours. Her friends had deliberately decided on going to the cave in the early morning because the streets would be empty of traffic and pedestrians.

Across the street, up on the hill she made out the shapes of Megan and Ciarra jogging in her direction. Megan was dressed in blue sweat pants and designer sneakers while Ciarra had on loose fitting casual slacks, a cardigan over a tee shirt, and sneakers. She wore a cap pulled down over her face and had a knapsack on her back.

"Good morning," they both said.

"It's going to be a good day," Ciarra said as she looked up at the sky.

"Yeah I have a good feeling myself about today. Rory, Andy and Tayo should be waiting for us by the school gate."

"Let's get going," Megan suggested. "They aren't going to want to stand around waiting for us."

They jogged in the cool morning air, each of them wrapped in their early morning thoughts. The quiet splendor of the morning enveloped Alex, heightening her senses and, as she jogged, a feeling of peace permeated her being. They continued jogging and upon reaching the school gate, they turned without hesitating through the gates. The boys were waiting for them and after sharing hugs and kisses, they wasted no time in moving purposefully up the hill. It was almost as if they were leaving civilization behind when they entered the bushes. Early morning dew had settled on the greenery; the darkness seemed to swallow them up.

"I can't see a damned thing," Ciarra whispered. "Can't we use the flashlights to see where we're going?"

"Not yet," Andy hissed. "We can't afford to let anyone see any lights here. Let's go a little further in and you'll get some light."

"Oh shit!" Megan screeched as she stumbled over a dead tree root along the path. She felt herself going down but Tayo pulled her back just in time.

"Careful, the slope may be slippery," Rory warned. "We can't afford for Megan to get a broken leg."

"Definitely not!" she confirmed.

Alex walked on. It was like her senses were especially aware of the sounds of the morning; crickets were chirping and frogs croaking. She was unable to suppress a shudder that ran down her spine. Rory stopped and turned around.

"Are you okay, Alex?" he asked.

She rubbed her arms.

"I'm frightened of the dark," she answered truthfully. The chills that were running down her spine were unbelievable.

He gave her a hug. As he guided them along the rocky path, he kept her hand in his. It was not long before Rory stopped and pointed the flashlight at a rocky shelf.

"Look up there. We can climb up and look down on the town. You can see for miles around. Below that is the cave."

They climbed up the rocky slope and looked over the vast expanse of Galloway in Castle Mountain. As Alex stood there gazing at the virgin land on which they stood, her mind raced with so many thoughts. She inhaled the cool air thinking that this was no man's land. She was so engrossed in her thoughts that she had to stifle a scream when she saw a shape emerge from the shadows at the entrance to the cave as if rising with the mist. Tayo clamped a hand over her mouth. After staring at the shape, she sagged with relief when she realized that it was only Octavius and Neil. Carefully, they slid down the rocks to the cave below. Ciarra clutched the back of

Tayo's shirt as she made her way down the jagged incline and Megan was extremely cautious as she let herself down. Alex followed Rory, almost clutching onto him.

Octavius was standing at the entrance of the cave stroking his beard when they all finally arrived.

"You rascals all made it I see," he said with something like pride in his voice.

He had been half hoping they wouldn't show but at the same time he was glad that they had had the guts to stick to their decision. They descended into the maze-like cave, which was now lit up by lanterns and powerful flashlights, thanks to Octavius and Neil.

"I truly hope there are no ghosts, rats or bats in these walls or holes in here." Ciarra's voice came out as a squeak. It was obvious she was nervous and afraid. Tayo began to laugh.

"Last time I was here, we saw spiders and frogs and you know what? We even saw a ghost. It tried to grab Rory."

Her eyes widened in shock.

"Stop it Tayo. You know that's not true." It was Alex's fearful voice echoing around the room that broke into Tayo's teasing.

"Come on guys; you are scaring me."

Megan started but as the light played on the walls and revealed the paintings, all fear disappeared. Ciarra and Alex were enthralled by the rare formation of the rocks. Stalagmites and Stalactites had only been words in her school textbooks until now. As they walked further into the cave, Alex remembered this was the area where she had gone so far with Rory. She looked up and saw him watching her. She remembered the touch of his hands, his smell...how it felt to have his lips on hers. She wanted it again.

"Alex..."

She heard him call her name and saw the look in his eyes. She turned away to listen to what Octavius was saying.

"Let's get what we came for and get out. I know the idea of exploring is tempting but for today, we need to move fast."

Andy had been right when he had said that this would be a very different experience. Ciarra gazed around. She suspected that any antiques they found would be priceless. She wanted to dig and explore... see what she could find. As she crossed the room, she ran right into huge plastic packages that served as a reminder as to why they were all there.

"Rory, come over here! There is a whole lot of marijuana over here," she said excitedly.

He walked over and pulled neat packages from the middle of the stash. He did not take any from the top. For a moment Ciarra wondered if they were doing the right thing but as she looked at the huge stack of marijuana, that thought went out the door. They were going to put the money they gained from this to good use. Giving those who were in need was way up there in her book. They filled two knapsacks with as much marijuana as they could and when they thought they had packed enough, they went in search of the money. Octavius had a pick and crowbar to work on the safe just in case they were unable to open it. Tayo was digging between the rocks where the earth seemed to have been recently trampled. Finally he shouted:

"Yes!! I've found some."

Megan rushed over to help him dig up wads of hundred and fifty-dollar bills. Everyone in the little group was giddy with the success of their adventure. Megan had no doubt about why they were taking the money. It would go a long way to making monthly payments to the basic school. Parents who could not afford to pay the monthly school fees would not need to worry so much if there was at least enough money for an entire year. All this was going to charity. Tayo's voice penetrated her thoughts.

"Can I roll a joint and smoke some of this? It's so tempting."

"Boy, get all this stuff together and let's get out of here. Furthermore your head may be too light to handle the good old sensimilla. I tell you I don't want to have to carry you out of this cave over my shoulder," Octavius reprimanded.

"Yes, you're right but I'm taking some for a joint," Tayo said stubbornly.

Alex looked at Andy and then at Rory. Amusement flickered across his face.

"Do you all realize that it can be said we're robbing drug dealers? Anyone would say that this is immoral and that we're wrong. This would just make people gossip. The way to hell is paved with good intentions." Alex started to giggle.

"I can just see Ciarra's father standing in Church praying for forgiveness for his unruly daughter and her mother crying rivers of tears for her poor child who has been led astray."

Sunlight and Dappled Shade

"Oh wouldn't you all like to see me brought to my knees by my proud papa who preaches brimstone and fire to all those who won't repent of their sins and who wants nothing more than to see me converted to follow Jesus and God by getting baptized?" Ciarra joined in the fun.

The image that this brought to everyone's mind had them laughing hysterically. Tayo sucked his teeth.

"Those who live in the lap of luxury have no right to condemn someone born to poverty. What do they know about being hungry because there is no money to buy food or pay school fees? I say later for what anyone wants to think."

"I second that," Andy agreed. "I wouldn't mind having a drag of weed myself. Like Tayo says, it may put me in the frame of mind to do some serious meditating."

"Save that for another time and place. Everyone, check to make sure that we aren't leaving anything behind. If everything is okay, let's get the hell out of here. We don't want daylight to catch us near here," Rory instructed before heading to the entrance of the cave.

Before they could make it to the entrance, the walkie-talkie crackled. It was Neil who had been left behind to act as lookout.

"There are two guys that I can see almost at the entrance at the cave. I couldn't see them before because of the heavy mist."

"What the hell! There is no other way out of the cave. They are bound to see us once they come in. What are we going to do?" Ciarra asked, her voice shaking.

"We may have to fight our way out of here. Who knows what may happen?"

They all stood, undecided.

"Don't worry; our ancestors will guide us out of here."

Alex didn't know why she said it but it suddenly felt like a voice was speaking through her.

"We are all getting out of here," Alex continued.

Megan sat down suddenly on the floor of the cave.

"I would like to see how we are getting out without being seen and exposed. We are either going to die or go to jail."

"Shut up Megan. Keep your mouth shut, if you can't help with a solution." Mass Octavius turned around. "Come on all of you. Follow me."

Alex's fingers played with the pendant around her neck. For a moment she could not recall where she was. She felt as if she was in a dream and everything was swirling around her. For what seemed an eternity, Alex stood still, staring into the night as if waiting for a sign. She felt as if someone was tapping her on the arm. She turned to face the figure that seemed to be floating before her. It was the woman from her dreams and she was mouthing something that Alex couldn't hear. She felt an inexorable pull and found herself walking toward the woman who beckoned.

The others followed Alex as if mesmerized by the halo that seemed to surround her. Alex walked slowly and deliberately, following the woman whose dark shadow was enveloped by a floating light. *Queen Nanny*, Alex thought. *High Priestess of the*

Maroons. There was a warm feeling on her neck but she felt no fear as she accepted the guidance of her ancestor. The woman floated ahead and Alex and her friends followed.

They were in a different part of the cave that they had never seen or even known existed. Alex thought of all the ghost stories she had been told; about good and evil, demons and gods. Miss Etty had told her that there was more to this cave than anyone believed and that she had a special gift - a special power to connect with the spirits as she had given her the special pendant. Now she knew what it was for. She saw more clearly this time, the beautiful, dark-skinned woman who turned and smiled at her as she led them away from trouble. The woman smiled one more time as she floated away and the rocks gave way to a stretch of dried earth, which led to a clump of bushes.

Alex stopped in her tracks because it seemed like a dead end but the shining light continued and Rory walked ahead pushing at the branches and brambles. He could now see daylight as he pushed through, urging the others to follow. They were out of the cave at the opposite end. At first they all stood unsure of which direction to take but then they spotted the light in the Church. Alex hauled herself through the opening and was greeted by the cool morning air, soft on her cheek. She looked behind but the woman had disappeared with the light of day. Alex touched her pendant and thanked her guardian angel.

Ciarra stumbled through and crumpled to the ground.

"Alex, what in God's name was that? It was the weirdest thing. It's as if you had a light on top of your head. Tayo and Andy, did you see what I saw? I'm thankful to whatever got our asses out of there because we were in a lot of danger."

Tayo made the sign of the cross.

"I agree with you because we might have been killed and buried right there. I saw a ghost for the first time because it must have been a ghost. How else did we get out? None of us knew there was another entrance." Megan had her hands on her knees to prevent her legs from shaking. She felt as if any time now she would pass out.

"There is a lesson for all of you children. Never criticize what you don't know or can't explain. Alex was the one who helped to guide us. The spirits chose to help her," Mass Octavius explained.

Rory turned and looked at Alex with a smile. He took her hand in his and gave it a squeeze. Once again she touched the pendant around her neck and whispered a *thank you* to those who had gone before her. Rory dragged Ciarra to her feet.

"Let's keep going and get away from here. We have come too far to get caught."

They continued to descend the steep rocky path at an almost breathtaking speed. They left the cave behind, walking steadily towards the hill and hiking past the Gardiners' orange grove. Next they looped back past Thompson's Cottage and this route took them back to the street by the standpipe just before Harper's Grove. The air had lost its chill and a mild breeze rustled through the leaves on the trees. The darkness had faded and the sun was making its appearance. Many of the large trees were overgrown with creeping vines. Birds flitted among the flowering shrubs and smaller trees and right before Alex's eyes, a bluebird perched on the branch of a tree, followed by a doctor bird. The songs and calls of the birds rang in their ears as they trekked home. They jogged the rest of the way as they always did. They didn't break from tradition but went their separate ways, Alex with the bag of money, Rory with some of the marijuana and Octavius with the biggest bag of all. Later on, they would meet to sort everything out.

By midday, they were back on the road to Octavius's house. Miss Etty had just finished pinning the last piece of the clothing on the line and then emptying the water to one side of the yard to allow it to run down the drain that Octavius had made to prevent it from settling in a puddle. She smiled in delight as Alex, Rory and the rest of the group stepped into the yard and thanked the Lord that they had made it safely to and from the cave. She made a sign of the cross praying that now they would have no need to go back to that place.

They sat together for hours, sipping ice cold lemonade while butterflies of every hue flitted back and forth and doctor birds fed on nectar from the flowers in the garden. Two little blackbirds perched on the steps in the warm sun. Everyone helped to count the money, while discussing a plan to sell the marijuana and spend the money for worthy causes. Alex decided that since everyone had worked together, each person present including Miss Etty would receive one hundred dollars that same day to spend any way they chose.

Octavius took charge of the marijuana. He would be the one to pass it on discreetly to his brother who knew how to get it sold. They would send a half of it at first to see how the trade would go and if the exchange was done with the minimum of fuss; then they would proceed with the second installment. Alex and Rory would keep the second half, which would be divided in two equal parts between them. Once every week, everyone would verify that the money was intact unless instructions were given to spend any of it. It was a satisfactory arrangement for everyone. They would make anonymous donation of a monthly check that would supplement the salary of two teachers in addition to supplying books, slates and pencils and providing lunch for the students three times a week. They thought about recruiting another adult into the group but needed to think carefully who this person would be. A few suggestions were mentioned but it was decided that they would return in the morning to finalize those plans.

On Saturday, while Alex was walking through the vegetable market in front of her grandmother's shop, she heard Miss Leah gossiping with Dottie.

"Dottie, I heard that Bongo Man and Fiat sorely beat the boys who were trying to rob them."

With her hands akimbo, Dottie asked:

"So why did they catch the people who tried to rob them and let them get away with their ganja? No, something is not right about the story. Start from the beginning."

Before she could answer, Miss Kettley who was selling thyme and scallions and carrots joined in the conversation.

"That's not the story I heard. I heard that Bongo Man got robbed but they didn't catch the thieves. I heard that they know who robbed them and that they are surely going to retaliate."

Alex eyes almost popped out of her head. She didn't know what to do so she asked:

"Who got robbed, Miss Leah?"

"Girl, those drug dealers, Bongo Man, Fiat and Lindie. I heard that somebody stole their weed and money." She started to laugh. "I heard that they know who did it but I am certain they don't know a thing. Do you think if they knew that they wouldn't have gotten it back already? I am sorry I don't know who robbed them because I would be that person's best friend. I could surely use some of that money." She laughed some more.

"Not you alone, Leah. I could use some of that money myself." Dottie lowered her voice.

"From what I heard, Fiat and his gang think that it was some boys from Ducketts who robbed them. Dottie and Kettley, why didn't we think of doing the job?" Leah sucked her teeth.

"Nobody knew where they had their money and ganja hidden. It has to be one of their own friends who robbed them because only someone close to them that would have had that information."

Five minutes later Alex was flying up the hill to give Ciarra the news of what she had just heard. It didn't take them long before they were on their way to Rory's house to round up the troops to report the news. Rory remained calm when Ciarra gave him the news that Bongo Man had sounded alarm about having been robbed. As far as Rory and Tayo were concerned, they were only trying to get a reaction from the people who had taken their things. They had no idea who had taken their belongings.

"The only way they can pinpoint the culprit is if one of us reveals what we had done," Rory said. "We must all keep our heads together and focus. While we are all here, let's throw around some ideas."

-CHAPTER 10-

R ory sat on the steps of the verandah and waited for Tayo. Luck was on his side. His uncle had let him borrow his car to drive into Montego Bay. He looked up at the blue sky against which white clouds floated. It was going to be a scorcher today. He looked around. The early morning traffic had already thinned and by this time, traffic was light. Where the hell was Tayo? Rory had gone to pick up Tayo who was not at his mother's house and there was no way he was going to drive his uncle's car on that rough road where Tayo's grandmother lived to find him.

He and Tayo had been friends for a long time. Recently Tayo had developed an interest in the Rastafarian religion and immersed himself in learning everything about Marcus Garvey. He closed his eyes as he recalled the image of Alex as she lay beneath him. Someone slapped him, jerking him back to reality.

"Hey man! Snap out of the daydreaming. Only God knows where your thoughts were."

He opened his eyes to see Tayo standing in front of him with a smile on his face and for a minute Rory had the urge to punch him in his face. Here he was waiting patiently for an hour and enjoying his thoughts and in one minute, Tayo had destroyed his peaceful moment.

"Where were you, man? I came looking for you at least an hour ago and you're just showing up."

Tayo touched fists with Rory.

"Brother, you know how waking up in the morning is when I sleep over at Granny's. I have to do this and that for her before I can get out."

With Rory at the wheel, they headed to Bogue Heights to meet with the Manager of Desnoes and Geddes, the home of Red Stripe Beer. They were going to pick up the beer and sodas that Desnoes and Geddes was donating for their fun day. They joined the traffic leaving from Bethel along the narrow street of Galloway and Chester Castle before the road opened up into a wide highway. They opened the windows and the breeze tickled Rory's skin.

"I'm going to miss all of this when you are gone, my brother," Tayo said. "I'm thinking of finding a job in Kingston after graduation. It doesn't make sense to come back to B Town. All our lives are changing. I might even go right back to get a Bachelors degree. It makes no sense to waste my brilliance."

They had just passed Montpelier where the old railroad station used to be. People never used to take mini buses to Kingston, to Spanish Town or up the line. They used to take the train or the diesel as they called it.

"I can understand what you're saying," Rory answered. "For the first time it has sunk in. I never felt that I was leaving anything behind being away at University in Kingston because we would always come back here every holiday or even on weekends. It was you and I in the same dorm and everything. We would link up with everyone: Ciarra, Megan and Alex but now I feel as if I am losing something. I don't know how to put it in words. Playing cricket and juggling school was one thing. Finishing college and going away for long periods of time is something else. Maybe one of these days when I'm away in Pakistan or Australia if I ever get there, you guys can come to visit."

"Yeah when you get famous we can come to watch you play - especially Alex. I hope she won't go off and get married to someone we don't know. We don't want a total stranger taking away our dear friend." Tayo looked closely at Rory as he said this. "As for Megan, she is already on the map as the top track and field athlete. The Olympics is her next stop and Ciarra will design clothes for us to wear."

"You know what? I can always come home for a visit from time to time. It's not as if I'll be living in Timbuktu. You know what I mean?" Rory was driving with greater speed now. "Why do you say that about Alex? Right now she is only interested in becoming an attorney. Do you know something I don't know because if you know anything you'd better spill it right now?" Rory had not noticed that he had raised his voice. Tayo smiled at Rory.

"No man! I don't know anything but Alex is a nice girl and if you really like her, you need to let her know especially since you won't be around much...but then again, you may want to sow some wild oats."

They drove along in silence leaving Montpelier and the wide open road through Mount Carey around some deep curves then into the town of Anchovy past the police station that had been recently built, and the policemen who chatted up the women in the area. The road narrowed with culverts on the right side of the street where the water ran off. Rory held the steering wheel with a steady hand as they came to Long Hill.

It was a dangerous, steep, narrow, winding strip overlooking seemingly endless deep gorges and gullies where there was no overtaking, even though some reckless souls who had no fear of endangering their lives and others' would try to go around other cars. There was a story about one of their classmates, Stephan, who was driving one of those big tankers down Long Hill when the truck slipped over into the gully. People said his grandmother's spirit had been with him that night because he jumped out of the truck and luckily a tree stump broke his fall. The story took on a life of its own and from all reports he became a big-time believer in God and the Church right then and there. Tayo felt relaxed at the feel of the wind blowing through the window and looked out ahead. He sighed at the beautiful view laid out before him. Down below was Reading with its beautiful, shimmering, blue sea that ran from there along the coast to Lucea.

"Sometimes we forget how beautiful our country is," Rory pointed out as he drove pass the villa. "I remember when my uncle took me over there to meet his friends one evening when I used to go to Cornwall College. He let me have a beer sitting out there by the bar with the waves rolling gently onto the rocks."

"Yeah I remember that was the day you left my ass at school and I didn't stop needling you until finally you got your uncle to take us there. It was fun - me drinking a Red Stripe Beer and all, walking on the beach like I was a big shot." Tayo laughed at the memory.

They merged into traffic and went with the flow, after which they turned into the wide impressive driveway of the beverage company where they stopped by the security station at the gate and gave their names. The gates opened allowing them in. Mr. Brown, a short, stocky, light-skinned man stood up and shook their hands when they entered his office.

"It's good to meet young people who want to make a contribution to their community."

They made small talk for a while before getting down to business.

"So what prompted you two to think about a fun day not only for children but also for the aged, even though you have no money as you put it?"

Rory looked at Tayo from the corner of his eyes and knew exactly what he was thinking. He covered his mouth and coughed.

"I am sorry. It was a friend of ours who first thought about it. Her name is Alex. Her mother and grandmother own a store. Every weekend, her grandmother gives away food to those who are not able to leave their homes because they are sick or have little or no money. We were sitting chatting one evening and she commented that there must be a way to get people out for at least a day. She wanted to have as many people as possible participating in a fun day and here we are asking for your help for charity."

Tayo continued where Rory left off.

"The Baptist Church does a good job of helping but they have never been able to take it this far, so we thought about it and decided that we would like to do more to spread some joy. As our sponsor, the Desnoes and Geddes, name will be all over the place. I personally love Kola Champagne soda."

Mr. Brown looked at how earnest their faces were.

"This Alex sounds like a smart little lady. I'm sold on your idea but I'm surprised you didn't ask for more. How about if I add a few boxes of Guinness Stout? Since you kids are here, would you like a tour of the facility to see how things are run?"

"Yes, we would," they both answered. "Thank you so much for your time, Mr. Brown."

He stood up to escort them to the next room where their tour began. Mr. Brown promised that one of his drivers would drop the boxes of sodas, beers and stouts the next day, which was perfectly okay with Tayo and Rory. They drove out of D&G making a right turn and headed into Montego Bay. Rory decided not to take the highway but to take Barnett Street and find the patty shop by the bus stop. Nothing had changed. Traffic was worse than it had been; people crossed the street whenever they wanted; they crossed against the traffic light and Rory cursed.

"Have you forgotten that you do the same thing that these people are doing all the time, Rory? Now that you're driving you're cursing like a sailor."

"As if you're any better," Rory answered. "but there is no way in hell I am this bad."

Peddlers sat on the sidewalks with a wide assortment of items for sale: anything from clothes to hair products. Men pushed carts with bags of ice and cooked food in boxes. Rory fought his away along in traffic, sighing with relief when they came to St. James Street. There was no reason for him to have taken this route, patty or no patty. They decided to head out to *The Pelican* to have lunch. An hour later, a satisfied feeling in their stomachs, they left Montego Bay to drive back into the countryside. Only *The*

Pelican. Years ago only a few locals dared enter those doors. How things had changed in this tiny island of Jamaica.

The Church and schoolyard in Bell Town had been converted into a fairground. On the grass in the Churchyard lines were marked for all the races. This was where the egg and spoon and the sack races for the children would be held. Beside the little school where the canteen was located there were six drum pans set up for grilling: two for chicken, two for pork and two for fish. Rice and peas, roasted yam and other food would be pre-cooked in the canteen. There were four bars located at the four corners of the schoolyard. By three o'clock on Friday afternoon, there was a big crowd of volunteers helping to set up tents and preparing for the big day on Saturday.

-CHAPTER 11-

For all the anticipation, the worry and the tossing and turning the night before the community fair, which was going to be a big event, the day dawned sunny and bright. How the time had flown. August had arrived and it was Independence Weekend. The little town was once again crowded with all the out-of-towners coming home for the holiday weekend. The morning sparkled. Alex sucked in a huge breath of fresh air. They were all together: Rory, Tayo, Ciarra, Megan and Neil walking noisily along the road toward the school yard.

The fact that Ciarra had caught Tayo red-handed with another girl was causing major headaches among the friends because of the arguing back and forth but today was the big day. Ciarra was riding piggyback on Tayo. Alex was laughing because Tayo had refused to admit that he was struggling with Ciarra on his back. Megan was walking alongside them, a bandana tied around her head and her precious bottle of water in her hand. Neil attempted to hold onto Megan's hand and managed to grasp her arm before she pulled away, swinging her arms freely.

Rory told Tayo to put Ciarra down before he dropped her or broke his back or worse yet, put a strain on that vital part between his legs. At the mere thought of that possibility, Tayo immediately stood still, sliding Ciarra from off his back, whereupon Megan made a noise somewhere between a laugh and a cough. Alex closed her eyes and raised her face to the sun. It felt wonderful--sun on her face and goofing around with her friends. What was better than this? She was surprised by the passage of time. The days had passed, then a week, then a month and now it was almost the end of the summer holidays. Soon they would be going in different directions; but today they were all together. These past few days had been idyllic, sweet. Rory no longer avoided her; instead he was always around teasing her, sometimes making her mad and sometimes making her laugh.

Minutes later, they arrived at the school yard. Today the men who were normally wielding axes were stirring pots over fires. The morning was already becoming hot and sticky but it did not prevent the crowd from converging on the fair. Babies, teenagers, old and young alike - all the villagers were out to enjoy themselves. Women held babies with their heads resting in the crooks of their arms; men sat in the cool shade of trees sipping on gin or rum chased with coconut water, while children frolicked about. Alex shook her head as she reflected on the fact that, here in Jamaica no matter what anyone said, doors would open faster for those who came from a more privileged socio-economic background and had a popular name, money and influence. Here she lived a fairly simple life but she also carried a bourgeois name associated with high class, wealth and privilege. She had a wealthy uncle who was a politician with connections all the way to the top, including the Prime Minister of Jamaica.

She shielded her eyes with her hands to avoid the glare caused by the whirring of the helicopter propellers as it made its landing on a small strip in the Churchyard. Dust and dry grass swirled up into the air. The noise heralded the arrival of the Honorable David DeCampo, Jamaica's Prime

Minister. Soldiers from the Jamaica Defense Force and Officers from the Jamaica Constabulary Force rushed to the chopper and stood guard while her uncle disembarked with the great public figure who referred to himself as 'Eli'. True to character, he was carrying the gift his father had received from Haile Selassie I, the late emperor of Ethiopia. This was said to be his good luck rod.

There were wild cheers from the crowd because most people were stunned at this unexpected visitor. Alex watched the Prime Minister stride powerfully through the awe-struck crowd to the podium. He looked gorgeous with his tanned complexion and she wished she were ten years older because she was in love with this man. She took him in: his formidable stature, his broad shoulders and the agility of his movements for a man of such imposing stature. His hair had a slight silvering at the temples that gave him an air of sober maturity and distinction. Everything zoomed into focus when Megan pinched her.

"Close you mouth and stop drooling. You have that look on your face as if you could eat him up right here, right now." Alex's mouth opened and then closed because before she could respond, Ciarra answered:

"I could eat him alive right here. I'm sure you could too, Megan. Oh how I wish I was older and accomplished. I would certainly make a play for him."

They all laughed hysterically at these words.

"Is this a private joke? Let me in on it."

Alex hadn't seen Rory coming. He put his hands around her waist and pressed his firm, sensual mouth against hers.

"I am not David DeCampo but you have me," he said with a smile on his face as he let her go.

People were stretching out their hands to shake the leader's as he made his way to the makeshift podium. He held up his rod and the people cheered even more.

"My people, it's a pleasure to be here with you today. As I look around, I see so much strength and love among you all. As a people, we have to work together for a better Jamaica. Many have deliberately misunderstood my call for change but this change is for us to make ourselves and our country better. My friends, I see an abundance of wealth surrounding me now because of the love that you have for each other. Hear me when I say that even though material gain is not the sole purpose of the human existence, on the other hand, poverty defeats all possibilities. Therefore the supreme challenge of our time is to work together to eliminate it from our midst. I believe that investing in agriculture, planting crops that we ourselves can use and export will allow us to be self reliant and independent because right now, we are too dependent on foreign goods. Many people distort my words and spread fear but all I want for my people is equality, dignity and justice."

The crowd was on its feet cheering. As the word spread that the Prime Minister was in town, villagers emerged hurriedly from their homes, not wanting to miss the unforgettable honor of being there in person to listen to this great man and to speak with him and shake his hand. At the end of the speech Mr.

DeCampo sat with the Baptist Minister, her uncle Harry and many of the villagers, chatting about sports and politics and sipping fish soup. When a mother set her little boy in his lap, he swayed the baby back and forth in his arms. The baby giggled and gurgled, holding on to his fingers. Auntie stood with her hands akimbo.

"Mr. Prime Minister, you know that many are saying that Jamaica is moving in a socialist direction because we have become friends with Cuba."

"I say to those people that Cuba is our closest neighbor. Sanctions have been imposed against this little country, Cuba, but none against South Africa, an economically powerful country that supports apartheid. Cuba is a respectful country that does not interfere in other countries' politics."

Prime Minister DeCampo responded not only to Auntie but to the crowd at large.

"I can't tell you how grateful Bell Town is to have the Cuban doctors," Auntie continued. "Many people who couldn't afford to go to the doctor now have access to free healthcare."

Mass Octavius knocked his pipe against his leg before looking at Prime Minister DeCampo.

"They're bombing airstrips and burning down ganja fields all because the American Government is busy trying to stem the sale of weed. That's foreign exchange gone down the drain. Car rental companies profit because people rent cars for business. Hairdressers profit because drug sellers give their women money to shop. What do they expect poor people to do when they lock down the trade?"

Prime Minister DeCampo chuckled.

"We'll make room to plant sugar cane and bananas and other crops."

The entire crowd began to laugh. David DeCampo was one of the upper class but yet he was a man who was willing to sit down and talk to the people at the grass roots level.

The rest of the day was full of laughter, love and mischief. At the end of day when the sun had long disappeared behind the clouds, the grounds were even more crowded. With work over, men and women had gone home to shower and come out dressed to the nines. Alex sat on the school wall in the semidarkness. With her eyes closed, she focused on some of the sounds around her: the music and the laughter. She opened her eyes and looked up at the stars that seemed to wink at her in a sky that was no longer blue but glossy black. Bending backwards, she watched the moon in the sky as if it were a boat sailing on water. She heard footsteps and turned to see Rory walking towards her, his shirt half unbuttoned. He wasn't smiling.

"I've been looking for you. Someone told me that they saw you with Nick."

"No, I'm by myself. There's no one else here. To think that I'll be gone in another couple of days. This time next week, I'll be in Kingston."

Rory took a seat next to her.

"Time flies. By the time you look around, you will be done with school and attending UWI. All of us: you, me, Ciarra, Megan, Neil and Tayo all have different paths now but we will find a way to get together as much as possible."

"Yeah, you're right," Alex answered.

"Come on," Rory said as he pulled her to her feet. "Let's go join the others but first I need a kiss." His mouth touched hers and their lips met. Someone cleared their throat and Alex and Rory sprang apart.

"I take it this is reason why we can't find you two." Ciarra was laughing. "Stealing, stealing, a kiss here and a kiss there."

"Oh shut up Ciarra. Wait until I catch you and Tayo together. It will be the scandal of the year," Alex said hotly.

Ciarra shrugged her shoulders and smiled even more.

"Come on," Rory held out his hand to Alex. "Let's go back to the party."

-Chapter 12-

T he very next day after moving to Jacks Hill, Kingston, Alex was sitting on the terrace in a lounge chair enjoying the breeze that was stirring the bougainvilleas and swaying the leaves of the palm trees when her uncle Harry laid out the ground rules.

"My requirement, Alex," he said, "is that you bring home As and Bs and I have to emphasize more As than Bs. I am not interested in seeing a report card with Cs. If you are going to be the first female Prime Minister of Jamaica, you are going to have to be better, smarter and brighter than the rest."

She stifled a laugh. *Her uncle had to be joking*!

"Prime Minister of Jamaica? I don't want to be Prime Minister, Uncle. I want to be a lawyer."

She looked directly at her uncle to see whether he was joking or serious but she saw that his face was serious. *Which student didn't bring home a C?*

"You being a lawyer, that's perfectly fine. As a matter of fact, your Aunt Bernice thinks it's a good choice but you have to do your best because I want you to attend the best law school."

"Uncle I know we discussed law schools some time ago. I don't want to go to Emory University in Atlanta or to NYU. I think I want to stay right here and attend Norman Manley Law School."

Her uncle laughed as she placed emphasis on *right here.*

"There's plenty of time to change your mind and you also understand that you will have to be careful with your personal life. We don't want any scandals ruining your chances of reaching where your intelligence has the potential to take you."

Alex half closed her eyes. *Hadn't she and her friends done the unthinkable?* She couldn't help laughing out loud at the memory of her and her friends removing marijuana and cash from the cave and then almost getting caught. Her uncle would probably have a heart attack and die if he were to ever get a hint of what she had been up to.

"Is there something I said that you find funny, Alex? Maybe you want to share the joke?" her uncle asked with a serious face.

"No, Uncle. It's just that at first when you said the part about me being Prime Minister, it seemed a little ridiculous. That's why I laughed," Alex answered.

"There is something called vision, my child. I am older and wiser so it's up to me to point you in the right direction. Having been in politics most of my life, I have some idea how you can succeed. It was never *my* personal ambition to be Prime Minister but I know what it takes. I see you as head of the leadership of this country."

Her uncle, the Minister of Finance and before that a renowned attorney, was one of the most respected men in politics. His affluent background had taught him how to make money. His wife, who was equally successful, was a franchise owner of one of the highest grossing duty-free shops in Montego Bay as well as the owner of a Public Relations firm in Kingston. Their daughter had chosen to move away to Miami.

All the while, Alex was pacing back and forth and thinking, *Prime Minister*. More and more it sounded appealing but politics could be dirty, and what about her privacy? She wouldn't have a life because she would have to campaign and attend political meetings. It was a whole lot to take in at the moment. On the other hand, she would take up residence at Jamaica House with everything at her disposal. Not bad for a girl who had grown up in the country. Thinking about Denham Town and Back Bush and Jones Town was already giving her a headache but you have to play the hands that you were dealt. Take some Tylenol and keep on doing your job. She looked over at her uncle thinking that he must have a lot of faith in her to even think that she could be at the helm of Jamaica's leadership or that she was a bright and innovative individual. She stood up suddenly and walked over to him and gave him a big hug.

"Uncle, you can say what you want. I have aspirations but nothing as grand as this."

"Girl, go and sit down," he said in a gruff voice, swirling the ice around in his lemonade. "You have always made me proud. You have it in you to be the next Prime Minister."

He patted her arm before turning and walking back into the house. Alex ran into the house and telephoned her grandmother. But Auntie didn't seem the least bit surprised and neither did Alex's mother. It was as if they had already known what the plan was. She hung up the phone with the feeling that they were all conspiring against her. She got her swimsuit from the closet, pulled it on and went downstairs and outside to the pool.

She stuck her toes in, watching the water slide over her brightly painted red toenails before slipping into the water. She floated on her back, looking up at the sky and wondering where Rory was today and what Megan and Ciarra were up to. Tired of swimming, she got out of the water, grabbed her towel from the lounge chair and dried herself. She wished that her friends were with her. She was missing Rory who was most likely off somewhere playing cricket. Right then, she thought out a plan: after sixth form she would see if her uncle and her mother would allow her to live on the university campus.

Alex's life underwent some serious amount of modification. She did not have to take the bus to school anymore. Gone were the days of walking all the way to Galloway just to ensure a seat on a bus that would be crammed with people anxious to get to work on time. She kind of missed the meaningless chatter that accompanied them to Montego Bay. Instead, she was chauffeured back and forth. If she was going to arrive late from school, she had to let her aunt or uncle know ahead of time and so for the next school year, she worked herself to the bone to get good grades.

She took up Economics, although she hated it. However, if she was going to be a Member of Parliament or even the Prime Minister, she would have to have some knowledge of how to balance a checkbook and eventually, a budget. She had male friends but since none of them closely resembled Rory in any way, she omitted the boyfriend part. Alex excelled in Spanish, English and History. She spent hours in the library reading up on slavery and the slave trade. She thought of the cave and how it must have been a shelter to so many of her ancestors.

Had they held secret meetings there? Had is been a place for lovers to consummate their passions without the prying eyes of outsiders? Had Nanny herself climbed those very hills, sneaking in through the hole that led to the underground? How many people, sitting relaxed on their upscale verandahs sipping lemonade and calling out to their helpers to bring more ice had had the experience that Alex and her friends had?

Alex obtained grades no lower than Bs and mostly As. She learnt about Chaucer and Shakespeare. On the holidays she went back to Bell Town to see her mother and grandmother. Rory was not at home much anymore because he was either in Kingston or away playing cricket. Whenever she was with Megan and Ciarra, she would hear about the things that they had done with Rory but he would not come to visit her and she refused to go to visit him as well. He would stay in touch by phone but there was no face-to-face interaction.

On Graduation Day, she was pleasantly surprised when Rory showed up at the Ceremony with Megan, Ciarra and Tayo. Her heart skipped a beat as he hugged her tightly.

"Alex, you know I wouldn't miss your graduation for anything in the world. It's been too long since I last saw you."

He was still holding onto her hand.

"You have always known where to find me so cut the crap, Rory."

Alex rolled her eyes.

"Don't roll your eyes at me. I hear plans are afoot for you to be the next Prime Minister of Jamaica. Just remember when you make it, we are all in this together."

Rory relished teasing her.

"Yeah, you heard right but it is a long time from now. My uncle gave me that pep talk the day I moved in and the goal has not changed. If I am not careful, I'll be a Member of Parliament soon," Alex answered.

She turned her gaze to where her uncle was standing with her mother and grandmother.

"You didn't tell me this, Alex," Megan said. "It would be really nice to have a personal friend in politics."

"Alex, there is a saying that to whom much is given, much is expected and that is what your uncle is saying. There is always one person who is chosen and you apparently have been chosen to lead your people," Rory said sagely.

"Enough of all this talk about politics! Are we going out to have a good time after we leave this place? I would like to have some fun," Alex said with a laugh.

"What kind of fun are we talking about?" Rory asked.

"The kind where we chat about nonsense, laugh and definitely drink something other than lemonade," Ciarra was trying to stifle her laughter but was unable to and burst out laughing instead.

-CHAPTER 13-

Three years later

J amaica had been at a standstill for the past week. People were more interested in the track and field events taking place in Berlin than in work. It was common knowledge among people of all ages that Megan Thomas was going to win gold medals for track and field for Jamaica at the Berlin games. People of every ilk in Jamaica always seemed to unite in their support for Megan and other Jamaican athletes to dominate in the events in which they were participating. The 200 and 100-meter races were locked up by Jamaica as far as everyone was concerned and so was the 400-meter relay for that matter.

There was a carnival atmosphere on the island - rum bars were full; cheering parties were taking place in homes across the country. In Kingston, crowds gathered in front of big-screen televisions that had been placed in the middle of Half-Way Tree. In Montego Bay, the sound of car horns were heard all over as motorcades were organized and people gathered in Sam Sharp Square to watch the games. However, there was no bigger celebration than in little Bell Town where banners with the map of Jamaica painted on them flew high and where Megan led the group of Jamaican athletes.

There were heated debates as to whether America could upset what so many knew was already written, that Megan could not be defeated in these games. In the United States, proud Jamaicans were waiting with bated breaths for the race to be run. At home,

Megan's parents' house was teeming with life as relatives and friends had their eyes glued to the TV. Outside, a red, green and gold banner waved in the breeze. Her mother paced back and forth nervously.

"Lovie, come sit down and stop marching," Mr. Thomas cajoled. "Win or lose, she is still the best so come sit down in the chair."

"What do you mean, *win or lose*, papa?" Megan's sister jumped in. "She will win. There is no doubt about that."

While all this was going on, all Alex could think about was Rory. That night in the cave seemed to be forever haunting her. He was going to be in Berlin. Last time she had seen him they had all been in Montego Bay at Doctor's Cave Beach throwing ball in the sand. She had gotten pissed because the boys were deliberately throwing the ball above the girls' heads, winning every time. Rory had picked off a ball meant for her by simply reaching above her head. He had then had the nerve to give her a hug and drop a kiss on her mouth and then even more nerve to smile. That was it, she was steaming. He had stood there, no shirt on with his six pack abs egging her.

"Come on Alex, if you bad touch me, touch me right here," indicating his chest as if they were still in primary school and looking at her in that sexy way of his.

She marched right up to him and poked him in the stomach; truth is she had really felt like punching him in the gut because he knew how to get under her skin. He had held on to her fingers sliding it down to the waist band of his shorts while holding her gaze. She had no longer felt like punching him. Instead she had felt that old familiar feeling that she had for Rory creep right up on her. Alex had smiled at him with that knowing smile after observing the increased bulge in his shorts. Playing ball had ended shortly after because Rory had to go take a dip in the water dragging her with him.

She shook her head clear and reached for the phone to call Tayo. She was leaving for Berlin with Tayo and Ciarra. Hooking up with her friends again was going to be the highlight of her year. They were all going to support Megan in her bid for gold and had every confidence that she was going to do it. Alex thought about the nights of training, pushing their friend beyond her limit until she was the best. The secret of the cave was still safe among them. Alex shuddered to think how brave they had to have been to pull off a stunt like that and not get caught. Bongo Man and Fiat must still be looking for their thief, probably beating up a few more people along the way.

Back in Berlin Rory, Ciarra, Tayo, Alex and Neil were sitting in the stands. Rory made an indication to Tayo with his head and, without blinking an eye, Tayo read the message. Tayo vacated his seat to sit beside Ciarra and Rory moved across to sit next to Alex.

"I could see that you were missing me next to you so, as you can see, I switched seats to be closer to you," Rory said to Alex.

Alex shook her head and sucked her teeth.

"What is it with you, Rory? You insist on bothering me all the time. Don't you have your hands full with all the women you are running around with? Stop messing with me. One day you might just get something that will turn you upside on your head."

Before Rory could answer Ciarra was pointing to the track.

"There is Megan." And all eyes turned to the field.

The Jamaicans were there to cheer their athletes on, win or lose, and there was a sea of Jamaican flags. Today there were no enemies; every Jamaican was a friend. Since the Olympics, Megan had won four gold medals with a world record each. What was she going to do today? Would she be able to break her own records?

It was amazing to see how far Megan had come from little Bell Town. When Megan began her so-called training, no one had any idea that she would be one of the most popular athletes in the world, smashing records and bringing excitement to track and field. Here she was now standing at the edge of the track. She was watching the many athletes gear up for their respective events when suddenly she felt overwhelmed and her confidence deserted her. Knees shaking and face in hands, she bent over and slid to the ground. Her coach immediately sat beside her and held her hands. For a few minutes, he allowed her to indulge her fears and then with a firm hand, he pulled her up.

"Megan, look at me," he demanded. "You fear letting everyone down but regardless of what happens, we will pick up and move forward but *dammit* pull yourself together. You have a race to win. Close your eyes and listen to the cheers of the crowd. Ciarra, Alex, Rory, Tayo and Neil are up there watching. All the love is up there in that stand for you so go win me a medal, girl."

Megan smiled at that thought. It had not been easy for her friends to come to Berlin but they managed to make it. Rory, as always generous, had purchased the airline tickets and paid for hotel accommodations for Ciarra, Tayo and Neil. Alex had objected to his spending any money on her and had opted not to come but her uncle Harry had decided that she should attend and had bought her a first class ticket and also paid for her hotel accommodations. The fact that Alex and Rory were at odds with each other was immaterial as was the fact that Megan was no longer seeing Neil. They had decided to put their differences aside; but after the games were over, the sniping between Rory and Alex would begin all over. It was plain to all except those two that their problem was the sexual tension and jealousy between them both; but you couldn't tell them that.

Rory was now a well known cricketer and he had had to fly into Berlin from Pakistan where he had been playing a cricket match. He had made a huge mistake by bringing his current flame along. He must have been a fool not to know that this would have only pushed Alex further away. Megan found this so funny that she began to laugh. It was just like old times when they were unknown teenagers in school who would get into all kinds of trouble and as usual there would be some drama between Tayo and Ciarra. This was the therapy she needed.

She walked onto the track and stood looking up in the stands. She spotted the flag with "MEGAN" boldly printed in gold and right away, she was able to pinpoint where Alex and the others were sitting. Wondering what was going on up there, she smiled to herself as she waved and blew a kiss. Suddenly she became impatient for the race to be over so that she could watch the fireworks between Rory and Alex. She turned away and focused her attention on the business of running. She rubbed her hands across her chest looking at her running gear that had been made by Ciarra. Her coach gave her a last-minute word of encouragement.

"Go and do your best."

That was what she intended to do. After all, she was standing here in Berlin where Jesse Owens' participation in the 1936 Olympics had been controversial because of his race. In the 1930s, Hitler wanted blacks to be excluded from future games and it was a time when segregation and discrimination were rife in the United States of America. Here she was in the same arena where Jesse Owens had achieved international renown against all odds by winning four gold medals, one each in the 100 meters, 200 meters, long jump and 4 by 100 meters relay. Today would be her day. They were called to the mark, Lane 1, United States, Lane 4, Jamaica's Megan Thomas, Great Britain, Trinidad and Tobago, Russia and on it went.

"And there is the start and Megan Thomas of Jamaica is in the lead and she is aggressive around the turn and she has pulled away, stretching the lead and maintaining it. She has dominated the race from beginning to end, setting a new world record for the one hundred meters." She threw her hands in the air as she crossed the finish line. She gave a celebratory jig and the crowd went wild. Up in the stands, her friends screamed and slapped each other on the back. They had helped her train years ago for this under ten point one seconds. Megan brought a world record to the Olympic Stadium and a gold medal to her country. Although the American women were the favorites who ran a smooth race, they had been left in the dust.

-CHAPTER 14-

Ciarra wanted no part of Tayo at the moment. She didn't want to see him, hear his name, absolutely nothing to do with him. He was a lying, two timing or three timing whore of a man. Just last week they had a physical fight after she found out some girl was having his baby. She had hit him then and he had pushed her causing her to go after him with her shoes. Of course she wasn't buying his bull shit story that all of this was a lie. It was happening too often where she was hearing that he was with this one or that one. She had finally figured out that he wasn't going to change any time soon. Her mother just last week told her they were too young to be so serious. If this girl was having his baby for real, she was through with him. She wasn't having any of that crap.

She was a secretary and a part time dressmaker. She had gone to secretarial school instead of going to the fashion institute as she had wanted because this was what her parents could afford. Sewing a dress and designing one was like second nature to her but she was scared to quit her job and move to Kingston where the fashion institute was without having a back up plan.

She was twenty two years old and living at home with her parents, which to her was pathetic. By now she thought she would have been living in a big house on a hill in Montego Bay and Tayo by her side; but this was not so. She missed Rory who was no longer living in Bell Town. Megan she saw but she was training hard, competing at different track meets and hanging with a different group and well, Tayo was living on his own and teaching high school. You would think that she would be spending more time with Tayo because he had his own place but no, it was not so.

There was always some drama going on with one woman or the other but at the same time he constantly told her how much he loved her and that she was the one he wanted. She had practically been dating him since her teenage years. He had been her first.

Everything was changing and she definitely didn't want to get stuck by herself in Bell Town. She couldn't remember when she spent so much time by herself. There was always Neil or Rory, or Megan; someone was always there. It truly sucked that they weren't around as much any more.

Megan was now a national celebrity driving around in her BMW and hanging out with her new beau Sam and his crowd. She was no longer Megan, her friend but some kind of celebrity who kinda wanted to leave her past behind because of some name dropping jerk. Rory tried to warn her about moving too fast with a fast crowd but she shrugged her shoulders and said life is about moving up and finding a guy with lots of money in his pocket. As a result of Sam they hadn't spent much time with Megan in Berlin.

Alex had invited Ciarra to spend the weekend with her up in Jacks Hill. The invitation couldn't have come at a better time. It was fashion week in Kingston and Alex wanted them both to attend one of those big name designer shows. Alex's Uncle

Harry had clout and had scored them tickets for the front row.

The house Alex lived in was beautiful with a deck wrapped around it and a long balcony above on the second floor where Ciarra's room was located. Burgundy curtains fluttered in the breeze that flowed through the open windows. Outside, butterflies darted from one window to the other. Her room was large and spacious with a huge four poster bed. Colorful rugs were scattered across well polished wooden floor. A small door led to her own bathroom, no sharing with anyone. White tiles lined the floor with a stand alone bath with a shower in the corner. A pair of doors led out to the balcony which was lined with flowers of so many colors. Adjoining her room was Alex's which meant that she could run across to her room.

There was a formal reception area that led into the dining area. Towards the other side of the house was a more relaxed and comfortable family room with a wide screen TV. At the back of the house was a garden where sunlight glinted off the clear blue water of the in-ground swimming pool. Later she was going for a dip. Ciarra couldn't understand why Alex wanted to leave her uncle's fabulous home to go live on UWI campus. She sighed to herself. If she lived here there is no way she would be in a rush to go live elsewhere. There was such a warm feeling throughout the house. It was truly a home. Uncle Harry's wife made you feel as if you are family. No snotty behavior. She was so engrossed in her thoughts she didn't hear Alex enter the room.

"Are you finished sewing your dress, Ciarra?" Alex asked. "We could just go buy one, you know."

Ciarra looked at Alex in horror.

"Buy a dress and I can make a better dress than what I am going to pay a bag of money for?"

Ciarra was not quite finished with her statement when Alex spotted the dress lying across the bed.

"Omigosh! This is the dress you made? This is gorgeous. I mean, I know you can sew your ass off but this is exceptional. You are going to get noticed today."

Alex was holding out the dress and looking at it in fascination. The dress was in colors of gold and black, simple, tight fitting but slightly above the knees, and sleeveless.

"Yeah, it took me sometime to get it right because I want to make my own fashion statement today."

Ciarra was laughing like old times. Later on, when Ciarra came downstairs, she could hear Uncle Harry's deep voice and Mrs. Keanon's infectious laugh. She made her way to the kitchen. As she approached, Mrs. Keanon clapped her hands.

"Look at my two girls. You both are going to steal the show today."

Alex giggled and Ciarra smirked.

"Auntie Keane, you always say the right things to make a girl feel on the top of the world," Ciarra said, still smiling.

"Come on girls. I am driving you guys today," Uncle Harry said as he looked at them and shook his head. "Looks like you guys were skimping on the material that you used for those dresses."

Alex and Ciarra looked at each other before cracking up.

"One thing I have to say Uncle you are always funny," Alex mumbled under her breath.

Fashion day kicked off at 9a.m. at Willowdene House in New Kingston and as Alex and Ciarra entered walking towards the front row, many turned around to stare. Ciarra looked around at the many chic celebs and some of the biggest names in fashion that she was rubbing elbows with. Wow, she thought, this is where I want to be showing my designs. There was one man who continued to stare at Ciarra and he was one of the biggest names in the fashion industry. His eyes drifted with leisurely and very male appreciation, taking in Ciarra's slender shapely legs.

Her dress, a short dress in black and gold geometrical patterns, held his attention. Alex he knew and, although she was a beauty, it was her companion who held his attention. He had to find out who she is.

Models strutted their stuff in flippy chiffon dresses, bright and short outfits with sculptured bodices. Itsy, bitsy, teenie swimwear caused the oohs! and ahhs! To float in the air even after the models had left the runway. Ciarra had her notebook and as each model left the runway she made jottings and notes regarding what she liked and what she didn't like. She made sketches and drawings of designs to be worn by skinny models and real people. It was the end of the show and Ciarra was still seated, frowning grimly at the sketch of a dress which didn't seem right. She sipped at the water someone handed to her without looking up.

"Your drawing has flair and I can imagine this dress coming alive."

Klein interrupted Ciarra as she concentrated on her sketch. She gave a startled screech.

"I am sorry, I didn't quite hear what you said before."

"I am a friend of Alex and her family. Why don't you introduce us?" Klein turned to Alex.

Alex could see the interest written clearly on Klein's before he masked his expression. Alex did the introductions as they walked out into sunlight. She sensed the interest that Klein had but she was still trying to figure out if the interest was in Ciarra herself or the designs that she had been sketching during the show. She felt a bit of unease at the situation.

"Ciarra is such a beautiful name," Klein drawled as he raised her hand to his lips. "Tell me, whose design are you wearing? It's a hot dress."

"It's Alex-Ciarra Designs," Ciarra quipped.

"Enlighten me. I have never heard of that designer."

Klein leaned forward, giving her the full benefit of his undivided attention.

"It's my designs. I not only designed this dress but I also made it. Alex and myself are in partnership," Ciarra explained.

The crowd swarmed around them. Photographers and celebs were clamoring for Klein's attention but, before he was dragged away he pressed a VIP PASS in Alex's hand for his after- party which was always one of the biggest bashes.

"Make sure you guys are there tonight."

He winked at them both before disappearing into the crowd.

"Do you know who that is?" Alex asked excitedly. "He is The Who of fashion."

"Did you hear him ask me about my dress?" Ciarra was hopping from foot to foot. "Tell me we are going to his party later tonight."

Later that evening Ciarra, dressed in a lime green strapless dress looking like she just stepped off the cover of Vogue, and Alex dressed in a chic deep red halter-necked dress stepped out for their after-party. Food and drinks flowed freely, designer treats, *Cointreau* cocktails were all a part of the night.

Ciarra was sipping on a Vodka Martini while Alex was drinking Mango *Mojito*, laughing at one of Coco's joke when Klein strolled over. My God, this man is one gorgeous hunk, Ciarra was thinking. She had seen him many times in the news and on television but up close he put his photographs to shame. He was infinitely better looking; as a matter of fact he was dizzyingly hot. Many heads swiveled to see who Klein was spending so much time in conversation with and why. Klein had his hand on Ciarra's arm and was looking at her with his soulful eyes.

"So, tell me, how do you come up with these designs of yours? That is a dress that I could see in the window of my boutique. It's chic and it's different."

Half an hour later Ciarra and Klein disappeared into the crowd. Alex sat down, looking around before she was approached by a familiar face in the crowd.

"Hi Alex, I see your friend disappeared with Klein. How about getting on the dance floor with me?"

"Okay, why let such good music go to waste."

While Alex was on the floor she craned her neck to see where Ciarra was but she was unsuccessful. After the song ended she went back to her table, scoping the room. Another hour and Alex was ready to go; but there was no sighting of Ciarra. Just as she was about to launch a search party for her, Ciarra came swinging her hips, flopping down on the chair.

"I am having a great time, you should be dancing. Come on."

Necks craned, people stared and Alex knew that this was going to make the papers in the morning.

"I am glad you are having fun but I am ready to call it a night."

"I am not ready to leave. Come on Alex, I am just having fun," Ciarra pleaded.

"I'll get her home all safe and sound if you have to leave," Klein offered.

But Alex didn't feel right leaving Ciarra with a bunch of people she had just met, but most of all, a man who had his woman. So she stayed and drank and partied. Hours later when they left the party, Klein walked them to the car. Alex got in, said goodnight and watched as he gave Ciarra a peck on the cheek.

"Oh he is a fantastic guy, Alex he has even suggested that I do some designs for him. Isn't that cool?"

"He is a married man, Ciarra. Be careful okay," Alex warned.

Alex picked up the paper the next morning and, sure enough, Ciarra and Klein were splashed over the paper. She read the article as she spread orange marmalade on her toast. *'Ciarra Johnston longtime friend of the Keanon's was front row at Klein's show smoking hot in a mini dress showing off her killer legs. Later that night they were joined at the hip while his current flame was said to be unavoidably absent'.*

She finished reading the article before dropping the paper on Ciarra's plate.

"Tayo is going to go ballistics when he sees this. But I am sure you know that."

She sucked her teeth.

"That's his problem. It's time that he get a dose of his own medicine."

She didn't care if Klein was married. She had fun last night. He was sophisticated, debonair and in that crowd of celebs and hot girls she had created a sensation and she received so much attention from Klein it made her feel good about herself. "Come see me at my office, call me. I would love to see you again," he had said. She was thinking that she would see him again. Show him some of her designs and seriously think about Fashion School.

-Chapter 15-

Alex peered through the window as the aircraft made its final approach. She watched as the Opera House, glistening like pink sails on the Sydney Harbour, came into view.

"We are finally in Australia," Megan muttered as she rotated her neck back and forth, trying to iron out the kinks in her neck. "Hey Ciarra, wake up. We are here." She poked Ciarra in the back of her head.

"Why did you do that?" Ciarra groaned as she rubbed her hands over gritty eyes. "I was in the middle of my dream about a handsome, rich devil."

She stopped in mid sentence as she realized that Tayo was straining to hear what she was saying and then whispered, a handsome devil like Klein Brooks.

"Hmm… I am not saying a word more on that subject but you should listen to Alex. Klein uses up people like you so you should stay away from him."

Ciarra sucked her teeth.

"Yeah, and pass up an opportunity to be seen with such a hunk. You didn't tell me not to accept the ticket he bought me so I could be here in Australia. "

Megan was shocked.

"That's because you didn't tell me, I assumed the money came from our secret investments. Trust me, I am telling."

Alex had briefly fallen asleep with images of Rory intruding into her dreams. She had woken up feeling edgy and irritable and was already in a spin in anticipation of seeing Rory. She slipped her shoes on as they taxied towards the terminal.

The airport teemed with passengers as they exited and then she saw him. Rory stood there waiting, dressed in faded blue jeans and a tee shirt that clung tightly to his well sculpted body. A tingle danced down her spine as he moved towards her and when his arms wrapped around her waist before his mouth descended on hers, her lips opened beneath his without any persuasion.

"Aw, man, come give me a kiss too." Tayo was laughing at Rory.

They pounded fists. Megan and Ciarra teased them before they moved towards the limousine which would take them to Belluvue Hill.

Megan pulled Alex away from the group whispering: "Klein bought Ciarra's ticket, did she tell you?"

Alex stood with her hands akimbo.

"No she didn't. I can only say that she should know how she is going to pay him back."

Alex sat in the stands in Sydney, Australia with Ciarra, Megan and Tayo chatting excitedly while they watched the cricket match as Rory stood at bat. They had shared so much, counting on each other to be there for good and bad times and for making the joy of any great occasion even better. For Alex, the bond of friendship would always be there; they had given her growing up years much sparkle and warmth and sometimes she completely forgot that she was an only child.

She had kept in touch with Rory, talking to him on the phone, congratulating him when he won a game, chit chatting about everything and nothing when he lost a game. She watched him from afar as he changed women like the months of the year changed. She was here now with the entire gang, fulfilling the pact that they had made three years ago when Rory was picked as a batsman for the West Indies cricket team that they would all join him in Sydney one day soon. Well the day had come and so here they were.

There had been much uneasiness between her and Rory since that night he had seen her kissing Nick but all she had done was retaliate when she caught him kissing Janet. They had had the biggest fight, throwing nasty words back and forth at each other. He called her a tease and she had called him a lying bastard. It was if he took great pleasure in bringing it up again and again and so they argued constantly when they were around each other.

There was a roar as the Australian team ran out on to the pitch, then the entire arena erupted as Rory, Davies, and Gerry came out on to the field. The Australian National Anthem was sung and, from the first ball was pitched the excitement wound the crowd to a fever pitch.

Megan screamed in excitement as Rory sent the ball flying as he hit it out of the stands for a six.

"Yeah, that's the way to do it," Tayo yelled out into the stands.

"Don't look now but isn't that the girl Rory was or is dating? She has been staring at us the entire time but it's more you Alex than us that she has been checking out," Ciarra said with amusement.

"She realizes that Alex is her competition," Megan chimed in. "I guess she knows that her days are numbered if Alex gets serious and take back her man."

"Hello, stop talking about me as if I am not here. Rory is not my man and never has been so you both can stop chatting all that nonsense," Alex responded with some heat.

"It's about time the two of you stop with the silliness and get together already. You both are wasting time. Rory need to kidnap you and take you to a deserted island. It's been what six, seven, nine years or more since you have been hooked on Rory. It's time to do something about it," Tayo joined in the conversation.

"I say amen to that. We aren't teenagers anymore, we are adults. He has been dating this one and that one but then it always come back to you, Alex. Rory cannot help himself when it comes to you. But the question is, how much longer is he going to keep running?" Megan said with a frown. The frown abruptly disappeared. "I know what the solution is. While we are here we are going to ensure that the two of you get together. It's the perfect time."

"I remember the night when Rory caught you kissing Nick. He was furious. It's a good thing I was there that night or he might have done something stupid. Talk about jealousy rearing its ugly head that night." Tayo had to bring up the past.

"He didn't catch me kissing Nick. I wanted him to see me and he did. End of story. He has kissed a helluva lot of girls and more. It's small wonder he hasn't picked up some terrible disease," Alex said in a nasty tone.

"Is that the green eyed monster rearing its head?" Ciarra said with a laugh.

"You had better not try to push us together, Ciarra. I am warning both you and Ciarra not to do anything stupid on my behalf. Megan, look at what you did to Neil. You dumped him for Mr. Hotshot and none of us could tell you a thing. He was hurt for months."

But Alex couldn't help staring out at the field watching Rory as he stood before the wicket waiting to swing at the ball. Her heart skipped a beat as wild excitement took over her body. He was drop dead gorgeous. Last night when he had looked at her it had taken all her will power not to plant a kiss on his sexy lips.

Rory was very much aware that Alex was sitting in the stands watching. For the first time in a very long time the group of friends would be back together. For the last two years they had been all over the place. He had travelled to Pakistan, India, Barbados whereas Megan had travelled to Germany and Philadelphia. Alex was in law school, Tayo was living in Kingston and Ciarra was busily using her hobby of sewing to make money on the side. The thought of Nick kissing Alex and her arms wrapped around him arose unbidden in his thoughts. He was angry all over again. For Christ sakes, he thought, get a grip and leave the past behind. He stood before the wicket as Ramjat bowled the ball.

Whack! The ball sailed outside the field.

Six!!! Another six. Rory took his frustration out on the ball. He was on fire, thinking to banish all thoughts from his head about that night. Alex was a hottie and dear Lord she had a butt on her and luscious looking breasts. He wondered who had been playing with what should be rightfully his. She was now twenty one years old but she had made it clear that he was just a friend. Tomorrow night she was going to be his date to the grand affair that was being thrown by the Sydney Cricket Association.

Alex's hands shook as she pulled the dress over her head. The silky blue fabric caressed her skin. It was seductive, daring. She wanted to be noticed tonight as a woman by Rory. It was all for him. Her excitement heightened. She felt wicked and sensual. The design was pure seduction. The dress left her back bare almost to the swell of her buttocks.

With each step, each breath there was the whisper of cloth over her hips and thighs. Her senses were heightened to a fever pitch. She wanted to feel what she felt with Rory all those years ago in that cave. She knew what his hands and mouth were capable of. All these years she was still a virgin but she kept this to herself. No one really knew because she dated and had fun but something always kept her back from giving herself to any one. Tonight she wanted to change all that.

She glanced at the clock and knew that it was almost time to go. Like in old times there was a knock at the door. She was barely able to open the door before Ciarra and Megan pushed their way in. Megan stood with her mouth open and Ciarra sank onto the bed. They were speechless.

"Mama mia. There is no way in hell that Rory will be able to resist you tonight. Girl you look heavenly." Ciarra finally was able to get the words out.

"You look wonderful, Alex," Megan gushed.

"Look at the both of you. The men will be feasting their eyes on the both of you tonight. And wait until Tayo sees you, Ciarra. He won't be able to take his eyes off you. And as for Neil, he will have his hands full with all of us," Alex said with sincerity before giving them both a big hug and slipping on her high heeled shoes.

"We'll meet you downstairs, Alex," Megan stated. We don't want to drive Tayo crazy tonight by keeping him waiting forever."

Rory stood waiting in the living room, dressed in an elegantly cut black tuxedo, watching the stairs as Alex descended them. Blue silk fabric caressed her full breasts, slender straps slid over her shoulders. The dress hugged her lush hips and slid down her legs in a fall of shimmering colors to her feet which reminded him of the colors of the sea. The long sapphire color gown on her was a statement of sexuality.

She was a temptress.

His blood was on fire and he knew that every man who looked at her tonight would feel the same. She was the most beautiful woman alive. He had a sudden erection and had to force himself to breathe through his lust. He extended his arm to her, staring at her with a sense of possessiveness and desire.

"I'll be the envy of every man tonight. You look fantastic but then, you always did," Rory complimented her as he escorted her to the car.

The party was being held in an exclusive boutique hotel in Double Bay. Money, money ran through her mind as Alex walked through the foyer and took in the tasteful furnishings, the fabulous floral arrangements. Everything oozed class. A frisson of fear mixed with the excitement of anticipation caused Alex's heart to thump almost painfully. She wondered if she would be able to compete with the beautiful girls that Rory dated. She had invested in this night.

The ballroom was huge and opulently decorated. Crystal chandeliers hung from the high ceiling. It was large enough to hold hundreds of guests and even more when the doors leading to the gardens were thrown open. The room was already filled with people. It was indeed a lavish affair. The band was positioned at the end of the ballroom just inside the open glass doors.

Guests were even now streaming in as the band started up. The chairman and his team mate Daniel looked up and smiled as Rory escorted Alex into the room, indicating that they should join him.

"And who is this angel by your side Rory"? he asked with a twinkle in his eye as he stared at Alex, then Megan and Ciarra. "Wait, let me correct that, there are three angels."

"Mr. Harris, Daniel, let me present my friends of many years. This is Alex, my date for this evening and this is Megan, Ciarra and you have already met Tayo.

Daniel bent over Alex's hand, bringing it to his lip and holding it for a fraction longer than Rory thought he should. Daniel looked at Rory with a smile on his face. The party was soon in full swing. Champagne flowed freely, society matrons with millions of dollars worth of jewelry moved around, ball gowns swished around and couples moved in time to the music.

Alex sipped champagne, chatted, laughed with her friends, having a good time.

"Come on, have pity on me and dance with me." Daniel held out his hand as the band played a new song.

Together they walked on to dance the floor. He was a pretty good dancer and Alex was having fun. Rory watched Alex on the dance floor, laughing, her hips swaying. She was no longer a teenager, no longer seventeen but twenty one years old. It was four years ago in that cave when he had almost lost his mind. He couldn't think straight. Daniel whispered in her ear and she smiled and nodded. He wondered what the hell was Daniel saying to her. She was like a light beckoning to him and he couldn't walk away from that beauty on the floor. His instinct told him that if he didn't make his move and claim what was his he would lose her; someone was bound to take her away from him and he could never live with himself if that guy was Daniel.

"This party is off the hook," Megan smiled at Rory, "and wipe that scowl off your face. It's only a dance, she is being polite. She will be back by your side in two minutes." Megan scanned the room. "Who is that handsome hunk over there standing talking to the chairman?"

"Ever heard of the Manillos? That is Jade. They have holdings in America, Australia. Moneyed," Rory explained.

"You have to introduce me. He is hot," Megan implored.

"Okay, let's go get a glass of champagne. On my way I'll introduce you and you can find a way to get him on the dance floor and then I have to go claim my girl," Rory responded.

"It's a deal."

Rory glanced over at the dance floor where Tayo and Ciarra were wrapped up in each other and Daniel was still patronizing Alex. Dammit, he decided, I am going to go get my girl.

The band started playing and the singer started singing Etta James song 'At Last'.

Alex was on the edge of the dance floor when Rory tapped Daniel on the shoulder, wanting to dance this number. Slipping his arm around her waist he turned her slowly, pulling her into his arms and whispered. "Dance with me Alex." He held her tightly, swaying to the passion of the song. He leaned down to speak in her ear and felt the whisper of his breath on her neck against her. His fingers stroked down her bare back sending shivers along her nerve endings as the band played.

They were caught up in the dance, consumed by each other.

"I can't take much of this much longer. We need to leave soon," Rory whispered in her ear.

She felt his erection against her belly, his body swaying with hers.

"Soon," she whispered.

As the song ended they headed over to the buffet bar, filled two plates and walked onto the patio.

"Hey guys." Ciarra sat next to Alex. "There are some fine men in this place. I am having so much fun."

"Me too," Alex answered. "Can't you tell?"

"We won't be here much longer, Ciarra. We are going to head out soon so if you don't see us don't panic, we are okay," Rory said.

"Oh stop, just because I got excited the last time doesn't mean I'll sound an alarm this time. All I know you had better take good care of my friend," Ciarra said with some attitude.

"I promise I won't do anything to hurt her."

Rory steered Alex through the crowd.

"We are going to my place so I would suggest you say goodbye to Megan and Tayo." She informed Ciarra, Megan and Tayo that she was leaving with Rory.

Megan kissed her and Tayo told her he loved her but only like a sister. She rolled her eyes at him and gave him a big kiss.

"Let's go," Rory said as he took her hand and they walked out together.

They walked through the foyer to the elevator where he pressed the button to the top floor and as the elevator swept them up to the suite, Alex realized she was shaking. Rory stopped in front of the hotel door, looking down at her before dropping a kiss on her lips. He opened the door and lifted her in his arms across the threshold, kissing her lips, her neck.

His suite was spacious and beautifully decorated with a wall of windows overlooking the bay and harbour beyond. He slid open the door that led out to the balcony and they moved to the balcony, standing at the railing breathing in the night air, gazing out at the view over the harbour.

"It's beautiful here," Rory said. "It always gives me a sense of peace when I sit here and look across the water. It is here that I sit sometimes thinking about you."

His sexy smile started a fire in her belly. He bent his head and then his lips came down on hers in a kiss so hot that every rational thought was banished from her mind. There had always been something sexy about Rory and when he held her in his arms she always felt safe. He was the embodiment of strength.

She had waited for so long. She had waited all this time for Rory because in her heart he was the one she had always loved. Alex would always have his attention and when his lips touched hers all thought of everything and everyone fled from his mind. She was his. Since she was sixteen he had tried to stay away from her, be the playboy that he wanted to be but he couldn't stay away any longer. His hand held hers around his neck as he continued to kiss her.

"Alex, baby. I have waited so long for this."

He deepened the kiss as he backed her up against the wall, lifting her. She wrapped her legs around his waist, feeling his hardness rubbing at her. Her hips arched into his as she writhed against him, wanting more.

He wanted to brand her. The need for her was twisting him inside.

He kissed her lips and sucked her tongue. She moaned in his mouth.

"Are you wet for me, Alex?"

"Yes." Her voice wasn't her own.

He stumbled across the room as he carried her towards the bedroom.

His kiss deepened as he brought her closer, one hand flinging back the sheet to make room for her in the bed. He kissed the side of her mouth, his tongue flicking against her bottom lip.

"Do you want me to stop?" he asked.

"No, don't stop baby. I need more."

They collapsed onto the bed. She felt the weight of his body pinning her to the bed as he held her in place, sprawling between her thighs, his hands holding her wrists as his lips continued to ravish her.

"No, don't stop," she groaned bringing her mouth to his in a hot melting kiss that said more than words could ever say. His tongue set fire to her mouth, each thrust thrilling her as she felt his erection between her legs. She opened her legs to accommodate him further.

His mouth moved from its onslaught of her mouth to her breast to suck on her nipple through her dress. It drove her to a frenzy. She watched him as he slipped the straps of her dress down past her waist, removing it. His head dropped between her breasts, his lips moving between them. An electric charge went through her body. He bent his head to each nipple, his tongue rolling over each tight point until she was writhing beneath him with want. She held his head to her, needing more.

"I have to feel you."

His hands moved between their bodies and searched for her heated spot, his fingers opening her gently as he felt her silky moisture.

"You feel so wet, so ready for me," he whispered.

She was beyond speech; all she could do was feel what he was doing to her. His mouth blazed a pathway down her body; he kissed her belly button, setting it alight before moving down between her legs where she needed to be touched.

Her body arched at the first hot flicker of his tongue. He did it again and again. Her scream rose high in the air. There was no way she could hold back the sensations that exploded in her body like a volcano. She had waited years for this and it was worth it.

His hand moved between her legs and his finger pressed against her opening. He inserted one finger and then a second. His fingers slid through the damp flesh, twisting, stroking, pressing in and out, stretching her, rubbing against her clitoris.

"You are so tight baby."

The shock of pleasure stole her breath.

"Rory," she whispered. "Please, I want more." Her pride deserted her; she was begging.

"I need to love you, Alex. You are mine, you will always be mine."

His hand gripped her thigh, spreading her legs wide. She watched him draw her hips along his thigh as he knelt before her. He reached for a condom and she watched her excitement building as he rolled it over his thickness. The thick head of his erection parted her as he pressed close.

The heavy head pressed against her opening, parted it and began to work inside her. She opened her legs wider as he came over her hugging her and then kissing her. His hips moved, shifted, moving in her stretching her, surging into her honeyed warmth. Lust was tearing through her and she thrust harder pressing him deeper. She flinched as he entered her and for a brief moment there was pain and then it was gone.

Rory's movements stilled and he looked at her with concern.

"You remained a virgin, Alex? Why did you behave as if you weren't? I am sorry for hurting you."

"It's okay. All these years I waited for you, Rory." She wiggled beneath him.

He groaned and sank forward, his control slipping. She moved with every thrust. At first he was cautious and tender and then he was moving harder, deeper stroking her into a never ending sensation. She couldn't breathe. He drove on. She had never imagined that it would be this good. She hugged him tighter, wrapping her legs around him. He filled her so completely. She kissed his shoulder, tasting the salty sweat on his skin.

"Hold me baby, oh God yes, hold me, Alex. I have waited for this for so long."

He touched her, inside and out, he held her to him, his hips bunching, moving grinding into her as the sensations of need began to tear through the last barriers of control.

"Rory." She was moaning his name.

She couldn't stop moving, feeling the pleasure building inside her, taking over.

"Oh God, baby. Alex. It's so damn sweet, it's so tight. I can't wait much longer."

She couldn't breathe. She felt the sensations pounding through her. She lost all control as the orgasm tore through her. She was writhing, twisting against him and dying from the pleasure of it all.

She knew that she had done the right thing by waiting for Rory all these years.

"Oh, Alex baby." It was such exquisite pleasure a man could ever know.

His orgasm rocked him and all he could do was hold Alex closer to him.

"Alex you have always driven me crazy."

Perspiration dampened both of them and between them flames of release burned.

They spent the night together playing catch up and when she woke the next morning he was laying beneath the blankets, his hand thrown against her chest. A smile curved her lips.

She propped her chin on her hands, just staring at him. His eyes blinked and his hand reached over, pulling her to him.

"Alex, you are a bad girl. I spent so much time thinking about who you have been with when you were actually still a virgin." He kissed her chin. "I love you babes."

Alex didn't want to get out of bed but Rory pushed open the curtains, waking her.

"Feel like seeing Sydney?" he asked.

She pushed up on her elbow, looked out the window at the bright sunshine.

"It can't be mid morning already."

"Come on sleepyhead, get up, get dressed and we will go have breakfast and then go explore the city. You cannot come all the way to Sydney without seeing something of the place. You'll enjoy it." Rory extended his hand to her.

She jumped from the bed.

"I am going to take a shower. I'll be ready in half an hour. Oh, what about Ciarra and the others?" Alex asked.

"They are fine. They know we spent the night together and I made the mistake to talk to Ciarra. She nearly took my ears off with her screaming."

Alex groaned and hid her face in her hands.

"So you can imagine all the questions that I am going to get from all three of them."

Rory screwed up his face.

"Yeah. I wouldn't want to be in your place today. I'll order up some coffee."

They had breakfast in a little café before he took her to Belluvue Hill, an upscale neighborhood where he was investing in real estate. He took her to Lady Bay Beach which was one of the earliest nudist beaches in Sydney and later that evening they went to the national park, right by Sydney's harbor where they watched the sunset as it shed a golden light over the great arch of the bridge and the Opera House. As twilight deepened, they watched the lights come on around the harbour. They walked in the Royal Botanic Garden where they visited the Herb Garden where herbs from around the world were displayed just so that Alex could verify that there was no ganja

in the midst being shown as a herb. It was a joke
they shared about removing weed from the cave
years ago. The garden was one of the most
breathtakingly beautiful settings that she had seen.

It was three nights of passion. Three nights of
pleasure that she had never experienced before and
probably would never experience again in her life.

-CHAPTER 16-

Megan was blasting the music in her car. She was looking forward to the polo match in Drax Hall, St Ann. It wasn't just a polo match today. It was an important match because the Jamaican team was competing against Argentina. Polo is to Argentina what soccer is to Jamaica. The game of polo had been introduced to Jamaica by the British army in 1882 and had made it onto the sports arena on the island. Megan's boyfriend, Sam Chin, was the one who had introduced her to the game. She was elated because classes at the University were over and she was now officially a graduate. This had been her goal all along. She had realized that she was not as brilliant as Alex and would not be able to get a scholarship and attend university for free but her friends had realized that she was a gifted runner and had pushed her to her limit to excel in that. She was in awe of the fact that she was driving a 500 series BMW. This was beyond her wildest imagination! Ciarra sat next to her in the passenger seat, rocking to the rhythm of John Holt's song:

> But if you continue to burn up the herbs, we're gonna burn down the cane fields.

"This song caused so much controversy back then. The people loved John Holt but the cops wanted to get him," Megan said.

Ciarra sucked her teeth.

"Sometimes we take these things too seriously. Life is not that complicated. People are the ones who make life complicated. It's just a song."

She kept singing and rocking to the beat.

"I haven't felt this free in a long time. There is no track meet to attend. No school. I am free."

Megan's foot hit the gas pedal and the car flew down the highway.

"Hey missy, take it easy because we want to get there in one piece. Klein and his buddies are going to be there and I don't want a scratch on my pretty skin," Ciarra warned Megan.

They looked at each other and began to crack up.

"The highlight of the trip for me was when I found out that Rory and Alex are finally a couple," Megan said. "I can't tell you how much I was hoping that those two would finally face the fact that they are in love with each other. She waited all these years to give in to him."

"That is a girl in love," Ciarra answered. "Alex was practically floating on air the entire time we were in Australia."

"Listen to this one!" Megan was singing along to another John Holt song: *Love and affection.*

Megan pulled into an empty parking spot, locked her car and together she and Ciarra walked towards the paddock where the horses were housed. They searched for Sam. They found him rubbing down his horse.

"Your horse look so sleek and pretty," Megan told him as she stroked the horse's flank. "She reminds me of a person."

"Not only is she beautiful but she has a lot of match experience and she's a natural at Polo."

The girls headed for their seats. Sam bent his head again, concentrating on buckling the leather straps when a shadow fell across his line of vision. He straightened up as a member of the opposing team stopped to wish him luck.

"May the best team win, my man," Sam said as he held out his hand to his opponent.

Sam walked away, swinging his helmet in his hands as he led his horse towards the shade of the tall trees that surrounded the grounds. His horse stood slightly apart from the others swishing her tail at the flies. Sam patted her on the rump, glancing at the other horses as they stood in the heat.

Sunglasses covered Megan's eyes as she watched from the stands while Sam stood together with his team mates who were wearing gold colored shirts with a smattering of green across the front. She looked around at the polo wives and girlfriends wearing designer duds and diamonds that dazzled in the sun. There were many beautiful and glamorous women in attendance.

"Megan, take a look at the chick to our left. Her boobs are practically falling out of her blouse." Ciarra was pulling on her arm.

"Girl, you know some of these women think that if they aren't exposed then they're not sexy enough."

A sudden burst of applause heralded the arrival of the teams. Megan clapped wildly as Sam rode out onto the field in his gold polo helmet. He looked so sexy in his white breeches and leather boots, gold shirt with a number three on his back. He was sitting in the saddle with an ease that was in contrast with the intense concentration on his face. The two teams rode onto the field as if they were in battle, mallet held in right hand like ancient warriors jousting. As they stood in the stands, they could feel the electricity in the air, the tension between the two teams; but Megan only had eyes for Sam. Ciarra had her eyes closed to what she called 'such violence'.

The game was now underway and as an athlete, Megan could understand the rush as the wild, thunderous hooves of the horses pounded the earth. The players pitched their galloping horses at each other and the animals clashed, while the mallets sliced through the air and the ball bounced around like a missile. The blood pounded in her ears as she shouted her encouragement as Sam flew down the field, pursued by another player. Number three rode directly in his path; the horses clashed and Sam bent low over the horse's neck. The umpire blew the whistle, signaling the end of the first chukka and the two sides separated, returning to the end of the pitch with their respective teams.

Minutes later, the grooms rode out onto the field with fresh horses and Sam slid onto the back of a mean looking horse.

"How many more chukkas are there, Megan? I always forget how many are played," Ciarra queried.

"There are six chukkas, so there are five more to go."

Megan watched as the players lined up, waiting for the game to recommence. Sam had his helmet off and his hair blew behind him in the wind. He looked like one of those karate fighters ready to slay the bad guys. As the Jamaican team scored, they applauded and as the Argentineans scored Ciarra applauded loudly.

"Those Argentinean guys are *muy caliente*." Ciarra kissed her palm to bring out her point. "I love hot blooded men. They get my heart pumping."

Out on the field, the battle continued. Sweat shone not only on the ponies but on the men who were determined to win this match. Sam took a vicious shot at the goal. They had lost the lead they had gained in the first half. And now Argentina was leading in the last chukka. He was so caught up in the game that when the umpire blew the whistle, he was shocked that the game was over. Argentina had won the game. Sam and his teammates rode over to embrace the other team and after much slapping of hands and backs they rode off the field to a great deal of applause.

"See you all at the party later!" they shouted to each other....

...The party was underway as Megan and Sam arrived. Fairy lights lit the Polo Club garden, setting the mood for the party. A series of colorful tents was set up in reds and blues. Guests moved from tent to tent, sampling the various foods provided and flitted from the wine bar to the other bars set up around the grounds. A group of people, his father included, surrounded Sam as he arrived, drawing him away and into their circle. Senya, the girl who his father had handpicked for his son, stood with the group of glamorous people. Then there were the other polo players who wanted to bask alongside him in their glory. Politely extricating herself, Megan walked away but she noticed that Sam had already turned away before she had had a chance to smile or say *see you in a while*. She went to the bar where she got herself a drink and stood watching the endless stream of people parading across the floor.

"Hey Megan," someone whispered in her ear. "If I were Sam I wouldn't let such a beautiful girl out of my sight."

She turned to see Rory smiling at her.

"What are you doing here?"

"Never mind, I'm glad to see you. What is Sam thinking leaving you by yourself while he gets rowdy with his friends?"

"It's not what it looks like, Rory. They had business to attend to, presentations to make, formalities to take care of."

"You're always making excuses for this guy, Megan. Why?"

Before she could answer he held up his hand.

"Okay, don't say it. I'll leave it alone. Come on let's dance."

Rory pulled her towards the dance floor. Sam followed her with his eyes as she moved around. He saw the ready smile she had for Rory and their easy manner together as they chatted. He picked up two glasses of champagne and turned towards them, placing his hand on Megan's hand. This halted their progress towards the dance floor. He pounded fists with Rory and they exchanged a few words about the game played earlier before Rory kissed Megan's hand and disappeared into the crowd.

"Would you like to take a walk outside, Megan?" Sam asked. "It's getting stuffy in here."

Her eyes lit up with pleasure in a smile that aroused Sam. Megan was experiencing the same arousal around Sam. It wasn't often that she felt so free. Sam placed his hand in the center of her back and guided her out into the softly lit garden. Almost by instinct, they veered away from the lights and into the darker area. A trellised rose arbor framed with well manicured hedges gave them the privacy they sought. Pulling her into his arms, he held her close as they exchanged a hungry kiss. Feeling the heat of their desire, they caressed each other.

"I want you, Sam," she told him.

He steered her towards a set of benches. He lifted her and seated her atop the bench. The caressing continued and she felt the sensual touch of his lips on her skin. She held him tightly around his neck as she longed for more. They could not resist each other any longer. With mounting excitement, they made love in the garden. This moment seemed to cement their relationship. He sighed as they walked back to the party. As they entered the party room, his father awaited him with Senya not far behind trying to drag him away; but this time it was Sam who kept his arm firmly on Megan's as he steered her to his father's crowd.

-CHAPTER 17-

The clock ticked on the mantel. Ciarra looked up at the time. It was 10 a.m. on a Saturday morning and she was busy sewing away. She nipped at the thread with her teeth, kept her hand on the material as it slid under the needle of the sewing machine. She had a ton of work she had to get through. She had to finish this hottie-hottie outfit in a few hours for Jen who lived up the street. The girl had a party to attend later that night and wanted to make a fashion statement.

Teeth gritted, Ciarra kept her focus on the task at hand. She had a goal so if this is what it takes to get into fashion, then so be it. She stayed up until all hours of the night and spent her weekends sewing clothes for her many customers. She was one of the very best dressmakers in Bell Town and beyond, and her popularity increased for not only doing an excellent job, delivering on time but her price was also modest. Her money she put away because the next semester was not passing and she wasn't enrolled in fashion school.

The time she had spent in Australia only served to spur her on. Rory had always pushed to do better and more and he served as a catapult, pushing their little group to do better. Sure, he had his messed up ways sometimes but at the end of the day you couldn't help liking the guy. According to him, none of them should be left behind. She wasn't a book person like Alex; she loved clothes and fun. The important thing, as Alex always said, is to know your strengths.

Megan became the top athlete in Jamaica partly because of the pushing of her friends. They honed in on Megan's strong point. From the time she was in primary school she was winning races, running away and leaving everyone behind so they decided to train her, make her better because they were all going to be somebody.

Klein kept in touch and she took her time to do a design or two that he requested. It had taken some doing to relegate Tayo to the back of her mind and focus instead on getting to where she wanted to be. From what she had seen and heard, first love rarely worked any way, so there. She consoled herself. She held the garment in front of her, twisting her head, this way and that before sliding it back on to the machine.

She had managed to stay one step ahead of Klein treating him with amusement because the more she resisted him the harder he chased. He had offered her a part time job but she was wary of packing her bags, leaving country and moving to Kingston to work for one of the richest and very good looking guy who had a reputation as ladies' man. He had invited her to the polo match in Drax Hall, St Ann and so she didn't refuse because Megan was also going to be there but if he thought that she was some little country bumpkin, that he could manipulate he had another guess coming.

Ciarra worked solidly for the next three hours. Her mother let her be and steered her brother away from her; but Ciarra needed to eat.

"Lunch is on the table, Ciarra," her mother called out from the kitchen. "You had better come and eat before you tumble off that stool from hunger. Your father wouldn't be pleased if he thinks that you are here starving and there is food to eat."

"Coming Mama."

Ciarra's belly was rumbling. It was one p.m. and she hadn't eaten. She rubbed a hand over gritty eyes and rotated her shoulders to ease the aches and pains.

"Don't let me have to come get you, Ciarra. Get out here now," her mother called out.

She walked to the kitchen, pushing aside the lace curtains at the window, looking out. It was sunny and bright. Banana leaves swayed in the wind. She dropped the curtain and turned towards the kitchen table. Her smile widened at the food set out on the table, and then she plopped into a kitchen chair. Mackerel with run down, boiled bananas and dumpling.

While she was eating there was some kind of commotion in the living room. She heard laughter and her brother's voice; but before she could even leave the table Megan walked in.

"Oh my gosh," Ciarra squealed as Megan crossed the room to hug her. "I was wondering when were *you* going to get here?"

"You know our friend Tayo. He wanted to make sure I got here in one piece so he drove me down. As always something smells good in this house to eat." Megan walked over to the stove like old times. "Got to get me some of this mackerel and run down."

She walked over to the cupboard, pulled out a plate, filled it with food and then sat at the table.

"I am going to be here all weekend," Megan said. "I spoke to Alex this morning. She wanted to come but she had a charity dinner to attend."

"I spoke to her too and she wanted to know what's going on, what are we up to and not get into any mischief while she is not around," Ciarra said. "As a matter of fact, come check out these two dresses I finished for Jen."

"Damn, Ciarra. This is off the hook. Did you do the pattern for this or you saw the style in a book and copied it?" Megan asked.

"Jen told me what she wanted and between us we figured out this style. I drew a picture of it for her. She said yep, that's it and I made it."

"You are gonna be in the big leagues soon. I ran into Klein recently and he was asking all kinds of questions about you. Of course I played it off on him. I gave him bits and pieces of information but nothing solid," Megan said as she laughed out loud. "That guy seems to be hooked on you right about now."

"Let's walk down to our tree stump where we can talk without my brother eavesdropping on our conversation."

They walked down to the end of the driveway where they sat on the tree stump. To the left they looked over at Alex's grandmother's shop abuzz with activity. Straight ahead they saw the square which on a day was busy like a major town. Buses dropped off and picked up passengers. Those who came to betting shop bought horse race and some just came to see what the hell was going on.

"Did Alex say what's happening with her and Rory?" Ciarra asked Megan as soon as they sat down. "They were so together in Australia but with her here and him all over the globe. I don't know."

Megan held her head in her hands.

"Those two just need to get together already. But did you see those pictures of him in the magazine with some skinny ass girl hanging all over him and then, to top off, they said his *fiancé*. This is turning into a nightmare for two people who should be together."

"Do you think she is okay?" Ciarra asked. "I try to talk to her but she hides her true feelings sometimes. She doesn't like to let on when she is hurt or down."

Ciarra had always felt protective towards Alex. It wasn't that she couldn't take care of herself. It was just that she hid her unhappiness and always tried to put her friends' feelings before hers.

"You are never sure with Alex, but I don't think she is okay," Megan answered.

"There are always ups and downs with life. I am going to see Klein again and if you tell Alex before I do, you know I'll pay you back in kind so don't even think about."

"Meet with him as in business or meet with him as in a date, Ciarra?" Megan looked at Ciarra suspiciously.

"It's business so don't worry, it is all above board and so what if I choose to go out on a date with him. It's my business," Ciarra answered defensively.

Megan took her time before answering Ciarra.

"Sometimes we think we know what we are doing but we are in way over our head. Oh my God, have you slept with him already? You know what, be careful you aren't the one to get burnt and that's all I am going to say. Subject closed."

Sunlight and Dappled Shade

-Chapter 18-

A lex couldn't believe what she was seeing and what she was reading. She was laying in bed catching up on her reading. There was all this propaganda in the papers about Jamaica going communist and all that nonsense. People were easily spooked when there was a whole heap of twisted information being given that they didn't understand. Auntie walked into the room.

"Look it's a prefect morning outside," her grandmother said flinging back the curtains. "Ms. Iris found out that you are here and doesn't want anyone else to read her letter so get up and get dressed. I made you salt fish fritters and fried plantain and here is Eve with some hot chocolate."

"Here is your hot chocolate, honey, and Leah got you some June plums so when you are finished eating come on down to the shop," her mother came in smiling at her.

Eyes half closed, Alex inhaled the scent of the rich creamy hot chocolate as Jamaicans knew how to make and broke into a big smile.

"Now I know I am home," she exclaimed, hugging her grandmother and her mom. "I haven't been here so long, Auntie, who has been reading Miss Iris' letters for her?" Alex asked.

"Your mother, but she likes when you do it. She says you add spice to it and don't forget Etty and Octavius can't wait to see you. They have missed you and the mischief that they help you and the rest of the group to get up to. So get it together. You have people to see and places to go."

"I have missed them too and they are getting up there in age. I guess Octavius is still smoking his tobacco."

Alex gave a small wistful smile.

"Remember the steps that led up to the verandah that was falling apart? Well, Rory sent a carpenter to fix and also to replace the worn out boards on the verandah. Although they resisted for a while, Rory added a kitchen to the house so that way she doesn't have to go outside to a fireside to cook. They didn't like it at all when he told them they were getting too old to do certain things."

Alex's mother was laughing so hard and then Auntie joined in.

"Alex, if you were here you would understand why we are laughing. Etty wouldn't let them in the house to fix anything. It took some time to convince them. It was a standoff." Auntie shook her head. "They are as stubborn as a mule."

Alex nodded in agreement. She got out of bed, yawned, stretched and headed to the bathroom. Twenty minutes later, clad in jeans and a blue top she raced down the stairs. She let her gaze travel over the ladies sitting talking to Auntie while they ordered their grocery. Miss Iris called to her to come give her a kiss, exclaiming that she hadn't even put on a pound on her slender frame. Alex laughed good-naturedly while they talked about her as if she was not there.

She helped Auntie in the store that morning as she always did. She noticed that they weren't using paper to wrap flour or sugar anymore but using small paper bags. This was much easier because if you didn't know how to wrap sugar and flour and cornmeal with the regular wrapping paper it was a problem. It had taken Alex quite some time to master that skill.

It took some time but eventually the crowd in the store let up and Alex was able to walk over into the bar. It didn't matter what the time is, there was always someone sitting on that bar stool drinking some form of alcohol. Her next stop was the piazza outside where the gossip was as rife as ever while the vendors sold their products of fruits, vegetables, escallions and thyme, and carrots.

"Come, chile, come get your tangerines and you already know there is no answer but yes where this is concerned," Miss Leah greeted, happy to see Alex.

They still treated her as if she was four years and not the adult that she thought she was; but she loved them all just the way they were. Simple, straightforward people.

The ground was steaming from the sudden downpour. As suddenly as the rain came so did it disappear. There was a damp, earthy smell as Alex made her way up the path. The air was heavy and humid and the sun, which had briefly disappeared, now beat down without mercy. Thank God I am wearing my straw hat, Alex thought.

She paused to catch her breath before running up the steps two at a time to give Octavius a big hug. Miss

Etty appeared in the doorway of the house, wiping her hands on an apron before dragging Alex close for a hug and a kiss. She pulled back and looked her up and down.

"There is such happiness surrounding you, Alex." Miss Etty shook her head and laughed a big belly laugh. "You are growing up right before my eyes."

Alex had the odd feeling that once again Miss Etty was looking through her, that she saw more than she let on and much more than she wanted her to know. She averted her face looking around at the changes. The house had received a do over, the outside was freshly painted and the floor boards on the verandah had been replaced. The doors were thrown open against the sticky heat of the day and the interior of the house looked cool and dim.

"Wow, I like all the changes you two have made to the house," Alex said as she walked around looking.

"Yeah, Rory helped us with some of the changes and since we went that far I planted some yellow hibiscus along the fence and keep it pruned. I copied the style from your grannie because I want to beautify my property so that when Etty sits out here in her rocking chair she has something pretty to look at."

Alex sat in the wicker lounger chair, her legs stretched out in front of her.

"We were all saying that you, Octavius should have been at the match with us in Australia. It was awesome."

"Me too old to take them long trip, my dear. I am quite contented listening to my game, sitting right here. My pleasure is that Rory is hitting them six and four all over the place. Give them white boys some work to do running for that ball. Rory always had an eye for you so I hope it's more than one eye him keeping on you these days."

"Hmph, you have a way of putting things, Octavius," Miss Etty said with a smile. Again Alex had the feeling that she knew more than she was saying.

There was no awkwardness when she visited, there was no sadness. Here were two people who were content with their lot. According to Auntie, sometimes Octavius would raise cane because Miss Etty would give away his best pieces of yam or dasheen. Whenever this would happen, Miss Etty would feign ignorance and pretend she didn't know what he was talking about.

"Let me get you some ice cold ginger beer. I made it especially for you, and a piece of duckanoo. Then you can tell us all about the studying that you are doing." Miss Etty patted Alex's shoulder.

She was back with a beer for Octavius and the ginger beer for Alex.

"So how is the school thing coming along?" Octavius asked. "Etty worries about you sometimes hoping you are alright and that everything is okay."

"Well I graduated from UWI and now I am going to New York where I'll be doing law. My uncle thinks that I am going to be the first female Prime Minister," Alex answered.

On the radio the announcer was talking about 'prips' and 'preps'. The preps being the wife and the prips being the sweetheart.

"In my days," Mass Octavius waved his arm and pointed to the radio, "we called the other woman the sweetheart but these modern days people dress up the name for the other woman. Whatever name you want to call it, sweetheart is what it is."

"Back to the argument of you being the first female Prime Minister. From the day you were born your grannie wanted you to run this country. She said with that bawling you did, impressing on everyone that you had strong lungs and that you wanted your presence known she said you were going to be someone special."

Alex almost fell out of her chair. Her grandmother had never told her all this. She had run to her, surprised that her uncle had this vision of who she was going to be but her grandmother had not breathed a word that she was the instigator in all this.

"My grandmother said this?" Alex said with some surprise. "She let me think that it was my uncle's idea."

"Your grandmother is a smart woman, Alex, and your mother has raised you right. You are probably too young to understand the influence that she wields. You are going to be great but as a result of this you will have to make great personal sacrifices. It has been my greatest delight to have been a part of all of your lives, Rory, Tayo, Ciarra and Megan and the others. You are all special."

Miss Etty stood up.

"I have something to show you."

Alex followed her down the hall where on a table stood books about black people; colored stones stood in a jar, silver and brass jewelry and a few pieces of sculpture. She pulled a book from the table, pointing to a page that was earmarked.

"This is about great women who made their mark against great odds."

Alex stood there sipping on her ginger beer and worked up the courage to ask:

"Can you do my cards, Miss Etty?"

Miss Etty patted the seat on the couch.

"Let me get my candles and a bowl of water. I won't read your cards but I'll help you to channel your energy. You have the ability to see things. You have the gift and the powers but you shy away from it. I'll help you to channel. You have to concentrate, to let your mind be free."

Alex lit the candle that was given to her before placing it in a holder. She dipped her fingers in the water and poured drops in all direction. Miss Etty took a sip of rum from her bottle before joining hands with Alex. She called on her ancestors, the spirits and the elements. Alex felt as if she was on the outside watching in slow motion. There was Nanny again, beckoning to her, to follow. She hesitated, but when she did it was to see Megan running towards the precipice. Megan was in trouble but, wait there was Rory but he was walking away from her. She jerked her hand away breaking the connection.

It took some time to focus and find her balance. Miss Etty sat for a while longer with her eyes closed. There was heartache in store for Alex and much personal sacrifice. What was she going to do about Rory and Alex? She squeezed her eyes tighter to get her balance before she turned to Alex with a bright smile.

"So did you see what you wanted to see?"

Alex shook her head.

"There was nothing about me. It's Megan that's in trouble."

"Megan is mixed up with the wrong crowd. She is losing her focus. What she had when you were all together real close is not so much there anymore. She need to get her center back or she will lose everything," Miss Etty said with a sigh. "Her talent alone is not going to keep her on top of her game. You, all of you used to work together to get her to where she is so you will all have to find a way to do that again."

"I don't know how we are going to do that because I am going away to law school. Everyone is doing their own thing," Alex answered. "Ciarra is involved with Klein and is making headway in the fashion world and me, well, I am here."

"Well, you have to find a way to help your friend."

Now that the rosy sun had slipped down below the trees, it was much cooler. Alex could hear the sound of the woodpecker in the tree. She missed Rory. How were they going to deal with these long absences, so much time spent apart in different countries? Soon she would be living in New York and only God knows where he would be.

As Mass Octavius walked her down the path to her home. Alex kicked furiously at a stone in her path. There were too many things that were just not right. Octavius looked at her and with wisdom and insight he said to her:

"With patience all things come. When it's the right time, don't worry, everything will fall into place and between me and you, no matter where Rory goes and no matter what he might do right now. Memba say me tell you this. One day he will come on home to you because you are his destiny."

Alex couldn't help laughing out loud.

"You have such faith in Rory. You haven't changed one bit because no matter what he does you are always on his side."

"I am in my prime now. I am old and that's why I see much more than you young people see. You come on let me get you home in one piece and don't kick no more stones. That is too pretty a shoe to get it messed up."

They walked together, laughing and chatting the rest of the way. Octavius was a good man, Alex thought.

A week later Alex landed in New York, her nerves stretched to breaking point. She didn't know what to expect because she was leaving her small close knit family to live with a father who had been more like a shadow that appeared, disappeared, and reappeared when the time was right. She exited the plane and walked briskly towards immigration. Clearing immigration and customs, she walked out to the lounge where there was a sea of faces, all waiting for that loved one to get off the plane. Her father stood with others leaning on the security ropes that separated the waiting area from the customs area.

He separated himself from the crowd, taking charge of her luggage and ushering her to his car. She rubbed her arms at the chill in the air. She hadn't expected this kind of cold coming from Bell Town and didn't have a coat, although it was only September. Her jacket was packed in her suitcase. Alex shook her head. It was going to be a real change living here.

As they drove along the Belt Parkway to Laurelton her father asked, "how was your flight?" to which she gave a polite "it was okay." It was an awkward feeling not knowing what to say to your own father.

The ride from JFK airport to his house was less than twenty minutes and her father spent the entire time drawing her out about her life that he didn't know about. Alex breathed a sigh of relief; she was hoping everything was going to be alright.

After finishing a first degree at UWI in International Law and Economics, Alex was glad to get away from Jamaica. There were too many questions being asked about Rory and his supposedly unknown fiancée and now that he had opened a sports bar and restaurant in Liguanea he had a tendency to drop in unexpectedly. She wanted to stay away from him so she was attending law school at NYU.

She had been feeling extremely down the first time that Rory had come to see her while she was attending University in New York. She was living with her father in Queens and things weren't going well between them. She didn't mind the fact that her father was a dictator but he was really mean at times, talking about him not being Salvation Army and he had no handout to give. Alex had found herself a weekend job and started paying rent to her dad.

After the first year she had found a place of her own in Laurelton. It was two bedrooms so she found a room mate. Whenever she couldn't come up with her half of the rent her uncle bailed her out.

Alex had completed her finals and was studying for the bar, her legs curled under her as she sat on the cushions on the floor with her back against the couch. She was hoping that in two weeks she would be done with law school and she would be able to go back to Jamaica.   Someone was knocking on her door. She stood up and promptly fell back on the floor. Her legs had fallen asleep. The knocking continued. She limped to the door and threw it open only to find Rory on the other side.

"Rory," she squeaked in shock. "What are you doing here? I wasn't expecting you. What would you do if my boyfriend was here?" She could not resist asking the question.

He ignored her question.

"I did call but your room mate said you were out. I left a message with her letting her know that I was in New York and I would come to visit."

She limped towards the couch.

"Did you hurt your leg, Alex? Why didn't you call me to let me know that you are not well? Dammit, you are supposed to let someone know when there is something   wrong."
She stopped in mid stride, surprised at his tone.

"Relax, Rory, there is nothing wrong with my leg. It's just that I have pins and needles after sitting in a cramped position for so long."

He stared at her as her breasts peeked through the T-shirt because that was all she was wearing. He felt his pants tighten which made him shift uncomfortably as he stepped forward. She wrapped her arms around him, avoiding his lips and attempted to kiss him on the cheek but he turned his head and their lips met. Her mouth parted as she kissed him back.

Her head said stop but she didn't want to. Not yet. That night in Sydney came back to haunt her- his mouth on hers, their naked skin together. Ecstasy like she had never known. His fingers slid beneath her T-shirt teasing her. His hand moved lower and she should have stopped him but she didn't. Sensations spun through her, hurtling her into forgotten pleasure. It had been so long since she allowed Rory to touch her like this. Hadn't he betrayed her trust a week after she had slept with him?

Rory pulled back, gazing down at her with an expression that contained both surprise and want. He had promised himself that he would stay away from her and just be her friend but when it came to her he couldn't seem to keep his hands to himself. It had taken so much in the past not to touch her, hold her, kiss her. He had blown it.

She pushed at his chest, slipping from his embrace.

"What the hell was that? I am not one of the women who share your harem."

She glared at him and ran to the bathroom. She had just embarrassed herself for Rory to see. When she came back into the room he didn't know what to say and he didn't want to make a bad situation worse. He looked at her; she was so vibrant, so alive and warm. He could not and would not lose her friendship but he couldn't stay here in this apartment with her, he had to get out.

"Alex, I came to see you because Andy is here with me. He wanted to get a few things for the restaurant so he is waiting for us in Manhattan."

"Well. Why didn't you say that in the first place? I'll just take a shower and get dressed."

He breathed a sigh of relief that she was still speaking to him as she left the room.

In about twenty minutes Alex was sitting in the plush leather passenger seat of the Mercedes Benz. She buckled her seat belt as Rory drove into Manhattan, taking the Cross Island Parkway and then the Grand Central, crossing over the Triboro Bridge and exiting at 59th Street. Andy was waiting in the lobby of the Marriott at 49th Street because Rory had called to let him know they were in the parking garage. She ran to Andy and he squeezed her hard and gave her a big kiss. He was grinning from ear to ear.

"I bet you never thought we would meet here in New York."

"You are looking so good, Andy. It is really nice to see you. So tell me how is the investment banking company going back home?"

"It's going along fine. But you look like a New Yorker. You carry a *Gucci* bag and you are in school. You definitely not feeling the student pinch."

Alex laughed.

"If only you knew. I could tell you stories that would make your head spin."

"We are going shopping and then my brother is taking us to dinner."

They walked out of the lobby and headed up Fifth Ave to Saks where Rory and Andy bought five pairs of pants each, suits and shirts.

"What do you think about this pair of pants, Alex? Do you like it?"

Rory didn't buy anything without asking her opinion. Eventually, she was picking out what she would like to see him wear with matching shirts and jackets. He wasn't shy to model them for her, getting a nay or a yeah. Alex was having a good time.

Andy dragged her to the women's section where they had her trying dresses and some pants that Andy claimed that he liked. Rory didn't want to use his credit card, afraid that Alex would refuse the clothes, but slipped Andy the cash instead. They then hit the Armani Exchange, Banana Republic and then Sean John.

Rory dragged her into Tiffany's where he gently persuaded her to accept the pair of diamond earrings that he wanted to see dangling from her ear. By the time they left Tiffany's they were starving and left it up to Alex to choose where they were going to eat. The Negril Village on West 4th Street was her choice so, after dropping off their packages at the hotel, they jumped in a cab and headed down town.

At the end of the evening they dropped Andy off at the hotel and Rory drove her back to Queens. They didn't speak on the ride back to her apartment. She instead looked out the window and watched the night lights of the city slip by. She had no idea what Rory was thinking. And she wasn't about to ask. It was late when they finally arrived at Alex's. Rory slid into a parking spot and walked her to the door.

"I hope you enjoyed yourself today."

Rory stood with his hands in his pockets, watching her closely.

"I did. Thanks so much for a wonderful day out."

She knew that she should say goodnight but it had been a long day so she invited him in.

"You can spend the night, Rory, but you sleep on the couch."

-Chapter 19-

Whoa!!! Hold up a second. I think there is something wrong with my hearing because I don't think you said what I thought I heard so, what did you say to me a minute ago?"

"You heard right the first time, Megan. You have been back from your big trip to Australia, you are always here and there with your friends who I happen to know don't like a bone in me. That is what Alex told me to my face. I said everyone knows that you are one of the best damn athletes to ever come out of Jamaica. You have been mentioned in every magazine that there is, even in *Vanity Fair* because you are like a speeding bullet. You have never lost a race. Just hear me out. Every one is expecting you to win, so the odds on you from a betting perspective is small. There is not much money to win. However if you should somehow lose the race a few of us would stand to win a lot of money."

There was a buzz in Megan's ear and her head felt swollen because there was no way she could be hearing something like this from Sam's mouth.

"Run that by me again, baby. How much money do you stand to make if I do this?"

He smiled, that sweet, sweet smile when he wanted something.

"I am talking over $50,000 dollars that we would all make and not Jamaican money. I am talking US cash."

"So tell me this, Sam. The rumors that have been flying around about you gambling away your birthright and then gambling money that belongs to your father and the hotels he owns is true?"

He held up his hands.

"Yes I do gamble, but I have it under control. I don't gamble what I don't have."

"Well, if you have it under control why would you ask me something so outrageous as to take a dive so you can fix your gambling debts? Why would you need to ask me such a question that could get me kicked off the track team and disqualified for life? You have no love for me at all, Sam. Is this what I mean to you? A meal ticket?"

"Well, are you going to help me out or what?"

She turned on him with all the fury of a demented woman.

"Help you out of what? A broken leg from owing gambling debts? They are going to have to break those legs because from what I hear your father has cut you off. No more signing of any checks because you have been draining his hotels of cash. You are one of the most hateful people that I have ever met."

He was not about to back down from Megan and his plan.

"You didn't mind being with me so you could hob-nob with the rich and famous. You didn't mind spending my money and now you think you are better than me, coming from country where your father plant yam."

Now she was really mad.

"You mean you helped me spend my money. *My* money that I receive for endorsements, for winning each race and setting records. You son of a bitch. This is my place so get the hell out of my face. You want to talk family. Your goddamn father who is so big on family is screwing your helper. So help me God, if you take a further step towards me, I will lay you out on this floor and use you to mop the floor."

He suddenly grabbed her and slapped her soundly in the face.

"You know what? All you are is a good piece of ass because I would never marry someone like you. You are beneath me, Megan, and one more thing, wait until I tell everyone that you and your friends stole money and weed from that cave."

Megan was shocked that he had dared to hit her again. She had always made excuses when he hit her. Ciarra and Alex had warned her about this jerk. Rory had tried to protect her, but she wouldn't listen. She had rationalized his boorish behavior over and over but for him to suggest something so evil, so foul was beyond comprehension.

"What did you say Sam, about weed? And where did you get that from?" Megan asked in alarm.

"Oh don't worry about where I get it from. I listen to your conversations and I can read," Sam answered with a smug look on his face. "Oh how them drug dealers would love to get a hold of this information."

Megan was beyond angry and, for the first time she hit him back. She picked up the first thing that came to her hand and smashed him on the head. She didn't care that he staggered.

"I am beneath you but you didn't mind stooping then. Remember all the days you went down there. Didn't you just love it then, slobbering all over it? Where are your friends? Call them to bail you out.

You are still here thinking that I'll change my mind or you would have been long gone. Is it that there is something so sweet, so delectable here that you find it so hard to leave? Get the hell out, Sam, before I really hurt you."

She watched him slink out of her apartment, nursing his aching head and glaring at her with evil in his eyes. She needed to call someone before that snake started running around, whispering in people's ears that she came to him with the idea to cheat. She didn't know how much she had hurt and she would die if he made the cops arrest her. She knew how the gossip mill worked. All it took was for this to fall on the wrong ears and she would be slaughtered. She couldn't allow this to happen.

Megan snapped her fingers. She would call Alex's Uncle Harry. If anyone would know what to do it would be him. She dug in her purse for his private number and pushed the buttons on her phone. She jumped when he said hello in that deep voice of us.

"Uncle Harry? It's me Megan. I am in trouble and I have to talk to you."

"Where are you?" he asked. "Can you come to me or should I send my men to get you."

She laughed in spite of the situation.

"No, not that kind of trouble. I can come to you."

"Okay then, I'll expect you within the hour," he answered.

She ran to her car, racing over to Jamaica House. His secretary must have been expecting her because she shooed her in immediately. Uncle Harry saw immediately the worry written clearly over Megan's face.

"Want some coffee or tea? Maybe something stronger might be best by the look on your face." He tried to lighten the mood. "Now tell me what's going on." Megan poured out everything and more, all the secrets she had been holding on to for Sam. She let all out and after she was through pouring out her heart she felt immensely better and did ask for a stiff drink.

"Don't worry yourself any further. I'll take it from here," Uncle Harry promised Megan.

After Megan took off, Harry picked up the phone and placed a few calls. The last was to Sam's father, Harry Chin. He had no intention of leaving a message or waiting for a call back. Wherever he was he wanted to speak to him now, immediately. He was put through immediately to him.

"Harry Keanon here, man. We have a few problems that need sorting out."

 To say the least Mr. Chin was shocked. He had no idea as to why he would have received a phone call from Harry Keanon.

"Harry, your boy has a huge amount of gambling debts and that is not the worst part, him like beating women and this is the last time he is going to lay a hand on Megan. So you had better do something about it now or someone is going to really hurt him. I have here a number for a rehab clinic in Miami and I have already been in touch with them so either you get him there or we'll have them pick him up, but he has   to   get   the   help   he   needs."
 "Explain to me what is happening, Harry." Mr. Chin's voice sounded faint on the phone.

"He has gone too far, trying to involve innocent women in his nasty deeds. You have to understand I protect those who I love so his recent doing doesn't sit well with me. I hope we understand each other," Harry barked into the phone.

"I'll see you in an hour if your schedule is clear because I have no time to waste in taking care of this problem. This is an embarrassment to my family. We need to set the ball in motion."

Over the next few days Megan was afraid to leave the house because she was afraid to run into anyone who might have heard the story. Sam called but she refused to pick up the phone. He left pleading messages. "Megan I am going to rehab and I am sorry." Who the hell does he think he is? "Megan, are you going to call me? Megan, I love you." She refused to pick up the phone. She was ashamed to talk to her friends. They had warned her on many occasions about Sam.

Her door bell was ringing and the person refused to go away. She peeped out the window and saw Tayo standing at the door. He stepped back, picked up a pebble, and threw it at the window. She might as well open the door because she knew he wasn't going away. As she opened the door he barged in pass her, looking around.

"What the hell is wrong with you? Don't you know that everyone has been worried sick about you? My God, I don't know whose ass I should kick, Sam Chin or yours. Look at you and this place. Megan, get your ass up and get it together. We are going to country."

Megan began to crack up. Tayo was always funny.

"You want to kick my ass, Tayo? Come try it," Megan invited.

"You know who would lose. I am no stranger baby. I've known you since you were wearing nappies. You scared everyone. People start thinking that something more than the ordinary had happened. I was the one dispatched with due haste to get over here to find you and I was told don't come back until I have you or find out what is going on."

"Oh stop lying. You didn't know me when I was wearing nappies." Megan rolled her eyes at Tayo but she was happy to see him, happy to see a friend.

"Tayo, Sam knows we took that weed from that cave. He must have searched through my stuff and found something because I didn't tell him."

Tayo shook his head.

"You wouldn't listen when we talked to you about that bway. Now he wants to bring trouble. We have to tell the rest of the crew that you let information like this slip."

-Chapter 20-

Whatever is hidden in the dark must eventually come to light. Ciarra was banking her hopes on the premise that no one would believe Sam if he dared to utter something so ludicrous that she, along with Alex and Rory had gone to the cave and removed weed and money. She didn't need no drug dealer to come looking for her. As a matter of fact, if there was more money and weed she had made the suggestion that they go back to relieve thieving Bongo Man and him gang of their loot. Alex was the lucky one because she was all the way in New York.

On top of this more problems were piling up.

For a while there Ciarra had been sleeping with Klein knowing full well that he was a married man but she didn't care. She wasn't sure if she really loved him or she just cared for him. Anyway it didn't matter. She was now someone to reckon with in the fashion world. At first she didn't know how to play the game but she eventually learned.

Nevertheless, she found herself murmuring to herself, "This can't be happening." She didn't understand how Mitzie, Klein's diva wife, had gotten hold of this piece of information and was threatening to release it to use it against her. She was paying her back for sleeping with her husband all those years. Someone once said that payback was a bitch. By now Mitzie should know that she didn't go down without a fight.

She lifted her stunned gaze to the mirror in her Miami bedroom suite. This was not the time to be away from her business and Jamaica. She was here on a buying trip for Klein but also for her own store. Ciarra rubbed her hands over her belly. Three years ago she had her son and she had known right from the start that it was Tayo's but she had been sleeping with Klein back then. She had hidden the truth from Tayo because they weren't together that night when they had forbidden, hot, angry sex. Her knees felt like jelly just thinking about what they had done that night although she had been seeing someone and he was with someone else.

It had been at a party that Rory was hosting at his house on the hill up there. She had been there with Klein and Tayo had been there with his girl. They had been watching each other while on the dance floor and, when they had some how switched partners, she had found herself flush against Tayo. He pulled her close- hip to hip and as usual the bump she had felt had come as no surprise to her.

He had baited her about her married man and she had laced into him about his air head woman. They were swaying together to 'When a Man Loves a Woman' by Percy Sledge and he was guiding her in a slow and sensual dance. He had suddenly blurted: "I want you, Ciarra."

"Even though you just said you hate me?" Ciarra asked.

"You said you hate me because I am a bastard but yet here you are in my arms dancing to the music."

He had grinned at her and suddenly she wanted to be here. There was an ache in her heart. His hands rubbed her butt and she shivered, her senses on high alert.

"Tell me you don't want me, Ciarra, and I'll let you go," Tayo whispered.

She couldn't, but she pulled apart when his woman came over to claim him. This pissed her off and the temptation was strong to hang onto him. She stepped away but not before Tayo saw the fury in her eyes.

Ciarra turned towards Klein and began to wine on him while Tayo watched over his girlfriend's shoulder. She hugged Klein closer, kissing him on the lips. They were wrapped in a tight embrace. A few minutes later Ciarra went to get a drink. She knew it was Tayo standing behind her and when he held her arm and pulled her up the stairs she didn't resist.

"What the hell are you doing, Ciarra, rubbing on some man like that? Have you lost your mind?"

"Tayo", she reminded him, "we are not together."

He pulled her into the bedroom and she made sure that the door was locked. He tilted her chin up, dipped his head towards her, his lips brushing across her mouth so lightly.

"I want to make love to you all night, Ciarra. I want to kiss every inch of your body."

"I want you too, Tayo," she whispered.

She had known that she should have walked away but she couldn't. She wanted him more than she had wanted anyone. He had picked her up, carrying her to the dresser. She remembered crying out with pleasure, begging him to take her. She had placed her legs on his shoulder in them damn sexy stilettos she had worn. Only Tayo could tip her over the edge like this.

She had made love to Tayo that night without using a condom. Big mistake!! She remembered him calling out her name. Lord, have mercy on my soul, she said to herself. That night she knew for sure that she had gotten pregnant. She had been tired, drowsy not wanting to move and Tayo had gone to the bathroom, bringing back a wash cloth, kneeling and cleaning her up with the soft cloth.

"Damn, I messed up your hair and your nice, sexy clothes." But he had straightened out her bra and her top.

She had kept putting off and dreading the day when she had to tell him. He had suspected but couldn't confirm it. The times when her son Fletcher had been around Tayo she had seen him looking at him as if he was studying him for a reason. Tayo had even asked point blank if Fletcher was his because he spoke like him, he had the same mannerisms and Fletcher gravitated to him. It was exactly the reason why she kept Fletcher away from him.

When she had become pregnant Ciarra had fled to Miami and stayed there for the last six months of her pregnancy. After the baby was born the DNA test had proven that Klein wasn't the father but he had kept her secret. It was becoming a mess. Obviously someone was stirring up a hornet's nest.

She walked to the window of her room, looking out at the scenery. Palm trees swayed in the tropical breeze. The waves danced rhythmically across the sand. It looked so peaceful in contrast to the turmoil raging inside her.

She had just spoken to one of the buyers at Klein's who was her bosom buddy and the news wasn't good. Klein's wife had suddenly gotten some spunk in her and was running around telling everyone that Fletcher was Klein's bastard son and he had better boot her from the company or else. She had better get her ass back to Jamaica to do damage control or she might lose what she had worked so hard to achieve in the company.

"Yes," she answered as the phone rang.

"Hello, Ciarra."

Ciarra felt the blood rush to her head as she slid onto the bed.

"Mitzie."

"You weren't expecting to hear from me, were you? Are you going to tell your son who his real daddy is or should I do the honors for you?"

She slammed down the phone. Ciarra closed her eyes, shame washing over her, knowing that for the last four years she had kept Tayo's son from him. The way he said her name made her want to go back in time to that night, to right the wrong that she had committed. Now she didn't know what to say or how to sort out this mess. Her phone rang again. It was Tayo.

"I really cannot talk now, Tayo. I will have to call you back."

His laugh so cool, so controlled reminded her of that night on the beach.

"What's going on Ciarra? I received a message that it was really important that I call you so I did and now you have to call me back."

"Oh yeah, I wanted to talk to you about Alex but I got the information I needed. I am sorry to have frightened you into thinking it was real urgent."

By the time Ciarra hung up the phone she was fuming. Mitzie, that bitch. It had to be her that had called Tayo thinking that would put the fright of God into her. Her phone rang. Thinking it was Tayo calling back she answered impatiently "Yes".

"You all forgot that I am on the board of directors, Ciarra? I have the power to boot you from the company. You are trying to take over my company. Well you will not."

It was Klein's crazy wife again. Ciarra was not about to let her push her around. After all the poor decisions that she and Klein had made, Ciarra had taken the company with her fresh, modern designs, her business sense and turned it around. She was going to go down fighting. How had everything changed so drastically? She still had time. She had signed a contract and they would have to pay dearly to get rid of her.

"Don't count your chickens before they are hatched, Mitzie. The only thing you did for Guille's Fashion was to spend the money so don't push me, Mitzie."

Ciarra slammed down the phone before picking it up again to call the airline.

Ciarra leaned back against the soft upholstery of the Mercedes as it sped along the highway from the Norman Manley Airport into Kingston. Klein had picked her up from the airport and, although the affair between them had ended a long time ago there were many who thought otherwise. It didn't matter how often they saw her with the reggae singer she was dating at the moment, the rumor persisted.

"My wife suddenly got up and start raise cane about you and me. I can't figure out what's going on in her head. It's like she hasn't known about other women that I have dated. She didn't give a damn as long as she had the money to spend."

Ciarra banged her head against the seat.

"I think someone is putting her up to this. The company has been clamping down on her with her spending so I don't know if that's putting a crimp in her lifestyle," he continued.

If the board ganged up against her and fired her Ciarra would limp away, not with her head down but her self respect would take a hit especially if everything came out about her son. She had her boutique but her designs, the company owned them.

The car wound through the busy streets, turning onto Red Hills Road and up into Kirkland Heights. She wanted to go straight home without any stops to see her son. She had some explaining to do.

"Klein, we have to figure out what I am going to do about my place in your business. It's almost time for the fashion week so I have much work to do and then I will have to figure out if there is still a place for me there because sooner or later it might come down to a major confrontation and I will have to kick your wife's skinny ass, and please don't even say a word."

"The newspaper would eat this up. This would be a coup for them."

Klein had the nerve to turn to her and say some crap like this.

"You are starting to piss me off," Ciarra said angrily. "You think this is funny?"

Klein held up his hand in a gesture of peace.

"Sorry I just wanted to lighten the mood."

This complication she didn't need.

Ciarra was hard at work in her small dressmaking shop. She had moved out of the main building that housed Klein's designs, wanting to put some distance between her and him and his wife. Getting involved with Klein after working alongside with him wasn't the smartest thing she had done. She was prepared for the crap that would hit the fan once her involvement got out so, with his help and that of three other coworkers, she had found a place to design and sew on her own.

-Chapter 21-

*I*t was the perfect day for a wedding. Laughter bubbled up in her throat, the result of pure happiness. Today she would become Rory's wife. Here they were, standing in front of the minister, the two of them and Tayo standing as their witness. What else did they need? What else but the love they shared, here in New York, far away from home? Guilty thoughts of her mom, her friends that she hadn't told intruded but she pushed it away. They would understand.

She floated through her vows, her hand unsteady as she held it out to him, her finger slightly raised to receive his ring. He caught her hand and held it firmly as he pushed the ring down.

"I now pronounce you man and wife."

"We've done it," he said as smiled down into her upturned face.

She loved him. Today was the start of their forever.

Alex stared up at the ceiling. It held no new revelations. It was still painted white. She shifted on the bed, rolling to the left. For the last two weeks she had been placed on bed rest. The baby was threatening to come early and the doctors were trying to prevent that from happening. The doctors had told her that at twenty four weeks the baby didn't stand a very good chance. So here she was, going into her twenty seven weeks. There was not much to do but read or let her mind wander.

No one had been able to tell when they attended her graduation from law school. She had kept it a secret and the times her dad had seen her she was all bundled up but now the secret was out. She wondered if she had passed the bar. She had done her very best because she couldn't and didn't want to fail, to go back a second time.

Her mind wandered back to when she had first moved to New York.

It was the second month living with her dad and she thought another weekend, another woman. She gathered up her books stuffed them in her book bag and called out to her dad that she was leaving.

"Les, I am leaving."

She never called him dad, daddy or papa. It was such a foreign word to her. She didn't have that connection with him. He was more like a relative, a cousin or a distant uncle. Her uncle back home in Jamaica was more like her father.

"Okay," he answered.

The door opened and Doraine stood in the doorway.

"It was good seeing you, Alex. Why don't we plan to go shopping next week?" she asked.

Alex nodded.

"You have my number so you know where to find me when you are ready."

Alex walked out the door. She couldn't understand why her father had so many different women. It was a different one every weekend. They weren't dumb women or ugly. They were all pretty, smart and had very good jobs. She especially liked Doraine because she was kind and sweet. Of them all she was the one who her father was hung up on. The thing is, while he was married he had been seeing her but by the time he had got divorced she had gone and gotten herself married because she was pissed off with him. A tangled web if you ask.

It had taken only six months for her to move out because it had not been easy living with Les. Added to that, coming from an island where it's hot year round, she was not prepared for the biting cold that left her toes and fingers numb.

The machines beeped constantly in the silence of the room. She placed her hand on her stomach, hoping fervently that she would have a healthy baby. She would finally have the family that she had dreamed of with Rory.

Her thoughts turned to Megan. She was annoyed that Megan had let Sam find their Achilles but that was nothing compared to how sad she was that her friend had tolerated licks upside her head from a man. She had never liked Sam and had suspected that something wasn't quite right between them. If she had ever known that Sam was hitting her she would have *siced* her uncle on him. Knowing Megan and the person she is it was hard to believe that she had allowed Sam to hit her more than once. If she had a girl there is no way she would stand by and watch a man hit her child and if it was a boy, there is no way in heaven that she would tolerate him hitting a girl. Hell, no.

Alex was drifting off to sleep when the door opened and a woman strode in, tall, hair flowing down her back, very light skinned wearing hipster black pants, a tangerine blouse, and looking vaguely familiar. The woman came closer into the room.

"Hello Alex. That is your name, isn't it?"

"Is there something I can help you with because I think you have the wrong room?" Alex answered.

She ignored Alex.

"I am in the right place. I came to see how you are doing." She held up her hand. "I am Lindsay and I am here to let you know that I am Rory's fiancée. We are engaged and we are going to be married. Since Rory didn't want to face you with this I took on the task."

Alex blinked and sat up.

"I thought you looked familiar. Lindsay Hamilton. That's right. Take your fake ass out of my room before I call security and have you arrested for threatening me."

Lindsay Hamilton shook out her hair for effect.

"Rory doesn't even think this baby is his so get it through your thick skull: he is mine."

"What did you say?" Alex sat up suddenly swinging her feet off the bed.

Lindsay stood hovering over her, waving her hand in her face. "You heard what I said. This baby is not Rory's and he doesn't want your jacket."

Alex slapped Lindsay's hand away and Lindsay pushed her. Alex fell back on to the bed. A cramp so severe sliced through Alex that she slumped in the bed. Not now. She didn't want to do this now.

"Let's hope that I'll be okay because I'll come hunt you down like a dog in the streets," Alex managed to get out.

The monitor was beeping, going crazy as Lindsay ran from the room, passing the nurse who was running into the room.

Alex felt something wet and sticky between her legs. Pain tore through her and she moaned as the staff raced around her. Tears drenched her eyes and rolled down her cheeks as her body contorted in misery. Loneliness swept over her as she looked at the concerned faces of the hospital staff. Dear God, let my baby be okay, she prayed. She was in labor and her baby was going to be born prematurely. She was in the grip of a nightmare.

Alex didn't hold her baby when he was born. The doctor said he was suffering from *tachycardia*, having retractions and in severe respiratory distress so he was intubated and placed on a ventilator. She was transferred to the ICU for complications related to the hemorrhage she had suffered.

For ten days Alex sat with her baby, looking at the wires and lines sticking out of his tiny arms and hooked up to life support. Rory was there every day but she had no urge, no reason to say much to him. Everything felt flat as if she was in a dream. He didn't understand her behavior; he didn't know why she refused to speak to him. She sat there looking like she didn't know what to do next.

Her baby didn't survive past ten days. That's when she told Rory it was over. She was done. She was all screwed up so she couldn't tell if the expression on his face was anger, relief or disbelief.

"What?" he exclaimed. "Alex, I know you are suffering but you refuse to talk to me. Why, what is it?"

"Go ask Lindsay Hamilton. She'll tell you."

-CHAPTER 22-

It was a little more than a month before Christmas and Auntie had placed her orders way ahead of time to get in her goods before the Christmas rush. Boxes of whistles and *fee-fee* were waiting to be unpacked. She had personally traveled to Kingston to get the dolls that she wanted. Last year the dolls with black or brown hair had sold like hot potatoes. The blonde haired ones were a little slower to go. This year she even had the ones that laughed or cried and said 'mama'. She had little wind up cars in all colors, firecrackers, *squibs* and all the little toys that the adults and children loved. She had learnt from last year when she ran out of toy cars and trucks.

Miss Eve picked up one of the tea sets. They were sitting in the living room of Alex's grandmother's house along with a few of the men and women of Bell Town. Everyone was starting to feel the Christmas spirit.

"I promised Karen's little girl a Christmas gift so I am going to put this aside and one of the little skinny dolls with black hair. It wasn't so long ago that Alex was playing with one of these." Eve turned the pack around and around.

"They grow up real fast," Auntie said with a sigh as she placed the Jacks set on the rack. I have to put these three sets away because Ruth and a few others are already paying down on their Christmas gifts."

"That reminds me. I have to put some more fruits and raisins to soak. Linnet said she doesn't have any fruits soaking so I promised her some. This Christmas is going to be big with all our wayward children coming in." Eve said with a laugh, "so we need more than one person to make Christmas fruit cake. I can't wait to see them all."

"You want something hot to drink?" Auntie asked to everyone in the room.

"Let me have some coffee if you have it. I prefer the one called Blue Mountain coffee," Miss Etty answered.

"See what I mean? She asked for the best coffee around these parts." Octavius stretched his legs. "No tea or regular coffee."

Auntie removed the cup from the cabinet and poured the coffee from the flowered tea pot. Miss Etty took the cup, poured sweetened condensed milk into the tea cup, and stirred with her spoon.

"I always thought that it would be the boys that we had to watch out for, that they would be the ones in trouble, but as it's turning out it's the girls who are the problem."

"There you go. That's because them boys been around us. Mass Kenny here can testify to that. They see how we live, simple and straightforward, no time for the drama that women like," Octavius said staring at the glass in his hand and refusing to meet anybody's gaze.

"See here Octavius, don't let me and you have a problem, you chatting fart like that." Auntie shook her head from side to side.

"Mass Kenny here will back me up with what I said. All them boys do is have a woman or two here and there," Octavius answered, taking a sip of rum from the glass, winking at Mass Kenny as he said this.

"Pass the rum over here, Octavius, and the coconut water. My mouth is getting dry from drinking orange juice without a drop of anything strong in it."

Mass Kenny avoided answering the question. They were outnumbered at least two to one and he wasn't about to start any fuss with his wife because he knew what side of the bed he wanted to sleep on when he got home.

"Take Megan for example. That girl is behaving as if her head isn't screwed on right. She is with this Chiney bway who seems to be changing the way she thinks. She has been behaving real uppity. We country folks have always been good enough for her but it's as if she is ashamed of where she is coming from," Miss Linnet said.

"And that's not the worst of it. He is a gambler who doesn't win but loses and that boy believes he wasn't created like everybody else. To think he would get away with treating Megan like he did. More trouble is coming but we are ready to deal with what comes." Miss Etty shivered slightly.

"No one hits any one of ours without consequences," Auntie said.

"Well, we are doing something about all this," Miss Eve gestured with the napkin in her hand. "Ciarra is with that womanizing married man Klein. Alex doesn't want to come home. I see Rory, Tayo, and Andy more than I see my own child."

"It all has to do with Kenny's son, Rory, and that no one can deny. That's why your child stays away. And as for Klein, Ciarra is quite busy herself, flirting and playing with this one and that one. Serves them right. She is only playing the game that they are playing,"

Miss Etty said. "It's time we give them all a good shake up. They have to be reminded of that bond, of what they all have in common. They were given a talent for a reason, to set examples for those coming behind and there is absolutely no way that they are going to destroy what was so freely given and bestowed on them."

Octavius leaned forward in his chair.

"Jimmy Cliff was one of the first artists to leave Jamaica for international waters but he never forgot his roots. His song 'Wonderful World, Beautiful People,' is well known all over the world. And then there was Bob Marley and the Wailers. They all had talent. Peter Tosh, Bunny Wailer. I remember when the song, "You can fool some people sometimes, but can't fool all the people all the time" was a hit and on everyone's tongue but even the great Wailers had disagreements and pressures. It was the pressures of the capitalists, record companies, international marketing and all that which led to the break up of the Wailers."

"Get to the point, Octavius." Auntie wasn't one to bite her tongue. "We all know there is a point in all this."

Octavius leaned back in his chair.

"The Wailers broke up in '74 and Peter Tosh and Bunny Wailer and Bob Marley went their separate way. It was the talent and skill that they all had that kept them going. The talent that they had didn't suffer. The name Bob Marley is recognized any where in the world that you go. Peter Tosh *Equal Rights and Justice* is sung daily. Bunny Wailer made a statement with his album Blackheart Man and his song *This Train*. The point is, all of our children that we are here discussing is just trying to be their own person right about now and they will come in to their own as the Wailers and Jimmy Cliff have done. Trust me, Alex or any of the others have not forgotten who they are."

Auntie got up and went to the refrigerator to pull out a bottle of iced water. She poured some in her glass and tipped a little Appleton in it.

"I agree with what you said, Octavius, but children also has to be guided. Alex's destiny is to be Prime Minister of Jamaica. This is not a chance happening. It is what is going to happen so we have to nudge it in the right direction. These young people nowadays take everything for granted. They don't think back to all the sacrifices that was made in order for them to have the freedom to do as they choose."

"We all say 'Amen' to that. Guidance is the key to accomplishments," Miss Etty said. "It's a long time that they haven't played cricket together."

They all looked at Miss Etty and clapped their hands.

"That is a plan right there. All of them together like they used to be. Let the planning begin," Mass Kenny pitched in.

"Did you all hear what happen to Vie? She is really sick. After all these years you would think that Rantie stop have her up but she is one woman who like to carry a grudge and George was never her man to begin with. We should pay her a visit," Auntie suggested.

"There is so much gossip as to what is wrong with her. Some say is Rantie obeah her but then I hear she have stomach cancer. The other day I saw her she was so skinny having lost all the weight she use to carry around with her," Miss Linnet contributed.

Auntie looked around the room, cradling her cup of fever grass in her hand.

"Time waits on no man. Alex is past twenty five going towards thirty. It is time for her to begin fulfilling her destiny."

Miss Etty shuffled the cards before pulling one from the pack and turning it face up. This was the second time she was reading the cards and the message was not good. For many years she had worried about the boys and feared for them, thinking that the girls would be alright. This was not so. They were hell bent on self destruction. From what she was seeing they were all in trouble. That boy Sam had not finished with Megan, he was looking for trouble but she, Miss Etty was not going to give him the chance.

The smoke swirled around her as the incense burned. She jumped up from her sitting position. Taking a swig of rum from the bottle, she blew it all directions. She clapped her hands and Ashanti came running into the room. Her missus pointed to the photo book sitting on the table with the girls' pictures. Ashanti lay the photo album by the basin with the water as Miss Etty began to chant.

"No evil shall befall those that I hold to my bosom.

Only God can take what's his, not you.

Begone, you Jezubel, Begone!!!"

Miss Etty was shaking because there was no way this bad ass spirit was going to get the better of her. She was going to protect her babies.

Ashanti started to shake the gourd and as she sang she began to stamp her feet in a rhythmic manner. Their voices blended together as they chanted. She poured the *Florida Water* on the machete and then struck the match, igniting a flame on the machete. Miss Etty swung the machete backward and forward, sideways until she was satisfied, and then with a smile, she slapped it on the ground.

"None that I protect shall come to such harm," she said quietly and with satisfaction. Miss Etty clasped Ashanti's hand and together they lifted their hands towards the sky.

-CHAPTER 23-

*T*he woman stood on the hillside, her arms outstretched, her face tilted towards the sun, her wide straw hat tucked on her head. In her hands a beautiful gold, green and red scarf trailed in the wind. The woman smiled as she held it out to Alex.

"It belongs to you Alex. I've kept it safe for you all these years."

Alex stretched her hand and touched the scarf as it fluttered in the wind.

"It's beautiful," she responded, "but why have you kept it all this time?"

Alex could feel the sun on her face and the heat beating down on her head.

"It's time for you to fulfill your destiny, Alex. We have given   you   time."
It was when the woman took off her hat that Alex realized that this was Nanny, her ancestor who had led them from the cave that day. Alex tried to explain that her destiny was here, but Nanny only shook her head.

Nanny laughed, her head thrown back so that the sun touched her dark face. She began fanning herself with her straw hat. Now Alex could see what she couldn't see before, the children playing together. Wait a minute; that was her with Rory and the others running in the schoolyard in all their wildness. A group of people standing by the crossroad, among them her grandmother and Miss Etty. She saw her child, her baby who had been here for only a while.

Sunlight and Dappled Shade

"Wait," she called out to his shadowy figure as he faded. "Wait."

Nanny turned to her even as she began to drift away.

"I could show you the future but I would rather show you the past. Open up a collection of memories that you seem to have locked away. Remind you of where you are coming from. Your future is destined and it's time to go home."

There was a pounding in Alex's head. She came awake as the alarm beeped its way into her subconscious. She switched on her bedside lamp, looking around in alarm. It was like Men at Work in her head, drilling away at their jack-hammers.

Thank God it was a dream, she said to herself as consciousness prevailed. Her eyes were caught by an item at the foot of her bed. It was a scarf the same color as the one in her dream. She couldn't remember if she had actually left it on her bed. It was becoming a habit now. These dreams were becoming more frequent. Was she somehow losing her grip on reality?

The dream weighed heavily on Alex all through the day. She thought about Rory and where he was. She thought about Megan and Ciarra, Tayo, her mom and her grandmother. Her thoughts were filled with back home. Home sick, that must be it; she said it out loud. New York was okay but she missed home. It was the Christmas season and by now there would be much hustle and bustle back home. Bottles of Sorrel laced with rum were perhaps being made right now. Christmas cake with fruits that had been soaking in liquor all year was being baked. Her mouth watered, but most of all she missed her family, and her friends. She missed hearing, coming from the kitchen her mother, grandmother and anyone else who came to visit, chatting away as they rubbed tons of cake batter, sipping some of the wine that was supposed to be for the cake. The smell of all that baking wafting through the air. Oh, God, she missed home.

Christmas was right around the corner and if she didn't book her ticket soon for Jamaica she knew that it would be booked for her. For months Auntie had been working on her about coming home. It was late, almost 7 p.m. but Alex was sitting at her desk going over documents for a case when the phone rang. It wouldn't stop ringing so she picked it up.

"Hello, Auntie," she said with surprise. "Why are you ringing me here and not on my cell or home?" Alex answered.

"I have been ringing you at home and you are never there so I figure that I would find you here, working yourself to death. When are you coming home for Christmas? The Christmas giveaways that we always do for the kids is coming up. This is something you should be a part of. You have been missing too many of these events, Alex."

Alex sighed.

"You are laying a guilt trip on me so I'll come home. So who else is coming home for Christmas? What about Megan and Ciarra? Aren't they doing their part and helping out? And what about the others?"

She didn't want to be dragged home to see people she hated or resented and Rory was at the top of the list. She had not seen him in four years, always making sure they were never in the same place at the same time. He was now living in Atlanta and, although Ciarra, Megan and all the others had been to his gorgeous home, she had refused to set foot in his house.

Alex sighed. She had been having so many dreams about the cave. That was in the past and she didn't want to dredge all that up. Remembering fired her up and brought back memories she would rather forget; but it had been an exciting time back then.

"If you are asking about Rory. I don't know if he is going to be here. I haven't seen him in some time. It's time you come home, Alex. You can do anything you want to do here. I know you are an important woman there but here is where you will make your mark. Your uncle has given you time, has given you the freedom to choose and to live your life but I reckon that time is up. Apart from all that, I miss you, baby."

"Okay, okay. I am coming home before Christmas."

Auntie's laughter came over the phone.

"I love you baby. So I'll tell your mother you will be home for the holidays."

As Auntie placed the phone in the cradle she rubbed her hands together in glee. "Yes," she said to the others, "she is coming home."

Alex had not been home for the last two Christmases and she was excited. She missed the Christmas cake and ginger wine, the drilling boys that went from house to house putting on a show like they were trained soldiers. It was the fact that people went from house to house, drinking and eating that made Christmas. She liked New York, she had a man and she worked with a prestigious law firm; but she was missing warmth, family. She stacked her papers, stuffed them in her briefcase and snapped it close.

She reached for the phone and dialed Ciarra's number.

Ciarra must have been running to get the phone because she sure sounded like some one who was out of breath.

"Ciarra. It's Alex."

"Hey girl, what's going on?" Ciarra asked.

"Are you going to Bell Town for Christmas?"

"Sure I am," she answered. "Miss Etty and your parents and mine want us home for Christmas. It's been sometime since you took your black ass home for the holidays."

"Is it just us or others have been invited? I am not sure what's going on. Paul, my boyfriend, wanted us to spend Christmas here but maybe I will drag him along   with   me."
    Ciarra was snacking in her ear.

"If you are asking if Rory is going to be there, I don't think so. He lives in Atlanta as you know. As a matter of fact he was inviting us up to have Christmas dinner there but I had to decline. Miss Etty and Octavius calls, I go. Hold on. I have a call."

Ciarra clicked back.

"That was Megan on the phone. She said to tell you that if she is going to Bell Town for Christmas, so are you. She said to call her when you finish chatting with me."

Christmas in Jamaica is celebrated from the beginning of December and the streets, the malls, the stores were all crowded. Traffic was brutal and Ciarra was having a hard time navigating it. She had no intention of driving all the way up to Manor Park now. It was brutal enough in Halfway Tree. She grumbled to herself after finally getting a parking spot. She had waited for ten minutes to get a spot.

"Do you believe how crazy it is?" she said to Megan as they walked along the plaza. "It is the same every year, people complain of not having any money but the stores are full. Look, do you see anyone without a shopping bag?"

"It's the holidays and it hasn't changed. The only thing that's changed is that I am not a child any more and I have money to spend." Megan did a jig and spun Fletcher around. "Look at the lights blinking on the Christmas trees. It's beautiful and do you hear the Christmas songs? Fletcher, I love Christmas. Your mom and Uncle Rory and Uncle Tayo and all of us used to spend Christmas together."

They moved along window shopping.

"Mommy is Uncle Tayo and Uncle Rory gonna be in country for Christmas? I would like to get them a gift. Uncle Tayo is always so funny. Auntie Megan, look." Fletcher pointed to the display in the window. "There is the scarf I want to get grandma for Christmas."

While Fletcher skipped ahead Megan looked at Ciarra.

"I don't want to keep your secret any more Ciarra. You need to tell Tayo that Fletcher is his. I think somehow Tayo suspects you. Do you think he is trying to get under your skin when he says things like Fletcher behaves like him or maybe Fletcher is his and you don't know? I think he tests you to see what reaction he is going to get."

"Oh, give it a rest, Megan. I am going to tell him soon."

"If you don't do it soon, Ciarra, I might have to tell him. I thought you would develop a conscience all this time but you haven't," Megan said with some heat.

Ciarra stopped in her tracks.

"What's your problem? Don't be getting on my case. It's the holidays. There is no reason to be so serious." Ciarra hugged Megan. "This holiday, let's go shop, from one store to the other. Fletcher, come back here. I don't want you to be so far ahead. If Alex was here, she would agree with me. Shop till you drop."

Alex was standing on a chair holding a star atop the Christmas tree.

"What do you think, Mrs. K, an angel or a star?"

Before she could answer Uncle Harry walked in, dropping his briefcase on the sofa.

"What do you think, Harry, a star or an angel at the top of the tree?"

He looked from his wife to Alex, weighing his answer carefully, not wanting to walk into a trap.

"What do you think, Alex?"

Mrs. K threw her arms in the air.

"Oh never mind, we'll do the star. It was the star that led the wise men to Jesus where he was born in a manger."

"Oh yeah, the star symbolizes, high hopes and high ideals. High hopes are what we have for Alex, that she'll reach above herself. It's time for you to wet your feet in the political arena, Alex. Here, hold on to my hand and come on down from that chair. Our neighbors are at the door, with a bottle in their hand. Let the celebration begin," he said with a laugh. "Matilda," he called, "will you let in the Baughs? They are at the door."

It was endless, the array of visitors and food. This was how Christmas was celebrated.

"So when are you going to Bell Town, Alex? Your grandmother is eager to see you and, since I don't want you driving from Kingston to the country, I have to make arrangements for the driver to take you."

"Come let's rock this Jacob Miller Christmas carol. *Deck the hall with lots of callie, trala,la,la,la,lala. Lift the pipe and let's be irie,*" his wife sang.

Alex shook her head at both of them.

"You two need to grow up."

She tipped on her toes, rubbing her uncle's head affectionately. The door opened letting the Baughs in with a bottle of liquor in their hand. There were more visitors coming.

"Matilda, do we have those ackee *quiche* hot and ready and that mango chutney to go with the roast pork? Let's put out the chicken wings. We are going to need food because when they start drinking, they also start eating."

Alex walked to the kitchen ahead of Matilda, opening up the jar of mango chutney and pouring it into a dish. Matilda was laughing so hard and then she was humming to herself.

"Alex, sweetie, it is going to be a good Christmas."

"Let's take a little drink, Matilda. I know you like Appleton. What do you say?" Alex prompted.

"Okay, here is my cup." Matilda poured herself a drink.

Alex winked at her as she left the room.

-Chapter 24-

T he streets were busy as if you were in Kingston or Montego Bay. Roadside work was given out every holiday to clean up the streets. Road banks were cleared. Big tractors had filled potholes and smoothed out rough patches in the street. Yards were cleared up and walls and tree roots and trunks white washed. Alex relaxed in the back of the car with her mother sitting next to her. Her grandmother sat in the front discussing the importance of putting the right ingredients in Sorrel as they rode to Bell Primary School to hand out gifts to the children.

It was Christmas Eve and Alex had been up from early morning decorating the school with Megan and Ciarra to give a festive air. Miss Etty and other volunteers were manning the refreshment booth. The driver braked suddenly as Mass Tom's son ran out in the street without looking first.

"Bway look weh yuh a go," the driver shouted.

The boys ignored him and kept at their game of tag.

The driver pulled into the school yard and Megan and Ciarra come running out to the car.

"Hi, Miss Eve, Hi Auntie," they said quietly, but they practically dragged Alex from the car.

"Come on, we have been waiting too long for you to get here. Ask Miss Etty. We were coming to get you but she wouldn't let us, not even to make a phone call." Ciarra was chatting away nonstop like a parrot.

"There are over a hundred kids inside waiting for their gifts. We have two Santas because we are dividing the groups into two, boys on one side, girls on the other," Megan said to Alex while she walked along at a rapid place as if she was in a hurry. "Slow down, guys. What's up with you two? If I didn't know better I would say you are both acting kinda funny. It's not like we haven't done this before. And another thing, you are walking too damn fast, slow down," Ciarra said.

Alex didn't see the look that passed between Ciarra and Megan. The children were singing Christmas carols while their teacher swung her hand back and forth in direction as if she was the conductor in an orchestra. In a corner of the room was a huge Christmas tree and sacks of gifts sitting on either side of the room.

There was an endless number of people to be greeted and endless gossip to catch up on. By the time Alex was through chatting with the Principal, twenty minutes had passed and by the time Megan rescued her from chatting with the Baptist minister another twenty minutes had passed.

"Where is the other Santa?" Alex asked. "I see the elves but no Santas."

"They are around somewhere," Megan answered vaguely.

The minister asked for everyone's attention and officially started the gift giving after saying a prayer. Memories of past Christmases crowded Alex's mind. Days when she and her friends were little and receiving gifts from Santa. It had become a tradition in Bell Town. She felt pleased at the delight on the faces of the children and vowed to make sure that every year the children of Bell Town had a Christmas party.

Octavius was looking through the window of his house when Rory and Tayo arrived. They drove up to the porch as he opened the front door. He looked at the two boys who had grown into manhood and felt proud, like a father. Octavius' hair was now iron gray but he still wore it in dreadlocks.

"Etty told me to conduct myself with dignity so I am walking around as if I am one of those old time butlers with my back straight." He shook his head and laughed. "After all this time she is trying to make an honest man out of me, an impossible task."

He was wearing a tee shirt and a pair of black jeans. Christmas carols blared from the record player as Tayo and Rory pressed knuckles with Octavius. Before they could enter, Octavius ushered them to the bamboo covered area in the back yard.

"My boy, you'll need a drink today before you see Etty," he said with a twinkle in his eyes. "You all needed to come home." He took a sip of his coconut water with his rum.

"This signifies trouble when we are summoned like this," Rory said with a grin, "but I can handle whatever comes."

"I am not sure what's coming so let me take a double drink," Tayo said pouring from the bottle of Hennessy he had in his hand. "I am glad we are the first ones here though. I sure as hell didn't want to be the one to have to break the ice. And as for you Rory, there is no dodging being in the same place with Alex today."

Sunlight and Dappled Shade

"You aren't one to talk about me Tayo. When was the last time you and Ciarra had a civil conversation? It seems to me there is a whole lot of crap going around," Rory said.

"Rory, children, it's too early to start bickering, wait until we are liquored up," Octavius laughed. "Don't listen to me. I am a sick old man who is allowed to say strange things and, Rory, don't be so sure that you have a handle on what's coming. Come let's go see Etty." Octavius stood up, patting Rory on the arm.

It was a view that Rory had looked at many times but never had his appreciation of the rugged beauty been more poignant. Bell Town had grown in the last few years. The narrow path leading up to Octavius's home was no longer a dirt track but a new road had been cut a few years ago passing by Octavius which now gave access to cars and motor bikes. Rory himself had developed and built a housing area with security. The houses offered a Jacuzzi, bathrooms and spacious living rooms. They had been sold as soon as the houses were placed on the market.

It was going to be an interesting evening.

He needed a breather. Tayo walked out to the back of the house and sat on the garden bench in the backyard, feeding the dog with pieces of chicken as it yapped and played around. Satisfied, the dog rolled over and curled up content with a full stomach. It was good to have the uncomplicated company of the dog. Sometimes those around him made life too difficult. Take today for example, he was sensing many undercurrents and tension already and everyone wasn't here as yet. He had problems of his own.

His cell phone was ringing. He looked at it, ignoring the ringing. The dog's ear pricked up, a low growl rumbling in his throat as he stared at the back fence which separated Miss Annie's yard. The iron gate began rattling. Tayo stood up at the sound of the gate scraping against the concrete. He hurried towards the sound. A little body came hurtling through the gate.

"Uncle Tayo!!!"

He was too stunned to reply. What the hell was Ciarra doing coming through the back gate? He stooped and Fletcher flew into his arms.

"You have grown tall, almost as tall as I am," Tayo joked, "and why are you coming in the back way?"

"Mommy stopped in to see Miss Annie. We brought her a gift and some food because we have a lot to go around. That's what Mommy said."

"Good man," Tayo remarked as he rubbed his head.

"See you later, Uncle Tayo. My cousins are waiting on me to start a game," Fletcher said as he ran towards the door.

He saw Ciarra standing there but he ignored her. He had nothing to say to her but hello.

"So you are ignoring me, Tayo?" she questioned. "You see me standing here and I haven't disappeared in thin air."

She balanced the tray in her hand.

Tayo looked up to the sky and muttered a prayer for Jah to give him strength. There were a few choice things he could have said to her but instead he said:

"I was sitting here in peace and here you come along as usual to disturb my inner peace. If you need help with that tray let me have it. I wouldn't want you to spill whatever is in it."

He took the tray and walked away while her heels click-clacked behind him as she followed him inside to greet the others.

Megan was happy with all the preparations: copper pots were on the stove and food in containers sat in food warmers. A marvelous array of dishes stood on the counter and the kitchen table. Three long trestle tables dressed in gold and green linen were set ready for dining. Miss Etty and Miss Linnet had everything under control. Megan tasted the Sorrel and held out a glass to her date, Dr. Marcus Hughes. He gave a thumbs up sign and asked for a full glass.

"I am already having a good time and all your friends haven't even arrived as yet," he commented.

"They'll be here soon," she reassured him.

She sent up a prayer that they would all leave any embarrassing events alone tonight. Satisfied she walked out on to the verandah. Candles in glass jars lined the edge of the verandah and, as Megan leaned over the rail she couldn't help grinning at the scene before her. Tayo was taking giant strides with a tray in his hand and Ciarra was behind him, pouting while trying to catch up to him.

"What you laughing at Megan?" Ciarra asked irritably.

"You. Who else?" Megan answered. "And a happy Christmas Eve to you, Ciarra. The Christmas spirit is here, Ciarra, so don't come here with an attitude."

Ciarra was wearing high heels and a sleeveless yellow dress belted at the waist. Quite the dressy lady that she was. Megan herself was wearing lime green linen pants with a gold silky knit top caught at her waist with a gold belt.

"Oh, girl, gimme a hug." Ciarra stretched out her arms to Megan. "It's all good, everything is going to be fine. So where is Alex? I can't believe she is not here yet."

Ciarra prayed that her secret would be kept one last time before the beginning of the New Year.

"Why are you out here by yourself? I can hear laughter and that voice I am hearing is definitely Rory."

"Did someone call my name?"

Rory Richardson stood there looking impossibly handsome in a pair of grey pants and a black shirt. He squeezed Ciarra tightly.

"Seems like you have expanded a wee bit up top." Rory joked.

Ciarra slapped him on his arm.

"I am going to my car. I left that record in there that I promised Octavius I would bring."

The person leaning into the car that had just pulled up straightened and the car door slammed. Rory turned towards the sound and his eyes fixed on the woman sauntering up the path, the warm breeze lifting her hair back from her pretty face. A face he would never forget in a million years. A face that had haunted him for the last three years.

It was Alex. She was walking towards him in a yellow chiffon dress. She was home, was the thought that flashed through his head.

Alex took charge of the container laying on the seat of the car, then straightened up and closed the door. She was late because everyone else had made it here before her. She hurried up the path and almost bumped into the figure leaning against the parked car.

She stopped dead in her tracks and felt her mouth open in wordless horror.

It was Rory!

Her mind suddenly emptied and for a few dizzying seconds everything spun out of control before it spun back into focus again on his tall, dark, very still stance.

No one had told her he was going to here. As far as she knew, he was in Atlanta.

Alex's heart seemed to have jumped out of her ribcage and into her mouth. Time and time again she had gone over in her head what she would say or do when confronted with this situation. There was no denying the powerful body, the broad shoulders and those mesmerizing eyes that were now boring into hers. She wanted to turn away but instead she stared back at him.

Sunlight and Dappled Shade

She hadn't seen him in so long; since they had buried their son.

Rory, she whispered in disbelief. They had all said he wasn't coming so what was he doing here?

Then he moved, straightening away from the car. Heat blazed a trail down her front.

"Rory," she breathed in a shaky whisper.

"It has been a long time, Alex," he returned huskily.

"Yes, it has been. What are you doing here?" she answered dryly.

His eyes narrowed but he ignored the question.

She met his gaze. Painful memories crowded her mind but the past was the past. She walked towards him, trying to get pass him. But he didn't move.

"I have always wanted to know what happened back then. You basically moved out of the apartment, wouldn't speak to me and left me without any explanations."

Her anger bubbled to the surface.

"You were married to me because I was pregnant and then you went and gave another woman a ring while I sat in a hospital room trying to save our baby."

A muscle jumped angrily in his jaw.

"And I thought you knew me," he said in disgust. "Maybe I need to remind you that you often said what a sweet boy I was."

She didn't get any further. In one move he closed the gap between them and brought his mouth down on hers.

"You look well, my wife. The years have been good to you." He pointed to the verandah. "We have an audience so you had better play nice."

As he straightened up she saw the look of self-satisfied triumph on his face.

"Damn you, Rory. I am no longer your wife." Alex hissed.

"Last time I checked we were still married."

Angry with Rory, she followed him into the house. As she stepped onto the verandah her anger fell away as she hugged and kissed everyone. They were all together again.

Miss Etty was clapping her hands.

"I need everyone's attention. I cannot begin to tell you how happy I am to have all of you here to celebrate Christmas. You have all grown into fine young people. I have watched you grow and have protected you as much as I could so now it is up to each of you to protect the other as we have all done over the years. Megan have been wonderful, she is responsible for most of the cooking so we all have to thank her. Okay, enough of me. Alex, will you bless the food before we sit down to eat?"

With the prayer said everyone sat down to dinner.

"This definitely tastes like *Jango* soup," Neil said as he took another sip of the hot seafood soup.

Octavius laughed.

"I added a touch more white rum to it than I should."

"The consensus is that it's better than the previous times you made it, Octavius," Rory added. "I'd drink another cup but I have to make space for all this food that I am about to consume."

There was enough to feed an army and for a period of time there was only the sound of a knife or fork clicking against a plate and exclamations of 'this is so good'. Octavius leaned back in his chair and began telling stories.

"Look at these two. Fletcher and your daughter Andrea fighting to sit on Auntie Alex's lap. These two really take a set on you. Alex. Auntie said you getting you practice for when you get married to that baseball player that you are dating up there in New York," Megan observed.

"Oh, he plays for one of those famous teams up in the States," Miss Eve clarified.

"I know you mean that handsome black guy Alejandro," Andrea squealed "He is such a hunk. Girl, Alex you have to hook me up with a man like that."

"Oh I love the Yankees, they have some cute guys," Ciarra said dreamily.

The glass that Rory was holding slipped from his grasp as Alex met his gaze.

"You are engaged, Alex?"

"Here we go," Megan said as she passed the dish with the pork to Ciarra. "Rory and Alex. They really need to drop the act about not caring what the other one did or what they are doing and jump each other bones and call it a day."

"No pork for me. And pass me the pasta," Ciarra said to Andrea. "I have to watch my weight. I tend to put on weight quite easily."

"Hah-hah, listen to this one, pass me the pasta. Ciarra, since when you call macaroni and cheese pasta and you don't eat pork? You couldn't have enough   of   it   at   one   time."
"Pass me the chicken and stop picking on me and what I eat," Cairra answered. "You like your size but I don't like thick or chubby for lack of a better word so I have to watch what I eat. Is something wrong with what I said?"

Alex ignored them and added macaroni and cheese to her plate. Megan watched with a smirk on her face. Sooner or later those two would be at it. Andrea found it hard to deal with the stuck up new persona of Ciarra and she refused to buy into this new person that Ciarra had become.

Tayo was busy thinking as to how to cut off Rory from the subject. He could see the hurricane blowing in from miles away. He felt it in his bones that today was the day of reckoning between him and Alex.

"You are engaged to someone, Alex? If this is so you need to talk to me about this."

Turning her head, Alex looked into Rory's face, shaking her head, willing him not to say anything more.

"Alex knows she cannot marry anyone," Rory bit out.

"You are so delusional, I swear," Megan laughed. "You don't own her."

"Why don't you tell her why I am not delusional, Alex? Hell tell everyone why I am not delusional. Go ahead. I dare you," Rory said angrily.

"Hey, Rory, man. Why don't you two go outside," Tayo was practically begging because he knew it was not going to be pretty.

Sunlight and Dappled Shade

"I want to hear what's going on so no one is going anywhere," Megan said leaning back in her chair.

"Don't start what, Tayo? Man shut the hell up if you don't have anything to say that I want to hear. It's been a secret for too long."

No, please, don't, Rory. The words formed on Alex's lips but there was no sound. She silently pleaded with him, begging him to stop. He was about to blow her up in front of everybody.

"What everybody in here doesn't know is that Alex is my wife. She is already married to me. We have been married so you see, she is not free to be anyone's wife but mine."

He saw the shock and stunned look on the faces of the people sitting around. He was done playing Mr. Nice Guy. If she wanted to pretend that she is an innocent he was not about to help her especially when they were touting some man she was messing with right here in front of his face. He was pissed.

It had every bit the effect he wanted it to.

Now he had everyone's attention. They were all sitting completely still in their seats as if they were watching an interesting movie, waiting for an answer. Her mother, her grandmother, Miss Etty all were watching goggle-eyed at the scene unfolding before them.

"Come again, Rory. Alex is married to you and all these years she never said a word to me and I am her friend?" Ciarra was the first person to say a word.

Rory had really thought that Alex loved him, that they shared this unbelievable bond. He had given her time to grow and mature because he loved her, but apparently what she had felt for him was a flirtation kinda love. Here today, gone tomorrow. She had married him in an act of lunacy because she was pregnant and scared of what her grandmother and her family and friends would say; an act she had regretted from the very beginning.

Yes, Alejandro would appeal to her. The tall, light skinned basketball player. She would always be in the spotlight, not to mention the status she would get from marrying such a man.

"I don't know about the rest of you but while I am waiting for answers I need another drink." Octavius shuffled over to the bar pouring himself a drink. "Etty, anyone want a drink?"

"Is it true, Alex? Are you married to Rory?" Auntie asked.

For a minute Rory felt a twist of pity as he saw Alex struggle to answer but then it was gone. If she was too ashamed to tell the truth then too bad. But then her head went up and her eyes flashed.

"Yes, it is true. We were married five years ago. I was pregnant," Alex answered quietly.

If Rory thought that his words had created silence it was nothing now like the freezing silence that had descended and Octavius began singing *tra la la,lalalalala la.*

Megan rounded on Alex.

"I can't believe we are friends and you two kept such a secret all these years and never said a word to anyone. Were you ever going to let us in on this secret?"

"I don't know if the marriage was really real or not. I'll tell you about it later," Alex said wearily.

"I am with Megan on this one," Ciarra said. "I can't believe you of all people was so deceptive Alex. Pretending you were so perfect and that you weren't married and now you are engaged to someone else."

For a minute Alex thought she was going to lose it.

"I am not engaged to anyone. Case closed. I might be dating the guy but not engaged," Alex snapped.

"Engaged. Whatever."

His shoulders stiffened and his eyes were boring into hers and all she could remember at the moment was Rory's eyes looking down into hers, the scent of his skin, the touch of his hands that first night in the cave when they almost went all the way, those sensual lips of his on hers. She could almost taste it.

"Alex."

She knew that tone. Knew by the way Rory said her name that he felt it too. She squirmed in her chair.

"So where did you two pretenders get married?" Ciarra interrupted. "And you more so than Rory is a pretender Alex. Fletcher don't be eating too much of that pork. It's not good for you," Ciarra barked as the little boy stuffed his mouth with roast pork

"Oh come on, Ciarra, let the child eat. He has a healthy appetite and it is Christmas." Tayo answered. "Come little fellow, you have food all over your face. Let me wipe your mouth."

"It's my child and I tell him what to do."

Andrea stood up.

"Fletcher and all you other kids go on outside for a moment. You know, Ciarra. You have been dumping on Alex since you found out that she is married and didn't tell any of you, but she kept her secret about herself. What about you, lying about *your* child?"

Andrea turned to Tayo.

"Fletcher is your son and it is time that Ciarra let you be a father to your son. She is sitting up in here behaving as if she is some chris miss. You are not no better than anybody in here, Ciarra. So start fessing up."

Alex was reaching for the Sorrel but her hand stopped midway. Megan's eyes were glued to her plate but the old folks looked on with interest, waiting for the pin to drop. It was getting more interesting by the minute.

Tayo turned around to look at Andrea and wiped his mouth with a napkin.

"Stop playing. I have asked Ciarra over and over if he is mine and she said no. Why would you say such a thing anyway?"

Andrea sucked her teeth.

"See, what she won't tell you is that Fletcher is your son and she has been pretending that he is not yours. Ask your other friends, they know."

She tipped the glass of Sorrel laced with rum that she had been drinking all evening to her mouth. There is a saying that whatever is hidden in the dark will one day be revealed.

"Is Andrea telling the truth, Ciarra? Answer me dammit," Tayo demanded.

"You bitch, Andrea. You hate me because I made it and you didn't."

Ciarra threw herself at Andrea but Andrea was waiting and smacked her. Ciarra hauled back and retaliated and the fight was on.

"I have been waiting to do that for a long time to knock some sense into you, Ciarra. Get off your pumps and pride. I have never lied about my baby daddy but you have."

They grabbed at each other, knocking into the table. Tayo dragged at Ciarra's arm.

"Is that the truth? Fletcher is mine and you have lied to me all this time? You frigging hypocrite, walking around and behaving as if I am the scum off your feet because I am a womanizer according to you. I could strangle you with my bare hands."

Megan's date sat looking on.

"Jesus, can't you guys act civilized for a change. We have visitors among us who doesn't want to hear about our dirty laundry." Megan's voice was brittle.

"Oh shut the hell up Megan. We kept it quiet that you had become a pill junkie. We helped you to get off that shit without anyone knowing. The day that you thought that Neil had slept with Andrea you were filled with jealousy and rage and don't you forget that you slept with Andrea's man as payback for her coming on to Neil so shut the hell up," Ciarra was screaming.

"Hey Tayo, let's take a walk outside," Andy suggested. "We don't want things to get out of hand."

Tayo shook off Andy's arm.

"It's already gotten ugly up in here. Rory, did you know about this?"

"No I didn't and I would have told you if I did. Believe me," Rory answered.

The thing with secrets is that no matter what you do, they will come to light and with Tayo standing there with that angry look on his face things were bound to get worse. Megan jumped up angrily.

"That was a long time ago. That has nothing to do with the fact that you lied to Tayo about Fletcher not being his. You chose to lie about it."

Neil was looking at Megan with a strange look on his face.

"You were angry, Megan because you thought I liked Andrea? I thought you said you didn't give a rat's ass who I banged."

"Oh for crying out loud, shut the hell up, Neil and don't say a word to me."

Miss Etty listened to the stories being thrown back and forth but not once did they divulge the secret that they all shared about the cave. They kept their silence. Auntie was mulling over the revelation that Alex had not shared any information about being married to Rory and neither had he told his parents. These kids sure knew how to keep a secret.

Miss Etty finally stood up, clapping her hands, bringing the attention to herself.

"Much has been said tonight and there is a whole heap of fences to mend and relationships to work on. Dinner is not over so no one is expected to leave."

She watched from the corner of her eyes as Tayo followed Ciarra out the door. She sat down as all the older ladies whispered among themselves.

"Let the young try and work out their differences but of course they needed to be pushed without them thinking that they were being pushed."

-Chapter 25-

There was a whole lot of blame to go around and the fallout between friends was huge. Rory wanted to throttle Alex for supposedly getting engaged to some man. Alex lashed right back accusing him of having constant bed partners. It was a mess. Auntie tried to talk to Alex but didn't get a straight answer, only a jumble of events; Octavius was playing referee between Ciarra and Tayo. Major headaches were going all around.

All the girls were thinking that their mistakes were not as huge as the other and pointing fingers. It was Rory who just could not deal with hearing that Alex was engaged that drew first blood. For sure they would all be at the Charity Ball and his calculated move was to walk in with no other than Lindsay, because of all the women in the world Lindsay was the last person on earth Alex would want to see him with.

It took a lot of time, money and effort to organize one of these impressive events which would be held the following night. Megan had worked hard to make the ball a success and it would have been impossible to pull it all together without the help of her friends. She knew it and accepted it that their lives were all intertwined. Ciarra, Rory, Tayo, Alex, Andy, Neil, their lives were always tied together no matter how much falling out there was among them. They always found their way back to each other.

Today on the eve of her event Megan was having lunch with some of her well heeled friends who had flown in for the occasion. From the balcony of the restaurant located on the water by Freeport they had a view that was breathtaking and magical. The sun shone and the wine flowed and the conversation which started out on a quiet note eventually took on a raucous tone. As she slid the last piece of pawpaw into her mouth, Megan leaned across the table and said in a dramatic voice:

"Now that we are done drinking we are going out."

Sharone, one of the biggest movie stars in the United States, stared at her in surprise.

"We are?"

Megan nodded.

"We are going to visit the Children's Hospital that this benefit is in aid of. It will be a good opportunity for you to see for yourselves why it is so important for such an organization to continue to receive your help."

They arrived at the hospital and were greeted by the nurses who gave Megan and each of her visitors a welcoming hug. Once inside they were given a tour from ward to ward and room to room. At one point Sister Chris, the singer, gave an impromptu concert and had the children clapping and laughing all over.

It was late when they finally left and Megan could see that the children had made an impression on her guests. Megan bit her lip and tried to imagine what Alex must have gone through when she had lost her baby. There were babies and older children dying because drugs and surgery cost a huge amount of money that many could not afford. She could only imagine the agony parents go through everyday. Yet the staff had been pleasant, smiling and easy to talk to.

"These children are so brave and fearless. They deserve all the help they can get," Sharone said as she dabbed at her eyes.

"That is why I host this charity event," Megan answered. "The least we can do is make sure that they have the resources and the comfort available to them to alleviate the situation."

They stood with other elegantly dressed guests on the deck as the boat glided through the water as the Sandals Island located on the Rose Hall coast in Montego Bay came into view. Since the Christmas dinner there had been tension between Megan and her new man Dr. Marcus. She had never told him that she had a problem with painkillers after she had hurt her knee running hurdles some years ago and he was not pleased that she had not trusted him enough to talk to him about this. She had been pissed off with Ciarra and the lot of them but tonight all those negative vibes were on hold. There was no way she could have done all this without the help of Ciarra, Alex or Rory or Tayo and the rest of her little *posse*.

Tonight Megan was surrounded by the very rich and some very beautiful people. There were glamorous Hollywood stars mingling with the locals, celebrities and the Jamaican aristocracy, international athletes, foreign and local singers were all out to support the annual Jamaican Children's Charity Fund.

Megan lifted her face to the breeze. She had the feeling that this evening was going to be extra special. She looked dazzling in this masterpiece of a dress. The straps were slender and the neckline scooped low. The back plunged to her waist showing well toned smooth skin. The fabric hugged her waist and then tumbled to the floor. On her feet she wore gold strappy heels. The look in Marcus's eyes when she opened the door made her feel amazing. He was staring into the distance, his arms on the guardrail. She wished she could read his mind.

"Do you do many of these charities?" Marcus asked suddenly.

"One or two. This one I do for the Children's Hospital every year. I realized that I could use my status as an athlete to do something more for my people," Megan explained.

He gave a brief smile.

"By the way, did I tell you that you look spectacular in that dress?"

She moved closer.

"Should I mention how easy it is to remove it?"

He stared at Megan, his eyes shining with desire.

"You are pure evil," he said softly. "I'll take up the offer later."

The sound of music and chatter floated through the air as the boat docked and they walked along the gang plank. There were softly glowing lanterns and fairy lights and the tiny island took on a quality of enchantment.

"Megan!"

She jerked to a stop causing Marcus to crash into her back, almost knocking her off balance. Sam Chin was bearing down on her and she was not happy.

"Hi Megan. You look fantastic by the way. I figure we would run into each other tonight."

He looked from her to Marcus who was standing quietly looking on.

"Sam, this is Marcus my date and Marcus this is Sam." She didn't elaborate. "Anyway I have to go. It was good seeing you. Make sure you spend some money tonight."

"Seeing it's for a good cause I will but even better how about I spend some on you?" Sam answered.

"Look I have to go but have a good time."

Marcus took Megan's hand as she proceeded along the path.

"For an ex he is pretty territorial," Marcus remarked.

"Forget him. He is the past. My interest no longer lies there. I am here with you and that makes me happy," Megan reassured.

No expense had been spared, with donations from various sponsors such as jewelry, trips, cruises, designer clothes, and gift certificates for spa treatments. As her guests walked up the path to the Indonesia themed restaurant and grand ballroom they were greeted with a glass of champagne or mimosas of their choice by waiters who stood in attendance. Little expense had been spared in providing an assortment of food, champagne, fine wine, top shelf liquor for the expensive ticket price.

There were colorful stalls set up in a semi circle along the shore from various cultures including Thai, Indian, Jamaican, and Japanese. Pre dinner drinks provided an excellent opportunity for committee members to work the party before entering the Thai restaurant with its soaring, flaming roof. At the end of the circle was a tent decorated like a private showroom with autographed T shirts from athletes, baseballs from famous players, jewelry in glass cabinets that held necklaces, earrings, bracelets, diamonds, sapphire where the auction was in progress.

Then there was an explosion above and everyone was staring at the sky and pointing to the fireworks which marked the beginning of the celebration. Mouth watering scent of food teased their nostrils. Marion, the director of the charity hurried over and immediately dragged Megan towards a display cabinet and removed a pair of diamond earrings, two carats at least.

"These are the earrings that you will be modeling tonight and it compliments this helluva dress you are wearing from Ciarra's creations."

Marcus looked at Megan with a question on his face.

"I am one of the models who will be wearing certain pieces of jewelery to attract attention. The idea is that when someone with a lot of money to spend sees how amazing these diamonds are and how beautiful this dress is they won't be able to resist buying them."

The media was in attendance and as Megan stepped into the centre of the ballroom welcoming everyone, cameras clicked away. Her message was heartfelt, asking everyone to help the children who suffer from birth defects, cancer, for those who are unable to afford the basic healthcare. She thanked everyone for coming, the guests, the committee, the sponsors, her friends and everyone involved in making this night happen.

There was a round of applause and then someone shouted.

"Who designed your dress, Megan?"

"It is designed by Ciarra from Klein's Creations."

As they moved across the floor, Megan introduced Marcus to people she knew and took the comments in stride that they looked good together.

"Your charity lady is trying to get your attention. I think it's time for you to go strut your stuff," Marcus remarked. He lowered his head, kissing her on the lips. "That's for luck and this one is for me," as he kissed her again.

Megan was smiling as she walked over to the woman with the clip board who steered her towards the group of women decked out in jewelry for sale. But the smile faded as Rory stepped into the room with a woman on his arm. Megan's eyes travelled to the spot where Alex and Ciarra were standing, following their eyes as they watched Rory walk in. She saw Alex move and prayed that she wasn't about to do something stupid.

The lights were dimmed just in time and then music flooded the room and the women sauntered to the front of the room. The spotlight illuminated Megan's radiance and the diamonds sparkled against her ears. All eyes were focused on the beautiful Megan standing in the center of the room. There was ripple of applause as the lights came up and Megan joined Marcus at the table.

"You were simply marvelous," Marcus bent his head even closer to her ear. "I can't wait to eat you all up."

"Sounds good to me," Megan answered, "but right now I am famished and furious," she added. There was going to be fireworks of a different kind before the end of the evening.

Alex could only stare at Rory in fury. Her thoughts suddenly ground to a standstill. Her heart did the same thing, every muscle she possessed locked tight and her eyes locked onto the woman with Rory. She watched Rory walk towards her with that devil-may-care look in his eyes and then he stopped in front of her; and then the look was gone. He bent and kissed Ciarra on the cheek while his date looked on with amusement written all over her pretty face.

"Hi, Alex, no date tonight? Where is the fiancé?"

The sizzling spit of Alex's anger held her prisoner. Mad feelings were running riot inside her. Her husband out in public with another woman, standing right in front of her, embarrassing her now that everyone knew. Rory took her hand and kissed her palm.

"You look beautiful as always, wife," he whispered in her ear before walking to the table.

He turned and looked at her before pulling out a chair for Lindsay. Hurt and jealousy was eating her up.

"Alex, get a grip, I can see steam coming out of your ears. What are you thinking and what is the plan?" Ciarra asked.

"I think I should deliberately spill some wine all over that nice looking shirt he is wearing."

Ciarra was trying not to laugh too hard at her friend.

"Weren't you the one who said you wanted nothing to do with Rory because he didn't have to tell the whole world you were married and all you wanted from him is a divorce?"

"Oh shut the hell up, Ciarra," Alex said angrily before storming off.

By the time the meal ended, excitement for the auction had reached fever pitch. The sound of a gavel hitting a table echoed around the room signifying the start of the auction. The bidding was spirited and there were many attempts between Sam and Marcus to outdo each other.

Alex watched as Rory stood up and left the table. She gave him a few minutes before she went after him.

"Keep his woman occupied, Ciarra, while I go do my thing," Alex whispered.

There was something different about this little island in Montego Bay where high society functions were sometimes held. No matter where you looked your gaze fell on the sea, the elegant building overlooking. Rory was standing in the dark looking out towards the water when Alex found him.

His eyes turned to her, steady, without a hint of apology.

"What do you want?" he asked roughly.

"So I see you are moving on, another woman on your arms if you like the bony type."

Rory laughed out loud.

"Alex, you followed me out here didn't you? Let's see… you wouldn't be jealous now, would you? Just the other day you were adamant about wanting a divorce."

"You are laughing at me Rory. How dare you?"

Alex went for his face. She was going to claw his eyes out. She did not care who saw or what the end result was. He caught her arms and she fought him like the hellcat she had always been. She lost the battle.

"Let me go. Don't touch me," she screeched.

It was so unexpected that before she even realized what was happening he had her up against him in a tight embrace and was in full, burning possession of her mouth. She was alive, that burning, dormant, seething cauldron of emotions spilling over and just as suddenly he pushed her away from him.

"I have proven my point, Alex, you can't stay away from me can you? You haven't quite gotten me out of your system, hmm?" He laughed, mocking her.

She was breathing hard.

"And so have I," she taunted right back. "You can't seem to keep your hands off me, can you?"

She smiled her brilliant smile before turning and walking away with her hips swinging. Rory watched her go. Being around Alex was never boring. He caught himself, dammit. What was the matter him?

-Chapter 26-

iarra's hand tightened around the doorknob, her pulse racing with a sense of dread. She rattled the door knob but the door refused to budge. Tayo had locked her in. She strained to hear if there was any movement outside the door but all was quiet. She was furious at herself for listening to her mom and coming here to talk to Tayo. She had followed him into his room when he refused to listen to her argument.

"I am going to ask you again, Ciarra. Is Fletcher my son?"

She bit her lip. An awful quiet hummed between them.

"Yes, he is your son and you damn well and know it too," she answered sulkily.

He looked angry enough to kill her with his bare hands and at that moment she wouldn't blame him.

"You are saying that I knew that he was my son? That's the way you are going to play this?" He slammed his hand on the dresser. "Do you have any idea what you have done to me, depriving me of my son for all these years? How could you be so evil?"

"I was going to tell you at the beginning but that's the same time when your bitch supposedly got pregnant. I was pissed and I wasn't thinking of the consequences and then I was going to tell you after that but somehow I never got around to it."

He shook his head and his mouth pulled into a grim smile.

"I can't believe I put you up on a pedestal all these years and you played me for a fool. I played around a lot and I was wrong but of all these women I loved you more than life itself. Maybe I played because I feared the power you had over me and I ran sometimes. You left me and you made a name for yourself but to punish me with my son..."

Without another word he turned and left the room closing the door and locking it behind him. Ciarra ran to the door, grabbing onto the knob. The door wouldn't budge.

"Tayo!!! Tayo," she was screaming. "Open this door right now. I am not done with the argument. Open the door, you asshole."

She pounded harder.

"This is kidnapping. I am going to have them throw your ass in jail if you don't open the door. Okay, I was jealous because you were screwing around and you were so happy about it and I got carried away."

"I am done talking to you, Ciarra," he shouted back.

"You can't keep me locked up in here forever and you know what I am going to do when you open the door? I am going to kick your ass."

"Really, Ciarra? You still have a terrible mouth. I thought you had grown up into a lady." She hated him at this moment like no other. She picked up the first thing and threw it at the door. The small vase shattered into a million pieces.

Tayo stood outside the door listening. He had not meant to lock her in but if he hadn't he would have her on that bed and his tongue in her mouth. She was his weakness; but she had made a fool out of him and now he wanted to anger, frustrate and punish her.

He was as hard as a rock and if he touched her he knew the urge to possess and to hold her would be stronger than ever.

She was a tigress. He moistened his lips as he remembered the last time they had been together. He had to lock her in to keep her from getting up in his face. This time he would not be able to walk away. He had played around but kept his heart intact. Ciarra was his heartbreaker. It was a bitter pill to swallow but she was the one.

All was quiet. He gently unlocked the door and stuck his neck in. She flew at him, grabbing for his shirt; but he was faster. He picked her up in his arms but she kicked and struggled, twisting in his grip and throwing him off balance so that he stumbled. They fell onto the carpet together, Tayo taking the brunt of it. A moment later he flipped her and she found herself on her back.

"Stop fighting me, Ciarra," he said in a harsh tone. "You are going to bring my son to live with me and if you want you can come too."

Rage and disbelief chased across her face. She wriggled beneath him but he didn't budge.

"You have got to be kidding. There is no way I am giving you my son and you are so out a line. What do you mean I can come too as if I am nobody?"

He grabbed her arms, forcing them above her head. He seemed to be on the brink of losing control.

"My son belongs with me. I need to raise my son."

"Okay, you can see him anytime you want to. Liberal visitation but he stays with me."

Sunlight and Dappled Shade

She arched her back and flexed her body upward shoving into the cradle of his. She felt his erection pressing into her sending fire through her body.

"Not good enough?" he answered. "You and my son come live with me."

He exhaled as she bucked against him. He wanted her. He bent his head and tasted her lips. His lips grazed the shell of her ear. He ran his tongue over the seam of her lips. She opened to him and his tongue invaded, tangling with hers.

She moved under him.

"Stop moving or we'll have to move to the bed."

She reasserted herself and tried to throw him off.

"Get off me."

"Your wish is my command," he answered and bounded up leaving her to get up by herself.

"I am serious about my son coming to live with me."

There was a knock on the door. He heard the intake of her breath and braced himself for whatever was going to come out of her mouth.

"That should be Megan with Fletcher. I didn't get around to telling you that I had asked her to bring him over."

He opened the door and Megan entered with Fletcher interrupting whatever he was about to say. Megan must have been telling him something because he was laughing.

"Mommy!" he cried. "I was just telling Aunt Megan a duppy story and she got scared. You are not afraid of duppy stories are you Uncle Tayo?"

Ciarra hugged him close, kissing him on his head. He started to squirm and she let him go. She licked her lips nervously.

"Sweetheart I have something to tell you. You love Uncle Tayo don't you?"

"Mommy, of course, Uncle Tayo is the coolest. Right, Uncle?"

Tayo reached and touched Fletcher's cheek and she didn't try to stop him. A mixture of pain and anger played across his face.

"Fletcher, I know you have called Tayo uncle all this time but I should have told you that he is your dad."

"He is my real dad and not uncle?"

Tayo bent to his level and held his hand.

"I didn't know I was your father until recently but I have always loved you as my son."

He dropped to his knees and held out his arms and Fletcher ran headlong into them. "I love you Fletcher and I will always be here for you," Tayo said, hugging him tightly.

"You are squeezing me too hard, Uncle Tayo. I mean daddy. Can I call you dad?" Fletcher asked.

"Of course you can call me dad. I would be really happy if you do."

The next few days were some of the most idyllic of his life. Tayo spent time with Ciarra and his son without any expectations but he continued his slow seduction of Ciarra's mind and body, taking his own time. He enjoyed brushing against her, touching her while pretending that his actions weren't deliberate.

The dance was driving him crazy but he was satisfied that he was driving her crazy also. Most importantly he was becoming more comfortable with his son. He tickled him, made faces, played with him. For the first time in his life Tayo felt content with being with one woman and his child. But time was up. Ciarra had deadlines to meet for her clothing line and he had to get back to work.

-Chapter 27-

Dressed in a light cream jacket and a pencil skirt, Alex sat on the tiny marble head stone of her son's grave. She had left parliament after the meetings and her uncle had flown her directly by helicopter to Bell Town. She ran her fingers along the engraving of his name on the headstone, gleaming white in the sun. Today was the anniversary of his death. She felt vaguely ill, no big surprise; the flu was going around. She probably had it too but she couldn't afford to give in to it right now. There was too much to get done. Alex sighed.

"Little one, I have so much to tell you. I made the mistake of not telling your grandmother and your great grandmother that I was married to your father. You can imagine what happened in the family meeting. I have to take responsibility for my part in this drama and I was reminded that I have a gift, the gift of bringing people together, of being a leader and that's it time I brought my butt home. Well I have been announced as a candidate for North East Westmoreland for the next general election."

She rested her arms on her thighs and looked around. She felt her eyes mist. Her heart swelled with the love she had felt for this little boy who had stayed with her for only a moment. He was happy, free from the needles and pain of suffering. She wished he was here but she hadn't wanted to prolong his suffering to make her feel better. That would have been selfish. He was somewhere standing guard as an angel to some little kid in need.

It had been tough watching them lay his little body in the small wooden coffin in preparation for the trip to the home he would never know. His tiny face had not had time to form itself but to her he looked so much like Rory. When she had arrived in Bell Town after the long flight from New York to bury her baby, no one but herself and Rory had stood at the graveside that misty afternoon. Alex, dressed in black with a wide-brimmed black hat on her head, had stood dry-eyed watching them lower him into the dark hole. Rory had stood on the other side of the grave. She had felt her knees buckle for a moment but had resolved not to weep. Her little angel had come to touch her life for a moment. And now he was gone. Alex had slipped out of Bell Town as quietly as she had arrived.

The graves were well tended and flowers bloomed hot and bright under the tropical sun; Sunlight and Dappled Shade. Birds and butterflies flitted around and the air was filled with the scent of jasmine. In her opinion there was nowhere more beautiful than Jamaica and she had wonderful memories growing up here. Why run away and leave it?

It was also muddled and confused. She had decisions to make and actions to back up whatever she decided. She jumped as a shadow suddenly fell across the sun. She squinted as she looked up. It was Rory.

"I hope I didn't scare you. I know how afraid you are of ghosts," Rory chuckled.

"That was when we were growing up. Not any more," she mumbled. "What are you doing here?"

He shifted his stance.

"He was my son too so I visit every year as you do on this day."

"I thought you went back to Atlanta," she answered.

"That's why there is a thing called airplanes so that one can travel between worlds." Rory pushed his hands in his pocket.

Drawing in a breath, Alex stood up and walked towards the chapel. After a few minutes Rory followed, making the back of her neck tingle. They used to spend so much time in this church yard and in this school yard.

Until now Alex had wrapped herself in the knowledge that she had moved on. She had a different life, a career she loved and a hot boyfriend. New York had gotten a hold on her but yet it was as if she was hiding from who she really was. Nothing compared to her life here and no man had even come close to Rory and the feelings for him she had locked away somewhere.

Looking into Rory's face with the sun in her eyes she felt the full impact of this new Rory with shock. Gone was the younger Rory she had fallen in love with. The new mature Rory. The mouth that she had kissed so many times before now had a hardness about it that gave her a chill. He was totally and devastatingly handsome. He was lean both physically on the inside and outside where it showed by the way he spoke and the aura she was picking up.

She didn't realize she was staring at the man in the sharply tailored suit in some expensive fabric that made such a statement about his wealth and how comfortable he was with the stunning sophistication with which he wore it.

"Do I have food in my teeth or something on my face?" Rory asked. "You are staring."

She pulled air into her lungs and forced herself to concentrate on what he had just said.

"No, you are fine. I was just thinking that our baby looked like you and you would have been good a father."

His body tensed inside that elegant suit.

"I cannot believe that you were not even aware that I visit my son." Something rippled across his face. "You walked away from me as soon as our son was buried and you hid yourself away refusing to see me, not taking my calls."

She touched his arm.

"I needed to be alone."

"Because you blamed me. You told me that I killed our child and that hurt deep down where I thought I would never feel such pain. Although I am a man, Alex, I do hurt you know." Rory removed his hand from his pocket.

Alex held onto his arm.

"I didn't really blame you and I don't. I am sorry for the things I said. I was just lashing out. I couldn't help thinking that you blamed me also." She let go of his arm and looked at her watch. "I am going to say goodbye now to our little boy."

Rory watched her walk away, his eyes narrowed. Blame her. He had never blamed. How could she possibly think that he would have blamed her?

Turning around, he saw she was about to bend down after kissing her finger tips before gently pressing them to her son's head stone. His throat tightened and he walked over, sliding his arm around her waist.

"Your mommy and your daddy love you and she wanted me to tell you that she is involved in government and you know what? Give it a few years she will be the Prime Minister of Jamaica." He touched his fingers to his lips and then touched the headstone.

"So what next, where do we go from here?" Rory asked as they left the grave.

The warm, familiar scent of him swirled around her senses; the hot sun pelted down on his bare head reminding her of the many times she had rubbed his head when he pretended he had a headache from the hot sun. She tried to relax but could not.

"We could speak to the Reverend about renewing our vows, doing it right, giving the people a wedding that they would love to see," Rory said smoothly.

The totally unexpected comment stopped Alex in her tracks.

"What? I am going to ignore that."

"I take it that for the moment this is not to your liking," he responded lightly.

She didn't feel like behaving anymore.

"I thought you would be running to get married to the woman you left in Atlanta." "Oops, we are still married. You would have to give me a divorce before I could marry anyone." His arm was still around her waist.

She wrenched her arm from him.

"Divorce..?"

For all the time that she had battled with letting go of the past she had never thought about divorce. It had not so much as entered her head. Divorce, she repeated to herself. It was sensible. It would bring closure to everything, freeing them to go on with their lives; but she was turned inside out.

Rory turned to face her, his hands coming to rest on her shoulder.

"Stop trembling, I am teasing. Come here."

He pulled her into his arms and held her there for a few minutes.

"Let's talk about your nomination for Member of Parliament because you are going to have all of our support. Tayo, Megan, Ciarra, everyone so after all the drama over Christmas we all have to pull together for this."

They walked towards the car park.

"I am already being attacked. There are discussions about my eligibility, my capability as a politician. People have been looking for my name on the voters list. I might have been away but my name is on the voting list. My uncle has always made sure of that so they can always search for dirt. One person wrote that I was born with a gold spoon in my mouth and questioning what do I know about rural life or my constituency."

Rory threw back his head and began to laugh.

"Ignoramuses they are. You of all the politicians do know what your constituents need. You grew up here and you have moved between two worlds for as long as I have known you. Country and town. It is funny because one of my fond memories with you and the rest of the crew is taking that ganja from that cave but even more so was that first night that we got carried away in that cave. Can you imagine if anyone should find about our adventures? They would have a field day."

Perspiration broke out on Alex's forehead. She stumbled. Rory stretched out his arm to steady her.

"Are you okay Alex? You don't look too well."

Alex grimaced. Her stomach rumbled. She was thirsty and hungry, not having had breakfast. As a matter of fact, she had not been eating or sleeping well these last days. Rory gave her a strange look.

"Seems as if you didn't have the good sense not to get pregnant by some playboy baseball player. This is exactly how you use to look when you got pregnant with my baby. If you are then you are on your own. You will have to call someone else to pick you up."

Car tires crunched over gravel as Rory sped off leaving her there.

"I am not pregnant, you fool," she shouted.

A few seconds later he screeched to a halt at her feet as he backed up.

"Get in."

Heat flooded her face as she slid in. He sent her a cool glance as the car picked up speed, all slick and smooth she observed with some resentment.

"I am hungry. I haven't eaten and I missed dinner last night," she explained.

Sunlight and Dappled Shade

A few minutes later they were turning into the drive leading up to his house. They came to a stop and the engine died. Rory climbed out of the car, coming around to her side and opening the door. She just sat there refusing to move.

He pulled her from the car.

"I really hope you aren't pregnant but for now let's go so I can get some food into you before you pass out on me."

She realized that Rory was holding on to his temper. Barely.

"I am not pregnant and there is no way that I could be pregnant and that is all I am going to say right now. Let go of my arm," she protested. She was tired and achy.

He did not loosen his grip but kept walking toward his house. He turned the key in the lock before pulling her inside and slamming the door. Then he strode off, leaving her there.

Miss Gloria came down the stairs a few minutes later.

"I had the blender going so I didn't hear the car. Sit down Alex before you pass out. I will be right back with some tea and something for you to eat. You poor child."

She rubbed at her arm while glancing around. She had never been to this house before. She was standing in a spacious living room with rooms leading off from both sides. With her curiosity getting the better of her she began peering into rooms. Not all were furnished. She walked down the steps which took her into another room where she could hear a kettle whistling. It was a kitchen. A huge, airy kitchen painted in cream.

"Come Alex, here is your tea, drink up and I have a chicken sandwich to go with that."

"Thank you Gloria, I am starving."

She sipped at her tea, thankful for something to eat. Rory walked into the kitchen minus his jacket. She couldn't help noticing his flat stomach and his long legs.

"Are you feeling any better because if you aren't I can take you to the doctor."

She didn't want to admit that she was ill. The room was spinning around and around.

Miss Gloria touched Alex forehead and exclaimed:

"Oh Jesus, she is burning up. Let me go get her some fever grass tea and in the mean time she need to lay down and rest."

From far away Alex heard Rory's voice.

"Dammit, Alex, you should have said something. You have a fever."

He lifted her from the table, bringing her to a bedroom.

"There I was thinking that I would have to strangle you if you had gotten pregnant for another man."

A few seconds later and she felt the soft bed with the cool touch of sheets beneath her. Gloria hovered nearby with a glass of water in one hand and a small pill in the palm of the other hand.

"Here take this, sweetie." She placed the glass to her lips.

"Thanks," she muttered as she swallowed the pill before sinking down on the pillows and rolling to one side of the bed.

Sunlight and Dappled Shade

She opened her eyes to find Rory sitting on the bed. He slid in beside her. Pulling her close to him, he held her until she fell asleep. Rory stared down at her sleeping face. Then he bent and placed his lips against hers. Slowly he rose and quietly left the room.

-Chapter 28-

Rory and his partner had been involved in wall to wall meetings with architects, builders and government officials for the last week in the Cayman Islands regarding the acquisition of a hotel. After the hectic negotiations and plans of the last few days, today was wind down day. For many the weekend was a time for relaxation, to take time out for family and friends, to catch up on what's going on.

It felt good to kick back with his friends that he had started out with. They had been carefree, reckless and broke but determined to succeed in whatever they choose. They had had some rough times but now things were level. He had moved back to Jamaica and had his office in New Kingston.

The sun was warm on the terrace as the group sat around shooting the breeze. Tayo sat with his feet propped up on a table while Megan reclined in an easy chair. Fletcher and his cousins were on the lawn kicking ball and having fun.

"I live all the way in Montego Bay and my ass got here before Alex. I don't believe that girl. This is Grovesnor Terrace, Manor Park last time I checked and it is not too far from where she is living and she hasn't put in an appearance as of yet," Ciarra complained.

"We are the early ones. Neil and Andy isn't here yet as usual. I swear they are the last to get anywhere and the last to leave." Tayo put in his two pence into the conversation. "I am sitting here for the rest of the day and I am sleeping right here too."

"Talk about the devil and here she is," Ciarra said as Alex screeched to a halt in front of the driveway.

She waved as she exited the car, looking up at the house. Large windows made the most of the view looking out over beautiful manicured grounds and garden. There was a beautiful stone fountain at the entrance to the garden. Rory watched her as she came through the gate wearing a pretty strapless sun dress. He was done playing games with her. He intended to take back what he had lost. He had given her time and he had sorted out his life, making way for what he planned for her.

"I see that look in your eyes, Rory, is there something you want to share with us all? Anyway it's time for you both to be serious. Let me know if you need my help," Ciarra said as she made a face.

As Alex stepped up on the terrace, Tayo greeted her.

"Hey Miss Member of Parliament. You kept your constituents waiting. Don't let it happen again." He handed her a glass of wine. "Come sit here in my chair. After all it's going to be your house soon."

Alex rolled her eyes at Tayo.

"What are you babbling about as usual?" She poked him in the head. "I don't know what you are talking about. Hey lazy people, that means you Ciarra, Megan and Andrea. What do you all have here to eat? I am hungry. I have been working on a case and got side tracked."

Rory looked at Ciarra.

"I told you she was going to be hungry. We have some ribs and chicken on the grill and just for you there is escoveitched fish and festival. Gloria fix us up with food."

"So," Alex said and sat on Tayo's lap before he could get up. "What's been going on, my friend?"

"You have more to tell now that the people have voted for you and you are officially Member of Parliament. I can't tell you how happy I am to have somebody in the political arena."

He gave Alex a big kiss. She slapped him and stood up.

"I am not talking about me. I am talking about you and Ciarra so don't avoid the question. And you back on campus doing your Masters degree." Alex held up her glass. "More power to you."

"Hey Alex, let's propose a toast." Ciarra held up her glass. "Here is to us, and health and wisdom to figure it all out. But I have to say I am proud of you. You are on your way to be Prime Minister."

"Here, here."

Glasses clinked and Rory kissed her smack on the mouth.

"To my woman. Much success."

Alex kept silent as there was a 'Here! Here!' to that.

"So, Megan, you started your own public relations firm? Here's to you, girl. Much love and all that. So how is Marcus, why isn't he here?" Alex asked.

"I can answer that," Ciarra said. "It's because Neil is coming, that's why. So don't even bother to front."

Megan sucked her teeth.

"You know too damn much, Ciarra, that is your problem," Megan accused.

"Yep, that's what I am here for, to know what's going on. Tell the truth, Megan, of all the guys you did it with Neil was the hottest, right?"

Megan didn't have to answer because Neil was walking up the steps.

Ciarra continued:

"Anyway, you all people. You heard it here first. I am quitting Klein's Creations and launching my own fashion house. I can't work at Klein any more. There is too much tension and if I am not careful I am going to have to beat Mitzie to a pulp and Tayo might suffer since he is my baby father and he is going to have to take care of Fletcher if I am sent to jail."

"It's about frigging time," Tayo quipped. "I get heartburn every time I think about your people over there and you know that I am talking about Klein and his dumb ass wife. I don't know who that guy hasn't screwed. You are way too talented to take whatever they dish out to you."

It was a good thing that Neil and Andy came in then one after the other and greeted everyone, changing the conversation. Andy couldn't leave the roast pork behind so he carted a big tray with him. Alex slapped hands with Andy because she loved the pork as much as he did.

Megan propped the pillow behind her head and leaned back on the beach chair.

"Let's talk politics. The General Election will be in another say four years and we want to see Alex as Prime Minister so we all need to strategize as to what we are going to do to make this happen."

Partisan politics is embedded into the very fibre and being of the Jamaican people. Those who are of the

Jamaica National Party called Nationalites are die hard members and those who are of the People's Leading Party called Socialists will live and die as the members they are. This is more entrenched in the older generation. Now those from the modern school of thought whose parents sent them to school to become educated are more in favor of the leader with the best rhetoric as to what changes they will make if they are elected as Prime Minister.

Alex kept much of her thoughts to herself while stumping for office. She understood what loyalty was for those who grew up in another era. Bustamante and Norman Manley created changes for many back then that the younger generation would never understand and so they would never cross the bridge to another party. Miss Etty and Mass Octavius, and her grandmother, represented a few of those people so she didn't set about knocking those for their stand. Miss Etty had told her to "understand the thinking of all will guide you in your quest for power, follow your instincts."

Politics in Jamaica could not only be dirty but violent and in so the country was divided. Alex's uncle stood solidly behind her and to touch her with the backing of so many in Parliament would probably bring the country to its knee. There were many corrupt politicians who were lining their pockets with the people's money; but there were good ones trying to make a difference.

Alex understood the culture of the Jamaican people. She was exposed to different worlds. Growing up in the country, agriculture played a major part of earnings for many. Farmers raised goats and cows which they sold to put money in their pockets especially during the holidays. From the cows they got milk which was a staple of life for many. Many such as Miss Lovely and her grandmother sold boxes of cocoa seeds by the inches to big companies who made hot chocolate and cocoa tea to bring in extra money. Banana was a major crop. Many planted crops of dasheen and yams so they wouldn't have to buy.

On the other hand there were the elite of Jamaica who had a great deal of influence over who ruled Jamaica. The elite stayed behind the scenes and manipulated the strings. They were in favor of a candidate who was polished, well spoken, smart and understood how to conduct themselves not only on a local level but on an international level as well. Alex had lived in New York and seen the workings of the Democratic and the Republican Parties to know that many, including the media, were able to sway voters also by manipulation. Alex had seen the workings of the wealthy and the educated and understood their logic.

The Jamaica National Party and the cynics were now recognizing that they had a formidable opponent because Alex was carrying her weight and she was fighting hard. She believed in education for all children because they were the future. When people are not educated they remain poor, having no skills. She had studied Marcus Mosiah Garvey, Paul Bogle and the other heroes who had fought and had given their lives for their country, and Martin Luther King Jr. because she was motivated by the thinking of many people.

"Well guys, you all had my back while I ran for Member of Parliament and now I am going for the ultimate, not just Prime Minister but the first female Prime Minister of Jamaica so I am going to need your help like never before. It's one thing to be a M.P. but it's another thing for me to run for P.M."

Ciarra started rocking her body to the music playing in the background and was singing along.

"Remember when we raided that cave because we needed money for the Basic School and to have that Bell day? Well, listen to this, there is too much violence happening around us and politics is at the heart of this. We hear about guns coming in. Someone is responsible for this and Alex not only need to take a stand but to do something about. Wouldn't it be something if we could confiscate one of these shipments, or like say blow up one of their airstrips?" Tayo suggested.

"What?" There was a chorus of voices.

"Just listen for a minute," Tayo implored. "Can you imagine, pulling this off? It would catapult Alex way ahead in the polls to take credit for something like this. We would be doing our civic duty for the country and it would give us an adrenaline rush."

Rory scratched his head.

"You got a great point, skipper. My heart has already kicked up a beat thinking about it. It would be like old times, the planning and the follow through."

"What you guys are thinking about and proposing is so far fetched. Do you hear yourselves, how ridiculous this sounds and even if it was feasible, I would be finished if it backfired," Alex said dryly.

Alex had been stumping hard. She talked about her goals for the people she would be representing. She talked about the foreign companies in the Free Zone who were taking much and giving little. Under her government they would be asked to do more, pay more to benefit the people. It was a new day for her and her family and friends. She was a woman who was interested not only in politics but the people she would represent. She had lived in Bell Town so she was in tune with much that was missing in that area. She was thrilled to have come this far.

Alex was putting her name out there. She decided that if she was going to win, to become Prime Minister she had better have a good strategy. Last week she had hosted a movie on financial planning; not a boring documentary but rather an interesting story of a man who went to the States on farm work. Every month he would send home money for his wife and kids but, instead of saving the money, his wife began to spend it on clothes and partying. For the last six months she had been spending her husband's money without any thought to what was going to happen in the future. Luckily she had a son who caught on to what was happening and he began to intercept the money, putting away some and giving her the balance.

When her husband finally came home, there was hell and bangarang because she couldn't produce half of the money he had sent home to her. The new so called friends had disappeared and the new man that she had met from foreign had left her high and dry. It was well attended and the women in Bell Town had much to talk about.

Then she had hosted a movie about family planning. It was about two families and their two teenage daughters and son and the choices they had made which would affect their lives for years to come. These functions were like social events with huge turn outs and the opportunity to talk politics. Megan interrupted her thoughts.

"Rory, we out of bottled water. Where do you keep them? I'll go get it."

"You sit and relax I'll go get it along with another bottle of wine," Alex volunteered. "Yeah. Where is it kept?"

"Downstairs," Rory answered. "I'll come with you, show you the changes I made downstairs."

Ciarra looked at Megan, Tayo looked at Andy and they all grinned.

Rory watched as Alex walked down the stairs with that sexy wiggle of her butt that always turned him on. His imagination ran riot. He walked towards the store room, removing the bottled water from the box and handed it to her, watching as her eyes avoided his as their fingers touched briefly. He felt the lightening bolt of awareness, the sensual heat of her body coming towards him, pulling him towards her like a magnet. His shorts tightened in the crotch.

"Rory I have been meaning to talk to you about this but now is as good a time as any. I want a divorce."

He remained silent for a few seconds before answering.

"If we are going to talk we might as well make our selves comfortable."

He walked to the table and pulled out a chair. He waited until she sat down then followed suit. He twisted the cap off the bottled water, watching as Alex drummed her fingers impatiently on the surface of the table.

"Alex, remember when we were kids, I would always tease you. I liked you very much from those days. I felt that there was something special about you, like you had a kinda spell over me. Sometimes I was downright nasty to you because I couldn't let a little slip of a girl have a hold on me. I was older than you so I kept my distance even though I wanted to stay really close to you. My mother said I couldn't "spoil you up" and you were too young." He laughed to himself. "That night in the cave I wanted to, only God helped me then because I was far from being a saint. I loved you even then."

She looked at him with wide eyes.

"I am running to become the Prime Minister, the head of this country. I can't have a husband out there running around. It's fodder for the headlines. I refuse to stand around while you have a woman out there running with. I have to clean up my life and move on from you."

He stood up, pushing his chair back and prowled around, coming to stand in front of her.

"I love you Alex, I have never stopped. I was young and I was traveling and playing a game I loved. There were many women. Yeah I was having fun but I swear I have always loved you and if you tell me right now that you no longer want me or that you no longer love me, I'll leave you alone and give you your divorce."

It was time for her to make some move.

"When I said my marriage vows, I meant every word I said. I vowed to love, cherish and honour you. I meant to keep those words and I still do but if you have or you are still seeing whatever her name is I am through."

He took a step towards her, tilting her chin up to look at him.

"I still love you, Alex. I have only you. Everyone is history. Christmas happened and you. I was reminded of what I had and what I have always wanted. You."

"I love you, Rory, and if you do I want this marriage for the rest of our lives."

She barely got the words out before his mouth came down on hers. Her mouth was on fire as soon as his came in contact with hers. He thrust his legs between hers, his legs moving forward against hers, causing her to back up until she was against the wall.

"I have never gotten you out of my head."

He cupped her face in his hands and kissed her deeply. The taste of her was exquisite, like fine wine, strawberries and cream. She moaned at the feel of his erection between her legs and gasped out loud when his mouth closed over one nipple, sucking and licking until she was out of her mind with wanting to feel him inside her. Her mind stopped functioning and sensations took over and the only thought that flashed through her head was that 'I am his and his only. There is no one else for me, only him. This is what I want and this is where I belong'. She moved against him to feel more of him.

His passion heightened. He couldn't take her upstairs or to the bedroom where he could undress her and take his time. He lifted her from the floor. She wound her arms around him. It had been a very, very long time and she couldn't wait. Her body pulsed with the desire that had been lurking beneath the surface of her skin for hours.

"Yes," he said as he grasped her thighs, bringing them around his waist.

He needed her, needed to feel, needed to bury himself inside her. Without breaking the kiss he carried her to the bathroom and sat her on the edge of the countertop. He put his hand between her legs, groaning loudly as he felt the wet heat of her against his fingers. He tore aside the scrap of silk called underwear she wore before sinking his fingers into her. He fumbled between unzipping his pants, freeing himself.

"Look at me, Alex," he commanded. "Say you want me. Tell me you want me. You are mine, you hear me. You have always been and always will."

She cried out with the sheer delight of having him so out of control, so intent on having her.

"All evening, all day I have wanted you. I want you, Rory."

He thrust forward and plunged into her, feeling her close around him.

"Say my name, Alex. Say it."

He was deep inside her, rocking against her.

"It's only you, Rory, only you," she cried.

He swallowed her cries. He felt her tremble, felt the pulse of her muscle as she came and then he exploded inside her, coming in a rush of unbearable ecstasy.

Jesus, he had been so out of control, so hot for Alex that he hadn't even taken off his pants. What kind of animal did she turn him into? He had totally lost his mind.

She sighed and then lifted her head and looked at him.

"Do you think they heard us? I felt like we could get caught any minute," she said.

"I know, but I couldn't wait."

He hugged her and brushed his lips against hers before setting her on her feet. He walked away and brought her a washcloth, gently tidying her so she was presentable.

"This is not enough. Spend the night with me. You are still my wife."

He encircled her waist with his arm, drawing her against   him.

"Why did you marry me, Rory?" Alex asked.

"I have always wanted you, Alex. That's what you wanted and you were pregnant. I would have preferred to give you the wedding of your dreams but time did not allow it. Passion was what had caused all the trouble from the beginning. Most of all, I loved you and still do."

He led her to the door and unlocked it. Turning, he caught her hand in his, holding it firmly so that she was forced to follow him up the stairs. So she took a deep breath, brought her chin up and marched up the stairs behind Rory. She only hesitated when she reached the top of the stairs and the buzz of conversation which was so loud a second ago faded into a murmur. Once more her hand was enclosed in his. Conversation died. Ciarra elbowed Megan in the rib. Andy, Neil and Tayo stared. All eyes turned towards them.

"Why is everyone looking so weird?" Rory asked. "You all know we are husband and wife. We never got a divorce and we have no intention of getting a divorce."

"Are you saying you two are back together?" Megan asked with hesitation in her voice.

"Yeah, she is giving me another chance," Rory answered as his arm encircled Alex's waist.

"Halleleujah!!!" Ciarra sang.

Rory's wife. In spite of all these years that she had spent being bitter and regretting their marriage, hating him because she thought he had been deceptive and blaming him for the death of their child- she was Rory's legal wife. She had always loved him and still did. Tayo picked up the bottle, poured a drink and passed it to Rory before pouring one for himself. Everyone stood up and began to cheer.

"What took you two so long? Jeez. I couldn't be happier for you both," Andrea piped up.

"Let's give another toast," Andy said.

"Here's to new beginnings, my friends," Tayo said.

Glasses clinked and everyone was talking at once and hugging Alex. Neil thumped Rory on the back and began to sing. "Back together again."

"Wait a minute. I'll be right back," Rory said as he went inside the house.

He came back with a jewelry box clutched in his hand. Opening it he held it out to Alex.

"I wanted to get you a ring which is fitting for a princess like you," he said with some hesitation. She stared as he gingerly removed the ring from the box and took her hand. Alex's mouth was still open as he slipped it on her finger, a rather large, sparkling, princess cut diamond that danced and shimmered in the light whichever way she held her hand. It was set high on a simple platinum setting.

"It's beautiful," Ciarra gushed.

"Yes, it is," Megan agreed. "Oh, I am going to cry."

"Thank you," Alex whispered. "I love it."

"I bought it a long time ago. I was waiting for the right time to give it to you." He kissed her hand. "I have waited a long time for this."

Alex looked at the ring. It was beautiful. The sex was great but she didn't want to live with anyone. She didn't want to have any more babies and maybe that's what Rory was expecting. She looked up from her contemplation to see Megan watching her intently.

-Chapter 29-

N ew York was cold and grey. Ciarra pulled her coat tighter around her. After the hot and sun drenched skies of Jamaica this was definitely a drastic change in weather. Once she got into the apartment that was leased for her on the Upper East Side, she unbuttoned her stylish coat, slipped it off and made herself a cup of tea to ward off the chill.

She wandered around the apartment, staring through the window as the last of the day sank over the horizon, the beautiful city of New York lighting up and chasing the dark away. Below, people scampered back and forth, some on their way from work, others out for a walk to a restaurant or walking their dog.

She was moving on from Klein's Creations. The company was losing money, not because they weren't making a profit but someone had been siphoning the money into their own pocket. Some one had leaked the paternity issue regarding Fletcher to the paper and the society page in *The Gleaner*, without naming names, had definitely had a nice paragraph dedicated to a fashion designer who denied father paternity. She could thank Mitzie for that. Then there was the issue with Tayo who carried a grudge because all this time Klein had pretended that he was the father of his son.

She was looking forward to the challenge of working with someone new, showcasing a new line that she had designed. Celebrities, fashion industry's finest would all descend on Bryant Park in a few days. After all it was Fashion Week in New York.

There was evidence to bear testimony that Fashion Week was almost here. Magazines such as *Instyle* had displayed signs on the Chrysler Building. There was a buzz going on at Bryant Park as the tents went up and workmen hustled to put in all the fixtures, the lighting, the essential décor. The air was crisp and cold and Ciarra was all bundled up as she strolled by the park. She shouldn't have been surprised, but she was, to see so many people out having a lazy Sunday in Bryant Park.

The tents sprawled and spread over Bryant Park. For this week the park was converted to a temporary fashion arena and the huge heated tents came complete with runway seating for attendees, backstage areas, lighting and sound. Ciarra and her assistant Lisa were caught up in the manic energy that buzzed in the air. The hottest designers were here to show their spring collection to the many celebs and *fashionistas* in the tents. 40th -42nd Street and Sixth Avenue was a beehive of activity.

Her models were also caught up in the excitement.

"How did you get Halle to come to a fashion week event, Ciarra?" one of her workers asked. "It's sooo happening here."

"And you are forgetting the beautiful Vanessa," Lisa added with a glint in her eyes. "Let's keep it together team."

Ciarra checked the listings, listened as Lisa made a last minute change.

"Okay, ladies, listen up. It's today or sometime in the future and we have today. The press is here, we all know they'll put us out there where the public can see our designs, what is going on, the fashion editor of all editors are here, she can make or break us. My style is fab but you all have to do your part. I spoke briefly to one of the writers from the *New York Times* and I scored an interview so I am going to let Lisa do the honors of handling that one."

Ciarra breathed in and out as she finished her speech.

"Oh no, Ciarra, that's for you to do. I am having palpitations. I am too nervous," Lisa answered.

"You will be fine. Ice runs in your veins when you do interviews. You are calm and collected." Ciarra squeezed her hand.

Ciarra listened as the brief introductory *schpiel* was given, then the announcement of the first category showing the *Ciarra* collection starting with Smart Casual.

All the planning and publicity had led to this moment and everyone held their breath as the music began and the model took the runway. Ciarra's designs were colorful, reflecting the Caribbean theme. The model was wearing a strapless olive green jumper and as she strutted along there was a burst of applause; colors, soft orange fitted jacket matched with a tight fitting khaki skirt, flirty, sexy dresses.

The *coup de grace* was the evening gown category. Ciarra went for classic glamour, a red one shoulder gown, fitted at the waist and then falling to the ankles, long sleeved evening gown, dipped sharply in the back and draped perfectly in the front, crystal beaded chiffon designs, slinky, figure hugging silk, spaghetti straps, each gown modeled drew more and more applause.

The final outfit was modeled and the model disappeared backstage. The *fashionista* called for Ciarra to take the stage, followed by the models. Ciarra had dressed in high heels and a soft orange top with black linen pants. She offered a dazzling smile as she indicated her models and called on Lisa to join her on stage. Gosh, Megan would love all this glitz and the spotlight. She wished that they were here to share in the rush she was experiencing right now. There was much applause as Ciarra made a final turn towards the audience.

"Wow." Lisa's voice was barely audible above the applause. "This is fantastic." They made a final turn towards the audience before disappearing backstage.

It was time to pack up the collection and they got down to it. Ciarra thanked the models, the behind-the- scene staff and everyone for their help.

"It's time for you to go mix and mingle, Ciarra, everyone is waiting for you and did you see that hunk Didier watching your every move? I have to say the flowers he sent you were gorgeous," Lisa added.

Ciarra emerged to find Andrea looking like a model herself and Andy waiting to envelop her in a bear hug. She was flabbergasted.

"You thought that none of us would be here to represent? Come on girl, that's why we all insisted that you had invitations for at least two of us. Tayo would have had our heads if we didn't make it here to support you and of course everyone send their love. Megan would have loved to be here but I am the one who was chosen to come see you. Here, Tayo sends this for you."

Andrea pulled an envelope from her pocket book and handed it to Ciarra.

"Now , go on and do your thing."

"Well done, Ciarra." Andy hugged her and then stepped aside to let her go mingle. Ciarra was on the verge of tears.

"Thanks, guys, for being here. It means a lot to me."

Didier stepped forward to hug Ciarra before brushing his lips to each cheek.

"You are a gem. Not only are you beautiful but very talented."

"Thank you." Her response was sincere.

"There are many who wish to talk to you so let me get right to it. Can we have dinner sometime very soon, like later this afternoon to celebrate if there isn't anyone special here who already gobbled you up?"

Ciarra laughed.

"Can I let you know?"

"Here is my cell and home and business number." He handed her his card. "I already have yours. I took the liberty of asking Lisa. I told her it had to do with business."
Ciarra shook her head.

"You men are something else."

Didier's eyes gleamed with laughter. She watched him leave and witnessed the many eyes that followed him. He was an interesting guy.

"Ciarra."

For the next forty minutes Ciarra was in great demand. She made her way backstage after speaking for a final few minutes to the press. Lisa, Andrea and the other girls had taken care of packing up and Andy was helping to cart boxes out the door.

"Look," Lisa was waving a list at her. "We have orders and requests for further showings." She was jumping up and down. "I think it's safe to say we did it."

Ciarra threw herself on the couch, pulling off her three inch heels. Her feet were killing her. For a brief moment Tayo flashed across her mind. They had mended fences because of their son but she wasn't sure how he felt about her on a personal level.

It was while they were sitting in a restaurant sometime later having cocktails and drinks that Andy casually mentioned that Octavius had been ill. Ciarra's brow lifted.

"Octavius was sick? He never gets sick. What's wrong with him? He finally caught a cold or did someone knock him over the head to get him to stop being so stubborn?"

Andy and Andrea exchanged looks.

"Oh no, nothing like that. He was watching Megan run tracks and he kinda keeled over so they took him to the hospital," Andrea answered.

Ciarra began to laugh and then stopped abruptly.

"I was assuming he was tipsy and tipped over but hospital? That would be too drastic a case. What's going on guys? It had to be something serious for him to agree to go to a hospital."

"He didn't have a choice because he wasn't conscious."

"Holy shit!" Ciarra exclaimed. "When did this happen?" She took a big gulp of her drink.

"He is home now and as feisty as ever. Actually he has ideas about you starting a clothing line just for him," Andy answered.

The thought of Octavius wearing designer clothes made just for him seemed far-fetched. Ciarra began to laugh hard. Octavius hated getting dressed up. He was a jeans and shirt kinda guy. Andy and Andrea breathed a sigh of relief. For now they wouldn't have to answer anymore questions.

"Oh, let me call him right this minute and let him know that I am coming home and he had better start wearing and showing off the clothes I design."

Andrea made a face.

"Good luck to you."

Two days later Ciarra and Didier sat watching a musical on Broadway. The dance was beautiful and compelling but as Ciarra sat watching, she was beginning to think that she really needed to go home. She felt detached from reality and there was something that was nagging away at her. She had the uneasy feeling that Andrea wasn't telling her everything. Well she knew someone who would.

She missed her little island Jamaica and as exciting as New York was with all these men who were at the moment fawning over her, she wanted her friends and the beach. She had made a decision; she was going home.

-Chapter 30-

There were times when Alex felt that the world was against her but her granny and Miss Etty kept encouraging her. The other night she had awakened from a dream drenched in sweat. It was as if she was back in the cave feeling trapped and there was the woman beckoning to her to come on, keep moving towards the air and sunshine that was out yonder. She had been so scared. Of course she had told Miss Etty who had done nothing but tell her to listen to the angels around her. It might seem tough now and the mountains insurmountable but she would eventually scale very mountain and hill in her way.

"Never lose sight of what your destiny holds, child. There is no one and nothing that can stop you from getting to Jamaica House because that is where the Prime Minister is to be found," Miss Etty once more reiterated.

The heat was murder and Alex was lucky to have gotten out of court early today. One by one Megan, Ciarra, and Andrea had quickly dropped whatever they were doing to meet up and drive out to Port Royal for some fish, bammy, and festival. The thought of sipping on cold drinks and feeling the cool breeze had them piling into Ciarra's car and heading out to Gloria's fish place for some relief.

The lady caller on the radio was saying "Mr. Thwaites, I don't have anything personal against the young lady, she might have a pretty face but that can't run a country. The only thing she can run is them two dry foot she have."

Ciarra was rolling around with laughter as she tried to keep a firm grip on the steering wheel.

"Gee, Alex let me see them two dry foot that you have."

Ciarra was back from her fashion show in New York and all four girls were liming, listening to each other vent.

"Well, she comes with great credentials," Mr. Thwaites replied, "and if you listened to the debate between her and the opposition she was quite brilliant. Destroyed her opponent who is a seasoned veteran in politics. I have to say I was impressed."

"Mr. Thwaites," the woman answered, "is it because you are a man why she brings you over to her side aready? She just come pon the political scene and expects people like me to vote for her? Tell the truth, sah, that no right."

"Oh, God, oh God, listen to that. She is a woman. I thought she would have some sympathy to your cause," Megan interjected. "Bway, Alex, I have been hearing some vicious story about your life. If I didn't know you I wouldn't vote for you black ass. I can't even tell you my story because of you and your damn politics."

"Sweetheart, don't blame Alex," Andrea joined in. "We all love to listen to Mrs. Gloudon and Ronnie because people say exactly what is on their minds. Some of it we find funny but I know, Alex, some of it hurt especially when they call you that pretty, empty headed bitch. You can't respond to everything but some you can address."

"On a serious note, Alex, " Ciarra said, "people will like you when you run around in the latest fashion and attend all the social functions because they can talk about your clothes or the man you are with but when you stand up for something that is meaningful, it sets you apart from the rest. You represent something deeper and because of that alone, people will dislike you so try and grow a second skin because you have to toughen up somewhat."

Alex looked at Ciarra because her insight into the situation was so true. The idea of a woman running for Prime Minister was something totally new and to some it might seem daunting. As she listened to Ciarra she was reminded that she was a force to be reckoned with; her aspirations were beyond some people's imagination and she would get there to that damn pinnacle.

"Turn the radio off, or down or change the station," Alex asked. "I want to hear more about your fashion show and your time in New York, Ciarra, and I want to know what's bothering my friend Megan. This is going to be interesting."

Alex you are so full of irritable today, jeez. Here let's listen to one of Neil's songs, the one about my special girl."

Ciarra slid the CD into the slot and Neil's voice drifted through the car. Alex leaned her head against the seat and let the music seep into her bones.

"Gosh, tell me that Neil is not the epitome of what sexy is?" Megan sighed in such a dramatic fashion that Ciarra suggested that she go audition for some kinda part in a movie. "It's the sex. It's killing me, man. Guys you know I like a man that can give it to me good but Marcus is not hitting it at all. After we finish with sex I have to use my fingers to get off."

Andrea's mouth opened wide.

"What? He seem so into you and here it is I thought you and the big time doctor was getting ready to settle down."

"Nay. He ain't hitting it and I have no time to teach a grown man a darned thing. If we should seriously be very serious as in getting hitched, I would have to cheat, definitely because he is not a good lay at all." Megan went on. "Call me crazy or selfish or whatever. Ciarra knows exactly what I am talking about because that is one of the reasons she cannot get over Tayo. He knows how to hit that spot. That is why he has always had so many women."

"Shut up, Megan. How do you know he is so good in bed? Did you try him or something like that?" Ciarra answered defensively.

Alex held up her hand.

"You tell us all the time and his women say he is good. Remember the time when we were peeking when they were pissing outside the little school. We glimpsed Tayo's and it was big."

Ciarra sucked her teeth.

"I don't know but I am trying hard to make amends with him but he is not paying me no mind. Furthermore I am back and he is in Barbados doing his Masters and Ph.D. I would have been depressed if it wasn't for Didier who is keeping me entertained, on the phone that is."

"Yeah, there it was. We all seem to be out of sorts. I thought we were on the fast track to taking care of the business of the illegal guns coming into my territory but it's been one thing after the other. Tayo is away, Rory is in England with his cricket thing.

Although we are back together everything seem so unsettled. I am getting discouraged with this running for office thing. It's no joke."

There was already a crowd when they pulled up to Gloria's. It is a small neighborhood and cars were parked all along the street, each creating its own parking spot, so Ciarra had to squeeze into a spot.

Alex slid out of the car and stood stretching her arms towards the sky. She felt restless, off balance. She was working hard, not only at the firm but campaigning with her party. She was lying to Rory about not being on the pill. She didn't want any babies, absolutely no kids. Alex felt a slight chill wash over her. Something wasn't right with Auntie. She knew because there were shadows but she was in denial, pushing it away and burying it in the edge of her consciousness. Sometimes the extra sensory perception that crept up on her was so very unwelcome.

"Hey Alex, are you okay?" Ciarra was looking at Alex in alarm. "You look like you are shaking."

Alex shrugged her shoulders. "It's like someone walked over my grave. She shook her head. "I am fine."

"Let's grab this table before someone else takes it," Megan suggested, resting her pocketbook on the table.

They sat waiting for their order to be taken. Megan tapped her fingers on the arm of Andrea's chair.

"Do you realize how lucky we are? Look at us, we can afford to take off early afternoon and come sit out here, in Port Royal while others are cooped up at work."

Sunlight and Dappled Shade

The drinks arrived and Andrea took a sip of her Red Stripe.

"Yeah man, now I am back on track. Back to the argument. You know what your problem is, Megan? I think you still have a thing for Neil. Tell me that is not true?"

Alex looked at Megan while sipping her Ting.

"You know, Andrea, you do have a point there. She was pretty flustered at that Christmas dinner when we said she wanted to get back at you for liking Neil."

"Mmmm-hmm. I totally agree with everything said."

Ciarra sipped on her wine.

"Fess up, Megan. Is it true? You still have the hots for Neil although you were the one who dumped him."

"You guys are behaving as if you all forgot why I dumped him. Remember he was in his third year at UWI campus. It was the weekend of carnival and we were all hanging at your uncle's house, Alex. That was when Neil met that record producer and to answer the other question, we all grew up together for crying out loud," Megan answered impatiently. "I'll always have feelings for him. Nothing can change that."

"Okay, let's rephrase that. Do you still want him, desire him?" Andrea persisted.

Megan hedged "It's hard to say. Anyway he is no longer looking in my direction so it doesn't matter, okay. Let's drop it."

Everyone was silent for a few minutes then. Andrea crossed her heart.

"He is hot, just thinking about him is making me, ahhm, never mind." Andrea pointed towards Megan.

"You stopped seeing Neil right around the time he made that record."

Megan nodded.

"I did the right thing. Neil was always one of those bad boys, such a rebel. We all knew he could sing but when he made that record, every time you turned around there was some woman up in that dorm. No way would it have lasted so I dumped him first. I was smart."

"Yeah, he is the one who ruined you for everyone else. It wasn't long after he got popular that he met some girl from the States and the dumb ass went and got married. He was lucky that he had Rory and Andy to come get him after that woman tried her best to get him locked up in New York and take his money. His ass wasn't so smart then. He certainly filed for divorce in a hurry. You could fly up to Atlanta under the guise of whatever and drop by to see him," Ciarra suggested.

Alex sat up straight as if she had just received an epiphany.

"Here we are fixated on men. We can do things ourselves. We have set aside the plans to blow up the airfield when we get a tip off about gun running but we have been looking at it the wrong way. One of us needs to learn to fly some kinda plane because we can take out whatever we want from the air."

They all turned to look at Alex in horror.

"Oh, my God! You are not serious," Ciarra squealed. "I am sick already with the thought."

"Hell no!" everyone agreed.

"We need a plan," Alex continued as if she hadn't heard a word anyone said. She continued sipping her wine.

Megan took big gulps of her wine. She sipped and sipped again.

"My decision making skills have temporarily deserted me."

"Well who is going to volunteer?"

"Don't even look at me." Megan shuddered. "I don't want to die in a plane wreck."

"I'll do it. My uncle can arrange lessons for me."

"That is a plan. That way we don't have to get anyone else involved."

Andrea frowned.

"Your uncle will never agree to this, you know that, right?" Andrea said, "But it sounds exciting and dangerous. I am in."

"So am I," Ciarra pounded fist with Alex and Andrea, "It will be like old times."

"Awright, I am in," Megan joined in. "Let's rope the guys in so we can do this, again. So now that we are settled on that, let's get back to the topic of Neil."

Megan allowed herself a brief fantasy interlude: Neil's mouth on hers, hot and devouring, her's answering while her hands roamed all over his hard body in desperation.

Ciarra pinched her.

"Where did you go for a minute there? We have been talking to you and you had this far away look on your face."

"Ouch, that hurts. I was having a hot day dream. You guys don't want to know," Megan answered.

"Good for you, Megan," Alex responded.

It was a little noisy and exactly what the doctor ordered. Alex leaned back sipping on her Ting. Her phone beeped. She glanced at it and before she answered she knew. The shadows that she had been keeping at bay, fearful of what she would see were there. The nerves in her stomach clenched into a painful ball.

"Hey, mom."

"Alex, can you get down here as soon as possible? Auntie is really sick and we had to take her to the hospital."

"What happen, mom?" Alex asked.

"She was helping Brother Arthur clean out that cluttered place of his and something cut her. She didn't say anything because she didn't think it was a big deal. Anyway I called your aunt and she is coming in on Sunday from Florida."

Alex's fork clattered to her plate with pieces of fish still attached to it. She stared in horror at her friends.

"Don't worry, mom, I am as good as there," she promised on a note of rising panic as she hung up.

Everyone was looking at Alex enquiringly.

"Alex. Alex, what is it? You are literally as white as a sheet," Ciarra asked in alarm.

"It's Auntie, she is really sick and my mom had to take her to the hospital. It's some kind of poisoning or something like that." Alex looked frightened.

"Okay, let's get the check and get out of here."

Megan held up her hand indicating she needed service.

"Oh God, what am I going to do?"

Alex picked up her fork, but her hand shook so badly she had to put the fork back down. She bent her head so her friends could not see the tears that were beginning to form in her eyes, and placed her trembling hands in her lap. People were starting to look.

"Come on, let's get out here."

Ciarra stood up and was tempted to ask those staring what they were looking at but this time she kept her mouth shut. She only gave them a dark look.

"I have to go to country now. I have to get there."

Alex didn't look too good. Her face was ashen and her movements were jerky. The cool, calm and often unfazed Alex was gone. Ciarra ran ahead to get the car. Megan placed her arm around Alex and Andrea walked alongside her, arms filled with hurriedly packed food.

"We are all coming country with you, so don't bother to think you are driving down there by your self. Let me get your cell. We have to call Rory right now."

Her mom was keeping vigil when she arrived. They hugged each other as if for reassurance.

"Mom, go with Megan. She is going to take you to get some fresh air," Alex could see the hesitation in her mother's eyes but she insisted. "Go on, mom, you need a break." Impulsively she reached over and hugged her again. "I love you, mom."

"I know, sweetie, and I love you too," her mom answered.

Auntie had smiled at her when she first came in, mouthing the words 'I love you, baby.' She had kissed her with a smile.

In the hospital room, she was alone with Auntie. She looked at her grandmother laying in the bed looking so frail and still. Alex had not noticed how old she had become. It was hard to imagine how this once strong, vibrant woman could be now laid so low. Alex took her grandmother's hand, so small, so tiny, and held it in the palm of her hands. She sat like that, unmoving for at least an hour. Then slowly, she lifted her hand, flexing it, trying to get rid of the cramped feeling in her hand. She remembered how Auntie's grip would tighten on her fingers when they were crossing the street or when she tried to hold her back from any danger.

Alex tried to smooth the bumpy veins on the small hand resting on the sheets of the hospital bed. Those hands had seen so much work in her lifetime and were resting for perhaps the first time in her life. She rubbed her hands across the still face of the woman who lay somewhere between consciousness and wakefulness. Why did she have to be the one helping others all the time? She should have just sent some one to Brother Arthur to help him clean up and now because of his frigging crap this had to happen.

For a moment, she rested her brow on her knees, fighting to clear her head. Rory, Megan, Ciarra, Andrea, her mom and others were all in the waiting room. They all were offering comfort and compassion and unity, but she had to escape. Their compassion was destroying her. It was too frightening and hurtful that she was losing someone she loved so much. She was useless against her grandmother's fight against death. She wanted to beg her not to go. But as she looked at the peacefulness on the woman's face, Alex knew. *Wait until morning, Auntie,* a voice seemed to whisper inside Alex's head. Alex was startled by what felt like a small squeeze from the hand she was holding in hers.

"Alex," Rory stooped in front of her, taking her hands and wrapping them around a cup of hot coffee. "Drink, sweetheart."

She shook her head but he wrapped his hand around hers, bringing the cup to her lips so she took a sip. He could see that her face was pale and glossy, her eyes red. He sat beside her, draping his arm around her shoulder.

They all took turns staying with her as the hours passed in that dream state so common to hospitals. People came and went. Miss Etty was there and so was Octavius. Mass Kenny and Rory's mom came and left. Tayo called every few minutes which kept her distracted. He had a new story to tell each time he called. There was the sound of footsteps as nurses came and went, the smell of antiseptic in the air so typical of hospitals.

Alex was tired today; she hadn't slept in more than twenty four hours because she knew the time was drawing close. She looked up to the sound of raindrops on the window of the hospital waiting room. It was said that the rain would come before your loved one slipped away. She crept quietly into her grandmother's room. She held her hand and told her one last time how much she meant to her, then she went back to the waiting room.

Rory was keeping her company and she fell asleep, her head resting on his shoulder. She felt his body tense and was awake in an instant. He held her hand as she looked towards the doctor.

He came in quietly, a handsome man.

"Mrs. Richardson."

"Yes." She braced for the news. Rory stood up.

"I am Doctor McGregor. I am so sorry."

-CHAPTER 31-

Neil alighted from the plane at Sangster's International airport and stepped out onto the tarmac. Less than half an hour later he and his luggage were speeding towards Auntie's funeral at the Baptist Church in Bell Town. He didn't expect to hit too much traffic, seeing that it was a Saturday afternoon. He would have preferred to have flown in yesterday but was unable to get out of his prior commitment. He didn't care about the money; it didn't mean that much if he was to miss this funeral. He would not be forgiven by his friends especially Megan.

Megan…

How would she react to him this time, today? Usually they pretended they were okay with each other, always bringing their dates whenever the other was present. She usually had the 'I don't care' attitude around him.

He must be getting old, maybe he was entering a mid life crisis. Maybe he was suffering from burnout. Being on the road so much, performing could become wearying on one's soul. These days when his thoughts would drift towards Megan, the girl who had dumped him, he would find himself with a smile on his face. She might be different today because grief usually changes one's perspectives.

He couldn't imagine what Alex was going through; she loved her grandmother with such a fierce love. Growing up together they had all experienced the deaths of people from Bell Town and beyond. But this was the first time someone this close to them had passed away. Alex's grandmother was always sending some treat for them: sweet potato pudding, Toe-toe, dukonoo. Sometimes she would slip in a soda or two. She had been like an institution in Bell Town. Even though they all were now grown themselves, they all still looked forward to arriving in Bell Town on their visits knowing that she would be in the shop, chatting up her customers, adding a little brawta in someone's bag because she understood what it meant not to have. Hard to believe she was gone.

As Neil walked towards the church door through which all of Bell Town was streaming, he made a vow. He wasn't going to leave this time until he knew for sure that there was absolutely nothing left between him and Megan, come hell or high water.

Breathe! Just breathe! Over and over Alex said these words to herself and knew without a shadow of a doubt it was the only way she could get through this dark hour in her life. The support of her friends had helped her along this far.

She rubbed her hand across her mother's back, offering reassurance. Her mother was the closest of everyone to Auntie. She had taken care of her. Alex could not imagine what she was feeling at this moment. Her Aunt clung tightly to her mom's hand. They would get each other through this. Tata sat next to her mom, looking frail and lost like he wasn't sure what was happening. No one would have thought her grandmother would go before her husband who had been sick for a long time.

Sunlight and Dappled Shade

Alex tried to focus on the program of service that she held in her hand but her hands trembled so badly she couldn't read a darned thing. The congregation was singing:

One glad morning

when my work is done

I'll fly away.

Alex stifled a scream that rose up in the back of her throat at the untimely end to such a beautiful life. It didn't make any sense. As her thoughts continued to wander her mouth hardened and she realized that she was very angry. Someone squeezed her hand. She looked up to see Megan and Ciarra leaning over her.

"You are making a face and it is not pretty. Pull your mouth in."

"I guess my unholy thoughts are showing on my face because I would love to murder someone right this minute."

Nothing today made any sense, not the formal surroundings of the church or the many people that were crammed into the church could capture the essence of what Auntie was about. The photo of Auntie that sat above the coffin stared back at her and Alex's over fevered imagination could swear that Auntie whispered in her ear: "It's okay, Alex, look around you." She looked around but there was no one other than the people who had filled the church to pay homage. A searing pain ripped through her. She willed herself to stay calm. What was she going to do without her grandmother? She was overwhelmed and felt a strong arm holding her tight.

Rory's grip on her arm was somehow keeping her calm.

As she looked around, she realized that all her loved ones were here, her mom, her aunt, Miss Etty, Octavius looking so uncomfortable in his suit. Alex could not resist a smile then. It would have to be someone or something great that would bring Octavius here in a suit. Tayo had flown in from Barbados. The church was packed to capacity and the crowd spilled outside. There were so many people come to pay their respects to this woman that they loved.

There was a rustle in the pews and she turned to look. It was Neil; she stared at him, his almost black eyes, his hair worn a fraction too long and she was pleased that he had come. He strode over, hugging and kissing her, whispering in her ear. "I am so sorry, not only for your loss but mine too. She would always raise cane when I would misbehave."

Alex whispered back, "Thanks for coming" and turned to look at the expression on Megan's face.

The minister was saying, "and now Alex will give the Eulogy." Alex stood up and walked to the front of the room. She took her time to look at all those who were sitting there.

"My grandmother raised me, brought me up to be the woman that I am." She paused and took a breath. "I cannot tell you why she is gone so suddenly but I can tell you why she was here. She was here to raise me up to help to guide me along that special path. She always told me that each person has their own path to follow and mine was to be the first female Prime Minister. Even when I didn't believe, she said she believed enough for both of us that I would succeed. Her belief in God was unshakeable."

Alex's voice seemed to fade away as Megan inhaled sharply on seeing Neil. It had been a long time since she had seen him in the flesh. Memories flooded in on her and everyone who had been in between seemed insignificant at the moment. She had watched his rise in the music business, heard his voice on the radio and on his CDs. Now, here he was, looking as good as ever and causing her emotions to do some kind of twirly-whirl. She tried to pretend not to notice him.

Alex concluded her eulogy of the woman who had raised her. Auntie's death brought home how fleeting life is. You spend so much time trying to make things right and just like that you are gone. She stepped down from the podium and returned to her seat. The congregation was still nodding and chorusing 'Amens'.

Alex had no intention of leaving her seat as the mourners filed pass the coffin. The music had stilled and now there was a hush, but her eyes were drawn to the coffin and to the faces that followed behind. She left her seat and walked with confidence to the coffin. She touched her hand to her mouth and touched the head of the coffin.

"I got your message, grandmamma. You have always been so smart. I know this is not goodbye because you will be watching over me."

The mourners filed out one by one and proceeded to Auntie's final resting place in the churchyard. For Alex it was the hardest thing to go to the graveside but she didn't want anyone to know. She stood a way off lowering, her face to her hands and letting her hair flood forward to hide her face. There was so much pain. It came from somewhere deep in her belly, sat there and rose. She tried to quell it but it shook her, causing her stomach to quiver. This was so hard. So hard. She could not imagine her life without Auntie, especially now that she was on the verge of achieving what Auntie had predicted to be her fate. Just knowing she was there every time she went back to Bell Town.

"Alex," Rory was calling her name.

Removing her hands from her face she squinted to see Rory standing there. Pulling in a deep breath, she straightened up, taking Rory's hand and walked carefully across the grass to stand next to her mother, feeling as if the letting-go stuff was beginning to crowd in on her from all sides. Tata sat on a chair someone had provided for him. Alex didn't say a word, or let a tear slip as the minister said "Ashes to ashes, dust to dust." She said her final farewell as they sang *"one bright morning when this world is over, I'll fly away.* In a sudden hush it was almost like she could hear the sound of angel wings passing in a *whoosh.* Auntie was going home.

Alex didn't mind walking. She had to marshal her thoughts together. The evening light was softly bouncing off the grass, the trees, creating a dappled effect. The flowers remained all color and scent, but inside Alex there was a tight knot of fury that she was holding on to. Somewhere a bird was singing its heart out.

Sunlight and Dappled Shade

Instantly it soothed her. A trek into the dampness, the same path that they had traveled years ago to the cave. She felt the tension seep out of her. She breathed deeply on the damp air, the sweet scent of fern. She felt herself relax, perhaps for the first time since Auntie died. Ciarra and Megan walked beside her.

"Remember that first time we came here? I was scared shitless," Megan said, breaking the silence.

The sun, what little of it was trapped in the tall green canopy the leaves created, the earth damp beneath their feet, which barely made any sound as they walked along the twisting path.

"You don't have to pretend that you are not afraid now," Neil answered. "All you have to do is to let me hold your hand or whatever else you would like me to do."

Ciarra couldn't help laughing.

"Some things never change," she quipped.

-CHAPTER 32-

The patterns were shifting and Miss Etty couldn't see beyond the shadows. She was in a state of madness. Something was going to happen, badly and she couldn't quite see it. Was she losing her powers? It was at the edge of her consciousness but she was being blocked. "Hell and damnation!!!" she screamed aloud.

"Etty, what is it?" Octavius asked, alarmed. He could feel the tension in the air also.

"Octavius, the spirits are beating around, but I can't hear them. They are trying to talk to me but I can't seem to tune in. I am too restless. It is Alex. I know it. She knows I have been looking into her, seeing into her and she is learning to block me. I didn't mean to teach her this well. Pass me a cigar."

Octavius slowly rolled the cigar, lit it with a match and passed it to Etty, but not before taking a deep draw himself. He should tell her what Alex and the rest of them were up to tonight. That was what was happening. Etty could feel it but she couldn't quite see it clearly.

"Eh, eh, Etty, did Rory tell you that they were planning to go over that place where we hear they bringing in the guns to set the place afire."

Etty went as still as a stone embedded in the ground. With her bangles jangling and skirt swinging she ran to her room.

"Octavius help me. I didn't want to do this but I have to. I have to intrude into Alex private world. There is danger ahead. Oh God, why didn't you tell me sooner?" she questioned.

She saw it, the blood that was going to be spilled. "Sweet Jesus, protect them," she cried, "protect Alex."

She shook the powder from the box and blew it in the wind while she called out the names and called the ancestors. She could see, but she couldn't see Alex.

Tropical darkness enveloped Jamaica. It was late as Rory turned off the road and drove through a pair of security gates that swung open by some invisible command. Megan found herself staring at the private heliport complete with hangar tucked neatly into the bowl of the hill. She shook her head. Alex's uncle had the contact to whatever you need. A helicopter stood idle on the concrete helipad. As they pulled up to a halt beside it she could see there was a pilot already sitting in the cockpit and Neil and Andy already waiting. Alex didn't say a word, sliding out the door as soon as the car came to a standstill.

"Everything is arranged. Money and privilege is a helluva of a thing," Megan remarked.

"Shut up Megan," Tayo barked.

With long-limbed grace, Rory climbed out of the car and turned to greet Neil and Andy. They all moved as with one purpose towards the helicopter. An engine started up, rotor blades roared into life immediately. Rory's hands grabbed Alex's wrist as they sprinted forward, the noise of the helicopter drowning out any sounds. They settled into their seats on the chopper. Rory and Tayo made their way through the door and into the pilot's cabin without giving any one a chance to say much. Alex sat back in her seat and by the time they finished reassuring each other that it was going to be okay they were lifting off the ground.

Under the cover of night they flew over their destination twice to ensure that there were no unwanted guests present on the small runway. They didn't want to get caught by gun dealers and be shot; but their small group of would be commandos meant business. By the time they landed at the airstrip Alex was wound up like a spring loaded clock.

A dim light bulb cast shadows across the compound, which sat on the lip of a low hill and the helicopter touched down. Immediately they slid out, bending low, knapsacks with charges and detonators on their backs. Alex shivered as a light wind danced over her skin. Bottles of all shapes and sizes stood guard around the property, like inanimate soldiers. The banana and mango trees lining the perimeter of the yard chilled their blood every time the leaves rustled. Megan was sure evil beings lurked in the darkness, shrouding the roots of the plants and trees. They eased in to the deserted warehouse lot.

"Megan, Ciarra, we have the building over there," Neil whispered.

They ran forward towards the building with its cracked windows. They were through the door before they realized that there were dogs.

"Oh shit, Neil, dogs," Megan screamed and began to run.

The dog gave chase, its eyes glowing pure evil in the darkness, yapping its jaws and showing its yellow, long teeth. Neil stopped suddenly and faced the dog. Holding his hand out, he zapped the dog with his stun gun. The animal jerked and fell. Neil and the girls dashed through the doors.

"I come prepared, sweetheart," Neil said with a grin, imitating some long dead movie hero.

Rory, Tayo and Alex had remained outside to set the charges. The silence around them was almost too good to be true. It seemed not even the crickets and night toads were around. Coordinating their movements, they quickly and quietly set charges to the perimeter of the runway.

"Rory, you have to see this, come on over here," Neil whispered into the walkie-talkie.

They raced towards the building.

"Shit, look at all these guns and ammo here heading for the streets. There is enough stuff in here to out fit the entire Defense Force," Tayo said, visibly shaken.

"Well, not this bunch," Rory answered.

"Someone is going to be real pissed off about losing their merchandise," Ciarra said with a nervous laugh.

"Let the sons of bitches be pissed. If they were here I would blow them to kingdom come too. All of this is for killing on the streets. Enough of the senseless violence," Alex answered with disgust.

"Grab any documents or evidence you can find people," Rory instructed "and let's move out of here. It's dangerous territory," he continued as he proceeded to set fire to the guns, buildings and everything in sight.

An explosion ripped through the air startling everyone and sending shivers down Alex's spine. Ciarra jumped and Megan screamed. Tayo looked at Neil. Was that supposed to go off that quickly? Neil shrugged.

"I hope you guys had a timer on that thing."

They looked at each other.

"Let's get the hell out of here before we get caught with our pants down. This is going to bring company down on us."

A line of flames was licking along the edge of the runway.

"Move," Rory was shouting at Megan.

They were all on their feet, racing towards the chopper when the explosion tore a hole in the side of the building, catapulting debris and flames onto the grass. The low heels of Alex's boot were silent as she ran onto the tarmac. Gunfire suddenly erupted from out of the bushes.

"Oh shit!!" Rory exclaimed, "We have company. They are firing on us."

"Move every one. Push it." Tayo grabbed onto Ciarra and pulled her along. Megan was way ahead.

"Go on guys, I'll run the other way as a distraction. They are gaining on us." Alex cried out. She didn't wait for an answer but began to run.

Rory watched in disbelief as Alex's body jerked and, as if in slow motion she fell soundlessly to the ground. A bullet had found its mark. Alex was hit. Rory had never felt so frightened, so angry in his life.

"Alex is hit. Alex is hit," Megan began screaming.

Ciarra closed and opened her eyes not believing what she was seeing.

"She is down, Rory, she is down."

Immediately Rory sprang into action and began running towards Alex. He pulled the gun from the back of his waistband and fired toward where the initial shots had come from. There was a responding slew of gunfire. Tayo and the others who had by now reached the helicopter started firing. Rory ran towards Alex under cover of their fire, his heart thumping in his chest, his mind praying to God that she was okay. No, not Alex, a voice was begging somewhere in his subconscious. He scooped her up effortlessly and ran back to the helicopter while they covered him.

He could feel the wetness from her blood. Alex was bleeding; he wasn't sure from where. Tayo took her from Rory's arms.

"Get in," Tayo pushed Ciarra inside.

"Everyone in?"

"Yes, all accounted for."

"Go," Rory shouted.

Megan tore her T-shirt, creating a tourniquet to stem the blood that was coming from Alex's side. Megan was all business. She turned Alex's head to the side to prevent any obstruction to her airway.

"She is unconscious," Rory said woodenly.

He could hardly get the words out. His mouth felt like dry dust. Why did they all agree to do something so stupid and place themselves in so much danger? The helicopter lifted. There had been no more gunfire. Maybe someone else besides Alex had been hit. The group gazed down as the night became lit up by the fire that was roaring below. Tomorrow there was certainly going to be hell to pay where someone was concerned.

"Think some people are going to be accused of double cross?" Neil asked.

"I have a feeling that's going to happen," Tayo answered.

Megan kept watch to see if Alex's chest was rising and falling and checked for a pulse. If they had only listened to her when they had first come up with the plan. Now Alex's life was in danger. Megan prayed her friend would be okay.

"Does she have a pulse?" Neil asked.

Megan nodded.

"But it's weak and she feels kind of clammy."

"Thank God she has a pulse." Ciarra finally was able to breathe.

Rory felt the anger rising in him again as he hovered over Alex. Her eyes were still closed but she seemed to be breathing.

"I'll make their life a living hell if anything happens to Alex. One by one I will find them and make them feel pain," Rory said through gritted teeth while he kept pressure on Alex's wound. "Wrap the blanket around her lower. Keep her warm."

"You know I'm there with you, Rory," Ciarra promised.

"We all there, Rory. Kill all a them," Neil reiterated. "Those dirty drug dealing, gun running bastards. They want to kill innocent people. Not in our town."

"Alex, I am here baby, I'll never let you go. Hang on, sweetheart, we are going to get you help. I love you so much sweetheart. Just hang in there for me, no."

"Did you make contact with Mr. Keanon as yet?" Tayo shouted to the pilot.

"Yes, he has been advised as to the situation. He is having a doctor meet us from Montego Bay as soon as possible. What's the nearest place to the house we can land this baby?" the pilot answered.

"We are going to land in the front yard of Octavius' house," Rory answered. "It's a huge piece of level land and few houses close by. By the time anyone realize what's going on you will have dropped us off and taken off."

"Alex is strong, Rory, she will make it, but we can't take her to the hospital here, it has to be someplace else," Neil pointed out.

"We are taking her home to Bell Town. Miss Etty has always been prepared for an eventuality like this. Too many questions will be asked if we take her to a doctor in town. We can't afford for any association to be made between us and what happened tonight."

"Roger that," the pilot responded. To Bell Town we go."

It was three o'clock in the morning when the sound of the helicopter approaching pierced the silence. Miss Etty rolled out of bed, blinking her eyes trying to orient herself. She rushed to the door and had it open with Octavius standing in front of her as the helicopter swooped in for landing. As it touched down, gentle hands lifted Alex and rushed her inside.

"Rory, and all of you," Miss Etty said, "will have to explain all of this to me sometime soon and not to mention her dear mother."

"To begin with, we weren't expecting anyone to be there. It was kinda of a surprise," Neil answered.

"Save the talk for now, son," Octavius answered. "We have a whole lot of work to be done," he said gruffly.

Miss Etty had her herbs and roots ready and, like a long associated team, she and Octavius worked hard to stabilize Alex. Sweat beaded Miss Etty's brow as she worked on the girl who had been promised a place in King's House. It must happen. The ancestors had ordained it. Nothing must get in the way of Alex, like her ancestor Nanny, leading her people to a better way. As the last light of the descending moon passed over the night sky they relaxed as the worst seemed to have passed.

-CHAPTER 33-

A lex lay stretched out on the small bed once occupied by Miss Etty's assistant Ashanti. The voices echoed from far away. There was someone in the bed with her. She could feel the warmth of her presence. There was a sweet smell that reminded her of the woman who had beckoned her and led them out of the cave. She had been there trying to shield her from the bullet that had entered her side. Nanny. Strong arms came around her and she was enveloped in a warmth that made her feel safe. There was no fear, no anxiety, no worry. There was Auntie standing by the steps. She was telling Alex to go back. She wouldn't let her go in through the door through which a bright light was shining.

Alex dreamed of the cave and its labyrinth of rocks in the sprawling cavern while Miss Etty used her herbs and powers of healing to bring her back. She was gazing down at the entrance of the cave from a great height. She looked around, realizing that this was one of the caverns that her ancestors used to use as a place of worship. Alex's gaze was drawn to drawings on the wall. She saw a figure silhouetted against the rocks and her heart began to pound in her chest. The moonlight fell on her face and her eyes narrowed, straining to identify the figure, which now turned towards her. It was Nanny. She raised her hand in greeting.

At this point in time Miss Etty realized that Alex's heart which had been beating erratically before had now slowed to a regular beat. An hour later the doctor arrived but the important work was already done. At this point the modern joined force with the alternative medicine.

Rory and a tearstained Ciarra sat opposite each other outside in Miss Etty's living room. Megan sat in a chair, leaning forward, waiting, her chin in her hands. Tayo and Neil had borrowed the doctor's car and gone to pick up one of their own. No one spoke, there was nothing to say. Rory's face was pale; his emotions had long ago retreated from his chest and were curled into a ball, somewhere in the pit of his stomach.

The door to the room opened and the doctor emerged, his jacket splotched with blood.

"How is she?" Ciarra asked.

"The next twenty four hours will tell. The bullet passed straight through her, which is good because we didn't have to dig it out."

"Tell what?" Rory exploded. "Whether or not she will die?"

The doctor shook his head.

"I can't promise you she won't die but we have eliminated that probability. You can go in now, but don't overstay," he instructed.

Rory picked up the bottle of rum from the table and poured himself a drink. He had been so terrified that for the last few hours his heart had hurt.

"Go in there," Ciarra and Megan urged Rory.

He approached the room with a mixture of elation and trepidation. Rory stared at the figure on the bed: her hair tied back with a scarf, a beautiful scarf in black, red and gold, her lovely features in her pale face caught in the soft light of the lamp. He looked at

Miss Etty and mouthed the words, 'thank you'. He held Alex's hand and bent, touching his lips to her cheeks.

"Thank you God," he said out loud.

Alex felt safe and warm. She was home. Auntie was standing by the steps waiting for her. Alex smiled as she saw her, hands akimbo, watching her as she walked up to her. She was tired and couldn't wait to get upstairs.

"Oh Auntie, why are you waiting for me here and not upstairs?" Alex asked. "I hope you weren't waiting too long."

Auntie blocked her path when she would have walked by.

"Don't be in such a rush, Alex. What's the hurry?"

She took a breath before she answered.

"I am tired and I need to rest."

"Alex, you have to go back. You cannot stay here. Let me show you something."

Auntie pointed towards the tree where troops of people were walking across mountainous terrain.

"What do you see, Alex?"

At first she couldn't see but then her eyes adjusted to the light. There were lines of people being led across the rough tracks and she couldn't believe it, the woman from her dreams, Nanny. It was her leading her people and, not far behind the dogs and the soldiers were coming.

"Let me tell you a story. In times of great stress and turmoil in Jamaica leaders were born and leaders were made. Many fought for freedom, Paul Bogle,

Marcus Garvey to name a few. Nanny as a woman was fearless. She fought hard to make wrongs right. There has been Bustamante and Manley who helped to lead their people out of poverty. They shouldered their responsibilities when they were called. Now it is your turn, Alex, to be a leader for your people. It's not your time to come home, sweetie," Auntie said gently.

Auntie held out her hand and there was her red, green and gold scarf. She wrapped it around her neck.

"Go on back, Alex. Be my brave little girl."

Alex held on to her grandmother's hand tightly and felt the strength return to her arms.

"I love you, Auntie," she whispered as she turned and walked back towards the light.

She could hear her grandma's voice. "I love you, my sweet."

Early morning dew glistened on the grass outside. Morning broke in the soft colors of white and pink against the pale blue sky as Alex opened her eyes. Her eyes fell upon the scarf clutched in her hands. She saw, like a flash bulb going off, the silhouette that stood between her and Miss Etty. As her gaze sharpened and focused the figure smiled and waved goodbye.

-CHAPTER 34-

S eated around the table in the conference room were the current members of Parliament and the opposing members of Parliament. Chairing the meeting was the Justice Minister.

"You have all been called here because of the incident last night, the blowing up of an air strip. You have all been given the same information that I have so we can dispense with introductions. This area or airstrip has been connected with the importation of guns and drugs. The police have denied carrying out any raids last night so that leaves us with criminals on our hands that are pushing against the bonds of our justice system."

Harry Keanon stared across the table at the other members of Parliament, his gaze a mixture of disbelief and disgust. An emergency meeting had been called in light of the so called airstrip that was blown up.

"My colleagues, are you trying to tell me that we have no idea who blew up an airstrip last night?" Keanon asked as he looked around the room.

"Harry, I can tell you that it might have been a radical from your party, the PLP," Brewster responded with his all too familiar sarcasm. "After all, your people are all out to pin blame on my sweet little party."

"We have tried...," Buchanan, the Minister of Security said.

There was no apology in his sharp reply as he braced his body in the chair as if conveying a sense of superiority over the others.

"We have tried to stem the arrival of illegal guns into this country," he continued, "but as we plug a hole more guns come in. It disgusts me to say this but some of us in this room have knowledge of this unforgivable act."

"Do you have proof of this, or does anyone have proof of this?" Brewster and his *compadres'* voices were loud.

"Yes, we have proof," the Security Minister answered.

"Whose proof? Yours?" Brewster scoffed at the Security Minister.

"The point is, we cannot have terrorists and criminals running around blowing up places. This must be a rival faction looking to displace the current criminals here and fighting for recognition. They must be stopped. We have a source that says there was heated gunfire and one or two might have been shot or killed and someone said they saw a plane," the Security Minister continued.

"Buchanan boy, what plane are you talking about? Will you please clarify? Who the hell are these people who can do what they do?" another Member of Parliament questioned rapid fire.

"We have photographs that show that the area has been destroyed. We have evidence of a substantial amount of guns that were also destroyed, drugs destroyed and two people who were injured were taken into custody. Needless to say, no one will be using that airstrip again," Buchanan explained.

Harry winced at the use of the word criminal.

"Whether we agree or not, there are now a few less guns on the streets and a few less plane loads of ganja coming in. I am not condoning the actions of these parties but I am looking at the brighter side," Harry suggested.

Brewster sighed.

"You are right, Keanon. The people are calling for an end to this nonsense. The media is breathing down our necks. We have to stem the wave of violence. This country of ours is too special for some crooks to destroy."

Harry leaned forward.

"No one has taken credit for what happened last night. It's been a guessing game. Let's get our law enforcement people in here. They need to be briefed on the statement that we need them to issue. They are going to issue a statement to the effect that they have been conducting some kind of surveillance in that area for some time and last night they conducted a secret, covert action in that area. The airstrip was blown up, men were apprehended and guns are off the street. Let's take a vote on this with a raising of hands."

There was a show of hands. A unanimous vote it was.

Harry Keanon breathed a sigh of relief and mentally made the sign of the cross while muttering, 'Forgive me, Lord, we have all sinned'. Alex's and the others' involvement was safe. Now it was time to go see his niece. He knew that she was in good hands but he had to see her for himself.

He had always prided himself in being a bit of a manipulator. It had served him well as a politician. He didn't really think of it as manipulation, anyway. Some people just needed guidance as to which way to go. This was what great leaders did. How else would people like Gandhi and Martin Luther King Jr. have got the people to follow them? For a moment he had held his breath after pitching his line to them. They had taken the bait.

As Harry Keanon rolled into Bell Town after his short flight from Tinson Pen to Montego Bay, he prayed that what he would find would be just as satisfactory. They said Alex had stabilized but he had to see for himself. After all, he had contributed to the situation. What had he been thinking, going along with their foolhardy scheme? Although he had been known to take a few risks himself in his time. That was part of the path to success, taking risks. Damn, but this had been more than risky.

Bell Town had certainly come a long way since the days of small wooden houses with a few concrete ones built by those who probably had relatives in the US. Rory had contributed a lot to that. He was a good boy at heart and Harry hoped he had stopped his womanizing ways for Alex's sake. Keanon parked the rental and walked up the steps to the verandah. Miss Etty smiled at him as he entered the cool, dark living room.

The smell of incense was strong in his nostrils. A disheveled Rory greeted him with a handshake and Ciarra and Megan each hugged him in turn. They made room for him to pass through to the bedroom in which Alex lay. Her eyes were closed, and there was a certain peace about her, almost as if she had died. But he could see her even breathing as her chest moved up and down under the thin sheet and he knew she was going to be alright.

Harry bent and kissed Alex's forehead. She felt warm, just right. He whispered a quick "Thank God" and crossed himself. He reached for Alex's hand as he sat on the edge of the bed.

"Alex, Alex, Alex. Your grandmother knew what she was doing, promising you to King's House. You are a strong woman. The blood of the *Coramantee* runs deep in you. You were born to rule and I am going to make damn sure that you do. Or my name isn't Harry Keanon."

For one moment it felt like she squeezed his hand but it might have been wishful thinking on his part. Candles burned all around her in the silence, the smell sickly sweet. Harry Keanon walked back outside into the light. The friends all sat solemnly in various positions in the living room. He looked at them.

"You all looking like somebody died. I don't want Alex waking up to faces like these. Come on, you all."

They straightened.

"Thanks for coming, Uncle Harry," Rory said, his hand outstretched.

"Go home go take a shower, man," Harry commanded, "clean up."

"Yes, sir."

"Glad you all here, though. Alex needs good friends right now. But fix your faces, man. She going to be alright."

They tried to smile as Harry Keanon walked back outside to the verandah where Miss Etty and Octavius were sitting. He stood facing them, his hands in his pocket.

"Etty, Octavius, you did a good job, man. Thank you both."

"We did what we had to do, Harry. We can't risk losing her," Etty explained.

"She strong, man. Alex not going anywhere for a long, long time," Octavius contributed.

As Harry Keanon walked back to the car, he realized how blessed his niece was to have the love and support of people like these. It was one thing to live in the lap of luxury with everyone and everything at your beck and call. It was another to have good friends who were there for you through rough times and good. Alex was going to be alright. He had no question about that now.

- Chapter 35-

Ciarra came awake to the sound of birds on chorus duty and brilliant morning sunshine blurring her vision but none of her other senses. Throwing off the covers, she looked around for Tayo. His side of the bed was empty.

Ciarra and Tayo were spending a few days in Bell Town while Neil had taken Megan with him on trip to Barbados. Since that night that Alex had been shot it was as if Neil was afraid to let Megan out of his sight. They had all been shaken because wasn't this the same reason they had decided to hide away here without interruptions? It was unthinkable that one of them could have slipped away. How would they have all dealt with such an event?

Her son, Fletcher, wasn't far away. He was at Ciarra's mother's house spending time with the grand parents. The connection between her and Tayo had deepened and it was as if she was that young, giddy girl who had fallen for Tayo all those years ago.

Following the smell of saltfish cooking, she stopped in the kitchen doorway and held back a sigh. Tayo stood in front of the stove, dressed only in a pair of shorts. He was every girl's fantasy come to life as he transferred fried dumplings, cook up saltfish and plantains onto plates. Goodness, was it any wonder she was still in love with this man after all this time? Remembering all they had done last night and this morning made her tremble all over. He looked over his shoulder.

"Do you want to eat inside or do you want to sit out on the verandah?" Tayo asked.

Sunlight and Dappled Shade

"Aww, inside is fine," she answered.

She couldn't believe that Tayo of all people had actually cooked for her. He was a new and improved version. She poured chocolate tea into a cup as he slid the plates onto the table.

"I am impressed. The great Tayo actually making me breakfast."

She picked up her fork and sampled the food.

"Damn Tayo, this tastes really good. I could get used to this," Ciarra remarked.

Tayo leaned back in his chair, staring intently at her.

"Are you wearing one of those push up bras, Ciarra, because you look a little heavier in your chest. You feel bigger too," he observed.

"I thought you like big boobs and damn stop looking at me like that," she answered a bit nervously.

She was panicking, wondering if he suspected anything at all. She was pregnant again with his child and she didn't know how she was going to break the news to him. Although she had not been with anyone else there wasn't exactly any commitment between the two of them. All this thing with Alex had stirred up so many emotions that she had tried to bury as far as Tayo was concerned. Tayo stood up.

"I notice everything about you. Something is different."

By the time she had polished off her food she was feeling quite contented. Seeing that he was finished, she picked up his plate.

"I'll wash up."

"So what time do we pick up Fletcher from your mom's house?"

"Later this afternoon," she answered.

She was done with the dishes and Tayo slipped his hand into hers pulling her towards the living room. He sat on the couch and turned on the radio. She lay on the couch, her head resting in his lap while they listened to the music. Tayo reached for her hand and placed it inside his shirt. An arrow of pain shot through her at the thought that he might be sleeping with other women. He placed his hands flat on her tummy, gently rubbing. He knew that she had always loved it when he did that. He had always known exactly how to turn her on.

"Why don't you move in with me?" Tayo asked.

It came from out of the blue. Ciarra's entire body shook. She was furious.

"Live with you? That is all you want from me? To live with you? Hell no, I refuse to."

She jumped up from the couch. Tayo didn't get why she was so upset.

"I thought you wanted to be with me. What the hell did I say that was so wrong?"

Anger coursed through his veins. Red hot.

"So you don't want me? I am not your millionaire designer, or your hip hop mogul."

Tayo was furious. He grabbed her wrist and spun her round to face him. Ciarra's head shot up.

"What the hell does that mean? What are you talking about?"

She took a breath, a deep breath.

"Tayo... I have something to tell you."

"Okay, then, spit it out. Whatever it is? I can't deal with it unless you tell me."

She chewed on her lip and began drumming her fingers on the table.

"I am pregnant."

The words fell into the silence like a grenade in a glasshouse. She saw the shock on his face and he took a step back as if the words had almost rocked him off his feet.

"Pregnant?"

His voice was hoarse. He looked at her in an accusing manner.

"Is it mine?"

She flinched at the question.

"What the hell kinda question is that?"

He turned away from her, rubbing a hand over his face. Then he paced the floor, back and forth, like a caged animal.

"Ciarra, is it mine?"

She gave him a disgusted look and walked away.

Tayo sat in the shade of the orange tree and surveyed the scenery in front of him, acres of land that belonged to Rory. It offered a terrific view. He looked up at the clear blue sky and as far as he could see there was blue. Flat roofed houses and fruit trees adorned the hillsides. His face was grim as it had been since the incident with Alex. It had brought home the fact that he was very in love with Ciarra and wanted all of her, not pieces and bits. He adored his son and it was time for them to come on home full time.

Panic was burning a hole in his gut that this child might not be his. He didn't know what he would do if this wasn't so. She didn't say it wasn't his. Karma is a bitch he thought to himself. He had played around and had done his part to destroy the trust Ciarra had in him. It was a bitter and sweet truth. Here it was that he was thinking that it was time to follow his heart and not his head and marry the only woman that he really loved and she was probably already gone. Tayo drank in the beauty of the picturesque landscape and the sound of a car interrupted his thoughts. It was Megan and Neil returned from their trip with Fletcher sitting in the back seat. The sight of his son warmed his heart and gave him hope. As soon as the car came to a full stop, Fletcher was out of the car and running straight into his arms.

Dinner was over and Ciarra hadn't eaten much. As they sat outside enjoying the warmth of the evening Ciarra was thinking I should tell him that this child is his- I should tell him. I need to take the risk and let him know. He has the right to know. The warmth of the island wrapped around her, kissing her body, the soft breeze playing against her skin. Fletcher was already fast asleep and Megan and Neil had turned in for the night. She eased back in her chair as the silence stretched. Tayo was watching her.

"Who is the father, Ciarra?" Tayo asked unexpectedly.

She didn't answer; she kept gazing out over the view, dim in the starlight, gazing out to the night. She could hear the rustling of leaves on the trees. He was sitting in his chair not moving, waiting for an answer.

"What if I said you are the father?" Ciarra finally answered.

She could feel the tension. Her eyes locked to his. Locked and stayed locked. She felt desire pour through her and saw the anger on his face before it was gone. He smiled at her and she recognized the look. He got to his feet. She watched as he came around to her, where she sat. He held out his hand to her. She placed her hand in his and he drew her to her feet.

For a long moment he just stared at her as if he was debating and then he bent his head and kissed her. It was bliss--sweet bliss. With skill he played with her mouth, deepening the kiss and she gave herself to the sensations. How long she stood like that she did not know, with his hands sliding down the length of her spine, his thighs pressing against hers while his mouth pressed against hers. Sensation flooded through her. She wanted more. For a moment she was lost. She was hot and felt secure with his arms around. Now she could feel the breeze against her skin as Tayo disengaged himself from her. She had no strength to move.

He started to speak, his voice harsh because he was jealous as hell and he couldn't swallow the possibility that she was pregnant for someone else.

"Ciarra, you like to play with me, don't you? Because if this child was mine you would have told me a long time ago. I can tell you this, I don't understand you at all. Damn, you have no qualms about doing anything."

She looked at him and took a step backwards.

"It is your child, you jerk. It is no one else but yours. I am pregnant for you but you are only too happy to believe that this is not your child I am carrying. It makes it easier for you to blame some one else."

She turned and ran, fleeing from this man who a few minutes ago she had wanted so desperately. Tayo stood in shock, good shock he called it. He stood staring out into the night without seeing anything. He welcomed the darkness and, although the warmth of the night wrapped around him he felt cold. He was an ass not to have given her pregnancy more thought. He felt relieved that the baby was his. He was going to marry this woman but she didn't know it yet.

-Chapter 36-

Alex woke from her recurring dream drenched in sweat. She lay there in that state just between being awake and asleep. The night was so very, very still. Off in the distance she could hear the muffled sounds of thunder and, as she sat up in bed she could hear the rain, drops of water hitting the window glass and dripping off onto the window sill.

It had been two months since the bullet had struck her; it was one of the best kept secrets. Only her inner circle knew the truth. Everyone else attributed her illness to some kind of virus. Oh, her poor mother had almost fainted when she was told about the escapade and her being shot that night. This had caused her mother to hover over her like a lioness over her cub.

The rain turned into a torrential downpour. She had fought so hard against her powers, not wanting to acknowledge that she had that gift of sensing and seeing things, the supernatural they call it. Miss Etty had helped her with that and for that she was grateful. These last days she had seen things which she now held as truth. She had come to accept the fact that she had to fight and to take a stand in the political arena. The Jamaican people needed a change. While she fought to come back from that brink of the unconscious she had been shown the path. Her grandmother and Nanny were always there.

She had been so babied and pampered by Rory, Ciarra, Megan, Tayo and everyone else that she had finally kicked them all out, telling them to go get a life. It was really sweet of them. Neil and Megan. Those two were as hot as the fire that was needed to cook dry peas. The door opened and Alex turned her head toward the door as Rory entered.

"What are you doing up at this time of night and sitting up in the dark?" he asked.

"It's not late. It's a little past nine o'clock. I had one of those nightmares again but I found the sound of the rain on the window pane has been quite soothing."

He held her tightly, kissing her on the cheek.

"Sorry I am getting home so late but I had to attend a function with Harry."

He switched on the light by the bedside. The light spread across the room, dissipating the darkness.

"Do you want to watch while I take a shower?" Rory asked.

"You have ten minutes for a shower, don't keep me waiting," Alex answered with a laugh.

"How about five?" Rory answered as he removed his shirt.

Alex's office was a little crowded at the moment. Her uncle stood towering over the small desk behind which Alex sat. Rory was standing behind her while Ciarra and Megan sat in the visitors' chairs in front of her. Her campaign manager, Micheal, a light skinned, curly haired young man with a Colgate Toothpaste smile had a slightly worried look on his face.

"I'm afraid Alex that, you are still behind in the polls."

Alex looked at the graph that her campaign manager was pointing to and then at the pessimistic look on the face of the volunteer who sat next to him. Alex looked at the man with disapproval.

"I never accept failure," she said coolly, "and I am not about to begin now. What we need to do is to change the slogan. This is more about what's needed and what the people want more than it is about me and my many degrees. Let my humility shine through. When I started with this campaign I wasn't sure as to where I was going or what running for Prime Minister meant, but now I do. This is my passion and I am in it to win. Anyone here who is not with me on this matter you can pack up and leave. If there is anyone who has doubts, now is the time to leave."

Alex's uncle interrupted.

"You heard the lady. Let's get to work. I expect you to deliver votes, Micheal, and if you can't, I will have to find someone else who can."

"You are making progress, Alex," he corrected himself as he saw the look of displeasure on, not only her face but the others. "We have made progress, since the campaign began to focus on education and the promise of the opening up of more jobs for the people. It's just not enough progress that we have surged ahead pass the opposing party."

Alex passed her hand across her face.

"So what you are telling me is that in spite of my policies being the same or better, Brent Markanos, that arrogant, corrupt son of a bitch is more popular than I am? Would anyone care to answer that question truthfully?"

Finally the volunteer piped up.

"People are saying that you are a woman, you are young and you have no experience."

"That is true," Alex answered. "Go on."

"You have to give something more, be much tougher. You being a woman make people skeptical as to your seriousness. Jamaica has never had a woman running for Prime Minister before. Also, show off your husband a bit more, a steady family life. It will go a far way."

"You are on to something there," Alex agreed, "but what the people saw was my lack of passion, my lack of fire. My lack of wisdom and focus has now changed. It's a new beginning. The people will see the new me and the tide will turn. This is my fight."

Alex thought about Nanny and what she had done for her people more than a hundred years ago. She had taken a stand to help free her people from slavery and, in her opinion, was one of Jamaica's founding fathers. Now it was her turn.

Alexander the Great had learned from Aristotle the philosopher and had become one of the greatest leaders of all times, creating one of the largest empires in ancient history. Well she had learnt too from the best, her uncle, her grandmother, Miss Etty and from those around her. She was ready to do battle with the best of the politicians and she was not prepared to die or be assassinated at a young age.

Her grandmother was gone but she would make her proud because she knew that she was around watching the moves she made. She carried the memory of her grandmother every day. If she, a good person could die why not criminals, thieves and villains.

Rory straightened his tie and chatted with a group of well wishers. He watched Alex lead the way through the crowd and onto the podium. She looked freaking amazing, he thought but he watched carefully. The auditorium was crammed with people from every corner of Kingston and St. Andrew. Her movement appeared to be casual, she would stop, exchange greetings, pause, laugh or smile but Rory knew better, she was a tough cookie. She was campaigning hard.

It was 7pm and there were those who came to hear her speak: bystanders, news media were out in full force, calling out questions, trying to snag a few minutes of recording to send out in the airwaves before the morning news. Alex continued to draw an audience; the skeptics were now turning to her. She scanned the faces behind the barrier and saw excitement, curiosity, interest.

"This way, Alex," someone touched her arm.

Alex let her thoughts play through her head. She turned, looking at Rory, the long rangy body, clad in a grey suit and her heart skipped a beat. It occurred to her that she would have this rush every time she saw him for the rest of her life. She took the stage, focused and enlivened by the crowd. Her uncle and other members of her party stood behind her. She raised her arm.

"I stand before you this evening because of the interest and the love that I have for my country, a land where my people was enslaved but fought for their freedom,

A land in which our native people were subdued.

I am here to tell you that we must now struggle to wipe out the violence that holds us in bondage.

Our children are the future and we must prepare them well for what is to come by giving them the best education, for violence is not the answer."

There was deafening applause.

She hesitated a moment for effect. "Together as a people we can accomplish much when our hearts and minds work together. Healthcare, better housing, will be at the forefront for my people if you elect me as the next Prime Minister of Jamaica."

The crowd cheered its approval, caught up in the electricity of the moment.

"We need to move forward, not backward. Once upon a time we would plant tomatoes and yams, be somewhat self sufficient but now we rely more and more on foreign goods. What about investing in some of our own crops?"

She raised her fist in the air.

"This city of Kingston, where we stand, the God fearing people who live here, should live in peace and harmony. This is our land, our heritage and we are proud of it."

The crowd erupted. Alex looked at the faces and the hope that she saw reflected generated by her message.

> "My people, we will stabilize our country because stability is the basis of everything and in so doing start the economic recovery that is of dire importance. I believe we can do all that we have set out to do. I love you all and God bless."

As Rory listened, his chest swelled with pride. Alex wasn't just good, she was darned good. She stepped from the podium as the crowd roared in approval. Security immediately surrounded her, escorting her from the dais.

Ciarra relaxed on a padded lounger on the beach, under a palm tree, looking out over the deep blue water beyond the white sand of Negril. The wedding of one of their old friends was over but Alex, Rory, Ciarra, Andrea and Tayo had decided to stay on at a neighboring hotel to where the honeymoon couple was staying in Negril. It was now the third day and it was hard as hell being around Tayo without getting into an argument; but she had to try for the sake of everyone.

Each passing day seemed more difficult than the last and she tried to not let it show, to be calm and rational, to hide from him the emotions that were rolling around in the pit of her stomach, to speak civilly to Tayo; but it was hard, so hard.

She watched as they played in the water, her son making a splash as he threw the ball at Andy. Tayo jumped to catch the ball, missed and made a splash in the water as Andy whooped with laughter. Tayo surfaced, grinning widely. Watching them sent a pain through Ciarra's heart she couldn't stop.

"Mommy, we are having fun, come into the water," Fletcher called out. He treaded water and ran across the sand to her. He pulled at her arm. "Come on mummy, let's show daddy that you know how to play too," and started dragging her towards the water.

"Mommy just wants to laze on the beach Fletcher, she doesn't want to play," Tayo's voice floated out to her.

"Come on mommy, let's show off on daddy."

Ciarra stood up.

"Of course I'll play."

Her son held her hand as she walked out into the water. Andy threw the ball and Ciarra laughed out loud as she caught it and threw it back. She laughed again. She could not stop herself as she splashed around in the water. She felt Tayo's eyes watching her but she was beginning to have fun, big belly and all.

Tayo tossed her son into the water with a huge splash and he squealed, full of fun and laughter. Ciarra stopped laughing. Realization hit and she knew in that moment that Tayo loved his son and his son loved him. She could see that, could not deny it that he was a good father, a father anyone would adore. I should tell him that this child is his. I should tell him. I need to take the risk and let him know. He has the right to know.

Self accusation burned in her. Tayo might not be capable of loving her as she deserves but he loved Fletcher and, to be honest, she knew that he would love this baby just as much. Watching them playing together and bonding sometime even made her jealous. As she stared at Tayo, her breath caught in her throat. She felt her stomach clench and knew that no matter how much she ran from it she was still in love with Tayo.

There was a knock at her door. Her head jerked around and she walked slowly to the door. Tayo was standing there.

"Look, about last night."

He stopped. She stared at him expressionlessly.

"Can I come in?" he asked.

"Why? Is it that you need proof as to whether or not the baby is yours? I am almost eight months pregnant."

He held up his hand.

"I don't want to talk to you, Tayo. I am leaving today for Kingston. There is no reason for me to stay here for another day," she said tersely and started to walk away.

A sudden pain lashed through her belly. Her steps faltered. She forced herself to keep going even when she heard Tayo calling after her. She stumbled and sank to the floor in a heap. Her throat felt tight and she gasped for breath.

"Ciarra."

The voice sounded strange. She could not hear clearly. She was in so much pain.

"Ciarra."

She heard the voice before everything went black.

Tayo paced back and forth. Here he was again and he hated hospitals. Jesus, please let her be okay, he prayed. Rory sat on a chair close by watching in silence.

"Do you know what's taking so long?" he asked Rory gain for the fiftieth time.

If it wasn't serious Rory would have laughed out loud. He didn't have anymore answers than Tayo did but his friend was learning a valuable lesson and finding out things on his own. He was only facing what he already knew: that he loved Ciarra deeply. Tayo turned to Rory.

"Well she and the baby had better be okay because I am going to put that ring on her finger; dammit I am going to marry her, Rory."

Rory stood up and pounded his fists with Tayo.

"Man, am I glad to hear you say that because you two were driving me crazy."

The doctor emerged from the room.

"What's wrong with her, doc?" Tayo asked.

"She is very exhausted and she needs to eat properly. I am advising rest for her. I did some blood tests to make sure that nothing more serious is going on but she should be fine. The baby's heartbeat is strong so the baby is fine."

Ciarra woke sometime later and for a few minutes she was disoriented. She looked around only to see Tayo sitting in a chair staring anxiously at her.

"Welcome back sleepy head."

"Hi" she said. "What happened?"

"I was talking to you and you fainted but the doctor said you and the baby are fine."

Ciarra sighed in relief, "thank God."

Tayo smiled.

"You are coming home with me and another thing as soon as you are well I am marrying you." Ciarra began to argue but Tayo put his fingers to his lips and shushed her before pressing his lips to hers.

"I love you, Ciarra Johnston. I love you and I love this baby. You have always been the one in my heart, the one that I truly loved. But I have been a fool and it's time that I behave truly as your man and yours only. Can you forgive me for all the damn stupid things I have done and said?"

"Let me think for a minute." With her hands at her cheeks she asked "are you are asking me to marry you or you are telling me?" Ciarra smiled at him. Then she reached out her arms, hugging him.

She wanted to go home, to be with him and Fletcher, to have him bring her breakfast in bed and rub her feet.

"Hold on a second. Let me get this is writing. That way I am holding you to what you just said."

Tayo rubbed her bulging tummy.

"Come here and lay your head in my lap future Mrs. Hunter. I love you baby and I will never stop loving you."

-Chapter 37-

Neil watched until Megan disappeared from sight. He didn't know what the answer to the question was or would be. Was this the end of the conversation about their relationship or was he prepared to take the next step?

Megan didn't look back. She was tired, drained. Traveling back and forth between Miami and Jamaica had lost its appeal. Living out of a suitcase was not her idea of living. But she had a business to run so she had to make the sacrifice of adjustment.

Megan kept a running conversation in her head as she checked in at the ticket counter and, with her carry-on slung over her shoulder, she made her way to the gate and then finally stepped onto the plane. Ignoring the buzz of conversation all around her she took her seat by the window, leaned her head back, and closed her eyes. Thank God Jamaica was only about an hour away. She was thinking about Neil. What was he going to do now? She had told him she had to go, she couldn't stay. She had her own business to run.

This very evening she had a commitment to attend the launch party for the opening of the new Fitness and SPA at the Golden Moon Hotel. She should have been there already since she was part-owner; instead she had been with Neil in Miami. The idea for the SPA had come from Alex who had watched Miss Etty using her herbs and natural talent. After Alex's shooting she had discussed with Miss Etty the importance of combining her knowledge of herbs with modern ways and investing in a business such as a SPA. Megan was then approached and with Ciarra and Tayo's input Miss Etty was in the business she loved.

Miss Etty wanted no part of the business end but in everything else she was a phenomenal part. It was Tayo, however, who had really gotten the project started. Tayo was multi talented, a whiz in Economics with an avid interest in African Studies and taught both subjects at the University level. It was the combination of Megan's knowledge about fitness, Miss Etty's knowledge about healing, herbs and know-how and Tayo's knowledge that had jump-started this project.

Megan had toyed with the idea of marrying Neil, pulling up roots and settling in Miami but over a period of time had realized that this was not what she wanted. She wanted to live in Jamaica. What would she do if he decided that he didn't want to see her anymore? She also had to decide if she would run the 100 metres dash at the Olympics or whether she would step aside and give her younger protégé the chance. Problem was, she had her heart set on the race and that win. She wanted to go out in a blaze of glory; but that was selfish on her part. It was a foregone conclusion that she was the last leg on the relay team, to take home that medal. The chance to kick butt one more time was pretty enticing.

She was awakened by a sharp jab in her side. The passenger seated next to her had accidentally struck her with one helluva sharp elbow. Megan gave her a vague smile realizing that the hour and ten minutes plane ride from Miami to Montego Bay was over. The plane bounced on the runway and then taxied to a halt.

Shifting carefully, she reached for her carryon. With her briefcase in her hand and her carryon slung over her shoulder, she negotiated the narrow steps to the tarmac. She was home. This is where she belonged. She plugged her sunglasses onto her face as she stepped out into brilliant sunlight. A welcoming breeze swirled around her and enveloped her. As Megan looked around her at all that was familiar her fatigue slowly began to dissipate. As she exited the airport she saw Ciarra waving, waiting to pick her up.

She was home, Megan kept saying to herself. She hastened her steps towards Ciarra and threw her arms around her.

"Oh Ciarra, I am so happy to see you and this little one," Megan said as she rubbed Ciarra's pregnant belly.

"Oh, it hasn't been that long, Megan, it's only been a few days," Ciarra answered with a laugh.

They walked through the small terminal to where Ciarra had parked her car. Barely stifling a yawn, Megan slid into the passenger side of the car.

"You don't understand, Ciarra, this traveling thing, back and forth to see Neil is tiring. I cannot keep running back and forth. I have had enough. I don't want to move. Staying here in Jamaica is fine for me."

Wearily, Megan moved her shoulders. Ciarra didn't respond immediately, concentrating on her driving.

"Have you told Neil how you are feeling? If you haven't as yet, that should be a starting point. Anyway you are home now. After we get to the hotel, if you need to rest that's fine, if not we can get something to eat and talk more about this. If you are worried about tonight, don't be. We took care of everything, Miss Etty knows more about these things than you and I."

Megan pushed her seat back, stretched her legs in front of her, and looked out the window at the many flowering shrubs interspersed among the trees growing along the highway. The colors seemed gloriously wild and unplanned. Megan smiled to herself. This was home; there were a whole lot of happy memories here.

It was easy to fall back into the old routine. Megan found herself savoring the beautiful warm evening, the sky paling to an opalescent glow as dusk descended. She couldn't have asked for better weather and setting for this launch.

Megan stared back at herself in the mirror. She wanted to look her best this evening. Neil, it's your loss, she said to herself. Her gown complimented her stature with its floaty style and gorgeous mix of varied shades of blue. On her feet she wore strappy stilettos and in her ears she wore a small pair of diamond earrings and a matching pendant which provided understated class. Carefully applied makeup with emphasis on her eyes and the soft color of chocolate mocha emphasized her lips, completing her look. Satisfied, she picked up her purse as there was a soft knock on her door. Standing there in all their glory were Miss Etty and Ciarra. Octavius, who didn't want to be a part of the fuss had stayed at home.

The event was being held in the garden closest to the SPA where the numerous guests converged and wait staff served drinks and *hors d'oeuvres* and fruit infused water, teas, dried fruits and nuts, fresh fruit, served in the lounge area of the SPA.

Men attired in evening jackets, a mix of upwardly mobile young people, industry heads, wealthy retirees, women beautifully dressed, exquisitely made up, some schmoozing, some gossiping, some keeping their eyes on their husbands, were all in attendance.

By the time dinner started, Miss Etty was deep in discussion with a number of guests about shrimp jambalaya as opposed to vegetable jambalaya, seaweed as opposed to mud wraps. People were having fun and found that Miss Etty had many interesting takes on different subject matters. The circle around her seemed to grow as the evening progressed. They were jazzed about how much she knew about ancient history and the present all mixed into one.

"She is brilliant", someone remarked, "Do we know who she is?"

Megan chuckled to herself, if only they knew.

The chairwoman of the hotel organization took the podium and introduced everyone, and presented her speech, lauding the importance of such a facility, where the past met the present by using old traditions of "bush remedies" to heal and nurture the body. To answer some of the questions asked, Nanny in her days used herbal remedies to cure and heal and also to stymie her enemies. These remedies included fruits, herbs, barks, roots and sometimes flowers, and this tradition would also be continued.

Guests were encouraged to take a tour of the SPA area along with a guide, where mini massages and drinks were also provided. Membership was also offered to those interested. They were treated to a delightful and enlightening tour of the SPA.

The SPA's treatment area was set amidst lush gardens and waterfalls, with the sound of the sea close by, giving guests the chance of having their rooms enclosed or open to their own private garden. The natural surroundings were classically incorporated into exquisite interiors with exceptional comfort and charming architecture, using opulent furnishings and calming scents.

There was entertainment throughout the evening, featuring a comedian from Barbados who had everyone laughing at his jokes and anecdotes, a parade of designer wear, and a surprise singer.

The wait staff was out in full force with trays balanced on their arms. Ciarra directed her models as they took to the catwalk, displaying a selection of the latest fashion in swimwear, evening wear, casual and formalwear. Then it came the time of evening where guests were ready to party and catch up with friends.

Megan looked around. The evening was a success but she felt empty. Romance, Megan thought, made a woman special. She loved the feeling of being romanced; but tonight there was no Neil standing beside her. He was the best kisser that she had ever had and the way he sang when he was mellow was a major turn on for her.

Megan separated herself from the crowd and sat quietly in a chair by the waterfalls. She just wanted a quiet moment to herself. Since she had stepped off the plane she had been going non-stop. Ciarra's voice came across the microphone but she wasn't listening. She had kicked off her heels and was rubbing her feet. There was a change in the music and then a resounding applause and then she heard it, the song she loved so much by Isaac Hayes and, wait a minute, the voice singing:

> I stand accused
>
> Of lovin' you too much
>
> And I HOPE, I hope it's not a crime
>
> Cause if it is, I'm guilty
>
> Of lovin' you, you...

"Let me tell you all, this one is for my partner and my woman, Megan."

Then he was singing his heart out. She automatically jumped up. She needed to find her friends, Ciarra and Tayo. They hadn't breathed a word that Neil had decided to show up.

Who would think that she would be so over the top about a man? Romance made your skin glow and your heart sing. Candle light, moonlight, white sandy beaches, palm trees swaying in the breeze, a handsome man, made your heart skip a beat.

There were a whole lot of happy memories here. And, although she knew that she should still be mad at Neil, she wasn't at the moment. Closing her eyes she fought off a wave of emotion. He had a way of sneaking past her defenses and seducing that heart of hers. Damn him he was making her smile.

-Chapter 38-

The general election campaign had electrified the people of Jamaica. The young female upstart who had the gall to run for political office had surprised the naysayers and those of the opposing party. Alex had won the grudging approval of even the hardcore political supporters of the JNP party with her smarts and her intellect, and had proven to be a tough cookie.

Today, being the day of the general elections, the nation was glued to its radio sets and television screens listening and watching for every tidbit of information connected to Alex and the election. The energy which had built steadily up throughout the campaign would end today in either an upset by Alex or the ruling party would trump her.

By 5a.m. Alex and Rory were up and ready to go face the day. She got down on her knees and prayed to God. She was not alone because in Bell Town her mother was on her knees also sending up a prayer for her. Her dreams last night had been quiet but somehow she had felt the spirits were with her. She had lain cradled in Rory's arms and had felt safe and calm.

At 6a.m. Election Day workers and members of the security force were to be found in the various locations that they were assigned to with an especially heavy contingency of law enforcement in areas prone to violence such as Trench Town and Tivoli Gardens, warring factions of Mountain View such as Nannyville and Backbush. By the time the poll opened at 7.a.m, all was in place for the voters.

The car swept into Alex's driveway and Uncle Harry alighted. He walked with a brisk step. Before he could touch the door knocker, the door opened. Her uncle was here to pick her up. 'Unity in strength', was the termed he used. She hugged him tightly. He smiled at her and held her hands in his much larger ones.

"Alex, I want to tell you how proud I am of you and if your grandmother was here to see this day, she would be even prouder than I am. I have loved you as my own child and no matter what happens, win or lose, which we won't, you will always be my child." He dropped her hands.

"I love you too, Uncle," she answered.

"Okay let's go face the day."

Alex and Rory were first in line to cast their votes. Alex clasped Rory's hand tightly. He had been a steady rock throughout all this, campaigning with a single-mindedness and intensity on her behalf. She squeezed his hand without even thinking, thanking him. People came over to shake her hand, to talk to her uncle and offer words of encouragement.

At 11a.m. there was a report from the Electoral Office of Jamaica that but for one or two glitches which were fixed, voting so far was going smoothly and that all of the polling stations had been opened on time. By mid day in the area of West Kingston there were long lines at the polling station where the ruling JNP representative reported a 60% turnout. This turnout had him in high spirits and claiming an early victory.

By 2p.m. in St Mary no one was claiming victory as there was a lull in voting, but both parties remained optimistic. The report from every area in Westmoreland was more than encouraging because by 3.30p.m. everyone who had a bus or car was driving the homebound and the elderly to polling stations to vote. Miss Eve, Octavius and Miss Etty brought out the church members from all religious denominations to vote. One eighty year old who had been a die hard JNP member said he had been voting for years for one party, but today he was satisfied that he was casting his vote for the right woman.

"I have been voting since my eyes were at my knees and I believe this is the right thing to do and I know that if Alex wins today she will treat us well, right here in Bell Town."

According to one reporter, "even the puss and even the dawg" was out voting for Alex. When asked why they were so in earnest to vote the answer was "Alex is our girl. See, we have telephone and running water which took us years to get here in this town. She is responsible for this." The mood was upbeat and even those from opposing parties showed a sense of friendship toward each other.

The day was not without incident as in areas of Mandeville, candidates for the Jamaica National Party expressed concern that some names were missing from the presiding officers' list and created a problem for these people to vote. Some small rural areas had people standing in lines in the blinding sun because initially there was only one voting cubicle, but by 11a.m the second cubicle was up and running.

By 5p.m. The People's Leading Party headquarters was beginning to see a crowd. Rory stood with Tayo and Ciarra in conversation with an ear listening to the radio and any news coming in while Alex talked to members of her staff. Reports were going out that insiders of the JNP were saying that they were ready to celebrate.

Uncle Harry paced back and forth, sat down to play cards, discarded the idea and paced some more. By 7p.m. there were reports that the PLP had 50% of the votes.

Harry sat at the head of the table listening to the results. Alex remained tense throughout the next two hours as the votes went back and forth. Her friends remained by her side. They were there for the long haul, whether she won or lost and at 9p.m. there was no longer any doubts that she had pulled it off. Thirty four seats so far to the JNP's twenty four, with 60% of the votes counted. That's when the celebration started all over the island.

Alex's uncle jumped up with a shout when the results were read, slapping Rory on the back. In Bell Town, Rory's mom and dad, Octavius, and Miss Etty, were gathered at Miss Eve's house and a shout of "yeah she did it" went up after they listened to the report.

Alex didn't realize how tense she had been, like a balloon blown up to its maximum but which, with one prick would deflate before you could count to three. She slid into the chair as her legs threatened to no longer support her. She had done it and she so wished that Auntie was here to see. She smiled as she pictured what the house was looking like in the country with her mom and Miss Etty and the others celebrating.

"Let's hope you have that victory speech ready, Mrs. Prime Minister," Tayo's voice broke into her thoughts. "I won't be the first to hug you so I'll give my brethren two seconds to hug you first and then all bets are off."

"I would say so," Megan and Ciarra said in unison.

It was jubilation and celebration that lasted long into the night. Alex had proof that when you had good friends and family standing with you anything could be achieved. She had her grandmother, Auntie, her mother, her Uncle Harry, Miss Etty, Octavius and, Jeez the list of those who had been there for her was too long. When she thought about it, the dreams had started with five lickle pickney: Rory, Tayo, Megan, Ciarra and herself. Of course Andrea, Neil, and Andy would definitely see red if they weren't mentioned. It took a whole village to raise a child because Mass Kenny and Miss Linnet, Ciarra's mom and dad, Megan's mother and father, the church had all helped to form and mold her.

Alex had fought hard and she had won the election. The people had spoken and she was the first female leader of the People's Leading Party and had made history by becoming the first female Prime Minister of Jamaica. It didn't matter which newspaper you picked up whether it be *The Daily Gleaner*, *The Observer*, *The Herald*, they all screamed the same story. 'History has been made', a woman by the name of Alex Keanon-Richardson will be the new person at the helm of Jamaica.

A week after the elections in a ceremony that could only be described as impressive with the many dignitaries present, and colorful as in the décor and colors worn, Alex Keanon-Richardson stood at her swearing in ceremony on the lawns of King's House. With an estimated 12,000 guests and thousands watching from home and abroad, raising the Bible,

Alex took the oath of office as Prime Minister of Jamaica, the first woman to hold that office. According to the Jamaica *Gleaner*, Alex had written a page in the history of this favored island by becoming the nation's first female Prime Minister.

In her speech Alex credited the past and the present for giving her the zeal, courage and the passion to step forward and to challenge others to represent her country. She thanked her ancestor Nanny for challenging slavery and colonialism thereby paving the way for her. Nanny could not even have dreamed of this day when a woman from this tiny island of wood and water would be just as powerful as any male world leader. She would be standing shoulder to shoulder with leaders of developed or First World countries, addressing organizations that had only been names in her school and college textbooks. Harry Keanon stood next to Alex like the proud uncle that he was. He cleared his throat as emotions swamped him. His niece was home.

Alex's swearing in would not have been poignant if her family and friends were missing. Miss Etty squeezed Miss Eve's hand and nodded her head in approval. Octavius whispered to Tayo that he could do with a drop of rum; all this goings-on was giving him a headache. Ciarra and Megan were busy whispering that they were now officially members of royalty, grinning like Cheshire cats.

Alex looked over into the crowd and gave her winning smile to her proud friends, whispering: 'Thank You'.

-Chapter 39-

Celebration

Honorable Alex Keanon-Richardson, geez, I got that all out in one mouthful," Megan laughed.

"What do you want from my life, my dear friend?" Alex asked in a playful tone.

"I got the memo. We are all attending church, next Sunday in Bell Town, no excuses," Megan responded. "It's going to be some church service," she continued with a chuckle.

"Hold on, Ciarra is calling." She clicked the phone. "Hi Ciarra, I am on the phone with the Prime Minister."

"Get the hell outta here", Ciarra answered. "Imagine that, the Prime Minister," the girls laughed together. "I got the message, church next Sunday," Ciarra continued.

"Yep, no excuses. Anyway let me call you back in a minute," Megan promised.

Although the church service started at 10a.m. at the Bell Town Baptist Church, there were always those who were late and Pastor would procrastinate for a few minutes to let those straggling in late get there before he started. On this Sunday, church was already filling up by half past nine. No one wanted to be late because their daughter, the Prime Minister was coming to church.

Octavius was fitted in his best suit, which was an honor because as everyone knew, he hated to be all dressed up. Mass Kenny, Rory's father and Ciarra's father Mass Luke, two of the deacons, were promptly at church by 9 a.m. Today there were programs printed detailing the service with an insert of Alex and a tribute to her.

The pews were filled with women wearing fancy hats of all kinds, shapes and color. Although worship was at the center today, dress and deportment were important because everyone wanted to put their best foot forward and if it called for outdoing the next church sister, so be it. Today the quieter, more sedate church service was being replaced by something livelier with different church bands and a whole lot more gospel music.

As old as Alex was, she was filled with excitement and Megan and Ciarra, not to mention Andrea, were definitely way over the top. It was as if they were back in school.

"Make sure you wear that bright colored hat, the yellow one," Ciarra emphasized. "Nothing tame. I am wearing orange so don't make me snatch off anything else on your head that I see if it's not yellow."

They giggled like kids.

At 10a.m. Miss Eve was picked up by the driver assigned to her. She stepped out of her door like royalty with her fan waving back and forth. A few minutes later the rest of the group was picked up, Miss Linnett, Miss Etty and Octavius grinning from ear to ear.

"Is there anything hard in here I can a drink of before we get to church?" Without waiting for an answer Octavius poured himself a drop of drink as he called it.

Rory leaned over and kissed Alex as they drove through the church gate.

"No more walking up this hill in tough shoes," Rory whispered. "We have come a long way, baby."

"Oh baby, give me a kiss and Amen to that," Alex said leaning over to Rory.

In the car behind, Ciarra looked at Tayo with a grin, remembering, and Andrea burst out:

"Don't start any reminiscing action here. Anyway, Fletcher is right, here so I know you won't start anything, Tayo."

In the next car Megan waved at those she passed as she pulled into the church yard. The driver stepped out and opened the car door. Alex alighted from the car in her yellow wide brimmed satin hat trimmed with a satin band around the crown and bow in front. Ciarra waved to her as she stepped out and walked towards her in her orange classic pillbox styled satin ribbon hat which was trimmed with a dramatic satin ribbon flower bow and feather with rhinestones at the side, Tayo holding her hand. Megan followed in her lime green satin dome shape fancy brimmed hat decorated with tiny pearls at the front with Neil by her side. Andrea stepped up with her purple Edwardian style tea hat. It presented a beautiful and colorful scene.

All along the landing and the steps people were lined off and a great big cheer and clapping resonated through the air. The crowd parted as Alex placed her foot on the first step of the church and as she walked in there was a huge portrait of Auntie sitting in the front of the church set up on an easel. Alex was moved to tears. Later she would find out that everyone including Uncle Harry wanted Auntie to be a part of today.

It wasn't a long and tiring church service. It was more a thanksgiving service for many, for Alex and friends and family and for all those in her community. Later after the service, hats were tossed, high heels were kicked off as everyone sat under tents and umbrellas at Miss Eve's house, enjoying the many stories of days gone by with much embellishment and the food that was plentiful. But the most important was the company of friends and family.

The tents were up and the food was ready. Chicken, barbecued, fried, and brown stewed was laid out. The smell of pepper tossed in with escoveitched fish was making the faint hearted hesitate but there were other choices of stuffed fish with Okra and fried fish.

Alex walked over to the pork, roasted with pimento wood and stuffed with rice, and took a step back in surprise. She looked around to see eyes tuned on her. Her father was present. Hmm, she said to herself, go figure.

"Miss Prime Minister, your uncle invited me and I wanted you to know that I am proud of you," her father said as he stood looking at her.

She reached up and kissed him on the cheek.

"It's Alex, okay? It's good that you are here. Look around pops, this celebration is what family, and I mean the friends that I recognize as family is all about."

Alex didn't harbor any resentment about her father not taking care of her or not being around. She had a good life, she was fine, and there wasn't anything to miss. In her opinion, sometimes too much was put on fathers who didn't know how to be one. It annoyed her more when others wanted to label her as being from a single parent home. Single parent my ass, she would say. Look at how many mothers and fathers I have around me. Her mother and grandmother and her uncle had done a good job by her. She was pleased that he was here but there was no depth of feeling where he was concerned. That was reserved for those who really mattered. She excused herself and walked over to Ciarra who had her head resting on Tayo's chest.

Rory walked over, placing an arm around her and whispered in her ears. In his usual decisive fashion, Rory grasped her hand, his long fingers closing over hers, "Come." It was like a command.

Ciarra's head snapped up.

"Don't be pulling her away, Rory, I know you guys are going to the cave. Are you insane?" Ciarra asked.

"Geez, there is no secret around here", Alex answered. She looked directly at Tayo. "You told, didn't you? Can't keep your mouth shut."

"Oh don't blame Tayo, honey. I told Ciarra", Megan answered as she sipped on her wine.

Ciarra eyed them sternly.

"Be careful you two. I am just jealous that I can't go anywhere, not with my big belly."

"Ah, Ciarra, I like having you right here and don't worry, the baby will be here soon," Tayo confirmed.

Excusing herself, Alex went with Rory.

"Are you sure you want to go to the cave?" he asked.

"Of course", she whispered back.

"Well, I was only able to get the first part of the cave taken care of. We aren't going to go into the far interior so that's okay. We'll have to find a way to slip away."

Miss Etty with her sixth sense walked over. She looked them up and down and, with a smile on her face, she told them to be careful.

It was evident that an attempt had been made to clean the first cavern of the cave. Lights flickered on the wall and onto the rocks from numerous candles that were lit. Rory looked around with satisfaction.

Alex gasped with shock as she saw the beautiful colored rugs that had been placed on the ground.

"Wow, this beats my first visit here. I can't find the words to adequately describe it so I'll say it's beautiful in a primitive way. Who did all this?"

Rory smiled.

"I wanted to do something special for you and with you. You have always loved this place. This was the first place that I really kissed you as if my life depended on it. I attempted to make love to you here for the first time. Stupid me," Rory said as he shrugged his shoulders. "This is where I first saw the evidence of your powers. This is where a lot of firsts began for us. This is where we all sealed our friendship: Megan, Tayo, Ciarra, Neil and Andy. I have loved you from the very beginning and that love is still here, bolder and brighter. It was always just you but you were young, too young. I didn't want to be the one to mess up your life. Alex, I didn't give you a proper wedding. Will you marry me again?"

He watched with satisfaction as her eye widened. She hugged him and stood on tiptoe and kissed his cheek.

"Kiss me," she breathed against his mouth, excitement building in her.

The flickering candles provided enough light for her to see, for her to make out the silhouette against the rocks. There was Nanny smiling at her and as her gaze sharpened, the shadow smiled and lifted a hand and then it was gone.

The answer that Rory received was not what he had expected. His tension level rose, although he couldn't understand why. He was already married to her so why wasn't she saying yes. His hand found hers; his mouth came down on hers, with punishing force, his kiss desperate and ravenous, trapping her cry of need.

"I'll marry you again, Rory," she whispered. "I love you and only you. All those years it was you and only you. That night in the cave, those many years ago I wanted to give myself to you to show you how I felt. I was angry when you didn't take what I was offering. I didn't understand. I have to thank you for waiting."

Her arms slid up around his neck and clung. Her shoulder pressed hard against the wall by the strength of his body and the force of his passion.

She forgot about being Prime Minister, she forgot everything except the need she felt for him. Excitement pumped through her body as he kissed her until all she could feel was the throb of his erection rubbing against her. She felt his hands slide up to cup her breasts as she opened her legs to feel him better. He used both hands to jerk her blouse open. They were aware only of each other.

He stripped her of her clothes and she felt the hard, cold wall of the cave pressed against her bare back; but she was oblivious to everything but his need and hers. It was raw, indecent but who cared? She felt his fingers slide between her legs and she moaned in frustration.

"I can't wait any longer, Rory, now, please."

Rory was breathing hard and without hesitation he lifted her, wrapping her legs around him and entered her with one hard thrust that brought pleasure and relief. She felt the force of him deep inside as she had never felt it before. She moved her hips and clung to him as excitement rippled and surged through her body, caring nothing except the need as it grew and grew within. Alex had never felt this intensity before as if Rory was touching her very soul.

He thrust deep and he did it again and again until her vision blurred and sensations so intense had her body jerking as if in shock and for a moment she ceased to breathe. It was as if she and Rory had fused together. She felt him shudder as he reached his own desperate climax.

She didn't know how long she clung to Rory until, dazed and disoriented she slid to the ground. The flickering candles, the cold wall of the cave, Rory gently touching her. It was if she had waited all those years to come back to this cave to be with Rory. It was more than sex, more than making love; it was a mating of the soul.

A shout from the mouth of the cave intruded.

"Rory," Neil and Megan were calling, "are you guys okay?"

"I hope you guys weren't hanky-pankying," Tayo echoed.

"Yes", Rory answered. "We are on our way out."

Rory pulled Alex to him one more time, gently hugging her.

"I'll always treasure this."

"Unfortunately reality returns and my presence is required elsewhere. I have a country to go run. I am better for having you beside me," Alex smiled up at Rory.

Rory touched a finger to her mouth. "Thank you, Alex, for making me a better man."

It was as if being in the cave together had somehow intensified and electrified their relationship. It was like an eternal bond had been cemented, here, where it had all begun.

-Epilogue-

The evening was cool as Miss Etty and Octavius sat on the verandah of their house watching the sun go down. Octavius puffed at his pipe. Etty felt a peace come over her. The spirits were quiet tonight. Alex was going to be alright. They all were going to be alright. Like Bob said, "Don't worry bout a thing cause every little thing gonna be alright."

The children had each achieved their destinies. Tayo and Ciarra were building their family, Neil and Megan finally realized they could not do without each other, and Rory and Alex were sitting in Kings House where they belonged. Youth and its many follies, she chuckled. Miss Etty sighed in contentment. Yes, every little thing was going to be alright.

Peenie Wallies dashed across the dark night. The toads and crickets were calling out. Somewhere a dog barked. Etty looked up at the sky as a stream of light streaked across the atmosphere and a shooting star faded in a blaze of colors. She wondered if it was going to be a boy or a girl. Alex and Rory didn't know it yet, but soon a little one will be running around the lawns of Kings House. Yes, Alex was going to make her ancestors proud.

Etty wrapped her shawl around her shoulders against the chill that was beginning to creep up on her. Octavius had dozed off and the pipe slipped from his hand. She picked it up, glancing at his profile in the gathering darkness. He awoke suddenly at her movements and seemed unsure of where he was for a moment. Then, he rose with her and, wordlessly they walked together into the house, closing the door behind them.

ABOUT DANTIE SMITH-BROWN

Dantie Smith-Brown was born in Kingston, Jamaica and grew up in a small town much like Bell Town, the idyllic setting of her debut novel *Sunlight and Dappled Shade*. She attended Montego Bay High School, forming long lasting friendships on which the relationships of the teenagers in her novel are loosely modeled. She majored in Language Arts and Social Arts at Teachers' College and taught at Excelsior High School in Kingston. Ms. Smith-Brown worked at Sandals Royal Caribbean Hotel before migrating to the United States where she pursued a course of studies at NYU Medical Center in the Respiratory Care Program.

Ms. Smith-Brown is an avid reader and travels extensively to Europe and the Caribbean. She has been featured in *The Jamaican Herald Newspaper*, *The Daily Gleaner*, and *The Observer* and is a participant in charity work, giving assistance to Cornwall Regional Hospital and Mona University Hospital and recently headed the Bethel Town and Neighboring Communities Association (BTANCA).

Currently she works as a Respiratory Therapist at a hospital in New York City and served as the Vice Chair for Respiratory Care, Local 768, DC 37. Ms. Smith-Brown holds a Bachelor of Science degree in Human and Community Service, majoring in Health Care Services Management. She resides in Long Island with her husband.

www.ingramcontent.com/pod-product-compliance
Lightning Source LLC
Chambersburg PA
CBHW022141010726
47493CB00002B/292